Totally Bound Publishing books by Cassie O'Brien

Single Books
The Girls' Club
From a Lady to a Maid
Ellie's Rules

I0646148

THE GIRLS' CLUB

CASSIE O'BRIEN

The Girls' Club
ISBN # 978-1-83943-869-1
©Copyright Cassie O'Brien 2018
Cover Art by PoshGosh ©Copyright February 2018
Interior text design by Claire Siemaszkiewicz
Totally Bound Publishing

Published in 2020 by Totally Bound Publishing, United Kingdom.

THE
GIRLS' CLUB

Dedication

For Gary — 1961–2012

Chapter One

The moon hid behind the trees to leave the path a dark trip hazard of exposed, misshapen tree roots for us to find. I grabbed Jules' hand to steady myself and giggled into the warm night air as I stumbled. Jules giggled beside me.

"Shouldn't 'ave had the last one, Ness."

"The B-52 or the pinta piña colada?"

Jules lurched against me as her shoe snagged and caught. I laughed and pushed her upright again.

"Both. Should'a got a taxi, though."

"Only gotta get through the par – "

Jules' chin hit her chest and her knees crumpled as the back of my head exploded with pain from a curled fist that I glimpsed out of the corner of my eye as my legs gave way. My butt hit the path and I joined my scream to Jules', kicked out with my foot and caught the thigh of the chunky male closing the gap between us with the high heel of my shoe.

"Fuck! You bitch!"

The man made a grab for my ankle. I brought my other leg up, kicked, caught his thigh again with the heel of my other *shoe and screamed louder. Jules' shrill cry cut off with a crack of bone on bone.*

"What the fuck you doin', man?"

"She's kicking me."

"Just shut 'er the fuck up!"

The man lurched forward and dropped his weight onto my legs, used it to stifle my struggles and cut off my voice with a hand clamped over my mouth and nose as I writhed beneath him. I fought for breath, aimed desperate fingernails at brown eyes beneath a knitted hat pulled down low and flashes of light swam before my eyes as a clenched hand connected with the side of my head.

"Get the fuck on with it! I've got the other one's jewelry and bag."

My arm was forced to my side and a heavy-heeled boot crunched down. My fingers were bent and twisted as my grandmother's eternity ring was yanked from my finger, my attempted high-pitched howl silent without air to give it sound. The chain of my necklace bit into my neck before it snapped. The flesh of my stomach caught fire as my belly bar was ripped from it without being undone. I curled into a fetal ball as feet ran away. I sucked air into my lungs in desperate gulps and my stomach heaved.

My butt hit the floor again and I woke, covered in sweat. I ran to my bathroom just in time to kneel and vomit into the toilet bowl. I straightened after my stomach emptied and my bedroom lit up over my shoulder.

"Ness? Another? So soon?" Jules asked from the bathroom door.

I nodded and flushed.

"I'll get you a water."

I ran the cold tap in the sink while Jules was gone, splashed my face and cleaned my teeth. Jules walked into my bedroom and handed me a bottle of mineral water as I straightened the duvet on top of my bed. I took the bottle and sat, legs out, my back against the headboard. Jules leaned back alongside me.

"So, walk me through your day."

I sighed and closed my eyes. Jules squeezed my hand.

"I know it sometimes seems pointless, babe, but it's got to be done. I'm sure there must be something that reminds you of the mugging and triggers a memory in your subconscious to make you dream about it, even if you don't recognize that something for what it is at the time."

I opened my eyes and drank a mouthful of water.

"It's been over three years since the attack, Jules. And still the dreams come and go for no particular reason that we can see. It does sometimes seem hopeless."

"Well, I'm not going for hopeless. Yes, the dreams appear randomly, none for three months then two this week, but that's the point. Something has got to be setting them off. So come on, girlie. Get on with it. Step me through your scintillating day in the back office of Belmond's of London."

I sat up straighter and squeezed Jules' hand.

"Thanks, Jules. I know it's tough on you, too, having to keep going backward. You were as badly hurt as I was."

"Yeah, but I don't get it all back in glorious technicolor when I'm asleep. So, yesterday, you got up, showered and walked to the bus stop. Take it from there."

I closed my eyes to concentrate and talked Jules through my very ordinary day. The queue at the bus stop, the passengers on the bus, a day at work in the office and we searched for a something—a pair of eyes that reminded me, a certain chunky body shape, beer on none-too-fresh breath, a piece of jewelry that looked similar to that taken from us — and came up with nothing, as usual. Jules put her arm around my shoulders when I finished.

"The trouble is that we've got so little to go on. It was so dark and once we were both down, we were in too much pain to take in the detail. But we're not giving up, Ness. We'll work it out one day."

I slipped my arm around my friend's waist.

"I hope so, because one thing I'm sure of is that I'm never going back on those tranquillizers the doctor gave me, even if I have to be like this until I'm old enough that I don't remember the bad stuff because my memory has leaked out through my ears."

Jules wrinkled her nose. "It was a bit like living with an automated puppet, babe. But the police have still got the DNA from under our fingernails. It'll make it better for both of us if they catch up with them one day."

I sniffed and rubbed my finger under my nose. "At least nobody will take us down like that again."

Jules sat up straighter. "Too right they won't. The Girls' Club has made sure of that. Anyone tries sneaking up on us like that and they're going to be the ones eating dirt, not us."

I let go of Jules' waist, picked up my phone and checked the time.

"It's nearly five. I'll try and get a couple more hours' sleep. If I go into work already yawning, I'll have nodded off at my desk even before the first coffee run at ten."

"Why don't you just tell the agency you'd prefer something else?"

I shook my head. "No, I'll have to see the rest of the six-month contract through at Belmond's. It'll look bad on my resume if I change jobs too quickly, although I could kill Liz at the agency. A challenging position in the finance department is what I asked for. A data entry payroll clerk is what I got."

Jules smiled and swung her legs off the bed.

"Yep, stunning use of your degree there, girlie. But you've nearly got the first month out of the way and at least you've got the Maisie, Annie, Jason thing to watch to stop you from falling asleep."

I slid down the bed and flicked my duvet over my legs.

"Well, Maisie was definitely the winner today by two coffees to one. And it's the big day tomorrow. The solid wall is coming down and the new half-glass one's going in."

I blew Jules a kiss as she turned my light out.

"Thanks, Jules."

"Night, Ness. See you in a couple of hours."

I slept and snoozed in fits and starts until the alarm on my phone trilled at seven and I arrived at work early enough to get a coffee from the machine in the corridor outside the office and take it to my desk. I nodded hello to Maisie and Annie, whose opposing workstations abutted mine then sat. They both lifted their faces and smiled when the main office door squeaked behind me.

"Hi, Jason," they chirped in unison.

"Morning, Annie, Maisie…Vanessa."

I watched their faces as Jason Peterson, my current boss, walked past my desk. Maisie and Annie turned their heads and gazed after him until he disappeared from their sight and shut his office door behind him. I waited. Maisie finally tore her eyes away and looked at me.

"The workmen will be in at ten."

I looked at the solid wall of Jason's office. Maisie followed my gaze and smiled.

"Vanessa, I think I'll take that workstation and you can have mine. We'll do it now before the office gets busy, if you don't mind."

"But, Maisie," Annie said. "What about me? We've always sat together."

Maisie dismissed Annie with a wave of her hand. "We'll still be opposite, but if I sit where Vanessa is, I'll be able see what Jason's up to without turning around. Don't worry. I'll keep you updated with what's going on."

I opened my workstation's drawer wider and took out the small store of stationery I'd accumulated during the first three weeks of my temporary contract while Maisie unloaded a rather larger accumulation from two years in a permanent position. I sat beside Annie, put my stationery away in less than a minute, picked up the cup tray that would allow me to hold multiple drinks and looked at Maisie arranging her pens and Post-it pads in her drawer.

"Is it too early for a coffee run? I could do with another dose of caffeine to wake me up this morning," I asked.

"No, that's fine. I'll have one, too." Maisie smiled.

I looked at Annie. She nodded.

"Okay. White without and white with one coming up."

I walked out of the office and into the corridor to where the drink machine stood in an alcove, tapped in the code for the first coffee and put the plastic cup in the drinks holder after the machine spat it out. The door from the office opened. Jason walked out and stood behind me. I looked over my shoulder and up quite a distance. Blond and at least six four, Jason towered over me, even with me in my heels.

I turned back to the machine and asked, "What code do you have?"

"Eleven. Just black, thanks."

I tapped in the code and offered Jason the cup when the machine finished filling it. Jason smiled his thanks as he took it and I turned to face the machine again.

"I see you've moved workstations."

I tapped in the same code as his for my own coffee and nodded.

"Yeah. I've swapped with Maisie."

Jason stepped alongside and looked sideways at me. "And that would have been your choice or...?"

I looked at Jason and saw from the half-smile tilting the corners of his lips that it was a question he already knew the answer to, so I gave him a reply he could take either way.

"Well, Maisie did say you've got a work crew in at ten. Perhaps she wants to face your office in case any eye candy appears along with your new windows."

Jason smiled. "Thought so. Never mind. It'll still be worth it to get out of the box."

"The box?"

"The office I worked in before this was open plan. I would have had the stud wall removed if I could, but our chairman, who still comes in and uses the office a couple of times a month, wouldn't have it, so we compromised on a half-way house."

"He does? But not this month then?"

"No. We're getting a month off for good behavior. He's away playing golf in Spain."

I picked up the coffees and turned in the direction of the office. Jason walked with me and opened the office door to let me walk in first. I thanked him over my shoulder and took the drinks over to Maisie and Annie, while Jason walked on and into his office for his last hour of not being on show.

I pulled my work tray forward and logged on to the payroll system. The workmen turned up at ten and Jason took his laptop into the meeting room next door to his office. The work was completed by lunchtime with the old stud partition coming down in sections and the new one going up the same way.

Maisie sighed as Jason walked into his new goldfish bowl. I spent the afternoon listening to a running commentary from Maisie to Annie every time he moved, only relieved by a short break to print three repetitions of hard copy of the data I'd input and leave them in the in-trays of other offices that might be interested in the figures. It was going to be a long week, I decided, when the following day I resorted to putting earbuds in and listening to music on my phone to escape the constant drone while Jason moved around the office, oblivious to the two sets of eyes that followed him everywhere. I bumped into him as he left the Human Resources office at four as I arrived there to drop off their hard copy.

"Are you okay? No problem, is there?" he asked.

I shook my head and showed Jason the report.

"No, no problem. HR just gets a printout of the figures I've input every day."

"They do?"

"And Facilities Management and Marketing. I've got no idea why. The same figures are available on the system."

"Thanks. I'll have a look at it. Let me know if you find anything else you're doing twice, will you?"

Two sets of eyes and one set of aching ears came to mind and I looked over my shoulder as I turned the handle on the HR office door.

"Two times everything where I sit in the office"—I slid my gaze down to Jason's tie. His gaze followed mine—"especially when you loosen that at lunchtime."

I opened the door, walked into the office and closed it behind me then put the timesheets in order for filing for the remaining hour of my working day. I spent the evening refreshing the playlist on my phone so I'd be ready to face another day of not listening to Maisie. When I went to bed, I said a quick prayer for no nightmares. Luck was on my side, because I awoke refreshed and ready to face Maisie and her antics once more.

At the office, the drone subsided once she became more accustomed to knowing that every time she looked up, she could see what was going on in Jason's office. I went to the canteen at lunchtime, bought a takeaway salad and took it to my desk. Jason walked through the office as I lifted the lid of it and glanced in my direction as he walked past, the whisper of a smile on his lips. Maisie revved up two minutes later.

"Annie, Annie, quick. Come around here as if you're looking at my screen. He's taken it right off. And the button. Oh, and the next one."

Annie walked to Maisie's workstation and stood behind her.

"Oh, he's stopped. Damn! Now, he's unwrapping his sandwich. What's he got in it today? Annie, can you see?"

"Something with salad. Um, maybe ham. Why's he smiling at his sandwich like that, Maisie?"

"I don't know. Perhaps one of the canteen girls has put a note in it. I'll find out if they have and let them know it's not okay."

I laughed. Maisie looked at me and I straightened my face.

"Sorry, Maisie. But really? Just because he took his tie off?"

I finished my lunch, worked through the afternoon, caught the bus home and let myself into my flat at six. Jules poured me a glass of wine when I walked into the living room and I flopped onto the sofa with it and caught her up on the latest Jason, Maisie and Annie episode.

Jules laughed. "Those two girls are a ditsy pair. All that over a tie and a button. I'd want a bit more than that."

I giggled and nodded. "I'll let you know if he obliges. You never know. Tomorrow it might be a third button or he might even roll his cuffs up."

"No, not a third button! The first two buttons are neck but the third's getting down to chest. I don't think he can go there in the office, not even to get you looking in his direction."

I picked up a cushion and threw it at Jules' head.

"Get out of here, you. He's just having a laugh."

Jules picked up the cushion and tucked it behind her back. "Really? Yeah, yeah."

I stuck my nose in the air and carried on watching the telly while I wondered if perhaps Jason did like me that way and whether I might like him that way, too.

Another night without nightmares passed. Instead, I had a dream with Jason in it. A vast improvement to waking up screaming and crying, to be sure.

Glad it was Friday, I went to work with a positive attitude, put in my earphones and worked to clear my desk for the weekend. When I got hungry at about one o'clock, I went to the staff canteen, saw they had run out of sandwiches so walked to the local mini-market and found a tuna-mayo wrap to graze on. Jason stepped into the lift as I walked into the lobby and put his foot out to stop the door from closing so I could get in. Jason looked at my carrier bag as he pressed the button for our floor and showed me his own.

"You were out of luck too, then?"

I smiled and nodded. "Yeah, and last Friday. Is it like a Friday thing?"

"A bit. If anyone's going to take a half day, it'll normally be a Friday afternoon. The catering franchise kept getting left with too much unsold food so they cut back on what they make on Fridays."

Our floor arrived. The lift doors opened.

"Are you getting a coffee?" Jason asked.

I nodded. Jason stopped at the coffee machine. "How do you take it?"

"The same as you, just black, thanks."

Jason tapped in the code, handed me the cup when the machine had done its job then selected the same himself. I sipped mine while Jason's drink was dispensed. He took his cup from the machine and looked at me. I gazed at his tie. Jason smiled when he saw where I was looking.

"Do you know if you re-positioned your screen and chair a few inches to the left, you'd be right in the way of somebody's direct eye line and they wouldn't be able to see straight into my office?" he said.

I laughed. "Oh, yeah. And what do you think the odds are of me getting to stay there for longer than ten minutes? About a million to one?"

"Why don't you do it, then, and I'll time it? Under ten and I'll get you a coffee this afternoon, over ten and you can get me one."

I turned to walk back to the office. "Okay, you're on. I'll move things around on my desk to make room to put my lunch on it when I get back. The time starts as soon as I move my screen. Coffee at three?"

Jason nodded and walked with me back to the office. I arrived at the office door first and, with my hands full, pushed it open with my hip. Jason took its weight from me and followed me in. Maisie looked at me as Jason walked away.

"What were you saying to Jason? Why was he smiling at you?"

I sat, moved my work tray to the side of my desk and took the paper napkins out of my supermarket bag.

"He was at the coffee machine at the same time as me and mentioned his new windows. I think he likes being able to see out into the main office now."

Maisie smiled and flicked a loose strand of hair over her shoulder. "Yes, I expect he does."

I unfolded the napkins, laid one in the center of my desk, moved my screen to the left and laid my tuna wrap on the napkins.

"Vanessa, you're blocking my view," Maisie objected.

I picked up my wrap, bit down on it and scooted my chair on its wheels to the left, in line with my screen.

"Sorry, Maisie. It's just while I eat this. I don't want to get mayo on my paperwork or my screen and keyboard."

Maisie walked around behind me and looked at my desk. "Really, Vanessa, you don't need that much room to eat a wrap."

Maisie moved my screen to its original position, walked to her desk and sat. "And move your head out of the way. I can't see through it, you know."

I smiled my apology and moved my chair to the right, carried on eating and drank my coffee. Annie looked over the top of her screen at Maisie.

"Are you going to ask her or shall I?"

"Oh, sorry, Vanessa. I nearly forgot. Most of us go out for a drink at the Barleymow after work on payday.

Everyone's welcome, temporary or permanent. Do you want to come?"

Annie added, "Quite a few people will be there. All the department managers normally pop in and get a round."

I looked at Maisie then at Annie and decided that a month of watching their obvious-but-getting-nowhere interest had left me feeling nosy enough to go and find out whether either of them stood any more of a chance with Jason outside of work.

"Okay, thanks. Yes, I think I will. I'll just let my flatmate know that I'll be home late."

My phone lit up as I messaged Jules.

I'm going for a drink after work. Back later to go to The Vine.

Work do? What are you up to, girlie?

Girls and him in pub after work. Going to go see how they get on!

I pulled my work tray forward and began to key in the numbers of hours worked from the cleaning staff's timesheets. Maisie whispered to Annie that Jason was on the move just before three and I watched him walk out of the office. He came back five minutes later with two coffees, paused and put mine on my desk as he walked past. I kept my face neutral as I thanked him. Maisie's gaze darted my way.

"Sorry. Didn't I say? I got Jason's coffee from the machine at lunchtime so he said he'd return the favor the next time he got one for himself."

I carried on with my work until Maisie and Annie picked up their handbags at five and headed to the ladies. I logged out of the payroll system, tidied my desk and they came back twenty minutes later with eyes done, lips pinked and push-up bras on duty. I tried not to cough as a tsunami of violets and candy floss hit my nose.

"Vanessa, don't you want to use the loo? I've got some lippy and things if you want some." Annie said.

"Thanks, Annie, I'm good. Ta, though."

Jason walked out of his office and Maisie's and Annie's gazes followed him to the main office door. I picked up my handbag, put my phone in it and zipped it up.

"Come on, Vanessa. Hurry up. We'll miss the lift," Maisie said.

Maisie linked her arm through Annie's and I followed them out of the office in time to see the lift doors close and the floor lights move downward.

"Damn," Annie muttered.

Maisie pressed the call button to ask the lift to return. I asked while we waited, "Ah… Jason hasn't already got a girlfriend, then?"

"He's never mentioned one," Annie said.

Maisie shrugged and pushed a long blonde curl over her shoulder. "And I don't care whether he has. I've seen a couple of those off in my time. Believe me."

I walked down the street behind Annie and Maisie toward a gaggle of smokers who stood outside a pub door. Maisie pushed the door open and I squeezed past the puffers and stepped out of the door again as fumes of beer hit my nose.

"We're a sociable bunch, especially if payday's on a Friday," Annie said over her shoulder.

"We're young at Belmond's — most of us, anyway. No kids to get home for," Maisie added. "Look. There's

Jason at the bar. Get over there, Annie. He's being served. We can add our order."

I followed Maisie and Annie as they swerved past tables and walked toward a bar of bodies, three deep, all trying to catch the eye of one of the bar staff. I could see why Jason had been picked out to be served. He was tall and easily visible. The barmaid gazed at him with much the same expression on her face as Annie and Maisie wore when they looked at him too.

Maisie squeezed up to the bar, stood beside Jason and peeked up at him from under her eyelashes, her voice all soft and breathy as she spoke. "Jason, hi."

I held back from the general scrum around the bar and watched. Annie moved forward to stand alongside Maisie. Jason tried to take a step back but with the press of people behind him, he couldn't. Jason asked, "Maisie, Annie. Would you like a drink?"

Maisie fluttered her eyelashes at Jason as she wriggled closer and maneuvered her breasts so they nearly rested on his arm.

"That would be lovely, Jason. Thank you. A vodka and Coke for me and Annie, please."

Jason looked at me over the tops of the heads. "Vanessa, a drink?"

"A glass of red if they've got one. Thanks." I dug around inside my handbag for my purse.

"Don't worry. I'll get these," Jason said.

Maisie smiled at Jason as he ordered the two vodkas and glanced at me then at Annie. "I'll help Jason carry the drinks, Annie. You go and stand with Vanessa. She doesn't know many people from the company yet. Look. She's been standing there on her own."

Annie pushed her way out of the crowd and huffed when she reached my side. "She always gets in there first."

"Does it do her any good?" I asked.

"No, not really."

"Well, if you don't think Jason's already got a girlfriend, perhaps he's a chaser not a chasee. I hate to say it, Annie, but yours and Maisie's interest is a bit obvious, if you know what I mean."

"You think?"

I looked at the bar. Jason picked up two glasses of red wine and I shrugged. "No idea, actually, but you could try playing it cool for a change. See if it makes any difference."

Maisie walked ahead of Jason and gave Annie her drink. Jason handed me a glass of wine. I sipped, expecting the worst and finding a good Rioja for a pub.

"This is good. Thanks." I smiled.

"Faustino One." Jason smiled back. "I bribed them to get some in. It's chateau de vinegar in here otherwise. Do you normally drink wine when you're out?"

Maisie interrupted before I could reply. "Vanessa, we're going on to Zero One after we've had a drink here. You up for it?"

"Ah, sorry, Maisie. No. I wasn't really expecting to come out straight after work. I've put it back a bit but I'm meeting a friend later for a drink."

"A boyfriend?" Annie asked.

"Afraid not. Just the girl I share my flat with."

"Jason?" Maisie asked.

I tightened my stomach muscles against the threat of a giggle as Maisie turned toward Jason with two extra buttons undone on the front of her shirt.

"Sorry, no."

Jason turned his head away from the full moons of Maisie's cleavage peeking through the gap in her shirt and toward me. I fought to keep the laugh off my face as he caught my eye and I bit down on my lip as he straightened his expression and kept his eyes focused on mine.

"Would you have gone if you'd not had other plans?" he said.

I maintained eye contact so he didn't have to catch another eyeful of Maisie.

"No. I had my fill of clubs like Zero One at uni—house cocktails and sticky carpets. And yes, I normally drink red wine when I'm out. I'd take a bottle of red and a wine bar over a club like Zero One every time."

"Even on a Friday night?"

"Especially on a Friday night. We've got a good wine bar near our flat and Friday is the best night to be in there."

Jason glanced at my near-empty glass. "Another?"

Annie swallowed the end of her drink in one large gulp. "Oooh, yes, please. I'll help you this time, Jason."

I gave in and let the laugh out that had been bubbling inside me since Maisie had undone her buttons then looked at Jason. "No, I'm fine, but thanks."

Maisie sighed and refastened a button as Jason walked with Annie to the bar. I sipped and waited with Maisie until Annie came back with two more vodkas and Cokes, then I took my phone out of my bag and checked the time.

"Maisie, Annie, sorry. I've got to run. Have a good time tonight."

I walked to the bar, put my wine glass down and turned in the direction of the street door as Jason exited the gents. He glanced over my shoulder as I walked toward him. I smiled and leaned forward to speak as we met at the people-free space near the door. Jason bent his face closer to hear me.

"Don't worry. Your fan club's not behind me. Thanks for the wine," I said.

I straightened, turned away and felt Jason's hand on my butt. I looked back at him and guessed from the look on his face that he'd put his hand out to touch my arm and reply but had missed when I turned, so I forgave him with shrug and a small smile and walked out of the door.

I caught the bus home and let myself in through the front door of our flat an hour later. Music was playing and Jules called out to me as I walked down the hallway.

"Hey, babe. Did you have a good day? How was the pub?"

I smiled and kicked off my shoes. "It had its moments. Let me have a shower and I'll tell you."

I washed the smell of beer out of my hair, toweled myself dry, slipped on my wrap and walked to the living room. Jules poured me a glass of wine as I sat beside her on the sofa.

"So, the pub?" she asked.

"Well…" I picked up my glass, tucked my legs up beside me and turned sideways so I could talk to Jules directly.

"They did their faces and all that in the loo first, then we went to the pub. Jason was at the bar, so they headed over and managed to wriggle in close." I sipped and laughed as I remembered. "Oh God, Jules, it was just so cringingly obvious—cleavage out, fluttery eyes, girlie voices. Maisie even managed to pop open a couple of extra buttons on the front of her shirt to give Jason an eyeful of the goods on offer, but it didn't do her any good. He didn't so much as look. In fact, he turned his head away so quick that I'm surprised he didn't get a crick in his neck."

Jules snorted into her glass. "You sure he's not gay?"

"No, I don't think so. A gay guy wouldn't bother hiding something like that. He'd just let the girl know he wasn't an available option upfront and outright." I widened my eyes at Jules over the top of my glass. "And besides, Jason's hand didn't feel gay to me when it landed on my backside as I left the pub."

Jules grinned. "What? How?"

"It's okay. It wasn't on purpose. I turned as Jason leaned forward to speak and his hand ended up on my rear instead of my arm. He looked a bit apologetic on the 'oops' front but not uncomfortable because it had been a girlie bum he'd touched."

Jules narrowed her eyes. "Ah…you did mention tall and maybe quite fit under the business clothes, I believe. And he does seem to have been looking your way quite a bit this week. You wouldn't happen to be getting personally interested back in that direction, would you?"

I wrinkled my nose and shrugged. "For sure, if he'd been dark and not blond. But as far as I can tell, Jason is friendly and chats with me because I don't behave like an idiot around him like the other two, not because of anything else."

Jules laughed. "Not all blond men are well-behaved in the sack, babe."

I sighed and rolled my eyes. "I must be plain unlucky then, because all the blonds I've slept with so far have handled me like I'm made out of glass."

"Well, being as you're a size four little squirt with a preference for guys twice your size, you're going to get some that think like that. Have you eaten?"

"Not yet. I think there's a bit of cheese in the fridge, though."

I investigated and found a lump of hard but not yet moldy cheese. Jules grated it onto the last four slices of our loaf and we grilled it then finished our glasses of red as we ate.

Jules' brown eyes sparkled as she put her glass on the coffee table. "So, Friday. Who are you expecting to be in to The Vine?"

I smiled. "I take it Ben is calling in?"

"He might well be, girlie. He was running a fitness session when I was in the gym earlier and I did just happen to mention we'd be there."

"Well, of my friends with benefits, Ryan's still away but I had a text from James yesterday saying he wasn't on duty this weekend, so I'm guessing he might be stopping by The Vine at some point tonight for a glass or two. I'll see how I feel about things if he does," I said.

Jules headed to her bedroom to get ready and I did the same. I checked back and front in the mirror after I'd strapped on my shoes. I checked out my hair, black and straight, lying down my back, skinny black jeans, shirt tucked in with a touch of cleavage on show, face made up with eyes emphasized by smoky gray makeup and false lashes, and the high heels of my sandals adding some inches to my height.

I walked into the living room and picked up my handbag. Jules walked in behind me dressed in blue jeans and a white shirt, her auburn hair long and glossy. I followed her out to the lift. Ten minutes later I pushed the door of The Vine open and sniffed leather, aged wood, a hint of spiced wine but no beer. I smiled.

"The usual?" Jules asked.

I nodded and followed her to the bar. Jules sat on the only unoccupied stool and held out her debit card while I stood beside her. John walked up behind the bar, took Jules' card and put it on the shelf behind him for the tab.

"Ladies?"

Jules ordered. "A bottle of Raimat and a couple of glasses. Thanks."

Our glasses and bottle arrived and Jules poured for us. The couple beside Jules moved and I jumped onto the empty stool beside her, put my phone in the back pocket of my jeans and nudged Jules when I looked up and saw the street door open behind me and Ben walk in, courtesy of the bar mirror.

He headed our way. "Jules. Ness."

I turned on my stool at the sound of Ben's voice and smiled into the dark brown eyes of six feet of gym-honed, black loveliness. I tilted my face and Ben pecked my cheek and kissed Jules. I waved at John for a fresh glass. Ben sat on the stool beside Jules.

Steve and Paula walked up behind us. Jules waved at John for more glasses. The street door opened and I smiled at James, my dark-haired friendly friend who inhabited my bed on a casual non-sleeping-over basis that left him in no danger of being unexpectedly kicked or vomited on by me when dreaming dark dreams. James kissed my cheek and I passed him a glass.

"Hey, the London baddies gave you a Friday night off, then," I said.

James smiled. He had brown eyes and was fit, although not quite as tall as I liked. The sex between us was good without being 'wow' and James and I met up no more than once or twice a month.

"Just about, Ness…although it was a close-run thing at one point. A late arrest."

"How did you get out of the paperwork?"

"I've got a new probationary PC. She stayed on at the station to finish it off."

Paula touched James' arm and he turned away to speak to her. I turned to talk to Jules, saw the street door open in the mirror over the bar and nudged Jules on her shin with my foot when two guys walked in and I saw who it was that led the way. Jules followed my stare to the mirror and she muttered, "Well-spotted, girlie. Where the hell did that one come from?"

I muttered back, "Ah, Jules…that's Jason."

"You've got to be kidding me!" Jules laughed so loud that Steve and Ben turned their heads and looked at her. I kicked her shin harder, glanced into the mirror and looked at his well-fitted jeans and white tee stretched across his broad shoulders with the sleeves tight around the muscles of his upper arms. I leaned closer toward Jules with the mirror's reflection in my sideways view and kept my voice low. "You can't see it so much in a suit. And besides, he's still blond. And it's probably only a coincidence that he and his mate have come in here."

Jules grinned and spoke as softly as I had. "Yeah, yeah. Don't tell me you'd turn *that* down just because he's blond."

"It's still probably just a coincidence that he's in here."

"Yeah, yeah, again."

I flicked my eyes to the mirror. John put two glasses down in front of Jason and stood an open bottle in front of him. Jason filled the glasses and slid one over to his even taller and bigger-than-him friend. His gaze moved over the faces at the bar and stopped at mine. Jules nudged me and I leaned closer. Jules moved her hair to one side to hear me.

"Okay and shit, babe. I'll admit it. I could definitely go there, but how do I find out if he's thinking that way too without it being obvious, just in case he's not?"

"Okay and shit back, babe. I don't know. The way we are, we've never had a guy turn up out of the blue then had to try and find out if they've turned up because they're interested or not, have we?"

I laughed into Jules' ear. "Double doggie dollops back at you then, girlie. No, we haven't, so I'm just going to sit here and behave as I normally would. Presumably, if it's not a coincidence that he's in here, he'll know what the next step is because I sure as hell don't, and I'm not about to make an absolute idiot of myself by guessing."

Jules started to giggle. "Doggie dollops? Where on earth did you get that phrase from?"

Ben swung around on his stool. "What's set you pair off?"

Jules laughed louder. "Doggie poo! And make it a double."

Steve looked over. Ben looked at him and shook his head. "Don't ask. Something about a 'double' and I don't think it's got anything to do with the latest trend in cocktails."

I joined in laughing with Jules. She climbed down off her stool, her eyes leaking. "Ness, take me to the loo before I wet myself, please."

I slid off mine and offered her my arm. "Okay, babe. Let's go before you totally gross Ben out."

Ben smiled. "Have to do better than dog poo and piddle for that."

I linked arms with Jules and didn't look in Jason's direction as I walked with her to the ladies' loo then waited for her to have a wee. We re-linked arms after she'd washed her hands then we sauntered out of the door. Jason said my name from beside me before we'd gone three steps. I stopped walking and turned toward him with a suitable look of surprise pasted on my face.

"Jason? What a coincidence seeing you here."

Jules turned a snort into a cough and walked on. Jason stepped closer and muscles in my stomach tightened as I took in the contours of a body only hinted at when covered in a business shirt, and he smiled.

"Isn't it? Tim and I were just out and about in the area and happened to see this place in passing. This is your Friday night wine bar?"

"Yeah. Jules and I don't live far. How was the fan club after I left? Did you manage to escape before the waistband got rolled over and the skirt went up a few inches?"

Jason laughed. "Is that what she'd have done next?"

"Well, you didn't go for the cleavage, so I'd have expected next on the list would have been to see if legs and short skirts were your thing."

"Oh, dear. She'd have been wrong both times."

I smiled and shook my head. "I won't ask. I can't let the cat out the bag by accident then."

I felt a hand on my shoulder, pulled my gaze away from Jason and turned to see that Paula was standing behind me.

"Ness, Steve and I are off now. We're not staying late tonight. We've got quite a bit to do tomorrow to get ready for the party. We'll see you and Jules around eight?"

"Sure. I'm looking forward to it."

"I can't wait to see what you turn up as this time." Paula looked over my shoulder at Jason. "Last time we did a themed night, we expected Princess Jasmine here and Ariel over there to turn up, but we got Aladdin's pet monkey Abu and Jafar's parrot Iago instead." Paula leaned forward and kissed my cheek. "Night, Ness. See you tomorrow."

I turned back to face Jason as Paula walked away, saw the question in his eyes and waited until Paula was out of earshot.

"Simba and Mufasa. We're booked in for the full face-paint job tomorrow afternoon."

Jason smiled. "I'd like to see the pics of that."

"You want me to send you some?"

"Yeah. That would be good."

I took my phone out of my pocket, unlocked it and offered it to Jason. He tapped on the screen and handed it back. I secured the keypad and smiled at him as I slid it into my pocket. "Watch out tomorrow, then. We like to turn up in whatever costume they're least expecting, so we've got a couple of shockers lined up."

"I'll look forward to seeing them."

Ben called my name and looked toward him. Ben flicked his eyes in James' direction. I looked at Jason. His gaze moved back from the other side of the bar, too.

"Um, I'd best get back."

"Looks like it."

Jason stepped close. I looked up and he put his head down and brushed his lips across my cheek. I stood for a moment against his chest, breathed in Hugo Boss and felt the brief touch of toned muscle against me and the warm, softness of Jason's lips on my skin. The combination of all three danced through me.

"Night. Have a good time tomorrow," he said.

I stepped away, let the breath out through my mouth and fought against the urge to act like the utter idiot I'd said I wouldn't be and kiss Jason back in front of the whole bar.

"Thanks. I will, and I'll see you in work Monday."

I turned and walked across the room toward Jules, sat on my stool and watched in the mirror as Jason finished his wine, stand up and walk to the street door with his friend. I let out a breath I didn't realize I'd been holding as the door closed behind them then Jules' spoke soft in my ear. "So...?"

I breathed back into hers. "So, he's put his mobile number in my phone and I'm going to send him some pics when we're ready to go tomorrow."

Jules laughed. "Well, that should let you know one way or the other whether he's interested or not."

I laughed. "You'd think."

Jules nodded at James, who stood behind us talking to Ben. "And what about him? That's why Ben called to you, by the way. James looked like he was on his way over."

"I don't think I can go there tonight, now. I'll make my excuses after I finish this glass and head off home."

"I'll be back with Ben later."

"And I'll be in bed with music playing loud in my ears. You're a noisy cow."

Jules side-swiped my arm. "Yeah, like you're not."

I laughed, finished my wine, told James I was going home alone with no offense caused or taken between friends, then walked home through the sultry London summer night air and home.

Chapter Two

I woke in the morning after a dream-free night and went to the kitchen to make the coffee. Jules appeared when the smell of it brewing made its presence known. I poured her a mugful and handed it over.

"Have we got time to go to the gym if it's going to take a couple of hours to get our faces done?" Jules said.

"I don't think so. I've still got to Skype home at eleven."

"Okay, let's give it a miss today. We can do extra tomorrow to make up."

"I'm going to shower, wash my hair and de-fuzz this morning. I'll use the shower hand-held to freshen up before we go out tonight."

"With you there, girlie," Jules said.

I refilled my mug, took it with me to my bedroom and spent the next hour and a half doing what was needed to make sure I had the smooth skin necessary for the outfit I would be wearing later, then spent half an hour's face time with my mum and dad.

Jules and I left the flat and made it over to the theatrical design studio in the West End by two. By four, two cuter-than-they-should-be lion faces looked into the mirror and laughed. Sharon, our makeup artist, handed us our headdresses, one black for Mustafa's mane and one gold and red for Simba.

"Now, you remember how to put them on? And don't forget to backcomb your hair so it blends in with the mane."

We nodded and took them from her. Jules called a cab while I paid the bill. We made it back to the flat by just after five and I took my second shower with the water tepid to keep my makeup intact. I pulled on my wrap, took my headdress into Jules' bedroom and we secured the headdresses into each other's hair. I looked at the time.

"Nearly six-thirty, babe. It's well past wine o'clock."

"Get the bottle open, girlie. Let's have a glass before we get dressed."

I laughed. "Or nearly dressed."

Jules followed me out of her bedroom and flicked the music on while I walked into our small kitchen, stood behind an open-arched wall at the back of our living room and opened the wine. I handed Jules a glass as Bieber floated out of the speakers.

"What will Ben say when he sees you?"

Jules grinned. "I think he'll probably choke and offer to lend me his jacket. You didn't plus one James in the end, did you?"

"Ah, no."

"So you could have plus one'd Jason instead?"

I snorted into my glass. "No way! My name's not Maisie, thank you. He only said he'd like to see a pic."

"Yeah, yeah. Get that wine down your neck and we'll get changed and do the selfies."

I swallowed the last of my wine, walked to my bedroom and pulled on a front-plunging, furry body suit that was definitely more Rio Carnival than Disney would ever allow. With my tallest heels strapped on, I fastened furry anklets over them and furry wristlets to drape over my hands then walked through to Jules' bedroom. Jules twirled in front of her mirror and pushed her own breasts—much larger than mine— lower.

"Woohoo, girlie," I said.

"Woohoo, you, too," Jules grinned. "Have you got your phone to take the pics?"

"Perhaps just a bit more wine before we do."

Jules smiled. "I haven't seen you this nervy over a guy in a long while, Ness. Jason's obviously interested. You should have just found out if he was free tonight and invited him."

I shook my head. "No way am I doing any inviting and looking like an idiot if I've got it wrong. Jason's said nothing about being interested, just that he'd like to see a pic."

"Then let's take some."

Jules passed me my phone and we posed singly, together and sideways then sat down to check the pics. I selected one. Jules facing front, me turned more sideways, the high-legged cut of my costume leaving a decent amount of bare butt cheek on display, my false tail perky in the middle. Jules looked at the pic.

"You're thinking butt?"

"Yeah, I'm guessing so, if boobs and legs aren't his thing. But first I'll send a pic of how we looked last time."

I scrolled through the photos on my phone and found me as Abu with a little chubby inflatable tummy in a hairy brown all-in-one and Jules in a bodysuit dripping with feathers with a huge beak on the mask on her face.

I named the pics 'Ness 'n Jules last time' and sent them. Two minutes later Jason's name and his message pinged onto my phone. I put my phone between and opened it.

Oh, ha and yep. Totally not Jasmine and Ariel. Ness, not Vanessa?

I clicked on the photo I'd selected, named it 'Yep, Ness 'n Jules this time' and tapped Send. The next message hit my inbox a couple of minutes later.

Bloody hell, Ness! Not sure I remember Mufasa looking quite like that in the film!

LOL. Shockers, eh?

Not sure my first thought was shock, although I did nearly choke on my wine.

Jules looked at the messages. "Oh, I'm definitely thinking interested here."

I smiled and tapped in my reply. "Okay, I'm thinking that way, too, but I've put enough out there for now with the pics. The next move's his."

LOL again. Cab here. See you Monday. Bye

Jules and I finished our wine while we waited for the cab to arrive, then we headed over to the party venue, the top floor of a pub near where Steve's family lived in Camden. Paula, dressed as an equally un-Disney-like version of Tinkerbell, squealed when we walked in through the door.

"My God! I don't believe you two! Steve, get over here and see what the mad muppets have come as this time."

Captain Hook looked in our direction and I grinned at Paula.

"Yeah, like Tinkerbell ever wore stiletto-heeled thigh-high boots or had a plunge to the waist neckline on her dress."

Paula looked down at her chest. "I know. Naughty, isn't it? But I've got a load of double-sided tape in here to make sure they don't fall out."

Ben, as Smee to Steve's Captain Hook, walked over with Steve, and if he didn't actually choke when he saw Jules, he did at least take in a deeper breath. Paula threaded her arm through mine.

"Come on, you lot. Let's get you a drink. We're picking up the tab for the bar."

Paula looked at me as we walked past Aladdin and two identical blue, air-inflated genies chatting to Snow White.

"And you haven't invited anyone, Ness?"

I shook my head. "No, not tonight. I'm happy enough to just have a bop around the dance floor with friends. You know Jules and I don't do nightclubs, so we don't get the chance very often."

Jules and I ordered our normal glasses of red wine while Ben asked for a bottle of cold beer. I took my phone out of my bag and snapped pics and a short video of the characters all around the room.

"Send them to me tomorrow, Ness?" Paula asked.

I nodded and walked with Jules to join the crowd on the dance floor as the music volume rose, relaxed in the certainty that anyone bumping into my back as I danced wouldn't be a certain brown-eyed, boot-stomping, never-apprehended male, and I danced through until one-thirty when our cab arrived. Earbuds in and music on after I'd removed my half-melted face paint, I fell asleep wondering what Jason had gotten up to on a Saturday night and whether he was on his own or had company.

I woke near midday on Sunday, went with Jules to the gym in the basement of our apartment block and put in an extra hour on the bike and the treadmill to make up for not going on Saturday. I found a message from Jason on my phone, which I'd left on my bedside table when I walked into my bedroom to shower.

Was the party good? Everyone turn up in costume?

It was very good, ta. No party spoilers not dressed. Got loads of pics.

Show me tomorrow? Eat lunch with me?

Eek! What? In your goldfish bowl?

Eek! Definitely not! Canteen or could walk down to Subway?

Canteen, I think. I can just happen to bump into you then.

Good. Bump into you tomorrow then.

I showered, did a couple of weekend jobs, put away the clean clothes the laundry service had returned to me in my weekly-wash hamper then walked through to the kitchen to make a pot of coffee.

"Do you want to go out to eat?" Jules asked from the sofa.

"I think I'm feeling too lazy. Shall we order in?"

Jules picked up her laptop and ordered pad Thai noodles and chicken satay to be delivered. Once it arrived, we ate it straight from the containers then did our normal amount of clean up. I lazed on the sofa and watched the telly, too full of food to move, but still went to bed thinking of lunch.

I was pleased to have a nightmare-free rest. I woke well in advance of my alarm in the morning, jumped into the shower, told myself off in my dressing table mirror for being an over-excited fruit bat and taking too much time over my daytime makeup, then sat there and used the extra minutes I'd gained by waking up early to make it perfect anyway.

I smiled at Annie when I sat at my desk and nodded at Maisie's empty workstation.

"She popped into the shop on the way in, but really she's loitering to see if she can spot Jason arriving for work and get into the lift with him," Annie said.

"And you're not with her?"

Annie shrugged. "No. I think all that's getting really quite boring. He's obviously not interested, so it's pointless." Annie leaned a little closer. "And Craig who works in IT asked me for a date in the pub after you left on Friday, so I went out for a drink with him on Saturday. Maisie's not pleased."

"Oh, I'm sorry. Not that you went out with Craig – I think you're right to move on – but I'm sorry if it's caused a bit of a rift between you and Maisie."

Annie smiled. "Thanks. I hope Maisie and I won't fall out over it, but I really enjoyed seeing Craig and I'm going to the cinema with him tomorrow."

"Ah well, I'd have thought Maisie would move on too. Sometime soon. I mean, how long can you keep it up if you're getting nothing back but the cold shoulder? Not for that long, surely?"

Maisie walked into the office ten minutes later. "No joy again. I wish I knew how he gets to work because I've never seen him come in through the main door."

"Is there another door?" I asked.

"The door that leads up from the underground parking bays, but he doesn't carry any car keys. I checked."

I looked at Maisie. "How did you do that?"

Maisie's cheeks flushed pink and Annie's gaze slid away.

"I mean, I've never seen any car keys — like in his hand or on his desk."

I picked up the drinks holder. "Why don't you just ask him how he gets here, if you want to know? Early coffee anyone?"

Annie nodded.

Maisie sat down at her desk and huffed. "Don't be daft, Vanessa. I couldn't do that. It'd make it too obvious that I was waiting for him to arrive. Yes, please, to the coffee."

I shrugged. "I'm not sure he's that clueless, Maisie."

I used the ladies then the coffee machine and saw that Jason must have arrived while I was in the loo. I handed the coffees out and sat at my desk.

"So, did you have a good time at Zero One on Friday?"

Maisie glanced over my shoulder. "It was okay. There was no-one particularly special in there, though. Did you have a good time with your friend on Friday?"

I pulled my work tray forward. "Yeah, it was fine. And Saturday, we went to a really good party. Fancy dress."

"Oooh," Annie said. "What did you go as?"

I thought *Mufasa*, but called up the photo of Abu and Largo from last year instead and showed it to Annie and Maisie without passing my phone over.

"That's Jules that I share my flat with. We've lived together for over four years now."

"She looks nice," Annie said. "Have you got any more pics?"

I bought up the short video where I'd swung my phone around the room that didn't include either me or Jules in it, showed them that then got on with my work until my phone vibrated with a message from Jason shortly before one.

Lunch?

Sure. I'll wait for you to go and bump into you about 5 mins after.

Do you want me to get you something?

Probably best if I get my own. Ta.

Jason walked past my desk and glanced down at me with the hint of a smile on his face. I breathed in a little deeper as I remembered Friday night's tighter tee, carried on with my work for a few minutes more then looked at Annie.

"I'm going to get some lunch. Do you want me to bring anything back?"

Annie shook her head.

"Thanks, but Maisie and I are going to Costa. Are you sure you wouldn't prefer something from there?"

"Ta, but I'm okay with a side salad today. Jules and I pigged out a bit last night on a Thai home delivery."

I rode the lift down to the canteen, picked up a side salad and a bottle of water from the self-service buffet and saw Jason's blond hair above the other heads in the room as I turned away from the till. I walked over and put my lunch on his table.

"Hey, fancy bumping into you here. Did you have a good weekend?"

Jason looked up, smiled and my heart did a quick double tap as I automatically smiled back.

"Yeah. I drove Tim down to Exeter. That's where I was when you sent the pics, catching up with some friends from uni."

I sat, pictured Tim from Friday and guessed. "And all of them are as equally big as you and Tim, I presume?"

"Uni rowing team catch up, so yes—and I'm the shortest."

I put my handbag on the floor beside my chair and opened my water. "Do remind me never to stand near you lot if I ever see you out and you're all together."

Jason smiled and took a bite of his baguette. I forked up a salad leaf and nibbled on the edge of it. Jason looked at my plate.

"Magnificent lunch there."

"Jules and I ordered food in last night. I'm still stuffed."

"Mopping up the hangover? Have you got the pics?"

I smiled and put my fork down. "No, no hangover. I drank mainly water because it was so hot, and yes."

I took my phone out of my bag, loaded the pics, bypassed those of me and Jules posing indoors and held my phone out to Jason. He didn't take it but put

42

his hand behind mine and held the phone steady between us. I swallowed, moved my thumb and pressed on the pic of Tinkerbell bouncing up and almost out on the dance floor.

Jason leaned closer and laughed. "Good lord, how did they stay in there?"

I laughed back. "Double-sided sticky tape, she said."

I skimmed through the photos and came to one of me with Widow Twanky lifting me up from my feet on the dance floor while I laughed.

"And that is who under the makeup?" Jason asked.

"Steve's dad, Dave, for his sins. He was nearly dead by the end of the night."

"Not the guy from Friday night?"

I moved my hand away from Jason's and dropped my phone into my bag. "James? No. He wasn't even there. He's not really part of the crowd that meets in The Vine on Friday nights."

I picked up my fork and Jason glanced sideways at me. "Ness, come out for a drink tonight?"

I looked at him. My heart jumped, thought *bed* and made mine an available option. "I'll be in The Vine sometime after eight if you should just happen to be in the area."

Jason smiled and picked up his baguette. "I will be."

I ate a little more salad, drank some water then put my fork down on my plate as Jason finished his lunch. He looked at my half-finished lunch.

"You must be really full after all that."

I picked up my water. "I can't eat big two days running, at least not until I've worked off the first lot at the gym."

"Which gym?"

"We've got one in the basement of our apartment block—and a small pool. It's not huge but it's okay for day-to-day, then Jules and I go to a couple of classes at the leisure center." I looked at Jason's shoulders. "You?"

"One near to where I live in Camden."

"That's where the party was on Saturday. God, how do you stand all the noise from the traffic?"

Jason stacked my salad plate on his. "Triple glazing. You don't get much in a dead-end road, I suppose?"

I picked up my handbag and pushed my chair away from the table, ready to stand. "No, there's no through traffic. You know the road I live on?"

Jason looked at me and smiled. "Your address is listed as part of the info the agency sent through. I took a little walk around the area, courtesy of Google."

"And just happened to come across a local wine bar?"

"Just happened to come across three. Went in all of them."

I laughed, reached for my water bottle and breathed in deeper as Jason reached it first and passed it to me.

"You go first. I'll get rid of the plates."

"Thanks. I'll see you later."

"See you tonight."

I took a coffee from the machine on my way to my workstation, put my earbuds in and didn't look up when Jason walked past ten minutes later. Music on, I worked through until five, let myself into my flat just after six to silence and an absence of Jules, headed for my bedroom and opened the wardrobe door. I called out as the front door opened. "Jules. In here. Help."

Jules appeared in the doorway. "Hey, babe. What's up?"

I moved hangers along the rail. "I'm meeting Jason in The Vine later. What the hell do I wear? It can't be anything too dressy. It's only a Monday. It should be jeans on a weekday, shouldn't it?"

Jules laughed. "Woohoo. Good for you, girlie. Calm down. Where has my 'take it or leave it' friend gone?"

I sat on the side of the bed. "I know. I'm acting like a bit of an idiot, aren't I?"

Jules nodded and smiled. "Jason's got under your skin a bit, hasn't he?"

"I think so. Who knew? If you'd told me that a couple of weeks ago, I'd have said you were losing it."

"Happens, babe. Are you hoping he'll come back here with you tonight?"

"Yeah. That's why I said The Vine."

"Then I'll ring Ben. I'll walk with you to the bar, make sure Jason's in there then I'll bugger off to Ben's."

"Jules, you don't have to."

"I know, but I'm going to. You really like Jason, so let's not do anything to put him off like having an audience next door listening in. Now, I'm going to pour the wine. You get your skinny, butt-hugging black jeans on but with a tighter top than a shirt. You're right. It's only a Monday."

I smiled. "Thanks, babe."

I rummaged in my chest of drawers and pulled out a black boob-tube top that had plenty of Lycra in it and didn't need a bra underneath, a thong and my skinny black jeans. Dressed, with my makeup on, I looked around my bedroom, plucked my high platform sandals off my pile of shoes and pushed the rest out of sight under my bed with my foot. Two dirty mugs stood on my bedside table and I picked them up and flicked the lamp on then skimmed my eyes over the top of my dressing table, gave it up as a lost cause and took the mugs to the kitchen. Jules looked up from the sofa.

"Wine's open. Best get the end of the satay out of the fridge. We ought to eat something."

I put the satay container down on the sofa in between us and Jules poured the wine.

"How many bottles have we got left?" I asked.

"There's still three in the kitchen but I had an email today. The next case will be delivered the day after tomorrow."

"Good. We can't be running out of the red stuff."

I picked up a satay stick to nibble on, sipped and sofa-bopped to the music alongside Jules, the way we often did before we went out for the evening. We left the flat just after eight and I pushed open the door of The Vine fifteen minutes later.

I waited with Jules just inside the door as she cast her eyes around the room to find Ben, and I saw Jason sitting at the bar, his focus on his phone. He was dressed in jeans and a tight T-shirt again and I appreciated the fit over his broad shoulders, ran my gaze down his back to a tapered waist and hoped he had an inexhaustible supply of body-hugging, tees.

"Ben's sitting over there at the table in the corner. I'll be home around one."

"Okay, babe. Text me when you leave Ben's."

I walked over to Jason, stood beside his stool and touched his shoulder. "Hey, you good?"

Jason put his phone on the bar, turned, smiled and leaned forward. I tilted forward to meet him and he kissed my cheek and put his arm around my waist, his hand resting on the small of my back. I kissed his cheek, leaned closer against the pressure of his hand and breathed in my favorite aftershave, soap and freshly shaven skin.

"I'm good. You?"

I stepped away and sat on the stool beside Jason's. "Yeah. I walked down with Jules."

Jason picked up the wine bottle in front of him and poured into the empty glass beside it. I looked and saw Raimat on the label. He followed my gaze to the bottle.

"Your friend Jules' friend was up at the bar when I came in. He saw me looking at the wine list and called across the bar to tell me what you normally drink when you're in here."

I picked up my glass, sipped and saw the smile in Jason's eyes. "Ben. What did he say?"

"That mad pair drink Raimat when they're in here."

I laughed. "I'll get him back for that one later."

Jason picked up his glass. His hand was twice the size of mine with long fingers and trimmed nails and his forearm, smooth with a light dusting of blond hair. I sipped and tightened my hold on my glass, fighting against the urge to reach out and touch him.

"How long have you known Jules?"

"Since day one of freshers week at uni. We'd both left it too late to get rooms on campus so we ended up in the same shared house. How long have you known Tim?"

"Since my second year, when I made the uni rowing team, along with Ian who we stayed with on Saturday."

Jason took my hand that wasn't holding the glass. "I take it that it's something you've never tried. You could never have rowed with these teeny things."

I breathed in deeper, left my hand in Jason's but adjusted the angle of my arm to cover my nipples' hardened response to his touch. "No, but I can peddle a mean pedalo, though."

Jason looked at my feet. "You sure about that? Would your feet even reach the pedals without those on?"

I smiled. "Hey, I can pedal in my shoes. I'm used to them. It's the land of little people down here without them."

"Just how small are you without your shoes?"

"Do you want to stand up? I'll show you if you like."

Jason stood beside his stool. I stood in front of him, the top of my head level with his chin, then stepped out of my shoes, sank several inches and found my nose level with the midpoint of his torso, the top of my head still a few inches short of his shoulder.

Jason put his arm around my waist and laughed. "Tiny girl."

I took a breath in through my nose when my muscles tightened as they reacted to the closeness of Jason's body to mine and the strength of his arm around me as I looked up.

"Five-three on a good day if I just blow my hair dry and don't straighten it. Five-two really."

I stepped away, climbed back into my shoes and sat on my stool. Jules stood on the other side of the bar beside Ben, who was settling their tab. She blew me a kiss and walked with Ben over to the street door. Jason took my hand in his, traced his thumb over the back of it and watched them leave. My nipples hardened again at his touch.

"Your friend's going home?"

"Eventually, via Ben's. There are four separate blocks behind the gates. Ben's got a one-bed studio a couple of blocks down from ours."

Jason turned to me as I answered. The outline of my nipples pressed against my top, inescapably in his eye line, and he moved my hand to his mouth and kissed my palm.

"Ness?"

My heart thumped at the touch of his lips and the warmth in his eyes so I breathed in deeper and asked, "You want to walk back home with me?"

He kissed into my palm again and smiled. "Very much."

I stroked my fingertips along Jason's jawline, took my hand back and looked at the bottle of half-drunk wine. "John will cork that for you if you want to take it home or he'll put it behind the bar for another time."

"Leave it here then."

I gestured to John, who brought over a cork and a pen then corked the bottle for us. I finished my glass as Jason added his name to the bottle label. Jason offered me his hand as he stood. I put mine in his and walked with him out of the door into the light of the bar illuminating the pavement and on into pooling darkness lit by the glow of the streetlights. Out of the glare, in between two streetlights, he stopped walking.

"Ness..."

I looked up, turned into his arms and tilted my face up as he pressed me close to his chest. I put my arms around him. Jason put his lips on mine. I explored his mouth with my tongue and tasted warm, sweet breath with a hint of wine. We broke apart as a passing taxi caught us in its headlights and hooted.

Jason smiled and I giggled. "Oops. I haven't been caught doing that in public view since Spotty Luke around the back of the bike shed at school," I confessed.

Jason laughed, held my hand and we walked on. "Spotty Luke! Who caught you?"

"Head of Year. Easy catch, though. Everyone used the back of the bike sheds for a bit of brace tangling. Didn't you?"

"I daresay some did, but as I went to an all-boys' boarding school, it was never my thing."

"Boarding? Did you like it? I always just went to school from home."

"It wasn't quite all it's cracked up to be in books and things, but most of the time, it was okay. Like anything, some good times, some bad but overall more good."

We arrived at the gates to my apartment block and I pressed the release button on the gate post. Jason glanced up at the darkened football stadium behind our apartments.

"How do you find that on match days?"

"Not a problem. There's no shortcut to the stadium through here, so all we get is the occasional fan who's tried his luck and has to be let back out."

I tapped the code into the keypad at the entrance door to my apartment block and walked ahead of Jason into our hallway when I let us in to my flat.

"That's Jules' bedroom on the right and this is mine on the left."

I stepped through the doorway and Jason followed me in. Jason slipped his arms around my waist. I dropped my handbag, turned, wound my arms around his neck and opened to his tongue. Jason moved his lips to my neck when our mouths parted.

"You need me to use anything, Ness?" he asked.

"You don't need to for me, but if you want to anyway, that's fine."

"No, not with you if I don't have to."

I reached up and ran my hands over his shoulders. Jason threaded the fingers of one hand through the back of my hair and cupped my butt with the other. I moved my hand to the bulge at the front of his jeans as we kissed, traced my fingers over the outline of his stiff cock then tugged at his zip.

"You want to lose some clothes?" I asked.

Jason stepped back, pulled off his T-shirt and dropped it to the floor. My heart rate stepped up as I gazed at his torso, firm with muscles and toned but not over-worked, with a light sprinkling of golden hair on his chest. I took my boob-tube off over my head. Jason's irises darkened as he gazed at my nipples, pink and hard, and my breasts, not large but full, round and generous for the small size of the rest of me.

I worked the strap of my sandals down with each foot, kicked them off and unfastened my jeans. Jason eased off his shoes, unzipped his jeans and pulled them, his boxers and socks off in one go. I looked at Jason's cock, stiff and in proportion to his large frame, and breathed in hard as I wriggled out of my jeans, taking my thong off with them.

I stepped forward into Jason's arms, his erection rigid against my belly, the hardness of his thigh against the bare skin of my pubic mound, my face level with his chest. Jason moved his hands over my shoulders and down my back to my butt.

"Beautiful," he murmured.

I pulled his face down to mine and pressed my breasts against him. He opened his mouth for my kiss and urged my hips closer as I explored the firm contours of his back.

I stepped away as we broke apart and sat on the side of the bed. Jason walked closer. I leaned forward and grazed my fingernails down the inside of his thigh, put my mouth over the head of his shaft and sucked. He tasted warm and smooth with a hint of lemon soap. I sucked harder, cupped his balls and grasped his cock. Jason's breath hitched in his throat.

"Ness, stop. If you carry on like this, I'm going to come in your mouth."

I ran my tongue over his cockhead and lay back. "I'd have liked that."

Jason lay beside me and kissed my lips. "Would you now?" He kissed my jawline, under my ear and down my neck. "And what else would you like?" he murmured.

He put his hand on my breast, his mouth on my nipple and sucked, cupping the fullness of my breast and squeezing. I tilted my breast forward.

"Yes, that. Don't make it nice."

Jason sucked harder. I arched my back as he lightly bit my nipple and the sensation tingled between my legs. "Oh, yes…good."

He pinched hard enough to feel, but not painfully, and it sent a shock wave of pleasure through my groin. I mewled in the back of my throat.

Jason kissed my neck. "More?"

"Yes, more."

Jason fastened his mouth on my nipple and his hand on my breast and I moaned, throwing my head back as he sucked and bit and squeezed, his every touch enough but not too much. The sensation built until I panted.

I stroked over his butt cheeks, circled underneath his hip, grasped his cock and moved his foreskin up and back slowly with a little pressure.

Jason tracked his finger through my wet center then pushed it inside me and added another when I parted my legs to urge him deeper. My breathing quickened as he touched and explored. He raised his head. "Now?" he asked.

"Yes, now."

Jason lay over me, replaced his finger with his cockhead and pushed his shaft inside me. My breath caught as he stretched and filled me, his words a soft whisper near my ear. "Oh, baby, that feels good."

I met his hips with mine and wrapped my legs around his thighs. Jason thrust faster. I pressed my fingers into his back, tilted my hips higher for his cock to hit deeper and the friction built. "Jason. Yes…that's good.

Breathing hard above me, he increased the pace. I met his downward movements, panting, back arched, eyes closed.

His muscles tensed, his thrusts shortened and he moaned, "Oh, God, baby…yes."

The throb spread from my clitoris, pulsed out and through my pelvis into the top of my thighs and I writhed as my orgasm shook me. "Jason…"

I stilled, my breath coming in gasps as the waves of my orgasm rolled on. Jason breathed short and quick and I held him to me. His heart was beating as fast against my breast as mine was beneath it. He kissed my neck, eased his cock out, rolled to his side and took me with him. I lay on my side, curled against him with his arm underneath me and breathed him in—Hugo, a little sweat and the unmistakable musky aroma of orgasmic sex. *Lovely.*

Jason stroked my back. "You were beautiful, baby."

I kissed his chest. "You're pretty damn gorgeous yourself, Mr. Peterson. Thank you."

Jason ran his hand over my shoulder and down my back. I relaxed under his touch and thought how easy it would be to fall asleep held securely in his arms until the reality of my unconscious aggression hit, when my nightmare would put an end to my dreamy abstraction. I eased away from Jason and reached for my wrap at the foot of the bed.

"Do you want a glass of wine?" I asked as I covered myself.

"Please."

I tightened the belt when I put my feet to the floor. "Back in a minute. I'll just use the bathroom."

I closed the en suite door behind me, used the loo and took a quick peek in the mirror to check that my makeup hadn't smeared all over my face. Jason had sat on the side of the bed and re-dressed when I walked back into the bedroom.

"The loo's in there whenever you need it."

I walked to my dressing table, picked up my brush and ran it through my hair. Jason walked up behind me, slipped his arms around my waist and looked over the top of my head at the muddle of cosmetics on its surface.

"What do you do with all this stuff? I wouldn't have thought you had enough face to fit it all on."

I leaned against Jason and smiled. "Work makeup, evening makeup, weekend makeup… All the things I need to get it on and all the gear I need to chisel it back off again."

"And do you never put the top back on anything?"

I laughed. "But then I'd only have to take it off again the next time I used it."

I put my hairbrush down in the middle of the mess, turned, stood on tiptoes and lifted my face. Jason bent his to mine and kissed my lips.

I took my phone out of my handbag, offered Jason my hand and led the way down our hallway and into our living room—a large, square space made more spacious by the complete absence of any dining room furniture, our compact kitchen behind the wall tucked into the corner.

"And this is the rest of it," I said.

Jason's gaze moved over our sofa, L-shaped and covered by us with throws and cushions, and the feature wall with its covering of photographs in different frames of differing sizes. I noticed Jules' abandoned shoes in front of the sofa, toed them under the coffee table and picked up the used wine glasses and empty satay container from the top of it.

"I'll just get rid of these and get the wine."

Jason smiled and looked at the French windows. "Thanks. I see you've got a balcony."

"It's so warm. Open it up if you'd like. I'll bring the wine out there."

I took the dirty glasses through to the kitchen, poured wine into two fresh ones and took them to the balcony. Jason leaned against the balustrade rail, looking outward at the looming shape of a darkened Stamford Bridge. I passed Jason his glass and stood alongside him.

"I can't believe how quiet it is here compared to mine. There's barely a hum from the traffic, even though the Fulham Road's so close. My flat has got the patio doors and a Juliette balcony but I wouldn't open them."

"I know. When Jules and I moved in we thought it was a bit too quiet, but now I love it. And we can get outside, even if it is only this little bit."

Jason moved closer to narrow the gap between our arms and we gazed out at the night lights blinking in the darkness, not high enough to spot any of the illuminated London landmarks but still a sparkling city nightscape that could have been used as the backdrop for any number of movies. Jason moved his head and looked farther out.

"An easy commute into work, too."

I smiled at him as I remembered Maisie's loitering at work earlier. "How do you get into work?"

Jason looked at me. "I bike in usually. Why?"

"Somebody at work has been trying to find out and bump into you when you arrive."

He smiled. "Oh, they have, have they? Well, it's unlikely that they will. I come up in the secure lift from the garage in the mornings. Where have they been hovering? By the main entrance? Reception?"

"Outside the front doors, I think. And it's not a 'they' now. It's just the one. Annie has started seeing Craig from IT. She's going to the cinema with him tomorrow night."

"Good. Getting there then. Is the other one close to giving up yet?"

I shook my head. "Not showing any sign of it. What will you do if she doesn't?"

"I'll have a word with Jenny in HR. She'll know how to tell her it's going nowhere without causing offense, but it would be a lot less awkward all round if it just stops without anything ever needed to be said."

"I don't think she gets it. The way she looks, I don't think she gets many guys turning her down."

"She must get some. Everybody does."

"So, who's been turning you down?"

Jason put his arm around my waist and kissed my shoulder. "I thought you might after I managed to goose you in the pub on Friday."

I leaned closer and tilted my head. Jason moved his lips to my neck. "You still asked."

Jason urged me closer. I turned and stood against him. He said, "I wanted to from the first day you walked into the office. I just didn't know where to look for you out of work until you mentioned your wine bar when we were all in the Barleymow."

Jason's cock hardened as he pressed against me and I ran my fingers over the bulge at the front of his jeans. "You want more?"

Jason stood his glass on the balcony table, took mine, put it beside his and put his arms around me. "Yes, more."

I traced my fingers over the outline of Jason's erection. "You maybe want me to sit on this for a while?"

Jason tightened his hold and put his lips on mine. I took his hand, walked into the living room and over to the sofa. Jason glanced at the living room door. I pulled the belt on my wrap and the front of it parted. Jason moved his gaze to the swell of my breasts.

"Jules will text before she leaves Ben's and she won't come in here if the door's shut."

I tugged on the zip of Jason's jeans. He pulled his tee over his head, eased his erect cock out of his jeans and boxers, shrugged out of them and sat. I stood in front of him and dropped my wrap to the floor. Jason leaned forward, cupped my butt, stroked down my center, put his head forward and tasted.

"Sweet, baby. You taste good. I like bare."

I straddled Jason as he sought deeper with his tongue. He brushed his fingertips over my hardened nipple. "More or sore?"

I kissed his lips. "More. It will let me know where you've been tomorrow when my nipples rub inside my bra."

Jason pinched my nipple. I pushed my breast forward for more. He grazed his teeth on my shoulder as he worked on my nipple with his fingers—a tug, a soft touch, a harder pinch, a sensation of pleasure followed by a brief nip of pain that rippled through my stomach and into my groin.

I breathed faster, sat straighter and moaned as he squeezed my breasts, sucked on my nipple then used his teeth to tug.

I raised my hips and grasped his erection. Jason released my breast. I tilted my pelvis higher, eased the head of his cock into my wet center and closed my eyes as the width and length of his shaft stretched me. I put his hands on my hips.

"Do you want to set the pace?" I asked him.

Jason held my hips and moved me forward. I put my hands on his shoulders and rocked on the hardness inside me, his cock hitting deep as his grip on my hips asked for me to move faster. Jason breathed harder. His hands squeezed.

"Ness…"

I moved faster on Jason's shaft, tilted my hips to feel his cock on the sensitive spot inside me, ground down and shouted as his cock rubbed against it and waves of sensation throbbed and spread through my groin. "Jason! Oh, fuck!"

"Oh, God! Ness…yes." He groaned.

I rested against his chest, panting as blood pulsed through my pelvis in time to that pumping through my heart. Jason held me to him, the rise and fall of his chest mirroring that of my breasts while he stroked the back of my hair. "Beautiful."

I raised my head, kissed his lips, eased off his cock and picked up my wrap. Jason reached for his clothes and put his boxers and jeans back on.

"I'll just use your bathroom?" he asked.

"Sure. Help yourself." I said.

Jason picked up his tee and pulled it on over his head as he opened the living room door. I looked at my phone, saw no message from Jules so left it on the coffee table and used my loo after Jason.

He stood looking at the photographs on the wall when I walked back into the living room. I walked over, stood alongside him and saw that he was looking at a photo of the peeps in the garden at home—me and Dad, small, compact and dark, Mum and Jilly—willowy, blonde and, at five feet nine, taller than both of us.

"That's the peeps."

"Is that your dad? You look like him."

"Yeah, and Jilly looks like Mum."

"Jilly?"

"My younger sister."

My phone vibrated on the coffee table. "That'll be Jules." I picked up my phone and read her message. "She'll be home in ten."

Jason put his arms around me. "I'd better go, Ness. It's getting late."

I put my arms around his neck and opened my mouth, closed my eyes and pressed in closer as I tasted and didn't break away until the front door rattled. I let Jason go and he sat on the sofa and put his feet into his shoes. I walked to the living room door with him as Jules walked down the hallway.

"Hi, Jason. You just off? I'm Jules, by the way. Ness, I'm going to put some coffee on. Do you want one?"

I nodded then walked with Jason to the front door and stood in his arms with mine around him.

"See you at work tomorrow, Ness."

"Code's seven-four-two-six to open the gates. See you tomorrow."

I opened the front door and watched Jason walk toward the lift before I shut it and went to find Jules. She turned around in the kitchen, raised her eyebrows and gave me the big eyes.

"So, I've got the coffee. Get in there, you, and spill it."

I laughed, followed Jules into the living room and sat on the sofa while she filled our mugs. Jules handed me mine then sat beside me.

"So…?"

I sniffed my mug and sipped. "So, he's every bit as gorgeous naked as you would hope from seeing him dressed."

Jules looked at me and asked the question with her eyes. "Every bit?"

I gave Jules some big eyes back. "Oh, yeah, for sure. You sit on that bit and you definitely know what you've sat on."

"And the sex was...?"

"Good. Actually, for me, really good. He knew exactly what I wanted and just how far to take it. My nipples are zinging, even if I'm not walking the walk of the tender in other places too."

Jules snorted into her mug. "You're a kinky cow sometimes, Vanessa DeRay."

I rolled my eyes at her. "Oh, yeah, yeah, Julia Henderson. And this from the woman who I happen to know likes a bit of a fanny slap herself."

Jules laughed and I joined in.

"Besides, I'm not that bad. I'm hardly into 'fifty fun things you can do with cable ties and rope', am I? I just like sex that pushes it a bit."

"So, I'm presuming you're thinking that Jason might, too?"

"I'm thinking he might. And if he does, he'll know exactly how far he can push it—which, let's face it, neither Ryan nor James do."

"Neither of them have really done it for you, have they?"

"No, not really. They're both pretty good straight up, but the first venture over the line with them was enough to warn me that neither of them knew the difference between 'sexy, ouch' and 'ouch, ouch, that bloody well hurt'."

Jules smiled into her mug. "Actually, Ryan quite did it for me even if, as you say, he was a bit straight up."

"He'll be back from Thailand soon. You thinking of going there again?"

Jules shook her head. "No. I might not be ready to find Ben's overnight toothbrush in my bathroom yet but I don't want anyone else but him in my bed. Did you make any plans to see Jason again?"

"Not really. We just said we'd see each other at work tomorrow."

Jules finished her coffee and put her mug on the table. "Hands off after being skin to skin... How do think that's going to go?

I put my mug alongside hers and laughed. "God knows! It makes me glad Maisie swapped desks now, though. I might have sat there all day gazing into his office and picturing him naked, else."

"Let me know. I'm going to hit the sheets now."

"With you there, girlie."

I turned off the lamp and followed Jules to the hallway, used my bathroom, got under my duvet and drifted off to pictures of Jason in my head, feeling his touch as my nipples rubbed against the sheet and the faint smell of Hugo Boss made itself known to my nose from my quilt.

Chapter Three

I walked into the office just after nine. Jason looked up from his laptop and watched me with a grin. My back toward Maisie, I smiled back at him then sat at my desk.

Annie did the coffee run at ten and I worked my way through the jobs in my tray until eleven, when Derek walked over from the group of workstations that ran the accounts payable section, stood by Maisie's desk and waited for her to notice him — his brown eyes fixed on her, a slight pink tinge on his cheeks.

Maisie carried on writing then looked up. "Yes, Derek?"

"Oh, hi, Maisie. I was wondering... I mean, I just wanted to ask. If it's not too much trouble..."

Maisie tapped her fingernails on the desk. "Derek, just get on with it. Spit it out. What do you want?"

"Ah. Um... I've got to go to a meeting with Jason and some of the sales and marketing team but the settlement checks have got to go out in the lunchtime post. Could I borrow Vanessa for an hour to do them for me while I'm in there, please?"

"And why have you got to go the meeting if I haven't? If sales and marketing are involved, then I should be, too. I'm section leader of sales commissions, after all."

Derek's cheeks turned a little pinker. "It's all to do with a big order we're going to bid for. If we get it, there won't be any commission as such but I do have to make sure the invoicing is ready to go."

"Well, I suppose you could have an hour of Vanessa's time if the meeting is to help Jason. Vanessa, is your input up-to-date? You don't have a backlog there, do you?"

I looked in my work tray. "I'm not behind, so there's nothing here that can't wait for an hour."

"Well, okay then. Yes, Derek, Vanessa can spare you an hour."

Derek's smile lit up his face and he looked different, more awake and lively rather than serious, hesitant and shy.

"Maisie, thank you. You've really helped me out. That's so kind of you."

Maisie flicked her hair over her shoulder and smiled. "Yes, it is, isn't it? I'm always happy to help in a crisis. I'm sure Jason will appreciate it."

I followed Derek to his workstation and sat in his chair. He stood behind me and showed me a batch of freshly printed checks and settlement letters.

"Just match the check to the supplier letter, mark it off in the ledger and envelope it up. If you can get them to the post room by twelve, that would great."

Derek looked at the girl at the next workstation.

"Do you know Jess? She'll help you out if you get stuck on anything."

I smiled at Jess, blonde like Maisie but with fine, short hair cut in a straight line above her shoulders. Jess smiled at me as Derek picked up a notepad and pen from his desk and walked away.

"Vanessa, isn't it?"

I nodded.

"Just shout if you need anything. It must be nice to get away from the Queen Bee for an hour."

"Queen Bee?"

Jess flicked her eyes in Maisie's direction. "The one all the guys buzz around and my, my, doesn't she just know it?" Jess nodded at Jason's office. "Well, all except the one that drives her mad and cheers the rest of us up to no end."

"Maisie's been okay to me so far. I didn't realize she's not very popular."

"You wait until you've known her longer. She's wound up several guys in the company then just dropped them. And she always seems to pick on a guy that another girl likes, gets them running after her instead then dumps them when she's proved her point."

"Ouch. Annie's just started seeing Craig, but Maisie wouldn't do that to her best friend, would she?"

"I wouldn't personally bet on it, but this time Annie's probably safe. Craig's already on Maisie's 'done and dusted' list and I've never known her to go back for seconds."

I looked at the company name on the first letter and pulled the batch of checks forward to find a match. "I'll keep an eye out."

Jess smiled. "I'm just glad I can watch from the sidelines. I've got a boyfriend outside of work and he has nothing to do with this place."

I picked up an envelope as I found the match, ticked it off in the ledger and folded the letter and check into the envelope. It took me much less than an hour to match them all and I looked at Jess as I gummed down the last envelope.

"Can you tell me where the post room is, Jess? I've not been there."

"Ground floor. You know, in reception where the photo is of the Gabriella necklace?"

"I've seen several photos of jewelry with the name Gabriella on them in reception. Is Gabriella the name of that line of jewelry? The necklace is on the big blow-up of a magazine cover on the wall just inside the entrance door, isn't it?"

"That's the one. Gabriella's the name of the jeweler who designed the pieces in the photos, not the jewelry itself. The door to the left of the photo of the necklace is the post room. It's a secure entry point because some of the deliveries are for the workshop on floor two, but just press the buzzer. Someone will come to the door and take the post from you."

I smiled. "Okay. Got it. Thanks, Jess. It's been good to do something different."

Jess nodded at Maisie. "Wander over for a chat anytime you need a five-minute break."

"Thanks again. I might just do that."

I picked up the envelopes, dropped them off in the post room and was back at my workstation before the hour was up. My phone vibrated as I returned to my desk with a message from Jules.

Hey, babe. How's work and J? You still coming to girls' club Tonite?

I haven't seen J to talk to yet. Absolutely, the club. See you home.

I heard voices behind me as people walked out of the meeting room a few minutes later and a message from Jason arrived in my inbox twenty minutes after that.

Coffee?

Sure. See you at the machine

I waited for Jason to walk past my workstation, gave him a couple of minutes to clear the office, followed him out and stood alongside him at the coffee machine. Jason handed me a cup.

I smiled up as Jason smiled down and my heart rate sped as my body responded to the remembrance of his touch, the feel of his skin naked against mine, the hardness of him inside me and the way the green of his eyes warmed and darkened as he stood looking at me.

"You good, Ness?"

"Yeah. You?"

A door banged farther along the corridor and I pulled my gaze away as Jason did the same and put the code for his own coffee into the machine. I took in a deeper breath to steady my heart rate and sipped from my cup. "Long meeting?"

"Wasn't it? And it created more problems than it solved. I've got to fly out to Spain later this afternoon. There are some issues I've got to sort out face-to-face with our 'I can't possibly leave my golf' chairman."

I smiled. "No sun and sangria for you, then. What time do you fly?"

"I've just booked the flight. Four-thirty. I've just got time to get home, pack some gear and make the airport. Are you home tonight? I'll call you?"

"Sure. I've got a class with Jules at the leisure center from seven until nine but I'll be in after that, sometime around ten."

We walked back to the office and Jason left it again twenty minutes later, his laptop bag in his hand. Maisie gazed after him.

"Well, where's he going at this time of the day? He's not down on the staff movements listing as being anything other than in the office this week."

Days of Maisie speculating on Jason's whereabouts loomed large in my mind as I watched the unanswered question pass across her face, so I told her. "Spain."

Maisie's eyes widened and she stared at me. "Spain! And just how do you know that, Vanessa?"

"I saw Jason at the coffee machine and that's what he said."

A flush rose on Maisie's cheeks. "Well, really! And you know that and I don't, do you? I'm not sure you should be by-passing me and talking directly to Jason like that, Vanessa."

I kept my face neutral but held Maisie's eyes as I answered. "I'm not bypassing you for anything to do with work, Maisie. It was just a conversation between two people that happen to work in the same place, and if Jason talks to me then I'm going to answer him. One thing I am *not* going to do is ask your permission to do so. And you can take that as a given, whether it's Jason or anyone else I happen to be conversing with."

Maisie's gaze slid away and she looked down at her hands. "All right, all right. But I'm still in charge when it's anything to do with work."

"If it's about the work I'm employed to do here then fair enough. Point conceded."

Maisie lifted her head and smiled. All signs of displeasure were gone from her face. "Sorry if that was a bit over the top and all that. It's just that, you know, I like him. When did he say he'd be back?"

I shrugged and pulled my keyboard forward. "No idea. Jason didn't say and I didn't ask."

I worked through until five, wished Annie a good time on her date with Craig and caught the bus home. Jules, sitting on the sofa eating pasta salad from a supermarket container, waved her fork at me as I walked into the living room.

"Yours is in the fridge. I went for the chicken and bacon tonight."

I slipped off my shoes, walked around them to the kitchen, collected my salad and took it to the sofa. "Thanks, babe. I didn't fancy lunch."

Jules swallowed her mouthful and smiled. "I thought you might have worked up quite an appetite after your workout with Jason last night. How was it today?"

"It was okay. I didn't see a lot of him. He was in a meeting all morning and flew out to Spain this afternoon. He said he'd call me later. I had a little bump with Maisie, though, over whether I need her permission to talk to him."

"Ouch and oh dear. What's she going to say when she finds out that you're doing more than talking with him?"

"It will be messy, I think. She went a bit over the top today when she found out I knew Jason was going to Spain and she didn't, but I'm not jumping the gun on that one. I've slept with Jason just the once and that's the way it could stay. I've made no plans for second helpings and neither has he."

Jules speared a mouthful of pasta on her fork. "Yeah, yeah."

I joined Jules in taking a mouthful of pasta. "Maybe...but nothing else has been arranged by either of us yet."

I changed my business skirt for street clothes after we finished eating and walked with Jules to the leisure center through thick summer air. Jules pushed open the door to the gym come basketball court come five-a-side pitch. Ben stood on the far side of the room talking with half a dozen other women that included Paula, and he looked up as Jules let the door swing shut behind us.

"I think you two are the last. I've had texts from the girls away on holiday and there's quite a few missing."

Jules and I took our places and Ben set up the first scenario—a lone woman walking, an attacker coming at her from behind—and the group took turns to stop his attack with a hand or a foot chopped down on whichever of the disabling pressure points on his body we could reach.

Ben moved on to an attempted handbag snatch and we hit his pressure points with minimal damage until he launched himself at Jules with a muscled arm around her throat as we all milled around waiting for him to set the next scene.

Jules reacted instantly, didn't try to break away but spun within his hold to face him, put her hand between his legs and smacked firm and hard on the pressure point under his testicles. Ben gagged but didn't vomit as he lost consciousness. Jules kneeled beside him, waited then swiped his arm with her hand when his eyes fluttered open.

"You know I hate that one, you silly sod!"

Ben sat and took a deep breath in. "I know. That's why I did it. You've been holding back because it's me. You can't do that."

A tear sparkled in the corner of Jules' eye. "I've got better things to be doing with your bloody bollocks than that, thank you!"

"Then concentrate. We're not here for the fun of it, are we?"

I left them and walked over to Paula. "How is his sister?" she said.

"A lot better, but the anniversary's coming up."

Paula reached out and squeezed my hand. "Makes me glad mine was only an attempted bag snatch."

I returned the pressure of Paula's hand. "Makes me glad that violent as ours was, it was still just a mugging and not anything sexual. Jules and I might have been left with a couple of hang ups but thankfully not any issues on that front. Want to walk back? I think Jules and Ben could be a while."

Paula smiled. "Sure."

I let myself into our flat just after ten, wiped the sweat from my face and turned the shower to cool, then turned it down another notch as I stood under the spray and felt Jason's touch from last night when the cold water hit my nipples.

With a towel around me, I took a glass of wine and my phone to the balcony, sat on a patio chair and willed the phone to ring. It obliged a little after ten-thirty. I smiled when I heard Jason's voice. "Hey, how's you and hotter-than-here England?"

"Hotter but not sunnier, I think. I'm out on the balcony and even up here it's like I'm wrapped in a furry blanket rather than a towel. It's going to tank sometime soon," I told him.

"Just a towel?"

"Yeah, just the towel. Hang on." I tapped on my camera icon, adjusted my towel to show the swell of my breasts, added a pair of Jessica Rabbit big, red puckered lips to my face, took the pic and sent it. Jason laughed on the other end of the line.

"Beautiful, but did I have to have the lips?"

I smiled at my phone. "You could have had the big, pink, licky tongue instead. How was your flight? The hotel?"

"The flight was as uncomfortable as short-haul economy always is but, thankfully, only a couple of hours of nearly eating my knees. The hotel's just a generic, could-be-anywhere place."

"Aw, not a swanky, five-star golf resort?"

"No, not for me, but I'll be visiting one in the morning for a breakfast meeting. There's a trade fair coming up and one half of the sales team is pulling one way and half the other. There'll be a lot of upfront costs involved if Mike Parker's team get their way. It'll be quite a big financial risk for the company."

"And Mr. Belmond has the final say?"

"Up for negotiation."

"Is he easy to work with?"

"No, not always. If he makes a decision, he doesn't like to backtrack and change his mind. He's quite stubborn like that, but I'll make sure he's up-to-date on the financial consequences for the company either way."

"Good luck with that one, then. Let me know how it goes?"

"I'll phone you tomorrow. You going to bed now?"

"Soon. When Jules gets home. You?"

"I ought to. Breakfast is at six. What do you wear to sleep in?"

"This hot and sticky? Just skin."

"Mmmm. I think I might fall asleep picturing that."

I laughed. "Oh, will you? Then I shall try picturing you in your anywhere-in-the-world hotel bed. Night. Good luck for tomorrow."

"Night, Ness. Speak tomorrow."

I blew a kiss down the phone, cut the connection and took my empty glass back inside. Jules walked in through the front door as I put my glass in the kitchen. I called out to her. "You okay, babe? Ben?"

"I'm fine, Ness. So's Ben now. I'm going to take a shower."

"Do you want anything?"

"A water would be good."

I took a bottle of water out of the fridge and Jules pressed it to her face after I handed it over in her bedroom. "This sticky weather's getting to me today. I'll shower and get into bed. Did Jason call?"

"Yeah. I've just finished talking to him. I'm on top of the duvet tonight with the fan beside the bed on full blast. I'll see you in the morning."

"Night, Ness."

I walked into my bedroom and adjusted the head of the fan to blow onto my body on the bed. My phone vibrated as I lay down on top of my duvet and I opened a message from Jason to see a selfie of him sitting on his bed, his back resting against the headboard, dressed in jeans but no top, the start of his smile tilting in the corners of his lips. I read the text underneath it.

Wish I was where you are. x

I replied.

Mmmm. Wish you were too. x

I left Jason's photo on my phone screen, propped my phone upright on the table beside my bed and fell asleep looking at it.

* * * *

I arrived at work in the morning with my face already beaded with sweat from a five-minute walk from the bus stop. The humid atmosphere outside seemed to infect everyone with a lack of energy, even in the cooler interior of the office. Time dragged, with Maisie sighing every time she looked up at Jason's empty office, and I gave up at four and told Maisie I would make the time up another day, to her languid agreement.

I picked up two tuna salad bowls and a bottle of cold white Chianti after I got off the bus, took the coldest shower I could bear when I got home then flopped onto the sofa with our standing floor-fan blowing over me. Jules came home at five-thirty, took one look at me then went and did the same.

"I didn't stop at the shop," she said as she sat at the other end of the sofa to me. I stood and moved the fan to point in her direction.

"It's okay. I did. And I picked up a cold bottle of white."

Jules moved her face closer to the fan. "I could do an icy white tonight."

"I'll get us a glass. Tuna salad. Do you want to eat yet?"

"Not yet. Later, when it's cooler. Have you heard from Jason?"

I walked to the kitchen, brought back two frosted glasses of white and handed one to Jules.

"Not so far today, but he said he'd call later. He sent me a pic last night. Do you want a look?"

73

Jules grinned and held out her hand. I loaded Jason's pic and passed my phone over.

"Woohoo there, girlie. That's fit. Better not let Maisie see that on your phone. She'll scratch your eyes out."

"I won't, but whether it's me now or someone else in the future that Jason's sleeping with, I'm pretty sure it won't ever be Maisie. For whatever reason, she obviously doesn't do it for him and I'm starting to wonder whether that isn't a lot of the attraction for her. I've been hearing that she's used to having her pick of any guy she wants at work and now she's got one that's said, 'no thanks', or rather hasn't even taken enough notice of her to even get to that point."

"And she's very pretty, you said?"

"Very. Think walking, talking Barbie doll, about five-seven, with natural, blonde curls right down her back."

Jules handed me my phone. "See if you can sneak a pic of her on that tomorrow. I'd love to have a peek."

"Sure. I'm sure it'll be easy enough. I'll just ask."

Jules and I finished our wine and she refilled the glasses while I searched on the telly for something to watch and came up with two old episodes of *Buffy* to take us back to our teenage years. We ate our salads and finished the bottle during the second episode. I flicked the television off at ten-thirty.

"I'm going to take a second shower and catch up on Facebook on my bed," I said.

"I think I will, too. There should be some stuff on there from Mark and Simon. Their runway show was last night."

"See in you the morning, babe."

"And you, girlie."

I goosebumped my skin under the cold stream, loaded Facebook on my Mac, sat on my bed and watched photos of two of the most beautiful men on the planet fill the screen, modelling next spring's fashion in a high-end hotel in Las Vegas. I scrolled through the pics, sent Mark and Simon my likes and my phone vibrated with a call from Jason just after eleven.

"Hey, Ness. How are you? Did you have a good day?"

I smiled at my phone. "I'm good, although it was like the day of the living dead in the office today. Don't tell the boss, but I'd had enough by four and legged it. You?"

Jason laughed. "He won't blame you at all. He did something similar himself this afternoon and snuck off for a few hours of sun by the pool then jibbed out of dinner and called room service."

"You did get some sun then. What about the sangria?"

"I stuck to a cold beer. And I've had my payback. I've burned my back. I couldn't reach the middle of it when I put on the sun screen."

"Aw, babe. Were there no little señoritas around to offer to rub your sunscreen on for you?"

"Well, now you that you mention it, the waiter that brought my beer looked like he might offer, but he wasn't my type. I've never quite been able to go for someone with that big a moustache."

I laughed. "I don't blame you. Moustaches tickle, let alone the fact that you'd probably have found a bit of last night's dinner lurking in it. How bad's the burn? Your skin hasn't blistered, has it?"

Jason snorted into his phone. "Who have you known that kept a ticklish late-night snack in their facial hair?"

"Ibiza with the girls. Probably about number four on my 'ew, you've just grossed me out, time to a do a bunk' list."

"Oh, God! How many on the list?"

"Oh, yeah, yeah, you. How many on yours?"

Jason laughed. "Pick any number from one to oh, God, I can't remember."

"Back at you, then. How was your meeting this morning?"

"So-so. I've left Peter some figures for him to look through tonight and he's left me with something to think over, too. He wants me to release one of the company's assets to offer as part of the deal our sales and marketing team is putting together for the trade fair and I'm not sure it's either worth it or the right time to do so."

"How will it be at work if you have to turn him down? Will you be okay?"

"I'll be fine. Don't worry. He's used to me saying 'no' on this one. I'll see him at breakfast again tomorrow, then I'm out of here if there's room on a flight. Can I call around and see you if I get home tomorrow?"

I sighed. "Well, as you seem to have a lack of obliging señoritas and don't fancy a hairy waiter, I think you'll have to. Somebody ought to get some after-sun lotion on your back if you can't reach."

"Just my back?"

"Perhaps I'd better do all of you, just to make sure."

"All?"

I breathed in deeper. "Every inch."

"Then I think I'd better get online and see what flights there are. See you tomorrow, I hope."

I blew a kiss down the line, cut the connection and fell asleep thinking of the cooling effect of the peppermint and jojoba oil mix sliding onto warm skin.

* * * *

I called out to Jules when I was dressed and ready for work in the morning. "Jules, have you got that oil that you had made up when you got sunburned when we went away?"

"Yes, babe. It's in my bathroom. Help yourself. Who needs it?"

I walked into Jules' bathroom, took the oil from the cabinet over her sink and tipped the bottle sideways to check that there was enough left.

"It's for Jason. He caught the sun on his back yesterday."

Jules grinned. "And you're going to rub that on for him, are you?"

I smiled. "Oh, yes. I'm hoping so. Jason's going to try and get back today."

I put the oil on my bedside table, headed out into unstirring air and arrived at work half an hour early to make up some of the time from my missing hour. Maisie looked at me already logged on and working when she and Annie walked into the office just after nine.

"You've started early." She yawned.

"Just half an hour. I'll work through lunch for the other half, if that's okay?"

Maisie sat and opened her desk drawer. "Sure."

I smiled at Annie as she sat beside me. "How was the movies with Craig? Good film?"

"Really good and we went for a pizza after. We're going bowling on Saturday. I might, sort of, see if he wants to stay over then."

"Good for you. Jules and I are out on Saturday. We're meeting up with a couple of the girls from uni, having a few drinks and something to eat in town."

"Lovely," Maisie said. "I don't know what I'm doing yet. Annie and I would normally have hit the town but now…"

Pink crept onto Annie's cheeks. "Sorry, Maisie. But we can still go out on Friday."

"It'll have to do, I suppose, but I hope you're not going to start seeing him both weekend nights." Maisie glanced over my shoulder at Jason's empty office. "Well, not until I'm sorted with Jason, anyway."

"I wouldn't do that. Maisie. We're still best friends."

Maisie pulled her keyboard forward. "Good. I'll have a think about what we're going to do tomorrow night then."

I carried on working and kept an eye on my phone as I worked. It vibrated with a message from Jason just after four.

Out of here shortly. Flight 7 UK time. Let you know when I've landed?

Sure. Have a good knee-chomping flight. Hope all on time for you.

I smiled at my phone as I put it down. Annie looked at me.

"Good news?"

"Just a message from a friend to say they've managed to get a flight and they're on their way home."

I pulled my keyboard forward, printed copies of my daily input and managed to spend nearly an hour dropping them off by using the stairs rather than the lift, then I remembered Jules' request for a picture as I put my stationery in my desk drawer.

"Maisie, Annie, would you mind if I took a pic of you and the office to show Jules so she can see who and where I'm talking about when I rabbit on about work when I get home?"

Maisie smiled, tweaked her hair with fingers and shook her head to loosen the curls down her back.

"Sure. Having trouble getting it over in words, are you? A pic'll get it out there for you all in one go. I'll perch on the side of the desk for the first one."

Maisie sat her butt on the edge of her desk. I lined up my phone, nodded 'ready' and Maisie smiled, pouted and peeked coyly up through a whole range of selfie poses one after the other without stopping while I tried to keep up tapping on my phone.

"There. That should do it." She smiled. "I'm always being asked to do that. Follow me on Insta if you want. I've got over a thousand followers now."

"Thanks, Maisie. I've got some good shots. Perhaps a last one with Annie, if that's okay? Then if I take a wide-angle from your desk, Jules can see a bit of the layout of the office."

Annie stood beside Maisie and I took the photo and one that showed our workstations and included Jason's goldfish bowl. I smiled goodnight to them when I left, made my way home and opened the front door to our flat just after six with two plates of microwavable noodles from the local shop. I called through to Jules' bedroom door over the noise of water running in her shower.

"I've bought noodles for supper."

"Thanks, Ness. I bought us a salad but I'd rather have the noodles. We can have the salads tomorrow. Did you hear from Jason?"

"Yeah. He's on his way home. He'll let me know when he's landed."

Jules walked out of her bathroom wrapped in a towel. "Then I'll walk over to Ben's later."

"No, Jules…"

"Yes, Ness. I'm sure Jason doesn't want to hear me and Ben bouncing around in the bedroom next door yet, not before we've even said hi to each other properly."

"He'll have to get used to it if we carry on seeing each other. We both live here. Other guys haven't minded."

"Other guys have known you and me socially first. Jason doesn't. Take the breathing space, at least for tonight. See if you can get Jason to The Vine tomorrow night so we can say hi."

"Okay. I will and thanks, but only this time. Jason's got a list of casuals so long he's forgotten who's on the end of it, so I should imagine he's done a good bit of bed bouncing in flat shares before."

Jules laughed. "Haven't we all. But take tonight anyway and after that, I'll resume my own bed bouncing activities as normal."

I blew Jules a kiss, dropped the noodles off in the kitchen then showered, plaited my hair wet, dressed in a short sundress and looked through the office pics on my phone until Jules came and sat beside me on the sofa. I passed her my phone and Jules laughed as she scrolled through them.

"How many did you take of her?"

"No choice, babe. She posed like a pro, one after the other without stopping."

Jules stopped on a shot of Maisie standing upright that showed her hourglass but slightly top-heavy figure, peeking back coyly over her shoulder at the camera.

"Hmmm. I see what you mean about Barbie. I can see why the guys fall for her, but I can also see why some don't."

I looked at the pic with Jules as she turned my phone one way then the other.

"See? When you say Barbie, I think plastic, and when I look at this pic, I think plastic — like she's too carefully put together, artificial, not quite real. I can think of a few guys that wouldn't go for that."

I scrolled to the picture of Annie, straight brown hair that looked good off her face, hazel eyes, the type of girl who could model jumpers for Pringle with a couple of cute spaniel puppies running around her feet.

"I suppose so. What about Annie?"

"Perfect foil. Destined for the house in the country, a Range Rover, several kids and an Aga when she's done the city-life bit, if you ask me."

I smiled. "Yeah, I can see that, but at the moment she's just mesmerized by Maisie, the sort of 'my best friend's so gorgeous' thing. I think she's floating back down to earth, though, from a couple of things she's said to me."

I scrolled to the last pic and showed Jules the workstation set-up with the goldfish bowl behind them.

"Yep, I can get it now. I'll know what you're on about from here on in."

"I'll delete this set now. I can think of better pics I like to look at on my phone."

Jules laughed and poured wine into two glasses. "Yep, and you don't have to tell me which one. Pull the fan closer, babe. I think I'm melting."

I obliged and Jules caught me up on her work in the art gallery, her mum, her grandma's ongoing war with her own hearing aids and Ben, and a bit more Ben, then some more Ben. I topped up our glasses with the last of the bottle around nine.

"Oh, my, God! We'd better eat," Jules giggled.

I heated the noodles in the microwave, took them to the living room with a fresh bottle of wine, poured but didn't pick up my glass again until I'd lined my stomach.

"What time are you going down to Ben's?"

Jules looked at the time display on our sound system. "When I've finished this glass. Put something boppable on, girlie. I need to get these noodles shaken down a bit before I go out and do the real bouncy stuff."

I tapped Play on the iPad and bounced up and down on the sofa beside Jules as we sang along to the lyrics. Jules finished her glass and texted Ben to say she was on her way.

"Right. I'm out of here. I'll text you as I leave Ben's. What time do you think Jason might get here?"

"I'm not sure. If his flight's on time, he should have landed by now, but then there's border control and getting home from Gatwick, and I've no idea whether he's going home first."

"Let me know, but if he's late-late getting here, I'll do the normal and swing straight into bed when I get home."

"Have a good time, babe. I'll see you later or in the morning."

I put my glass on the coffee table as Jules closed the front door, took a quick look around the room, unplugged our laptops and pushed them out of sight under the coffee table with the shoes, walked to my bedroom and saw only two water bottles on my bedside table to get rid of. My phone vibrated in my other hand as I took them to the kitchen. Jason.

In cab. Come straight to yours from airport?

I breathed out as I read the message, thoughts of cancelled flights and delays leaving my head and images of Jason naked on my bed replacing them as I replied.

Sure. See you when you get here. Door code same as gate.

I looked at the time, hoped for just over half an hour, got real, left the front door on the latch just after eleven and heard Jason's voice twenty minutes later.

"Ness…"

"In the living room."

I walked to the living room door, looked down the hallway and breathed in deep as the real-life man in front of me replaced the image in my head and smiled at me. I walked down the hall while Jason put his travel bag on the floor then put my arms around his neck. "Hey, you. Good flight?"

Jason put his arms around me and bent his face closer. "Hey, you back. No."

I closed my eyes as Jason put his lips on mine and pressed in close against his chest as he held me. I stroked my fingertips across his back when our lips parted. "How's this?"

"Needing you."

I traced my fingers down Jason's spine. "You want to come and get yourself naked on my bed, then?"

I put my hand in Jason's, took him to my bedroom and pushed the door shut behind us. I sat on the side of the bed and waited for him to come closer. Jason pulled his T-shirt up and over his head, walked nearer and my nipples pressed against the thin material of my sundress as I looked.

Jason released the button on his jeans, pulled the zip down and wiggled out of them and his boxers, his cock

83

stiff as he released it. I patted the bed and Jason lay face down on it. I kneeled beside him and kissed my lips over the pink V of warm skin in the center of his back.

"You're very warm, there. You ready for cold?"

Jason murmured, "Please…"

"No moving, then, unless I say. I might miss a bit else and have to start over again."

"Yes…"

I spread Jason's arms to each side and straddled his waist. Jason took a deeper breath in as I brushed my bare skin, damp in the center, over his and let him know there was no underwear under the dress.

I poured oil into my hands and stroked over the pink burn. Jason sighed as cooling peppermint shivered his skin. I massaged over the muscles of his shoulders, the bulge at the top of his arms and down to and in between each finger, then over his back and traced my fingertips down his spine. I cupped my breasts out of the top of my dress and trailed my nipples over the contours of his butt as I repositioned myself farther down his body.

Jason murmured, "Ness…yes."

I took more of the oil and worked my hands over the roundness of each butt cheek and traced my fingertip down the sensitive parting between them. Jason's breathing deepened as I paused my fingertip then circled the sensitive place in the center. I shuffled farther down the bed, put my face between his legs and sucked on the underside of his balls peeking at me. Jason moaned. He lifted his buttocks. I nipped his butt cheek.

"Uh, uh, no moving now or I'll have to start at the top again."

"Ness…"

I nipped again, poured more oil and moved my hands down Jason's thighs, massaged each calf, his heels, the soles of his feet and threaded my oily fingers in between in his toes.

"You want to roll over, babe?" I instructed.

I raised myself on my knees and Jason turned over, his cock standing away from his belly. My heart beat faster as I took my sun dress off over my head. The rise and fall of his chest increased as his gaze moved down my body and rested between my legs.

I poured more oil, moved my hands across the taut muscles of Jason's chest and down his belly. His stomach muscles tightened as I moved nearer his cock. I raised my pelvis and teased the tip of his erection straining to meet me with my wet pussy. Jason moaned.

"Ness. Soon. Please…"

My heart rate accelerated as the vein throbbed on his cock. I stroked my hands faster down his legs and over his feet then put the head of his cock inside me and moaned as I sank down on him.

Jason's eyes closed as I enveloped his cock. "Yes. Take me, please…"

I closed my eyes and rubbed my softness against Jason's shaft as I moved back and forth. He grasped my butt. I gripped his forearms and lost myself in the sensation as I bounced and rocked to the pressure of his hands. His muscles tensed as his hands tightened.

"Oh, fuck, yes. Ness…"

My moans joined Jason's as I ground my pelvis down and the throbbing pulsed out from the center of my mound and spread. "Jason… Oh, God! Yes…"

I lay on Jason's chest as blood rushed through me, his heart pounding against my cheek, him holding me close until our breathing slowed, then I eased myself away from his cock, moved up his body and kissed his lips.

Jason opened his eyes. "Shit. Ness, that was…"

I slid my breasts over and around the oil on Jason's chest. "Slippery?"

Jason laughed and slid his oily hands down my back. "I'm covered in the stuff. You definitely got every inch. What is it?"

"It really is a sunburn remedy. Jules had it made up when we traveled abroad. Her skin's very pale. Jojoba base with peppermint to cool and lavender to heal."

Jason rubbed his shoulders against the quilt. "Actually, it's pretty damn good."

I laughed and slipped up and down on his body. "And slippery and quite distinctively stinky. I'll go turn the shower on."

I kissed Jason, pulled away, jumped under the spray and handed him the soap to get the oil off when he joined me. I gave him a towel from the rail when he turned the water off, wrapped another around me and walked into the bedroom to find my sundress.

I picked it up to see oil all over its front, so I dumped it in my nearly full laundry hamper and pulled a clean dress out of the wardrobe while Jason re-dressed behind me. Jason looked at the bed.

"Do you want change the cover? I'll do it for you if you like so you can get it in the machine before it stains."

I touched the oily patches and found them not damp enough to have sunk through to the duvet underneath.

"Don't worry. I'll change it on Saturday in time for when the service wash goes out."

"You don't do laundry?"

I smiled. "Come through to the kitchen. I'll get you a drink and show you where we keep the washing machine — or don't."

Jason followed me out of the bedroom and I left the living room door open to let Jules know it was okay to come in if she came home. We walked to the kitchen. Jason almost filled the floor space when he came into it behind me. I pointed to a cupboard door under the work surface.

"The plumbing for the washing machines in there."

Jason opened the door to see the wine rack we kept in the space, full of bottles from our online delivery.

"See? A much better use of space."

Jason smiled and looked around the rest of the small area that included our oven, gleaming in nearly showroom condition.

"You don't cook either, then?"

"Of course we do."

I counted on the fingers of my hand.

"Beans on toast, egg on toast, cheese on toast, soup and toast... Oh, and instant noodles. Just don't look in our microwave if exploding beans aren't your thing."

I squeezed past Jason, goosed his butt on the way through, opened an overhead cupboard and took out two glasses.

"You going to tell me now you're a Domestic God that's got a kitchen out of a glossy magazine?"

Jason put his arm around my waist and kissed my shoulder. "Come around to mine tomorrow night and find out?"

My heart thumped at the image that bounced into my head as he asked. Me and Jules, my stomach on fire and bleeding, Jules missing her front teeth with blood running down her face, no phones, ringing doorbells, knocking on doors to ask for help and no one answering and the prospect of standing out on the street, waiting for my knock or ring to be answered, shivered down my spine.

I swallowed and figured out a side-step to avoid having to do so, as Jules and I always did since the mugging.

"Okay. But meet me in The Vine first? I don't know where your place is. Can we go back to yours from there?"

Jason put his other arm around me too, held my back against his chest and the tension left me as he kissed my neck.

"Sure. I'll come get you. Take you home with me from there."

I smiled over my shoulder as Jason took his lips away. "Do you want to grab the glasses? The wine's open on the coffee table."

Jason picked up the wine glasses, followed me out and sat beside me on the sofa while I poured. I tapped on the playlist and handed Jason his glass as Bruno Mars' voice came out of the speakers. I curled my legs up and turned my body sideways so I could see Jason's face. He rested his arm along the back of the sofa, twisted his body and looked at me.

"Did you have a worse flight back from Spain than on your way there, then?" I asked.

"Just a bit. On the flight out I had an aisle seat, but on the way back, a window with a bloke beside me on his way home from a stag do and so hungover that he snored and dribbled down his chin all the way back. How was it in work today?"

I laughed. "Ew, he sounds revolting. Work was okay but still half-asleep with the heat. Did you get done what you needed to?"

"Nearly, but I need to pick Nick Davies' brains tomorrow and get some final valuations. I'll have a look at the figures again when I've got them."

"Nick Davies?"

"Sorry, Nick's one of our goldsmiths. He's been with the company nearly from the start and the valuations I need are for some of the company's older commissions."

"And you'll have to tell the chairman either way after?"

"After the weekend at the latest. The trade fair's the week after. The sales team need a few days to prepare their bid, one way or the other."

I stretched and kissed Jason's cheek. "Good luck with that one, then. I hope it all doesn't get too sticky for you."

Jason put his arm around my shoulders and I tilted my face up for his kiss. My phone vibrated on the coffee table. I stroked my fingers down Jason's face.

"That'll be Jules."

Jason smiled. "I'd better get home and get unpacked. What time will you be in The Vine tomorrow?"

I sat straighter and Jason took his arm away. "Nine, nine-thirty. Do you need to call a cab?"

"It's okay. I'll flag one out on the street." Jason stood and I walked him to the front door, wrapped my arms around his neck and lifted my face to kiss him goodbye. "I'll see you at work tomorrow."

Jason lowered his face to mine. "But I don't get to do this at work."

I pressed close as Jason put his lips on mine, threaded my fingers through the back of his hair and opened my mouth. Jason held me tightly to him, one hand on my back, the other on my butt.

"Until tomorrow night."

"Until tomorrow, Ness. See you in the morning."

I opened the front door and let Jason out. Jules stepped out of the lift, glanced toward our front door and put her foot in the way of the lift door to keep it open.

"I'll hold it for you, Jason. This lift's got a mind of its own. It'll take ages to get it back up here again if I let it go."

"Powered by snails on a treadmill, for sure," I called down to her.

Jason smiled, walked toward her and thanked her as he got into the lift. Jules took her foot from the door.

"Night, Jason. See you again."

"Night, Jules. See you tomorrow."

Jules grinned as I closed the front door behind us. "You're seeing him again tomorrow?"

I smiled and followed Jules into the kitchen. "Jason's invited me over to his tomorrow. You want a coffee?"

"I'm too hot for coffee. Just a bottle of water from the fridge, I think. Are you going to be able to... You know...do it?"

I opened the fridge, passed Jules a water and took one for myself. "I got a bit of the shakes when he asked, but as I don't know where he lives, I asked him to meet me in The Vine first."

"Did he notice?"

"If he did he probably put it down to a bit of nerves, as in 'girl, new guy, first time at his place' type of thing."

Jules flicked up the cap on her water bottle and swallowed a mouthful. "You know, Ness. The more I think about it, the more this one's really pissing me off. I walk down to Ben's but only if I've called or texted him first to let me in. I'm nearly twenty-four years old. I should be able to knock on a bloody door!"

"I know, babe. But it was one of the things apart from the attack itself that was just so awful—the pain, the helplessness and no one answering. To stand there again brings it all back and I hate that."

"And so do I, but I'm starting to resent it more. Next time I go down to Ben's, I'm not phoning and if I shake on his doorstep or even if I puke, then so be it. I'm going to do it."

I breathed in deep and clasped my hands around my water bottle as they shook at the thought. "Then so am I—the next chance I get."

Jules glugged a mouthful of water. "Right. If we can do it this weekend then we will, but if we haven't by Monday, we'll go together and take turns to do it at Paula's. She knows what it's about. She won't mind."

I swallowed hard and opened my water. "Monday at the latest then, girlie."

Chapter Four

I showered the night stickiness away when I woke, made it to my desk before nine and smiled at Jason before I turned my back on him and sat down. The office door opened as I logged on and Maisie and Annie walked in. Maisie took lip gloss and a small mirror out of her handbag and stated the obvious while she checked her reflection.

"Look. Jason's back. He must have flown back some time yesterday."

Annie flicked her eyes toward Jason's office then at me. "Ah, wasn't your friend flying home yesterday as well, Vanessa?"

"Yes. They got home fine, thanks. Does anyone want a coffee?"

"I'll get them," Maisie said. "Jason might like one. I'll pop in and ask."

Maisie picked up the drinks holder, walked toward Jason's office and came back ten minutes later with only three drinks and handed them out.

"I've just seen Tom in the corridor. It's his birthday. Everyone's going to the Barleymow at lunch. I've said Annie and I will be there. What about you, Vanessa?"

"I won't. Thanks, Maisie. I don't do bars in the middle of the day. I'll stay and cover the phones for you if you like."

"Are you sure? I know someone's got to stay but Derek would do it. I'd only have to ask."

"No, really. It's fine. Thanks, though."

Maisie shrugged and I carried on with my work until the office emptied at twelve, took a Post-it pad and pen from my drawer as the first phone rang, answered the call and stuck a sticky note of the message on Jess' screen. I moved around the office and wrote down three more messages, glanced around waiting for another phone to ring then walked back to my workstation when one didn't.

Jason came out of his office, walked over and, with no one in the office to see him do it, put his hand on my waist and kissed my cheek. "Hey, you. You good?"

I leaned into Jason, breathed him in and kissed his. "Hey, you, back. Yeah."

I smiled as I moved my lips away, reached up and wiped a smear of my lipstick off his cheek. "Bit of a giveaway there."

Jason smiled and let go of my waist. "How did you get phone duty?"

"I volunteered. I don't do bars if I'm not drinking, and I don't drink if I've got to stop and get real again afterward. You didn't have to go, then?"

Jason perched on the side of my desk as I sat. "No. I only have to go on payday. I was just going out to get a sandwich. Do you want me to bring something back?"

The phone rang on Derek's desk. I picked up my pen and Post-it pad and smiled. "No, I'm good. Thanks."

I answered the phone as Jason walked out of the office, stuck the sticky note on the screen and the office door opened. Maisie walked in.

"Oh, hi, Vanessa. I came back because..." Maisie looked into Jason's office and frowned. "Where is he?"

I walked to my desk. "He said he was going out for lunch."

"Damn!" Maisie pulled her eyes away from Jason's office, sat in her chair, took her mirror out of her handbag and checked her reflection. "I looked for him in the pub, and when he wasn't there, I realized that if he was still here, you would be here alone in the office with him." Maisie looked up from her mirror and smiled. "Then it just absolutely hit me as three people in the pub all tried to talk to me at once. I think Jason is holding back with me because of all the eyes that are always watching me." Maisie dropped her mirror into her bag with a small laugh. "You know how it is. I've always got people fluttering around. There's never been a chance so far for Jason to catch me on my own. I was going to ask you to go and get a bit of lunch or something, to leave me alone in the office with him. Give him his chance to ask me out with no one's watching."

I opened my mouth and found myself at a loss for what to say. "Ah. Well. Right..."

Maisie stood and smoothed her skirt over her hips. "Never mind. The time will come. It's just a shame he's missed his chance today. I might as well get back to the pub if he's not here. I might even have missed him walking back here. He could well be there by now."

"Ah, yes. Okay. I'll see you later, then."

I watched Maisie walk out of the office door and wondered if I should have said that I knew Jason was seeing someone without mentioning it was me, before Maisie did or said something that would make her feel like a bit of an idiot if she found out later.

A phone rang on the other side of the office and I pushed the subject to the back of my mind until I could talk to Jules. The first people wandered back from the pub twenty minutes later. Annie and Maisie returned with the rest half an hour after that.

Maisie's eyes brightened when Jason walked through the office at three and she spent the rest of the afternoon speculating with Annie on the best way to let Jason know which bars they were planning on visiting when they went into town later that night.

I gave up at four-thirty as they debated the possibilities of writing a venue on the side of the cup if Jason wanted a coffee and I packed my desk away early in lieu of working through lunch.

"I'm out of here. Have a good weekend, Maisie – and you, Annie. I hope you have a good time with Craig tomorrow."

Annie's cheeks pinked a little. "You have a good weekend, too. And I'll, um…let you know on Monday."

I smiled at her, walked out of the office, caught the bus home, let myself into our flat and heard music playing. Jules called to me. "Woohoo, girlie. It's Friday, thank God!"

Jules, with one foot up beside her on the sofa, was varnishing her toenails when I walked into the living room. A glass of wine stood on the coffee table in front of her.

"You're ahead of me there, babe. Hang on. I'll get a glass." I brought a glass in from the kitchen, kicked off my shoes, sat and picked up Jules' nail varnish bottle. "Golden bronze. So, what are you thinking of wearing tonight?"

"I'm thinking it's too hot to wear jeans. You know how sticky it gets in The Vine when there's a crowd, so I'm going to wear a dress."

I put the varnish on the table, poured wine into my glass and topped up Jules'.

"Well, I was definitely going to go crop top to let a bit of air in around the middle, but you're right. It's going to be a hot one in there. Perhaps I'll wear my peach skirt with it rather than jeans. I'll see how it looks. I don't want to look too party. We're only going to The Vine."

"Then lose the crop top and go for your sleeveless shirt that ties above your waist. You'll still get a couple of inches of air around your middle but you'll look more summer than party in a shirt."

I chinked my glass on Jules'. "Okay. Yep. That should do it. I'll go and get showered."

Jules smiled. "I'll go and get dressed, too. We can catch up for a while with a glass before we head out."

I left Jules blowing on her nails and took my glass with me to my bedroom. After I'd showered and straightened my hair, I made up my face with a summer evening look, pale blue and silver on the eyes, plenty of black on the lashes and checked myself out in my full-length mirror.

My back view showed my skirt clinging in all the right places and the front, my shirt with glimpse of breast at the top and tied under my rib cage to leave a couple of inches of waist on display. I picked up a pair of chunky-heeled sandals along with my glass and walked to Jules' bedroom. Jules sat on her stool in front of her mirror, her hair up in a high tail.

"You look gorgeous, girlie," I said.

Jules smiled. "And you. Wine time?"

"For sure."

I followed Jules and we swung our legs up beside us on the sofa while we sipped.

"Go on then. You first. How's the fan club?" Jules said.

"Still down to one. Annie's going bowling with Craig tomorrow and says she might invite him to stay over after, but as for Maisie? Well, I don't really know where to start on that one today."

"Why? What's she been up to?"

"It's just that she can't seem to wrap her head around the idea that Jason just might not fancy her. It's like it's inconceivable to her. So now she's made up her mind that Jason steers clear of her because she's always surrounded by other people and is never on her own for him to ask her out. She's spent all afternoon trying to work out a way for him to do so."

Jules laughed. "She can't be that clueless, surely?"

"Apparently so. In fact, she nearly guilt-tripped me today when she was so obliviously certain of getting Jason into her bed if she just keeps at it."

"Because you're sleeping with him and she doesn't know?"

I nodded and sipped my wine. "Yeah, just for a while there I felt like a bit of a two-faced cow, but this afternoon I remembered something Maisie said to me when we went to the pub after work, and whether Jason's sleeping with me or the man in the moon at the moment, it won't matter to Maisie and it won't put her off."

"Along the lines of…?"

"Of me asking whether Jason had a girlfriend or not and Maisie replying, 'I don't care if he has. I've seen plenty of those off in my time.'"

"So…?"

"So, guilt trip over for me, as far as she is concerned. Maisie's going to do what she's going to do. *Que sera, sera*. How was your day? Ben?"

"The gallery was packed. I wish I could say with art lovers, but I think it's probably more to do with the fact that we're climate controlled to stay nice and cool."

I smiled. "Oh, dear. What? No sales?"

"A few postcards of the originals and several decent-sized prints, but I wasn't on the floor this afternoon. We've got two oils in a fine arts auction next month so I was in the back office helping to prepare the sales blurb for the catalogue. I heard a little whisper of something that sort of connects to your place."

"What? Belmond's?"

"Yeah. The rumor mill says that a piece of Gabriella's unseen original artwork will come onto the market soon."

"Gabriella? The same Gabriella who designed the original pieces for Belmond's?"

Jules picked up the bottle and topped up our glasses. "She didn't just design them but crafted them, too. All one-off statement pieces. Made the company's name for them. The finished pieces were beautiful but so was the artwork she did for the designs. Her artwork became quite collectable in its own right when she died so young and the market realized there weren't going to be any more—not like the actual pieces of jewelry, of course, but still."

"I wonder who's flogging it then? When did she die?"

"Over ten years ago, and I don't think it will turn out to be Belmond's. If they have a piece they want to sell, it would be out in the open on the market, not on the rumor mill. No, I think this will turn out to be a doodle on a beer mat or a quick sketch or something. You know the type of thing. Someone does a house clearance or buys an old handbag in an antique shop, finds a bit of paper in it and recognizes the artwork."

"Well, good luck to them, although I think you and I are probably the only two people I know that would rather have the paper version than the real one."

Jules laughed. "Absolutely. Never again will I wear anything valuable enough that someone would take a piece of me to get their hands on it. I'd walk a mile barefoot over hot coals rather than wear one of her pieces."

I chinked my glass on Jules'. "Make that two miles over hot lava for me."

Jules snorted into her wine glass. "I just can't believe that you've ended up working at a jeweler's, even if it is in the back office."

I laughed. "Or me. Get your shoes on, girlie. I think it's time we weren't here."

Jules did up the straps on her shoes. I put mine on, let us out of the flat and Jules pushed open the door to The Vine fifteen minutes later. I followed her in, looked at her and she back at me, as through the crowd we saw Ben and Jason standing together at the bar, Jason dressed in jeans and a short-sleeved shirt that did nothing to disguise the muscles of his upper arms.

"Well, I suppose they've sort of met already. Ben told Jason what wine to order last Monday," I said.

Jules smiled. "Man thing. They'll have recognized each other and nodded, then made a couple of remarks and now what sport do you reckon they're talking about?"

"Hmmm, it's the off season. So, cricket?"

"I wouldn't bet against it. Let's go listen in." I walked with Jules up behind Ben and Jason.

"His batting average is…"

Jules slipped her arm around Ben's waist. "Good, bad, indifferent but better than Cook's, Ali's or Broad's," Jules answered.

Ben kissed Jules' cheek. "Joe Root, actually." He smiled.

I tilted my face up for Jason's kiss and breathed him in as his lips touched mine, his hand on the bare skin of my back between my skirt and shirt. Ben picked up the wine bottle on the bar in front of him and poured some into two empty glasses.

My handbag vibrated. I took my phone out of it, saw a picture message from James and opened it, knowing any message from James would only be a mate's message that anyone could view. A female police constable in full dress uniform, her hair tucked under her cap, her face bare of makeup… An official portrait that didn't include a smile appeared on the screen.

My phone vibrated with a second message, the same woman in jeans and a tee, waves of chestnut-colored hair framing her smiling face and, underneath the picture, several bouncing emojis with their tongues hanging out. I showed them to Jason, laughed and passed my phone to Jules to look at with Ben.

"What do you reckon? The new probationary constable he was on about last week?"

"I'd have thought," Jules laughed. "We know about all the other availables at the station, don't we?"

Jules handed me my phone and I tapped in a quick reply.

You are such a bloody tart!

"James is in the police?" Jason asked.

"Yeah. Rapid Response Unit. He loves dashing about the place with his blue twinklers on."

"Does he live around here, then? Is that how you know him?"

"Ah, no. Not around here. He…um…" I stalled and looked at Jules.

She stepped in and brushed over how a victim support officer had called around to our flat a year after the mugging to give us a progress report on the ongoing investigation and that officer had been James. "Just a community liaison thing. James used to be on that side of things." Jules looked over my shoulder. "Paula and Steve are here."

I dropped my phone into my bag and murmured to Jason, "Tinkerbell and Captain Hook."

Paula and Steve walked over and I introduced them to him. Steve leaned on the bar and held his credit card out.

Paula smiled at Jules and Ben. "How's the butt, big boy? I bet you've got one hell of bruise."

Jules smiled. "Not that he'll admit it, but tweak the side of his butt and he'll yelp like a good 'un."

Paula leaned forward and hugged Jules. "Good take down, girl."

Ben smiled. "Yeah, it was. Well worth the price of the bruise."

"Do you all do a martial art or something?" Jason said.

Steve turned from the bar, handed Paula a glass of wine and nodded in Ben's direction. "Not as such. Ben runs self-defense classes for women. Teaches them moves they could use to give them time to leg it if they get jumped or something. Couple on the move behind you, Ness, if you want the stools."

"You take them for Paula and Jules. We're just here for a glass and heading over to Jason's soon."

Paula and Jules sat with Steve and Ben standing to each side of them. I put my glass alongside Jason's and leaned against the bar sideways. Jason rested his hand on my waist.

"How soon?" Jason smiled.

"About as soon as you can get a cab here," I replied.

Jason pulled his phone out of the back pocket of his jeans and ordered the cab. I sipped my wine. Jason cut the connection and picked up his glass. "About half an hour."

I threaded my fingers through his and smiled. "So, did any interesting drinks appear on your desk today?"

Jason traced his thumb over the back of my knuckles. "Funnily enough, yes. I nearly brought the cup with me to show you but I thought it might be taken the wrong way so I left it there for the cleaners."

"Maisie decided today that you haven't asked her out because you never manage to catch her on her own."

"Then I shall make sure that I don't."

I sipped. "Why don't you fancy her? She's got the looks, a fit bod. Most single guys I know would have at least dipped their toe in the water there, even if it was only for a one-off, one-nighter."

Jason smiled. "Not this one. I'll dig out a picture to show you sometime."

"Of what? An ex?"

"Nope. Not saying. You'll have to wait to see it."

Jason looked at his phone. "Shall we go and wait for the cab outside? I could pretend to be Spotty Luke for a while until it turns up, if you like."

I put my glass on the bar and picked up my handbag. "You'll have to shrink a bit then. Poor Spotty Luke wasn't much taller at the time than I am now." I slipped my hand in Jason's and walked up behind Jules. She turned on her stool and I kissed her cheek. "We're out of here, babe."

"See you later, girlie. Have you texted the peeps?"

"Not yet. I'll do it in the cab."

"Text me later and I'll watch for you to get home."

I gave Ben a quick hug. Jules jumped off her stool and gave Jason a peck. Ben and Jason nodded goodbye and we repeated the process with Steve and Paula. Jason slipped his arm around my waist as I moved away from the light spilling from the bar door. I stopped walking and tilted my head to give Jason access to my neck.

"Good job your work skirts don't cling like that. It'd be a bit more of a giveaway than a smear of your lipstick on my cheek."

I leaned back against Jason and wriggled my butt against the top of his thighs.

"Mmmm. There's always the stationery room. It's got a lock."

Jason moved his lips farther up my neck. "You bring the picnic rug then and I'll bring the packed lunch."

I laughed, turned and put my arms around Jason's waist. "Do you think anyone would notice if I just happened to have a nice cold bottle of champagne with me and a couple of glasses? What about the ice bucket, though? A bit much?"

"Nah. It'll be fine. No one in the office ever notices what anyone else is doing, after all. Far too busy, heads down, getting on with their work."

Stationary headlights lit up the pavement behind Jason and I pulled my arms back at the sound of a motor idling. Jason took my hand and we climbed into the back of the cab. I pulled my phone from my bag and lit up the screen as Jason confirmed his address with the driver.

"I'll just text the peeps. They won't know your location if they check their tracker."

I typed in a message to my dad.

Out in Camden. All okay. Love you.

"You let your parents track you?"

I tapped on my tracker app and showed Jason the map with mine and Jules' icons on it, now showing as a half a mile apart.

"Sure. And Jules does. It's not as if they can see or hear what either of us are up to just because they know where we are."

"What would happen if you forgot to text?"

I skipped lightly over the subject, knowing the plans my dad had made for such an event happening would seem over-protective to someone who didn't know why he would be.

"I don't forget—or haven't yet—but they'd give me a call then call Jules if I didn't answer. The chances of neither of us answering are pretty remote."

I dropped my phone into my bag and leaned under Jason's arm as he put it around my shoulders. The cab exited the traffic and pulled up outside an apartment block of similar age to my own, his brickwork cream rather than the red of mine, with more architectural detail but still low-rise like my building, at four floors.

I stepped out onto the pavement and walked with Jason through a pedestrian access gate set in a low brick wall topped with tall, black metalwork. Jason tapped the entry code in at the street door and I followed him through a square lobby with a porter's room to one side and over to a small lift. Jason pressed for the top floor as the doors shut. I looked at him.

"Have you got CCTV in this lift?"

"Not as far as I know."

I didn't drop my gaze from his eyes as I pulled on the tie on my shirt, undid the buttons on the front of it and cupped each of my breasts to sit above the material of my bra, my nipples ready for his touch. Jason's irises darkened as he pulled me close to his chest and reached for my breast.

"Jesus, Ness."

I closed my eyes to the soft pull on my nipple and the bell pinged as the lift arrived at Jason's floor. I stepped away, pulled my shirt together and followed him out.

He opened his front door, picked up a remote from the table just inside it and pressed. The entrance lobby lit, as did the first room on the right. I followed him into a sitting room, minimally furnished — blinds, not curtains. A giant sofa stood in the middle of the room, facing a large picture window. A coffee table was in front of it with a wall unit to one side that seemed to contain everything else.

I dropped my bag to the floor, let my shirt fall open and reached for Jason as he reached for me. I lifted my face to his lips as he pulled me against his chest, then let my hands roam over his back as I kissed his mouth and he threaded his fingers through the back of my hair while we kissed.

I moved away as our lips parted, slipped off my shirt, wriggled out of my skirt, unlatched my bra and let it fall onto the pile. Then I kicked off my shoes and sat on the sofa in my thong. Jason followed me. My heart rate rose as he stood in front of me, took off his shirt, undid the button then the zip on his jeans.

I pulled my thong down and off and sent it over the back of the sofa. He stepped out of his jeans and boxers, his cock erect, and kneeled beside it. I lay back. Jason traced around my breasts with his finger, kissed down my body and tasted between my legs. "Sweet, baby. I want more of that."

I parted my legs. Jason planted small kisses over my pubic mound then explored the damp creases inside it with his tongue.

I sighed. "Jason...yes."

He urged my legs farther apart and his tongue searched deeper. I whimpered as he fastened his mouth over the swollen nub at my center and sucked. He lifted his head and asked. "Now, baby?"

"Jason...please, now."

He lay over me, parted the damp lips between my legs with his fingers and eased his cock in.

"Ness, baby, that feels good."

I mewled as Jason's shaft entered me, pushed my hips up to meet his and wrapped my arms around him. Jason moved his cock inside me. I raised my hips, pushed against each thrust and arched my back to push my breasts harder into his hands as he squeezed.

"Yes, sweetheart. Fuck me back," he urged.

Jason moved his pelvis faster and picked up the pace of his thrusts. I tensed the muscles of my thighs, raised my butt up and ground my pelvis against Jason's, digging my fingers into his back, my heart racing, blood pounding through me.

"Jason, so good…"

He pumped harder, moved his fingertips to my nipples, pinching, and my orgasm pulsed out in waves. I shouted his name, my head thrown back, eyes closed. "Oh, God, Jason!"

He tensed under my fingers. His thrusts shortened and he groaned. "Ness. Oh, fuck! Baby…"

I panted as my orgasm rolled on, lowered my butt onto the sofa and softened my grip on Jason's back as he breathed hard into my neck. He kissed my shoulder. I ran my fingers over the smooth skin of his back and the roundness of his butt cheeks while our heart rates steadied.

Jason eased his cock out of me and lay on his side. I curled against him in his arm and breathed in our musk. He ran his hand over my shoulder then down my back, following the contour of my waistline and on to my thigh. I kissed Jason's chest, his shoulder, his neck. He moved his face to mine and kissed my lips.

"Good, baby?" he asked.

I buzzed my lips over Jason's. "Mmmm. Yes. Very."

"A glass of wine?"

"Please. And your bathroom?"

"Third door on the right in the hallway."

I picked my clothes up on my way to the bathroom, checked my face after I used the loo and re-dressed but without the bother of a bra. Jason sat on the sofa in his jeans with his arm along the back of it and his shirt on but not buttoned up. I sat beside him, curled my legs underneath me and Jason passed me a glass of wine, picked up his remote from the arm of the sofa and pressed.

Adele's voice floated out in the background. Jason tapped on his remote again and again. The track changed, two table lamps lit and a fan started up in the background.

I laughed. "Anything that little black box doesn't control?"

Jason smiled and put the remote on the arm of the sofa. "Lights, music, heating, air conditioning, telly. Doesn't make the beds or take out the rubbish."

I shook my head and tutted. "Is that all? I won't bother getting one then. I at least expected Bieber to pop out of the cupboard the next time you pressed it — transported through time and space, singing live."

"You must have a remote."

"Yep. I just sort of use these" — I uncurled my leg, wiggled my foot and held up my index finger — "to walk over to the device of your choice and press."

"Oh, do you now?"

Jason grabbed my foot, put my toes in his mouth and nipped his teeth along them. I squealed. He laughed and kissed where his teeth had been. I smiled when he let go of my foot, sipped from my glass and had a better look around the room with its walls bare of any art work or even a photograph in a frame, the 'everything else' unit with nothing on it that didn't belong there, every item neat and in its proper place.

"Have you not been moved in here long?"

Jason brought his hand from the back of the sofa to my shoulder, rubbed his thumb over the curve of it and trailed his fingers down the top of my arm. "No, I've been here nearly three years now. I bought the flat when I qualified. Does it look like I've just moved in, then?"

I moved closer and relaxed under his touch. "A bit. There's no clutter. It's like your things haven't had time to spread themselves around the place yet."

Jason smiled. "That's ten years at boarding school for you. You get one half-size wardrobe beside your bed to put all your gear in and you soon learn to keep it all tidy, because if you lose or misplace anything, there's no popping out to the shops. Instead, you get to go to matron's room and take your pick of whatever discards she'd managed to collect from stuff that got left behind when the upper years left at the end of the summer term."

I wrinkled my nose and sipped. "Ew. That sounds grim."

"A lot of the guys didn't mind but I always preferred not to. The spare uniform didn't ever fit. When Sam lost his trousers, he spent nearly the whole of one term in a pair so big he had to put a belt twice around them to cope with the spare material and keep them up."

I laughed. "How do you lose a whole pair of trousers?"

Jason took a mouthful of his wine. "Actually, when I say lose, I mean the first fifteen rugby team nicked them. They overheard him taking a piss when he'd missed an easy catch and lost a match, and everybody but Sam knew his trousers were in their changing room and they used them to wax their boots after the match."

I laughed into my glass. "Silly sod! He should have known better. Did you play?"

"Yeah. Rugby was compulsory. I was nowhere near the first fifteen, though. I was one of those kids that grew too tall, too quick, like I was just all arms and legs for a couple of years until I bulked up a bit and sort of grew into them at uni."

I looked at Jason, tried to imagine it and giggled. "Right… Where's the year book? Damn! I bet it's still at your peeps."

Jason shook his head and smiled. "No way am I getting that out. What's yours like? Please tell me you at least had a bit of puppy fat or something."

"Yep. Lots of it, and I had crossed eyes, knock-knees and a face full of zits. Now can I see yours?"

"I'll show you mine at the same time as I get to see yours."

"Then I shall bring mine back from the peeps when I go home for the baby bratlet's birthday next weekend."

"Your little sister? What day's her birthday?"

"Yeah, Jilly. She's seventeen on Friday. There's family dinner Friday night then Saturday she's having a mass sleepover. Jules is coming with me to give a hand. Can't leave the peeps to deal with the rampaging sixth form on their own."

"Good luck with that one. It sounds like hell."

I finished my wine and put the glass on the coffee table. "It won't be too bad. We'll half-and-half their vodka with water when we find it, get the possible pukers' heads over the pan and Jules and I will have a good laugh with the peeps while we do it."

Jason stood his glass alongside mine and kissed my lips. "Still sounds like hell."

I slipped my hand inside Jason's shirt and stroked my fingers over the contours of his chest. He put his arm under my thighs and lifted me to sit on his lap. I leaned against Jason's shoulder. Jason put his hand inside my shirt and circled my nipple with his fingertip.

"Do you ever drink anything stronger than wine?"

I tilted my head for Jason's kiss on my neck. He circled the roundness of my breast. I trailed my fingertips down his stomach toward the ribbon of golden hair below his navel that disappeared into the waistband of his jeans.

"Not often. Sometimes I'll have a brandy with a coffee with the peeps after dinner."

"Mmmm. Nice. You willing to risk one?"

"How nice will it be?"

Jason rolled the nub of my nipple between his finger and thumb. It hardened under his touch. "Very *not* nice."

"Mmmm. Yes, please then."

Jason smiled. "We need coffee then."

He stood with me in arms, scooped up his remote and carried me into his kitchen that was lit by light filtering into it from the hall. Jason stopped at the shadowy outline of a tall bar stool and set me on it, pressed his remote and ceiling spotlights flooded the room with white light. I looked at a kitchen four times the size of mine and Jules'. It was high tech, gleaming with high-gloss white cupboard doors, polished black granite worktops and a high-shine white ceramic tiled floor. I laughed.

"Oh God, I knew it. You've got a washing machine in its proper place behind one of those doors, haven't you?"

Jason put his remote on the breakfast bar and smiled. "Yep."

"And you use it, don't you?"

"Afraid so."

"And the oven?"

"Sorry."

I looked at the appliances in the kitchen and saw one that looked suspiciously like the one currently sitting at home in the peeps' kitchen.

"Is that one of those coffee machines over there that grinds its own beans?"

"Unfortunately so."

"I promise faithfully never to touch it."

Jason laughed. "Because?"

"Because the one at home took three engineer visits to fix after I asked it to make me a cup of coffee."

"What did you do to it?"

"No idea. But I'm like the kiss of death to anything like that. I'm actually banned at home from touching anything in the kitchen other than the toaster."

"No wonder you can't cook."

"Sad but true. Although, if you want to know anything about the fine dining range of pre-prepared pasta salads and any variety of reheatable noodles, then I'm your girl."

Jason put his arms around me. I kissed his stomach through the gap in his shirt.

"I'll have to cook for you, then." Jason traced his finger around the outline of my lips. "Will you let me feed you?"

I nipped Jason's finger with my teeth and sucked the end of it. "Yes."

Jason threaded his fingers through the back of my hair and kissed my lips. "Will you take it from my lips?"

I ran the tip of my tongue over Jason's bottom lip. "From here or anywhere else."

Jason put his lips on mine and I opened my mouth for his tongue, gave him mine and squeezed my arms around his waist when our lips parted.

"I'll get the coffee," he said, a little breathless.

Jason walked to the coffee machine, fiddled with various bits on it and stood two cups underneath the spout. The machine started grinding. Jason kissed my shoulder as he left the kitchen and came back with a bottle of brandy and two glasses, poured and fetched the filled coffee cups.

I sipped from my glass as Jason sat beside me and the liquor warmed the back of my throat. The coffee intensified the sensation from warm to hot when I swallowed a mouthful after the brandy.

"This is lovely," I murmured.

Jason sipped his own. "Isn't it? Take them to bed?"

"Yep."

I followed Jason, brandy in one hand, coffee in the other, to the darkness of his bedroom door. Jason pressed his remote and low downlights lit around the edge of the ceiling. I wandered in to shades of black and cream and put my drinks on the bedside table. Jason pressed his remote and Adele's voice played in the room.

"Clever," I smiled.

Jason put his drinks beside the bed and lay on it with his arm out. I nestled in it and he pressed his remote again. I giggled as the ceiling lights dimmed to be replaced by two floor level spotlights angled toward a mirrored ceiling above the bed.

"Oh, very cute, Mr. Peterson."

He looked at my face in the mirror. "You like?"

I looked into Jason's reflected eyes and smiled. "Very much."

I watched in the mirror as he took his shirt and jeans off and I matched his movements with my skirt and shirt. Jason gazed as my bare skin appeared while I drank in the beauty of him naked, the muscled power of his body next to mine.

Jason sipped from his brandy glass, moved his mouth to my nipple and teased the sensitized nub of it with his tongue, and I murmured at the tingle from the alcohol. Jason moved the glass downward, dribbled a little brandy into the apex of my thighs and stroked his fingers in between my legs.

I writhed as the alcohol touched the sensitive pink skin inside me. Jason sipped a mouthful of coffee, put his face down and sucked on the brandy, his hot mouth replicating the sensation I'd experienced when swallowing it. Jason lifted his head and looked into the mirror. "More?"

"Yes, more."

Jason stroked his fingers in between my legs and parted my lips to expose my reflected clitoris to my gaze, then dipped his fingertip into the brandy. "Ready?"

I held my breath and nodded.

Jason rubbed his finger over my clit and I bucked, shouted out and Jason sucked the brandy away. I moaned for more. Jason filled his mouth with coffee, took the hard nub of my nipple into his hot mouth and sucked then nipped with his teeth.

"Jason…"

I looked into the mirror. His reflection looked into my eyes, dipped a finger into the brandy and slid it into the wetness waiting between my legs. My voice caught in my throat as the burn tingled inside me and I moaned when Jason lay over me and the hardness of his erection replaced his finger.

"Jason, yes."

Jason moved slowly above me. The length of his shaft filled me, pulled back and filled me again. I lifted my pelvis to meet his and watched the rise and fall of his butt in the mirror, while he breathed hard.

"Jason, please."

He increased the pace of his thrusts. "Yes, baby. Tell me."

I ground my pelvis against his, my fingers pressing into his back. "Oh, God, fuck me hard."

Jason thrust with more force. His cock hit harder inside me. I held on tight and moaned as the throb built until the spasms of my climax pounded through my groin and spread.

"Jason... Oh fuck! Yes..."

He groaned as he thrust again and again and came with me. "Baby... Oh, fuck!"

I stilled, panting, my heart racing, my eyes closed. Jason kissed my shoulder, his breath short and quick in my ear. I held on tight until my chest steadied then moved my legs. He kissed my lips. "That was sweet, baby."

I opened my eyes. "Jason, you and I have a very different definition of 'sweet'."

Jason smiled as he rolled off me and held his arm out. "Matches yours of 'nice', then."

I moved into Jason's arm, rested my head on his shoulder with my arm over his chest and relaxed against him as he stroked his fingers through the length of my hair and down my back.

"Have you got stuff on tomorrow, Ness?"

"Mmmm. I've got a bit pre-arranged. Gym in the afternoon, then I'm out with Jules in Covent Garden tomorrow night with a couple of the girls from uni. You?"

"A squash match, then I said I'd meet Tim at the Sports Bar and Grill."

I looked at the window and saw the first fingers of daylight creeping around the edges of the blind. "It's getting light. I'd better get home. Can I use your loo?"

"You've got to go?"

I kissed Jason's chest. "I'd better. I won't be awake to Skype the peeps at this rate, let alone make the gym." I put my feet to the floor.

"Do you want me to call you a cab? The en suite's in the corner."

I picked up my skirt and shirt and walked to the bathroom. "That'd be good, thanks."

I used the loo. Jason called through the door as I looked into the mirror to see what state my makeup was in.

"They've got one just dropping off in the area. It'll come here after. About fifteen minutes."

"Okay. Thanks."

I finger-combed my hair, took a couple of eyeliner smears away from under my eyes with a piece of damp loo roll and walked into the bedroom. Jason sat on the end of the bed dressed in his jeans but not his shirt and I sighed inside my head that I wasn't able to still be in his bed curled alongside him.

Jason smiled. "Do you want anything before you go?"

"A water would be good. I'll text Jules and let her know I'm on my way."

Jason stood. "Water's in the fridge. Jules won't have waited up, will she?"

"No. She'll wake up for long enough to see me home on her tracker then go back to sleep."

I followed Jason out of the bedroom and picked up my bag and shoes from the sitting room on my way through to the kitchen. Jason passed me a bottle of water from his fridge.

I sat on a stool and unscrewed the lid. "Thanks. I could do with this."

Jason sat beside me. I tipped the bottle, let the contents slide down and didn't stop to take a breath until I'd drained it. Jason laughed. "Yep. You definitely needed that!"

I smiled. "I can do cold water or milk by the pint if I'm thirsty, although my stomach will now gurgle loud and clear over the taxi driver all the way home to pay me back for it."

Jason put his arm around my shoulders and pulled me closer. "You could have stayed and gurgled all over me if you'd liked."

I rested the side of my face on the warm skin of Jason's chest and put my arm around his waist. "I would have if I could, but I've got to go home."

I kissed Jason's chest, pulled away and picked up my handbag and shoes. Jason followed me to the front door. I lifted my face up for Jason's kiss, tasted him sweet in my mouth and squeezed around his waist when we broke apart. "Have a good night tomorrow. Talk soon."

"Have a good time with your friends, Ness. I'll call you."

I climbed into the back of the cab waiting at the curb, looked up at Jason's window as the cab pulled away and saw a shadow of him watching me go. I paid the cab when it drew up outside our apartment block, exited it to early morning summer daybreak and called softly through Jules' door as I walked to my bedroom, "Home, babe. Night."

Chapter Five

I opened my eyes on Saturday morning at ten-thirty to the smell of coffee and walked through to the kitchen. Jules pushed the plunger down on the cafetière and smiled.

"Hey there, girlie. How was it at Jason's? Good?"

I fanned myself. "Oh, yeah, for sure. He's got a mirrored ceiling in his bedroom and as for what that man does with a drop of brandy…"

Jules snorted and poured two mugs of coffee. "It's sounding like you two are pretty well suited on that front."

I smiled and picked up my mug. "I'm hoping so, babe. I've got to Skype the peeps at eleven. Do you want to go to the gym after?"

"Sure. We'll go down after you've spoken to them. I heard from Beth earlier. She and Mae will be in Scarlet's around eight."

"Great. It'll be good to catch up with them."

assie O'Brien

I took my mug with me to my bedroom, opened my laptop and used the bathroom while I listened for my Skype icon to ring. I tapped Accept when it did and Mum and Dad lit up my screen, sitting at the breakfast bar in the kitchen at home.

"Hey, you both okay? Where's Jilly?"

My sister appeared between Mum and Dad, poking her tongue out at me through a mouthful of braces. I stuck mine out at her.

"Hi, bratlet. You good?"

Jilly nodded. "You are coming home next weekend for my birthday, aren't you?"

I smiled. "Sure. I'll be home Friday. Anything in particular you want me to bring you?"

"That boutique shop by your flat that we went in last time I stayed with you had a white-gold charm in it. Do you remember? The horseshoe one with the little blue stones. I can't find anything like it around here or online."

"I'll see if they've still got it. See you Friday."

"Thanks, Ness."

Jilly's face disappeared.

"How many is she having for the sleepover on Saturday?"

"I've said no more than twenty. I'd like to try and get them all settled down by about two," Mum said.

"Sleeping bags in the telly room?"

Mum nodded.

"Okay. I'll do smores at one and get the horror flick on. What are you two up to next week?"

Dad leaned in closer to the cam. "I'm in Paris on Tuesday. Mum's coming along for the ride. Will you be able to keep an eye on my trading account when I go through the black hole if you're at work?"

I nodded. "I don't see why not. There's enough to do but the work's hardly taxing. I can load your account to my phone and keep an eye on it."

"I've got a price alert in place for American Small Companies at fifty dollars. It's close. I'll call you before I lose signal. If the shares hit the price when I'm underground, sell the holding."

"What time are you going through the tunnel?"

"Around ten."

"Text me when you want me to log on. You going shopping out there?"

Mum smiled. "I'll try and get Jilly something over there she couldn't get here for her birthday."

"I'll get the charm then. I know they've still got it. I see it in the shop window when I walk past on the way to the bus stop. I'd better go now. I'm due in the gym with Jules soon and we're out in town to eat tonight. Hear from you Tuesday, Dad. Bye, Mum."

I blew kisses at the screen, cut the connection and walked through to Jules' bedroom. Jules closed the lid on her wash hamper and dropped a handful of clean knickers into her drawer.

"The peeps okay?"

"All good. Off to Paris next week. Are you still coming with for Jilly's birthday next weekend?"

Jules smiled and closed the drawer. "Of course. I wouldn't leave you to fend off the baby bratlet and her friends on your own."

"Thanks, babe. Gym in ten?"

Jules nodded and I walked back to my bedroom, changed into leggings and a T-shirt and spent the next two hours sweating with Jules on every piece of equipment our gym possessed. I checked my phone when I walked into my bedroom to shower and saw a text from Jason.

You having a good day?

Yeah. Good, thanks. Just back from the gym. Did you win your match?

Tough match so yes, but only just. What time are you out?

Scarlet's at about 8. You?

7ish. Have good time tonite.

And you.

Jules called through her bedroom door as I walked out of my bathroom wrapped in a towel.

"You dressing up or down tonight?"

"It's so sticky out. I thought perhaps my halter playsuit, but I'll dress it up with strappy heels."

"I'll go with a skater skirt then but dress it down with ankle boots so we don't look too girlie."

Dressed and good to go, we made it to Scarlet's just after eight. Beth and Mae sat at a red-topped table in front of the bar with a tall Tom Collins in front of each of them. I looked at the menu after we'd kissed all around, and sat beside Jules.

"Do you want to order from the small plate menu and share?"

"Sure, but nothing too sticky like the chicken wings. I always manage to get them all over my face," Beth said.

We settled on the halloumi with red pepper, mac 'n cheese fingers and chicken Caesar salad with four forks. The room filled as we ate and caught up with the highlights of Beth and Mae's latest trip to Zante. I put my phone beside my glass and glanced at it from time to time. It lit with Jason's name as the deejay raised the music level to twelve.

Hey, you. You still out?

At Scarlet's but moving on soon. You?

I glanced at Jules as I tapped Send to the beat of louder dance music. Jules flicked her head toward the street door and I nodded. Beth and Mae smiled as Jules and I stood and picked up our handbags. They knew we didn't hang around when a venue turned more nightclub than bar.

I blew air kisses and followed Jules out of the street door. We managed to flag down a black cab as it lit up for hire after dropping people off only five hundred yards down the road. My phone vibrated as we climbed in and Jules gave the driver our address.

Where are you off to next?

I showed the message to Jules.

"Is it too lame to say we're going home this early? Should I say we're going to a party or something?"

"Ness, don't bother about lame. Just get it out there. Our little nightclub issue is a minor one compared to the rest."

I nodded and replied.

Scarlet's too 'club' after midnight. I don't do clubs so am in cab on way home.

It's still early. Call in for a drink? I'm home.

Jules looked at my phone. "Here's your chance, then. Are you going to do it?"

My skin goosebumped at the thought of standing out on the street. I breathed in deep and pictured Jason, nodded and replied, my hand shaking as I typed.

Hey, you. Yes. Be with you in about 20.

My phone vibrated one minute later.

Hey, you, back. Waiting for you.

I leaned forward as I read the message, spoke to the driver and asked for an extra stop before our apartment block. Jules squeezed my hand.

"Right, girlie, I'm doing it, too. I'm going to knock at Ben's and see if he's in and up without texting or calling him first."

I squeezed Jules' hand and laughed as the cab approached Jason's apartment block and realized I should have taken his text literally. Jules laughed too when we saw Jason's tall figure leaning against the half-wall and iron-work railing beside the pedestrian access gate.

"I'm still going to do it," Jules said.

"And I'm still doing Paula's on Monday, then."

I kissed Jules as the cab pulled up. Jules blew kisses from inside the cab as I shut the door and walked over to Jason. I slipped my arms around his waist, lifted my face and he opened his lips to mine. He skimmed his hand over my butt cheek and ran his fingertip across my bare thigh where my playsuit finished.

"You naked under this little short thing?"

I nuzzled my mouth on Jason's chest through his tee. "Yep, it's hot and nobody would know unless they get as close to me as you are now."

Jason rested his hand on my butt. "I bet someone got close and snugged up behind you in the crowd at the bar."

I slipped my hands into Jason's back jeans pockets and squeezed.

"Not going to happen. I don't like people standing close if I don't know them. I take steps to avoid it. It's why I don't do clubs or any venue that gets too crowded."

"The Barleymow last week?"

"Was fine. I knew a lot of people there. It's a crowd full of complete strangers that sets my teeth on edge."

Jason kissed the top of my head. "You get knocked off your feet in a crowd or something sometime because you're so small, Ness?"

I kissed Jason's chest and smiled upward. "Yeah. Getting knocked off my feet and getting hurt because of it just about sums it up. Now, did you say you had some wine in there or shall we stay out here and continue to delight your neighbors?"

"Just one more for Mrs. Noakes, then. She'll have her nose firmly pressed up against the window. I'm sure she's being waiting for me to do something scandalous ever since I moved in."

I wrapped my arms around Jason's neck and giggled as he kissed my lips, lifted me, threw me over his shoulder, patted my butt then walked to the street door, holding me with one arm while he used the other the other to tap in the entry code. Jason stood me on my feet inside the entrance lobby.

"Right. If she wants any more than that she can get herself over to Amsterdam for a floor show like everyone else."

I laughed and slipped my hand into Jason's as he called for the lift, put my bag on my shoulder and cuddled in around his waist when the lift doors closed. Jason cupped my butt with his hands.

"You got a case of butt love there?"

Jason squeezed. "Cutest little one I've ever seen or laid my hands on."

I nipped my teeth on Jason's neck. "So, would you like to do my butt?"

"Yes, that."

I kissed his neck. "You want me to bend over the back of your sofa, maybe?"

Jason pressed me closer and I breathed deeper as his cock hardened against me. "Please."

I stood straighter as the lift floor pinged. Jason took a key out of his pocket and let us in. I followed him into his softly lit sitting room and dropped my bag to the floor. His irises darkened as I pulled the tie of my halter top and it slipped away from my breasts. I put my finger on the button that held the shorts half of my playsuit up and together.

"Shoes on or off?"

Jason's chest moved as he breathed in. "On."

I unfastened my shorts and held the two halves together. Jason kicked off his shoes and peeled his tee off over his head. My heart rate sped up as his torso appeared and it raced on when he unzipped his jeans. I dropped my shorts and stepped out of them as Jason took his jeans and boxers off. I turned, naked apart from my high-heeled shoes. He murmured as, with my legs together to keep my butt cheeks pert and tight, I bent over the back of the sofa.

"Baby, you're beautiful."

Jason put his hands on my hips and his lips on my back. He kissed downward, dropped to his knees behind me and sucked. I whimpered as his teeth grazed first on one cheek then the other.

He sucked harder then stroked his fingers over the fullness of my cheeks and traced through the crease underneath them. I clutched at the sofa and moaned, eyes closed, as he slid a finger into the wetness between my legs. I moved against it. He put a second finger in and nipped with his teeth. I writhed against his fingers as his mouth moved over my flesh.

"You want me in you, baby?"

"God, yes. Please, now…"

Jason stood and put the head of his cock in me. I braced my arms against the sofa as he held my hips and moved his shaft in. His pelvis hit my butt and I moaned as his balls slapped between my thighs. He pulled his shaft back slowly then pushed forward with more force.

"Jason, yes."

He repeated the movement over and over until the tension built and my body cried out to feel his thrusts, fast and hard.

"Jason, more, please."

Jason eased his cock back. "Baby, that feels good in there."

I whimpered as Jason pushed his shaft forward — sweet torture, inch by inch. "Jason…"

"Yes, baby. Tell me…"

"Oh, God… Just fuck me, please."

He kissed my shoulder. "Yes, baby. I'm going to fuck you hard now." He pulled his pelvis away and slammed his shaft in fast. I moaned.

"Oh, God, yes. Please, more…"

Jason thrust in, again and again. I raised my hips higher, with my hands fisted on the back of the sofa and my eyes closed. I panted as the throb built between my legs. He reached down and found my swollen clitoris. I shouted as he rubbed and teased it until I came. "Jason… Oh, fuck!"

Jason thrusts shortened as he followed. "Ness…yes…yes."

My breasts heaved and my heart pounded as Jason stilled, eased away from me and moved his hands to my waist to steady me on my heels as I panted. I loosened my grip on the sofa and Jason scooped me up, walked around it and sat. I leaned against his arm, my cheek resting on his chest. He reached down, undid the straps on my shoes, eased them off my feet and held me close.

"That was sweet, baby. I don't think I've left any hickey marks on you."

I nuzzled my lips into his neck. "I wouldn't mind if you had. I'm not planning on going out dressed in my Mufasa bodysuit again any time soon."

Jason stroked his hand over the side of my butt cheek and down my thigh. "I'd like to see that again sometime, and not in a pic."

I kissed Jason's neck. "Then you will, but I'll lose the wired tail—unless getting a good poke in the eye actually floats your boat."

Jason laughed and I sat up straighter. "Ah, no. Not much, thanks. Do you want a glass of wine?"

"Please. I'll just check on Jules and use your bathroom."

I put my feet to the floor and picked up my playsuit on my way to the bathroom. I checked my face in the mirror and saw one of my false lashes unsticking in the corner of my eye, so I pulled both of them off and flushed them down the loo.

Re-dressed, I walked to the sitting room and sat beside Jason on the sofa. He passed me a glass of wine and I smiled as he pressed his remote and Justin Bieber's voice floated out of the speakers. I curled my legs up beside me, sipped, took my phone out of my bag and didn't have to check my tracker when I saw the message on it from Jules.

Whoop, whoop. Did it! Tell you tomorrow. xxx

Jason curled his arm around me as I smiled and dropped my phone into my bag.

"How was Scarlet's? Did you eat?"

I twisted sideways so I could look at him as we talked.

"It was good. We haven't caught up with Mae and Beth for a while. They've been away. We all shared some bits off the small-plate menu. What about you?"

"Yep. A really large steak off the very big plate menu."

"And the bucket of fries and all the sides?"

"Oh, yeah. I would have preferred to cook it myself but it was a pretty good ribeye."

"I bet that's what my dad cooks on Friday. Not steaks—there'll be too many of us—but as a roast."

"Your dad cooks, then?"

I pictured Dad at home in the kitchen and smiled. "Yeah. It's like his thing. My mum can cook but gets all the boring weekday stuff while Dad takes over at the weekends and when we've got guests in."

"How many will there be?"

"Lord knows, but at least fifteen. It depends on how many of them need to stay over. If the taxiable ones are coming, it'll probably be over twenty, and it's a safe bet they will. Any excuse for the bottles to be open and the horde always turn up."

Jason laughed. "The horde."

"Yep. There's loads of us. Come round to ours on Friday and they'll be stuffed in every nook and cranny. What about you? Your mum and dad? Have you got lots of family?"

Jason sipped. "No, not a lot and not close. My parents weren't young when I arrived, so there's only me – no brothers or sisters and no grandparents left, just an aunt and a couple of cousins that I don't know very well. You sort of don't when you're away most of the time at boarding school."

"What about your mum and dad? Do you see them often?"

"Ah, no. My mum and father had quite an odd relationship. They never married or lived together as such, although they always were, if you see what I mean. When I was young, I lived with my mum in one house and my father lived in another one three doors down from ours. They just sort of visited each other – or maybe not for a while, if they'd had a row."

"Did they argue a lot then? Is that why they couldn't share the same house?" I asked.

Jason nodded. "I didn't realize it until I was older but yeah, they argued a fair bit. They were very different people. My mum was high spirited and laughed a lot but could hold a grudge for just about ever if someone upset her. My father is reserved but can get quite loud, stubborn and arsy if he doesn't get his own way."

I put my hand over Jason's. "Ah, I don't know if I should ask but...was or is?"

Jason picked up my hand and kissed into my palm. "So, here comes the messy, slightly awkward bit."

Jason took his arm from my shoulders, leaned forward and pressed the side of the coffee table. A drawer concealed in the frame slid out. Jason took a glossy brochure from it and handed it to me.

"Inside cover," he said.

I took the brochure and saw a Belmond's sales and marketing promotion, opened the front cover and looked at a photograph of a tall, lean man with waves of thick white hair and a familiar pair of green, green eyes. I read the caption over the top of the photograph — *Our Chairman, Peter Belmond* — and I bit down on my lip to stop myself from laughing.

"Okay. I get it. You're Peter's son," I said.

Jason laughed and I let my own laugh out as I handed him back the brochure.

"I know. My parents lived the way they did for years before I was born, but when my mum fell pregnant with me, she thought they ought to get married and my father refused. My mum changed her legal name in court when she found out she was pregnant with a boy because that was what my parents were like. They didn't just row but scored points off each other as well. You won't know it now when you meet my father at work, but they were both volatile and competitive with each other and not in a happy-ever-after way."

I sipped my wine and considered the 'is' and the 'was'.

"So, that's your dad. What about your mum?"

Jason leaned forward, put the brochure back in the drawer, took out an eight by ten glossy photo and passed it to me face down so could I read the writing on the back. I ran my fingertip over the writing. "Your mum was Gabriella?"

Jason smiled. "Yeah, she was. People don't make the connection between us because when she changed her name, she never actually used it in public. She continued to live and work under her original name, Gabriella Delaney."

I stroked my fingers down the side of Jason's face. "I'm so sorry. It must be awful to lose your mum so young. I can't imagine it."

Jason held my hand to his face and kissed the back of it. "It's been a long time now, Ness. You get used to it after the first two or three years. You still wonder how it would have been, what they would have thought about certain things, but you stop looking over your shoulder for them. This photo is the one I said I'd dig out for you last night."

I turned the photo over and the first thing I noticed was Jason's mum's hair, wilder than Maisie's but still a mass of natural blonde curls that fell right down her back. The similarity ended there when I looked closer. His mum, naturally beautiful with little makeup, could have featured in any seventies magazine under the heading 'free spirit' or 'wild child'.

"It's the hair? That's what turns you off Maisie?"

"Absolutely. I could never go anywhere near the bed front with someone whose most outstanding feature reminds me of my mother. It would just be too weirdly yukky."

I smiled and handed Jason his photo.

"I suppose it would. She doesn't look much like your mum apart from that, though. You don't keep any photos out on display?"

Jason slipped the photo into the drawer and shut it. "No, I don't leave personal stuff out in view. It doesn't bother me who knows that they're my mum and father or who doesn't, but I can't be trotting that particular piece of history out too often."

"How does it work in the office with your dad? Do neither of you acknowledge your relationship when you're in there?"

Jason shrugged. "We just keep it professional. It's easy enough to do. We don't really know each other that well. I might have seen a bit more of him before I went away to school but I went at eight and I didn't see a lot of him after that. I don't call him 'Dad'. I never have. Just Peter."

"Jesus, Jason. Eight. That's young."

"It might seem like it, but when you get to school you find the place is full of kids just like you with ambitious parents working flat out, it doesn't feel strange and I liked the routine of it all, preferred it to living in the midst of the perpetual warfare at home."

I swallowed down the last mouthful in my glass and stood it on the coffee table. Jason looked at the bottle. I nodded and he topped up our glasses. I picked mine up and relaxed under his arm.

"It's funny sometimes how you hear a name then it keeps popping up, isn't it?"

Jason picked up his glass. "As in?"

"Your mum. Jess told me to look for the Gabriella necklace when I needed to find the post room, then Jules mentioned her when she got home from work yesterday and now you tell me Gabriella's actually your mum."

"Jules mentioned her? How?"

"Jules' degree is in fine arts. She works in John Southall's art gallery now. They got a back-office buzz yesterday that something drawn by your mum has been found somewhere."

Jason frowned as he sipped then put his glass on the table. "Really? Did she say what?"

"She didn't know. Is it important?"

"I don't know about important, but it is odd. I didn't think there was any of her artwork out there that I didn't already know about."

"Call tomorrow if you want to ask Jules about it. I'll stick her on the phone."

"Yeah. Thanks. I think maybe I should."

I reached out and teased away the frown lines between Jason's eyebrows with my fingertips. He moved my hand to his mouth and kissed the ends of my fingers. I took his hand to mine, kissed it, put his finger into my mouth and sucked. His irises darkened as I did.

"You want my mouth?" I asked.

Jason threaded his fingers through the back of my hair. I put my glass alongside his and straddled his lap. Jason moved his lips to my neck, under my ear. "Your lips. Your mouth on me. Yes."

I trailed my fingers over Jason's chest through his open shirt and down toward his groin. "I shall enjoy that."

I kneeled between his legs, popped the button on his jeans and moved his zip down. Jason inched his jeans and boxers over his hips and freed his stiffening cock. I pulled them off, put my hands on his thighs and my mouth on his balls then ran my tongue over and around each one, licking down the smooth skin of his erection and over the sensitive point where his foreskin joined his shaft. Jason leaned his head against the sofa back and closed his eyes.

I wriggled a little and positioned the center of my pussy to touch my heel, put my hands around Jason's shaft, covered him with my mouth and sucked. His breathing deepened as I increased the pressure of my grasp.

I moved my hand faster with a small twist as it met his cockhead and rubbed my clitoris against my heel to the rhythm. Jason's stomach muscles tightened and tensed. I took my hand from the base of his cock, tugged gently on the skin under his balls where the nerve endings met, sealed the vacuum of my lips around the head of his shaft and sucked harder, keeping up the rhythm of my hand.

Jason groaned. Salty warmth hit the back of my tongue and I slowed my hand movement and milked Jason's shaft into my mouth, moaning as I tasted and swallowed to the throb of the muscles tightening between my legs.

I released Jason's cock from my mouth, kissed its moist end and rested my cheek on his thighs. He reached for me and I cuddled into his side as he swung his legs around and lay with his head on the arm of the sofa.

"Oh, baby, you're good at that."

I kissed Jason's neck and smiled. "Beautiful for me, too. Mark would be delighted if I told him—which I won't. He's an outrageous git and would rib me for just about ever."

Jason opened one eye. "Mark?"

I kissed the end of Jason's nose. "One half of Mark and Simon, the couple that live in the flat below ours. Me and Jules bumped into them in the lift the day we moved in and they sort of scooped us up and sorted us out while we found our feet. It's how we ended up using The Vine. They'd turn up on our doorstep on a Friday night and drag us out for a bottle or two."

Jason opened both eyes. "How old are they? They sound like they've been a couple for quite a while."

"Oh, for years. They were both only about twenty when they hooked up. Do you want to see a pic?"

Jason nodded. "Yeah. Go on then."

I reached over the edge the sofa and scrambled around in my handbag until I located my phone. Jason sat straighter and put his boxers and jeans on while I scrolled to my favorite pic of Mark and Simon — Mark, dark-haired and olive-skinned, Simon, blond and packed, leaning against each other back to back. The camera had caught the perfection of both of their faces as they stood sideways on with their heads turned to face front for the cover shot of a fashion magazine.

I handed my phone to Jason and his eyes widened slightly as most did when they first saw Mark and Simon together — so much beauty packed into one couple that it didn't seem quite fair.

"Blimey! That's the neighbors, is it?"

"Gorgeous, aren't they? They've been really good mates to me and Jules."

"How good? Good enough to give you a few tips on what's good or bad on the oral front, I'm guessing?" Jason handed me my phone.

I put it on the coffee table and smiled. "Yeah. The subject came up a while back when we were all fairly pissed round theirs. Jules had just handed out one of the world's worst blow jobs."

Jason laughed. "World's worst?"

"Oh, yeah. For sure. On the eye-watering, over-enthusiastic front…"

"Ouch."

"Definitely. Like most girls, me and Jules were bloody awful at giving oral until we got a guy tutorial, and those two know it from both sides."

"Well, I've certainly had some I could have lived without by the time I left uni and returned the favor to a couple of girls, at least. So, they gave you a heads up, did they?"

"Oh yeah, they sure did. I don't think me and Jules had laughed as much in ages as we did that night around theirs with the stuff they picked to demo on."

"Like?"

I giggled as I remembered. "Like if you cut the top off a condom it replicates a pretty good foreskin on a vegetable of your choice. In Mark's case, a fairly obvious cucumber. In Simon's, a gnarly old parsnip he found in the bottom of the fridge. The pair of them deserved an Oscar for their can of whipped cream finale. They're in Vegas doing a runway show at the moment. They'll be back next week."

I looked at Jason's window, saw daylight around the edges of the blind again and kissed his lips. "It's light outside. I'd better call a cab."

Jason tightened his arm around me. "Do you want me to call the local one? Have you got things planned for today?"

"Please. I'll text Jules and tell her I'm heading home. I'm heading straight for my quilt when I get there. Call me later if you want to speak to Jules?"

Jason nodded and spoke to the cab company while I tapped in a message to Jules and put on my shoes.

"They're not that busy. They won't be long."

I picked up my bag and walked with Jason to his front door, put my arms around him and lifted my face. Jason held me close and kissed me goodbye. I walked down the hallway toward the lift and a woman's voice called to me as I got into it.

"Hold that lift, will you?"

I stepped back out and kept my foot in the way of the door while I looked down the hallway for the owner of the voice. A motorized mobility scooter came toward me, a slim woman with short, layered gray hair, dressed in a white shirt and linen trousers, sitting on it. She reversed it into the lift when she reached me. I stepped in after her and the doors closed.

"Thank you, dear," she said. "That's so much nicer of you than the girl he had in there last month. She pretended not to hear me when I called and I'm sure she must have. I spoke clearly enough."

I smiled. "You're welcome."

The lady carried on speaking as if I hadn't said a word. "And I don't know about you, dear, but as much as I love red roses, I really prefer to see them in a vase and not tattooed all down an arm. And as for the one with the piercings—I see you don't have any, by the way—just what is the attraction of having them through your lip *and* nose *and* eyebrow? I liked Caz, of course, the one he went out with for—oh, it must have been at least two years—but they broke up after Christmas last year. And even so, she had her oddities. Did you know she wouldn't press any of the lift buttons without using a tissue so she didn't have to touch them?"

The words ran out and the lady looked at me and smiled. I kept my face straight against the giggle trying to make its way out of my mouth. "Ah, no. I didn't. I'm Ness, by the way."

"Lovely to meet you, dear. I'm Mrs. Noakes. I just can't sleep these hot summer mornings so I get myself up and out. They start to set out the market around six, so I go and watch them set up their stalls. They all know me down there and chat with me and somebody will always offer me a cup of coffee."

The bell pinged as the lift arrived at the ground floor. I got out first and held the door so Mrs. Noakes could drive herself out. She called over her shoulder as she motored toward the street door. "Nice to see someone with some lovely, long hair too, dear. Much better than the one before the roses, with the short brown bob. Now she would have looked better if she'd just let it grow past her shoulders a bit."

The street door opened and closed behind the electric cart and I waited a couple of minutes for her to drive away before I started to laugh and let myself out, too. The taxi stood at the curb and I got into the back seat of it still giggling as I watched her motoring down the road. I gave the driver my address, looked up at Jason's window and saw the outline of him watching me go. My phone vibrated less than two minutes later.

Have you just bumped into Mrs. N?

I giggled at my phone and tapped back.

Oh yeah. for sure. Still laughing here. Taxi driver thinks I've lost it!

Oh God! What did she say?

The words that lady can pack into a 4-floor drop! No stopping her.

Tell me when I phone later?

Lol. Yes. Does she keep a running list of your girls or just edited highlights?!

Bloody hell! I'm not that bad.

Mmmm. My butt is telling me you have been, are and it hopes you will be again. x

Baby, with u, as bad as u like. x

Think I might fall asleep picturing that.

Sweet. Picturing you too.

I paid the taxi driver and opened the front door just after six-thirty, heard Jules call my name and poked my head around her bedroom door. She yawned at me from her bed.

"Ben walked me back here then went home around five. I take it you haven't been anywhere near a bed for actual sleep yet?"

"Never mind that. You *did* it. You called at Ben's without phoning."

Jules smiled. "Yeah. It was fine. I felt a bit shaky on the doorstep but it was worth it to see the look on Ben's face."

"Surprised, was he?"

"More delighted, I think — that it was his door I picked."

"Because he was the person you most wanted to see that you did it?"

"Yeah, that type of thing."

"Well, he was right about that, wasn't he? It was the fact that you couldn't just walk down to his that really pissed you off."

Jules yawned. "Yeah."

Jules' yawn set mine off. "And you're right. I've been up all night and I'm knackered. I'm hitting the sheets now. I'll see you this afternoon."

Jules nodded and turned her face to her pillow. I used my bathroom, climbed under my quilt and didn't wake until the smell of coffee hit my nostrils a little after two. I wandered through to the living room. Jules sat on the sofa with the cafetière standing beside two mugs on the coffee table. She pushed the plunger down as I walked in and sat beside her.

"How was your night with Jason? Good?"

"Yeah. Good. Wanna check my butt cheeks for teeth marks?"

Jules poured and passed me a mug. "Kinky cow."

I looked at Jules over the top of my coffee mug. "Oh yeah, you. Was that my free-standing full-length mirror I saw beside your bed when I peeked in your room earlier?"

Jules let out a giggle. "Okay. Got me. Yes, it is. Great three-way view if you line it up with my full-length and my dressing table mirror. I take it if you were up all night, you still haven't mentioned your sleep-over problem to Jason?"

"No, it hasn't got to that point yet, but I can see it coming."

"How do you think it'll go down?"

I wrinkled my nose. "What? A lover that either goes home or kicks you out of bed in the middle of the night? I don't know, babe. I not sure Jason's the type of guy that would go for that for too long. Why should he? Have a look at the assets. It's a pretty good list. I met his neighbor in the lift this morning and she was an absolute hoot, but from what she said, Jason has plenty of girls in and out of his place and other ones don't have the shit in their heads that I've got."

Jules squeezed my arm. "Don't be too sure that Jason will leg it, Ness. Ben hasn't."

"I'm not. I don't know Jason well enough to predict how he feels about anything yet. I like him enough to carry on for a while and see how he feels about things, but"—I finished my coffee and put the mug on the table—"I'm telling you now that the least sign of the way I am being a problem for him and I'll let him go first, because one thing I'm certain of is that will hurt a damn sight less than when Tim disappeared over the horizon."

"Tim was a bloody git with no bollocks!"

"No, Jules. It's not a guy problem. It's ours. All we can do is keep an eye out and save each side a bit of pain all round when we seeing it coming."

"Well, if we find out what sets off the nightmares, it won't be a problem, will it?"

I laughed. "Being as we've been trying to work that one out for the last three years, Jason might be in for a long wait. He wants to have a word with you when he phones later, if that's okay?"

"With me? What about?"

I smiled and poured myself another half mug. "You'll like this one. About the rumor on the Gabriella artwork that you heard at work."

"Because of the Belmond's connection?"

I gave Jules the big eyes over the top of my mug. "Maybe a bit of that, but mainly because it turns out that Gabriella is also Jason's mum."

"Shit! You're joking!"

"Nope. And his father is Peter Belmond."

"Bloody hell!" Jules laughed. "How come people don't know?"

"Because Jason's parents had a complicated relationship. They weren't married, never lived together, argued like demons and now Jason's mum is gone and he's not close to his father. He said that he doesn't care who knows but prefers not to have to keep explaining the situation since it was so messy."

"Well, sure. I'll have a chat with him about what I heard, even though I don't think there's much more I can add to what I told you."

"Thanks, babe. I got the feeling this is more important to Jason than he said out loud, so I think it's better if he hears it from you directly rather than second-hand from me. I might get something wrong or miss a bit." I put my feet to the floor. "I'm going to run for a while. Pump the blood a bit. Are you coming with?"

Jules put her feet up on the sofa. "Nope. I got quite enough exercise last night, thanks. I'm flopping here and catching up with stuff on my laptop."

I smiled and walked to my bedroom, pulled on leggings, a sport top and running shoes, took my phone to the living room and handed it to Jules. "I'll leave this with you while I run."

"Sure. Do you want me to answer or let it go to voicemail?"

"Either. Up to you."

I let myself out of the flat, took the stairs rather than the lift and opened the street door onto stifling, still air. I began to jog, picked up the pace and found myself wet through with sweat even before I got to the first corner. I kept up the pace and followed my normal route, our apartment block and the next two — a square mile circuit.

I gave up after the fourth go-round, bent over, rested my hands on my knees and caught my breath. I jogged back home and Jules called my name as I opened the front door.

"In a minute, babe. I'm leaking here. I need to jump in the shower." I soaped up, rinsed off, dressed in fresh leggings and a T-shirt after I rubbed dry then walked through to the living room. "God, that's better. Did you want me?"

Jules held out my phone.

"Jason was on the line when you came in. I said you hadn't heard me call you and you were in the shower. He said to ask you to call him back when you're free."

I took my phone. "Did Jason ask you about the Gabriella artwork?"

"Yeah. I told him what I'd heard at work and I think you're right. There's something more bothered in his voice than the words he's saying. I said I'd have a discreet ask-around at work tomorrow to see if I can find out any more."

My stomach gave a loud rumble. "I'll call Jason back after I've eaten or I'll just gurgle all over him. I'm starving. Shall I order a pizza delivery?"

"Yeah. I could just go for gooey melted cheese right now. Hawaiian on my half with extra cheese, please. We've got some *Celebrity Juice* shows recorded to watch, haven't we?"

I nodded, called up the pizza delivery app on my phone, ordered the largest size with double everything on it and Jules flicked on the telly. We watched the first episode of *Celeb Juice* and laughed until the tears ran while we waited for our pizza to arrive then stuffed ourselves through the second episode until I closed the lid of the pizza box, my stomach full of melted cheese.

"It's going to hurt to move but I said I'd call Ben. I'll flop on my bed and do it," Jules said.

I picked up my phone. "I'll call Jason while you do."

Jason answered on the fourth ring. "Hey, you. You good? Jules said you'd been out for a run."

"Hey, you, back. I'm good, and yes, but it's so muggy out there that I only managed four miles and I've just undone all my good work by eating the biggest, sloppiest pizza in the world. You had a chat with Jules?"

"Yeah. She said she'd have another poke around for me in work tomorrow and I'm having a little dig around from here."

"This is worrying you, babe?"

"It's bugging me a bit. If, as Jules thinks, it's only an old sketch or a doodle, then fair enough, but the only other pieces of Gabriella artwork that aren't already out in public are owned by me and held at my bank."

"They should be secure then. Are you thinking forgery?"

"I don't know yet—theft, forgery or just an undiscovered sketch. They're all an option at the moment until I get some more information. I've got a couple of phone calls I can make this evening. They should tell me a bit more. Jules said she'd call you tomorrow at work to say if she'd managed to find out anything else."

"I'll come and brave the goldfish bowl as soon as she does."

"Thanks, Ness. So, Mrs. N this morning?"

I laughed. "What a woman! She doesn't even stop to take a breath, does she? Were your ears burning?"

I heard the smile in Jason's voice. "Lungs of steel, for sure. Now, spit it out, you."

"Okay. I'll give you the quick version. I can't match her lung capacity. Ready?"

"Yep."

"So, here goes…" I took a deep breath and rattled it off. "Mrs. N prefers her red roses to be in a vase, not inked, wasn't too keen on the girl with the piercings, likes my hair better than whichever of your girls had short, brown hair, can't sleep on hot mornings, was off to the market where she knows everybody, liked your long-term girl Caz that you broke up with last year, although she was a bit bewildered by her reluctance to go anywhere near the lift buttons without a tissue."

I puffed out as I finished and Jason laughed.

"God, has she stitched me up or what? And that was the quick version, was it?"

"Oh, yeah. Cut at least in half. It's just as well you don't live in a high-rise. She might have had time to cough out the lot."

"How do you know that wasn't the lot?"

I smiled at my phone. "Because last time I looked in the mirror, I didn't see the word 'idiot' written all over my face."

Jason laughed. "No, never that. What are you up to tonight?"

"Working off the weight of a pound of runny cheese and smoked sausage in my stomach by flopping on the sofa and laughing at Keith Lemon until my muscles hurt from doing it. You?"

"I'm going to make my phone calls then I'm going to actually cook something that might even include something healthy like a vegetable."

"Hey, I've just had my five a day if you count the tomato sauce on the pizza and the tray of deep fried onion rings we had delivered with it."

"How you and Jules don't both have absolute faces full of zits beats me. Enjoy Keith, baby. I'll see you at work."

"I hope you find out what you need to know. See you there tomorrow."

Jules walked into the living room as I blew a kiss down the phone and we sat on each end of the sofa with our legs stretched out, drank coffee and laughed until our eyes poured as we watched more Keith until eleven. I rinsed our coffee cups and left them on the side, ready for the morning while Jules disposed of the pizza box and I slept through until my alarm at seven, dream-free again.

Chapter Six

I walked into the office in the morning, put my bag down beside my desk and smiled at Maisie and Annie.

"Did you have a good weekend?"

Annie's cheeks tinted pink. "Ah, yes. Saturday was… Well, I had a good time. Thanks."

Maisie looked over my shoulder at Jason. "No, not really. How about you?"

"Yeah. Mine was good. Jules and I went to our local wine bar on Friday, and Saturday we went to Scarlet's to eat and had a few drinks with a couple of girls we were at uni with. Yesterday we just called a pizza in and flopped in front of the telly."

I pulled my work tray forward, took out the weekly paid staff's timesheets and arranged them in alphabetical order. Maisie tapped on her keyboard and the printer whirred into life an hour later.

"Right. I'm not happy with these figures. I'm going to the office to get them checked," she said and picked up the hard copy.

I looked at Annie as Maisie walked away. "So, how did it go with Craig on Saturday?"

Annie smiled. "I didn't want to say too much before, with Maisie not having a boyfriend of her own at the moment, but I had a fantastic time with Craig. I haven't laughed so much in ages. Maisie's great. I'm lucky to have her as my best friend. But she doesn't just sort of muck about, have a good laugh and take the pee out herself, if you know what I mean."

"I'm glad you had a good time. Are you seeing Craig again soon?"

Annie nodded in the direction of Maisie's desk. "Not that I'm saying much. I don't want to rub it in, but I'm seeing him tomorrow night and he'll be staying over again because that bit was bloody good, too."

I laughed and straightened my face as Maisie walked past me and sat at her desk.

"Silly of me. I'd transposed a couple of the figures on my spreadsheet. Jason spotted it straight away. He's on the phone now. It sounded like Mr. Belmond, although Jason called him Peter and I've never heard of any of the staff here use his first name."

"I expect they have to speak quite often now that Jason's taken over from him as Finance Director, but Mr. Belmond's still the chairman. That's probably why," Annie said.

"I suppose," Maisie shrugged. "But Jason didn't sound either friendly or particularly happy when he started to talk to him."

I stood and picked up the drink carrier. "Coffee, anyone?"

Maisie and Annie both nodded and I walked out of the office.

Jess came out of the ladies' loo and walked over as I arrived at the machine. "How goes it on your section?"

I put the first filled cup in the carrier and asked the machine for the second. "Good, thanks. It seems to be going well for Annie with Craig."

"And the other one?"

I shrugged and took the next filled cup from the machine.

Jess looked sideways at me. "She thinks Jason's looking at her when he glances out of his office, doesn't she? But he's not, is he? He's looking at you."

I shrugged again. "I wouldn't know. I've got my back to him."

Jess laughed. "A little laid back on the oblivious front there, I think. Not that I blame you. If he was looking in my direction, I'd keep that fact well away from the general office gossip too, let alone the Queen Bee. Mind you, evil cow that I am, I'm quite looking forward to watching the hissy fit she'll throw if she ever gets wind of anything going on between the two of you."

I laughed at Jess. "Oh, thanks for that one, I don't think."

I put the third coffee in and turned to walk back to the office.

Jess walked with me. "I'm just saying, though. Watch out for those fingernails coming for your face if there is or will be, especially in the ladies."

I nudged the office door ajar with my hip. Jess reached over my shoulder and held it open for me to walk through.

"Thanks, Jess. I appreciate it, but don't worry. Maisie won't be doing anything like that to me."

I handed Maisie and Annie their coffee and Jess walked on to her own work section. My phone vibrated with a message from Jason as I sat.

Bump into me at lunch?

I smiled at my phone and tapped back.

Sure. 1ish again?

Maisie looked over my shoulder.

"He's got his phone out. I wonder who he's messaging? Perhaps I should have written my phone number on his coffee cup on Friday instead of the name of the bar we were going to."

I opened Jason's text and out of the corner of my eye saw Annie glance over her shoulder at the goldfish bowl then at me as Maisie started speaking again.

"Damn! I should have thought of that. Of course, I should have given him a way to send a couple of cheeky messages and establish a bit of contact first rather than just expecting him to just turn up and ask me out face to face."

I read Jason's reply.

Sure, but Subway not canteen? Fewer eyes and ears.

And tapped back.

Absolutely. Eyes on swivel sticks round here today. Someone else might follow you out at lunch.

Abandon Subway then. Meet me in the underground garage by secure lift at 1:15?

Sure.

I dropped my phone into my bag. Jason left the office just before one. Maisie picked up her handbag and followed him out less than a minute later. I looked at Annie.

"Are you not going with Maisie for lunch today?"

"Uh, no. She's got plans of her own. I said I'd stay behind, sort of keep an eye on things and cover for her. Uh, just in case she gets an important call or anything, you know."

I carried on working, stood up fifteen minutes later but didn't pick up my handbag.

"I'm going to the ladies, Annie. Keep an eye on my bag for a few minutes, will you?"

Annie nodded. I walked out of the office, found the door to the stairs beside the lift, followed them down and opened the door at the bottom. Jason stood waiting by the brick pillar by the middle two lifts and smiled as I walked toward him.

"You were right. She followed me out but she can't follow me into the secure lift if I don't invite her to. I picked us up a sandwich in the canteen. We can eat in the staff rest area on floor two."

"They've got their own, then?"

Jason keyed in the security code on the pad beside the lift and the doors opened. "Yeah. Floor two's pretty self-contained. It's why I come up this way if I run or cycle in. They've got a lounge, restrooms and showers. Some of the goldsmiths work all night if they get wrapped up in a particular piece, then there's the night security crew working on four-hourly turn arounds."

I stepped into the lift and Jason keyed in another code.

"Why four?"

"It's the optimum attention span for night duty before the eyes start to close. It's better for the security staff to take a good, long break that they can sleep during, if they want. You didn't take the tour when you first started working here?"

"Ah, no. Do most people, then?"

"Yeah, there's nearly a hundred percent take-up. It's the only chance they'll ever get to visit this floor and see how the sparkly stuff is made, after all."

I pasted a false smile on my face. Jason looked at me and laughed. "You'd rather watch paint dry, wouldn't you?"

"While sitting on a bed of nails with a heavy weight on my head. Yep."

The lift doors opened and I followed Jason out.

"You're safe, then. We don't have to go into the workshop. Every room up here has its own secure entry point."

Jason stopped and keyed another code into the pad beside a door and I followed him into a soft-seated lounge, which was empty of other staff.

"It's full of security cameras on this floor, but they're only vision and not sound."

"I bet you've got some excellent lip readers tucked away somewhere."

Jason sat on one of the chairs. I sat to the side of him and took the sandwich he passed me.

"We only bring them in if security reviews the footage from the cameras and spots any unusual behavior, and even then, their reports only end up with me."

I opened my sandwich wrapper and found ham, salad and no sign of cheese. "Thanks for this. Did you get hold of who you wanted to last night?"

Jason opened his sandwich. "Yes, I did, and the more I find out, the more I think the answer is wrapped up in the trade fair that I went to Spain to discuss with Peter."

"How's that?"

"It's just looking like too much of a coincidence that the asset I've agreed to release to bump up our marketing package is one of the Gabriella designs I hold and the artwork for it will be coming out of the bank for the team to take with them."

"And it's valuable enough for someone to be thinking of making it disappear while it's out and about?"

"I'm thinking that way, and if so, I need to know who—someone here or someone who's got wind of it on the other side of things at the trade fair. I can't involve any official authority on the strength of a rumor, a couple of phone calls and a prickly feeling on the back of my neck." Jason chewed then swallowed a mouthful of sandwich. "So, I talked to Peter this morning and we decided that the only way we're going to find out more is for me to attend the trade fair as part of the team. Nobody at Belmond's—bar you and Nick Davies—knows I've got any personal involvement in any of this, so I should be able to keep my ears and eyes open without anyone realizing that I am. Peter's going to tell the sales team that he's sending me with them as he's given me his power of attorney to sign any contract *in situ* with a single signature."

"So, when's the trade fair?" I peeled the crust off my sandwich and bit off a mouthful.

Jason looked at my face as I chewed. "I'll wait for you to finish that. I've read your resume. I know you went there on your gap year and I know you are just about to laugh at me."

I swallowed. "Go on then. When and where is it?

"China. I fly out next Sunday."

I raised my eyes to the top of Jason's blond head and laughed. "Oh, you are going to get petted and photographed just about constantly. I'd recommend some hair dye and maybe a little fake tan for someone as blond as you. But really, it's not going to help unless you can work out a way to start walking around on your knees."

Jason laughed at me. "Oh, thanks for that one. I can hardly wait."

"Hey, you might like it. Nearly all the fondlers are female."

"Thanks again. Lovely."

I let my giggles subside, looked at Jason and saw a question in his eyes. "Is something else worrying you about going there?"

"Yeah, there is, because no matter why I'm really going, I've got to fit in with the team. The business is still there to be done and we've got to host a lunch and two dinners. I've looked on the net and found quite a difference in opinion on what's considered polite or not when eating. I wondered how you found it?"

"I saw a couple of tables of business types having dinner in the restaurant at the hotel where we stayed and it all seemed as formal and polite as you would expect. Subdued voices, lots of smiling, no laughing, a small toast here and there with a glass or teacup to another person to acknowledge a point of agreement... But outside of formal venues is where it gets crazy..." I laughed. "Oh, God. The noise alone. Bowl in one hand, chopsticks in the other. No one stops talking just because they're eating. Find a bit of something in your mouth you don't much fancy and get it back on the table to be cleared at the end of the meal and don't pause to stop talking while you do so."

"Sounds…ah, messy?"

"Very, and…"

Jason's phone vibrated. He took it out his pocket and looked at the screen. "Damn, I've got an incoming call in about fifteen. Talk to me more later?"

I nodded, rolled my sandwich crusts into the wrapper and dropped it into the bin. Jason screwed up his empty wrapper and sent it after mine. I walked after him to the door and he let us out.

"How long have we been?" I asked.

"About forty minutes."

"Oops. I thought I could get away with thirty with a coffee stop and bumping into someone in the corridor when I told Annie I was going to the loo. I left her watching my bag for me."

Jason smiled. "Tell her half the truth then. It was me you bumped into and I asked you about China because I knew you'd been there and we chatted for longer than you expected."

I stepped into the lift after Jason and he entered the code and pressed for our floor.

"I'll get a coffee then and you can go on in first," I said.

"No, I'll get one with you. It's only a couple of cups of coffee being brought into the office by two people who are allowed to chat and be friends and the rest of it is nobody's business but ours."

I walked with Jason to the coffee machine, tapped his code in for him and handed him his coffee while the machine dispensed my own then walked alongside him to the office. Jason held the door. I walked in and did my best to ignore Annie's stare as she looked up and whispered to Maisie. Jason sipped from his cup and carried on walking, seemingly as oblivious as he always was when Maisie's head swiveled in his direction.

"Do you know what time Jules is likely to call?" he asked me.

"She finishes work at four, so it'll be before then."

We reached my workstation. Jason smiled. "Thanks for the China stuff. I'd like to talk to Jules when she rings."

I nodded and put my coffee cup on my desk. "Sure. I'll bring my phone in to you when she does."

I sat in my chair as Jason walked away, picked up my handbag, looked for my phone and rummaged deeper with my hand when I didn't see it.

"I thought you were only going to the loo. Have you lost something?" Annie said.

"I can't find my phone. I didn't take it to the loo with me, did I?"

"I don't think so," Annie said.

I patted the lining of handbag to check my phone hadn't slipped under it.

"Can I borrow yours for a minute, Annie? My phone's got a tracker on it. Jules will be able to look at the map at her end and tell me where I've left it if I give her a quick call."

Annie leaned down and rummaged in her own handbag.

"Sure. Oh, hang on. I think I see something under Maisie's desk."

Annie dropped to her knees in the desk's leg space and crawled forward then backed out with my phone in her hand.

"Yep. Here it is. You must have missed your bag when you dropped your phone in it before you went to the loo. It must have skidded and gone under Maisie's desk. You must have done more than go to the loo, though?"

I smiled at Annie as she handed me my phone. "Thanks. I bumped into Jason in the corridor. I went to China with Jules on my gap year and Jason's going there next week. He had some questions. It's very different over there, so we chatted for a while."

Maisie huffed. "First Spain and now China. He hardly seems to be in the office nowadays. What's he going there for?"

"That sales and marketing thing that Derek went to the meeting for. I don't know who, but there seems to be quite a few of the staff going. Jason said a team."

"How long for this time?"

"Oh, sorry. I didn't ask. Do you want me to when I take my phone in when Jules calls?"

Maisie smiled. "Please. And he wants to talk to your, um, friend, does he?"

I crossed my fingers under the desk and trotted out another little half-truth. "Yeah. Jules as a red-head stood out in China and attracted a lot of attention from the local population. Jason will too because he's blond, and even more so because he's so tall. The attention can be a bit overwhelming."

Maisie shook her head and her curls rippled down her back. "I've heard that the people in the Far East are fascinated by blonde hair. It's really true, is it?"

I looked at Maisie and spoke only the truth. "Maisie, if you went there, you'd cause a riot on the streets. They'd be falling over themselves just to touch you for good luck or get a photo with you."

Maisie laughed and waved me away. "Get out of here! Would they really?"

"Yeah, really they would."

"Oh, God! I wish I'd known sooner. Can't you just picture it? Me and Jason walking down the street out there, arm in arm. What a sales and marketing opportunity! Is it too late now for me to suggest it, do you think?"

I looked at Maisie, noticed the brightness of her eyes and put the brakes on. "Maisie, I think you'd be better off finding out if Jason would like to be on show like that. From what he said to me, he's not looking forward to it. You might enjoy it, but I don't think Jason likes being the center of attention."

Maisie fluttered her hands at me, staring off into the distance, unfocused on any of her current surroundings. "Think of the business it will bring in. I've pictured it so many times, what we'll look like when we're together. What a couple we're going to make. God, it's just going to go viral on Facebook and Instagram when I post our beachwear shots…"

I nodded at Annie to intervene. She gave me a small shrug. I looked at Maisie and raised my voice a little. "Maisie, stop. You're not going out with Jason. It takes two to make a couple, not one and a load of wishful thinking."

Maisie blinked and focused her eyes on me. "Oh, yes. Silly of me. I'm getting ahead of myself again. Ah, well… It would have been stunning. Never mind. There'll be another time."

Maisie pulled her keyboard forward and got back to work. I glanced at Annie and spoke out of the side of my mouth.

"If you're her best friend, have a word with her outside work before she steps over the line and embarrasses herself."

Annie looked sideways back at me and whispered, "I can't do anything with her when her eyes go all bright like that, but it doesn't last long and she soon comes back down to earth."

"I hope so, because I know it and so do you. Jason's not going anywhere near her."

Annie sniffed. "He still might. And if he does and she gets her way, it'll all be over with and Maisie will be back to normal."

"Annie, he won't or he would have done so by now. Just try and talk her down a bit. Don't let her show herself up. There must be so many guys out there that would fall over themselves if Maisie so much as smiled at them."

My phone vibrated on my desk with the call from Jules. "Hey, babe. How did it go?"

"Good, I think. Is Jason around?"

I looked over my shoulder. Jason was holding the handset of the office landline to his ear. "On the phone at the moment. Can you hang on and chat for a few minutes?" I asked.

"Sure. I've got some information he wanted and I've had bit of a laugh getting it," she said.

"Go on. Spill it, girlie."

"Well, you know John's got a bit of thing about my boobs?"

"Yeah. And the way your nipples poke through your top when the air con's on."

Jules laughed. "So, I perched on the side of his desk under the air con blower when I was pumping him for a bit more info on the rumor and he was…

I smiled at my phone. "Drooling over your nipples."

"Absolutely. I don't think he took in a word of what I was asking him but he did give me the answers I wanted as he drooled."

I glanced over my shoulder. "He's put the landline down now. I'll walk you in, you outrageous flirt. See you and your nipples tonight, babe."

I walked over to Jason's office as Jules laughed. "Yeah, yeah, girlie. It takes one to know one. Go and poke yours in Jason's direction."

Jason looked up from his laptop and nodded at the chair in front of his desk. I sat, passed my phone over and listened to a one-sided conversation that on Jason's side seemed to comprise the words 'hmmm' and 'yes'. Jason handed me my phone when he'd finished talking and frowned. "Damn. Jules is pretty certain the rumor originated in the UK, and from what she said, it is getting to be a little more of a certainty. The whispers have described the actual item on the artwork the team is taking with them."

"So, you're thinking that if the artwork is about to disappear, it'll be an inside job?"

Jason nodded. "There just aren't that many people that know that any new artwork even exists. I didn't even know until a couple of years ago. Mum left everything she owned to me when she died but it was all held in trust and administered by the bank until I was twenty-five. Not even Peter knew she'd left a last portfolio of designs until I told him when I started here six months ago."

"Why only six months?"

Jason smiled. "I never had any intention of working here. I'd had enough of the in-fighting between my parents over Belmond's when I was young to want to come anywhere near the place and I'd just been offered a partnership at the private practice where I worked before. Then Peter told me he wanted to retire from the day-to-day running of the company. Pulled the whole emotional 'your mother would have wanted' guilt-trip thing on me and here I am."

"So, you're here because your mum wanted you to be?"

"She never said so outright but she left some notes for me with her portfolio. And yeah, I think she expected me to care enough about her work to see it made in the way she would have wanted. To do that, I have to be here on site and see it through from design to finished product."

The phone rang on Jason's desk. I stood as Jason reached for the handset. "Come back to mine after work, Ness? I'll cook."

I consigned knocking on Paula's door to the waste bin for another day as I looked into Jason's eyes and nodded. I walked out of his office to my workstation and tapped in a message to Jules to tell her I going straight to Jason's. My phone vibrated with a message from Jason just before five.

You ready to go?

Sure. Just need to pack away my desk.

I'll come get you in 5.

I logged out of the payroll system, put my pens in my drawer, picked up my bag and dropped my phone into it. Jason walked over as I stood from my chair and threaded my arm through my handbag strap.

"Are you just leaving? I'll walk down with you?"

"Sure, if you like."

I looked at Maisie and Annie putting pens and paper away in their desk drawers. "See you tomorrow. Night." I walked out of the office door and Jason looked at me as it swung shut behind us.

"Okay, double-quick time on the walking pace and we should be able to get into the secure lift before she makes it out of the door behind us."

I sped up and had to take two paces for every one of Jason's longer strides. He reached the lift first and tapped in the code as I caught up to him. I smiled as I walked into the lift.

"Well-rehearsed routine, there."

Jason tapped in the second code to get the lift to move. "I've been getting a lot of practice lately."

"She got quite bored when you were out of the office in Spain and that was only for a couple of days. She's pretty high maintenance on that front. Longer in China might just do it. How long are you away for?"

"I fly out Sunday, back on Friday, but we don't land until the early hours of Saturday morning."

I wrinkled my nose. "A week then. I'm not sure that'll be long enough to do the trick."

"It's plenty long enough from where I'm standing."

I looked up into his warm, green gaze and nearly forgot to take my next breath as I smiled back. I stepped out after Jason when the lift doors opened and looked around. "How are we getting back to yours? Two on your bike?"

Jason smiled. "I'll leave it locked up here. We're not quite dressed for it, I think. You okay to take the tube?"

"Um…"

Jason put his arm around me and squeezed my waist. "No one's going to get close or come up behind you if I'm standing in the way."

"Okay, then."

Jason offered me his hand. I looked up at the security camera.

"Out of work hours, Ness."

I slipped my hand into Jason's, walked alongside him out onto the street and into the thick, muggy air with more than a hint of gray rain on the edges of the clouds above. I swallowed hard as we reached the underground station and I saw the press of commuters pouring into it. My heart started to race.

Jason squeezed my hand. "No rush. Let them all swirl around us."

I moved closer to his side as we walked through the ticket hall, the busy crowd passing either side of us. He stood close behind me on the escalator and my heart pumped harder as the sweat-filled whoosh of hot air hit me as we moved farther underground. I stood against the back wall of the platform with my hand in Jason's until a distinctive hum told of the tube arriving.

"Let them all get on first. If it's too crowded, we'll wait."

I waited, walked after Jason to an open carriage door, jumped on and stood with my back against the glass privacy screen. Jason stood facing me, his hands on the handrail to either side of my waist, his body big enough to make mine nearly invisible.

He looked down. "You okay?"

I breathed in his scent. "I'm good. How many stops?"

"Only four. It won't take long."

I counted the stops and swallowed hard as I faced the crowd waiting to get on. Jason held my hand, his frame large enough to make people step out of his path rather than meet it head-on. I began to breathe easier again as we exited the station.

I looked up as we started to walk along the Camden Road, the sky above us a much heavier gray than it had been when we'd left work. Jason followed my eyes.

"It's going to tank, isn't it?" The first heavy drop hit my shoulder.

Jason looked at my handbag. "You got an umbrella in there?"

I shook my head. "No. You?"

"I biked it in this morning."

I shrugged as the second and third drops hit the top of my head in quick succession. "Oh well, it's only rain."

The next drops had no gaps between them. The first rumble of thunder sounded and the deluge started. Jason stopped walking.

"Here. Take my jacket."

I laughed and turned my face up into the rain. "No, it's fine. I quite like a good drenching when it's been this hot and sticky."

Jason smiled. "I don't think it would do you much good anyway. The rain has already soaked through it and onto my shirt."

We walked on. I saw a sizable puddle forming in a dip in the pavement and jumped, landing both feet in it and adding another pint of water to Jason's trousers, which were already clinging to his legs.

Jason looked at me as I laughed. "Right, that's it. The next one's yours and I've got much bigger feet than you do."

Jason stomped his foot down into the next puddle and managed to get his splash up to the tops of my thighs.

"Unfair advantage there. What size are your feet?"

"Fifteen, but it's not cheating. I only used one."

"I'll let you off then, even though mine are only size three."

Jason put his arm around me. "I think this suit's heading straight to the charity bag."

"Hey, baggy knees and sagging pockets... It's a good look. You might be setting next year's fashion."

Jason nipped his fingers on my butt in reply as we arrived at the pedestrian gate to his apartment. He keyed in the code, pressed for the lift and we rode up, leaving a puddle on the floor. The bare skin on my arms goosebumped at the change in temperature. Jason opened his front door, put his laptop bag down and picked up his remote. "Hot shower?"

My teeth joined in with my arms and started to chatter as I dropped my handbag beside Jason's laptop. "Please."

I followed him to his en suite. He turned the shower on and I kicked off my shoes, stripped off my sodden clothes, left it all in a heap and ran in under the steamy water. Jason hung his suit jacket, peeled the rest of his clothes away from his skin and left them with my clothes on the floor. My heart beat harder at the sight of him naked, walking toward me.

I moved to one side of the shower stream and pressed my now-warm body against his still-cold one. Jason wrapped his arms around me and I picked up the soap from the chrome rack screwed to the tiled wall beside the shower pole.

"Want me to do your back?"

He smiled and turned around. I lathered my hands, reached for his shoulders, soaped them then moved my hands down his back, over the cheeks of his butt then kneeled. I lathered Jason's legs, ran my fingernails under the crease of his butt, cupped his balls in my hand and stroked my soapy fingers over them. His cock hardened.

I re-soaped my hands, moved to Jason's front, lathered his chest and teased his nipple with my lips as I moved my hands down his stomach, into the creases of his thighs and down the length of his erection. He threaded his hand through the back of my hair. I tilted my head for his mouth and worked my hands up and down the length of his shaft.

"You want me, baby?"

"Yes, you inside me."

I grasped the shower pole and took the only position possible with our height difference that would allow Jason to enter me without the height of my shoes — bent at the waist, my butt raised. Jason moved behind me. Hot water rinsed both of us as he stroked between my legs then entered me.

"Jason, yes…"

He grasped my hips and pulled me toward him. I gripped the shower pole, held my hips still and my arms absorbed the impact as Jason thrust. I pushed back against him, as he pushed into and pulled out of me, harder and faster. I panted as the friction built, put my hand over his and moved it to my pubic mound.

"Slap, please…"

Jason slapped on the soft flesh of my mound and I writhed at the blood rush. "Oh, Jason…" He did it again and my voice caught in the back of my throat as the sensation spread through my pelvis and into my thighs with the thrust of his cock. Once more and I cried out as my muscles tensed and tightened in spasms through my groin. "Jason! Oh, fuck!"

Jason held my hips tighter and his thrusts shortened. "Ness, baby. Yes!"

I whimpered in small squeaks as Jason stilled behind me and my pelvic muscles throbbed and contracted. He eased his cock out and held me as I straightened. I leaned back against his chest until the rise and fall of my breasts steadied. He kissed the top of my head and reached for the shampoo bottle.

"Turn around, baby. I'll wash your hair."

I turned and smelled green apples as Jason worked the suds down the length of my hair and rinsed it then washed his own. He turned the water off, handed me a towel for my body and another for my hair then wrapped one around his waist.

I stood on tiptoe and kissed his lips. "I'll get my hairbrush from my bag."

I found it and brushed my hair as I walked into the bedroom. Jason stood in front of an open wardrobe door. I sat on the side of the bed and looked at a shelf stacked with perfectly folded T-shirts and thanked the god of inexhaustible supplies as I put my brush down on the bedside table. Jason opened a drawer and took a Lycra sports top out of it.

"Do you want to try this? It's the smallest thing I've got."

I took it from Jason and pulled it over my head as I stood. It fell nearly to my knees and sleeves that would have been short on him came down past my elbows. I twirled. "Sexy?"

Jason kissed my shoulder. "Always, baby—even if you were dressed in a sack."

I smiled, stood on tip-toes and kissed his neck.

"Smooth, Mr. Peterson. No wonder you've got such a long list pinned on the back of Mrs. N's door."

He bent his head down and kissed my lips. "Couldn't say it if it wasn't true, though."

I looked into his warm green eyes, wrapped my arms around his neck and asked for his mouth. He opened it and let me in. I kissed his cheek when our lips parted and let him go. Jason picked out trackies and a T-shirt from his wardrobe, dropped his towel, covered his beautiful body and took the damp towels back to the bathroom.

I picked up my handbag from the hall, followed Jason to his kitchen and perched on a stool at his breakfast bar.

"Wine, Ness?"

"Please."

Jason took glasses out of a cupboard, poured from an open bottle and pressed his remote. I picked up my glass as the opening notes of *Yellow* came out of the speakers. Jason opened the door of the fridge side of his refrigerator-freezer.

"Is chicken okay?"

"Great, thanks."

"Pasta or stir fry?"

I smiled. "You're not supposed to give me a choice. Whichever one you can sneak a healthy vegetable into."

Jason took a chicken and packets of vegetables out of the fridge, put them on the worktop, opened a cupboard and lifted out a wok.

"I can sneak just about every vegetable I've got into this."

A chopping board and a long-bladed knife joined the chicken.

"Do you want me to help?"

Jason held up the knife and light glinted off the blade. "I think not, given your cooking skills are limited to the blunt edge of a wooden spoon."

I picked up my glass and sipped. "Excuse me. Jules and I do actually own a cheese grater and a bread knife, you know."

Jason opened the butcher's bag and laid the chicken on the chopping board. "And do you use them?"

"Only if there's no sliced or ready-grated in the shop."

Jason smiled. "So, what about your dad? What does he cook? Just the steaks and Sunday roast?"

"No, he cooks like a demon. Makes his own pasta and bread. It drives my mum mad."

Jason bought the knife down and did something unpleasant that the chicken, if breathing, really wouldn't have liked. "Why?"

"Because she's a really good cook, too, but only gets to be the helper. I think that's why Jilly and I are useless. We've never had to bother."

The track on the speakers changed to Ed Sheeran's *Thinking Out Loud* and I smiled as I thought of my mum and dad dancing around the breakfast bar in the kitchen to it the last time I had been home.

"This is my peeps' favorite song. They dance to it whenever they hear it. I thought Jilly was going to curl up and die when it came over the sound system in the supermarket and they started waltzing around the freezer section to it."

Jason stopped chopping and looked at me. "What? In the middle of the day in a shop?"

"Yep. And Jilly's just at the age when your parents are just so, so embarrassing. My mum's never found her height a reason not to wear a six-inch heel and my dad? Well, you've seen the photo. He *says* he's five feet eight but, like me, he's lying by at least an inch."

Jason put the chicken to one side, took a clean chopping board and a smaller knife out of a drawer and set about reducing various vegetables into small, bite-size pieces.

"What does he do?"

"Stockbroker. Well, that's what he started out as, but he did okay in the eighties so now he keeps a small office open in London for a few private clients and mainly stays at home managing his own portfolio."

Jason suspended his knife work again. "How old is your dad? He looked quite young in the photo."

"He hit fifty-five last month."

"He did a bit more than okay in the eighties, then."

"Yeah, he did. Then he travelled around the world on a year-long ticket and met my mum. I was born in ninety-three and Jilly just before the millennium. I've got to keep an eye on his trading account tomorrow at work for half an hour while he loses contact with the outside world as he goes through the Channel Tunnel, if you see me keep looking at my phone."

Jason sliced baby sweetcorn into chunks. "What will you be watching?"

"Astra Fund Management. If American Small Companies hits fifty dollars, he'll sell."

"What did he buy at?"

I took my phone out my handbag and unlocked it. "I didn't ask. Hang on. I'll look."

I called up the DeRay website, logged on to Dad's account and scrolled down the holdings. "Oh, nice one.

Only twenty-seven and the price is up at close of business to forty-five twenty."

"That's his live trading account?"

"Sure. If the price hits while Dad's underground, I'll put the trade through for him."

"So, you know all about the business and trade for your dad but you didn't follow him into the brokerage side of things?"

I logged out of the account, smiled and put my phone on the breakfast bar. "No, probably for the same reason that you're an accountant and not a jeweler. Knowing how to do it isn't the same as being good at it. The best brokers and fund managers have got an instinct for when to buy and sell their shares, which I haven't. I might trade on Dad's account but only according to his instructions."

Jason picked up his glass and drank a mouthful. "Yeah, you're right. The best jewelers have got a delicate touch and I'm not built for it. It's why I've been reluctant to release any of Mum's designs. There just hasn't been anybody as skilled as her that could make them, and that was one of Mum's notes on the portfolio to me. *'Don't have them made just for the sake of it.'*"

"So, you changed your mind because…"

"Nick Davies has a nephew that started work for us a few months ago and he's good—really good. Nick worked with Mum and he's an excellent goldsmith, but he knows he could never have re-created one of her pieces. But Harry's got the touch. I think he could."

"And he'll be making the new piece here in the UK?"

"Yeah. The artwork might be going with the sales team but the technical drawings on how to do so will be staying at the bank."

Jason heated oil in the wok until it smoked then dropped the chicken into it, poked it around for a while, added pieces of veggies, noodles and various seasonings then emptied the wok onto one large plate and brought it over to the breakfast bar with two forks. I looked at the forks.

"No chopsticks? You could have got a little practice in to be ready for next week."

Jason sat beside me and handed me a fork. "Not tonight. I'm too hungry. I'll fiddle around with some later in the week. That's what else I wanted to ask you about. What's the food really like there?"

I speared a piece of chicken on my fork. "Not like here. We eat a Westernized version. They wouldn't eat so many different sticky sauces all together in one meal, even at a banquet. It's all rather more subtle and delicate." I stopped speaking, chewed Western-style on my fast-cooling piece of chicken and swallowed. "This is really good."

Jason swallowed his own mouthful. "I think I'd better hope for a good room service menu for later, then. Delicate, bowl-sized portions aren't quite going to do the trick."

I smiled and speared another piece of chicken.

Jason speared a piece of corn and held it up to my lips. "Vegetables, you."

I opened my mouth and took the corn off his fork. He twirled his fork through the noodles then kept up my intake of vegetable pieces as we finished the plate between us. Jason stacked the dishwasher after we finished while I sipped from my glass and watched him.

"Do you want a coffee and something else to drink?" he asked.

I looked into Jason's eyes and saw a small glint of future mischief in them. "What something else?"

"Cointreau with lots and lots of ice."

I smiled. "Okay."

Jason set his coffee machine off to grind, left the kitchen and came back with a bottle of Cointreau and two glasses. He filled them with ice from the dispenser on the front of his freezer and poured the liqueur over it. My phone vibrated as he sat beside me.

I took a sip of coffee, then one of ice-cold orange and coughed when I swallowed. Jason patted my back as I spluttered and unlocked my phone to see a message from Mark. I put my phone where Jason could see it and opened the message.

Flying home tonight. Vine tomorrow? Be there please, my angel. I can't wait to give you x's and love and hugs. x

I glanced at Jason. "Wanna meet me in The Vine tomorrow night?" Jason looked into my eyes and I couldn't keep the laugh out of them.

Jason smiled. "Yeah. I'll be there."

I picked up my glass and swallowed some Cointreau with more care than I'd taken over my last mouthful. Jason took my hand and laid it in the center of his.

"You like that I'm small for a girl?"

"Yep. When a guy's going to be tall, as a teenager you get to grow the big feet and hands first. It makes you as clumsy as hell. Then the arms and legs shoot out in all directions and suddenly you're all arms, legs and feet that you don't know what to do with and keep tripping over."

I looked at Jason and laughed. "I can't imagine it."

"Believe me. I spent several years looking like the perfect material for a clown. I had absolutely no chance of getting my hands on anything that actually breathed until I went to uni."

An image of a skinny Jason with a blow-up doll popped into my head and I giggled. "So, what did you get your hands on then that didn't breathe?"

Jason squeezed my butt. "Pack it in, you. Not what you're thinking. What I got was a severe case of the *Buffys*. I caught an episode when I was about fourteen and there was Sarah Michelle Geller flick-flacking all over the screen — tiny, neat, perfectly in control of her little bod and that just did it for me. I spent the whole of that summer locked in my bedroom watching the box sets one after the other and repeated them at least the next two summers after that."

"Until you went to uni?"

"Yeah. I met Emma in fresher's week. She looked nothing like Buffy but did at least breathe and was about as experienced in bed as me. We fumbled our way through the beginner's manual for quite a few months before we broke up."

"And you broke up because…?"

"Because I started rowing, used the gym and bulked up quite a bit, and she *didn't* use the gym and bulked up quite a bit."

I laughed and ran my fingers down the muscle of Jason's upper arm. "And made up for lost time after?"

Jason laughed his eyes into mine. "Absolutely."

"Well, I might not row, but if girls turning summersaults are your thing…"

"You can do them?"

"Gymnastics is a natural choice for very small girls to pick for their after-school club. That or ballet — and I was never into the itchy, pink frilly stuff. I made it to county level but couldn't train for a few months when some injuries put me out of action at nineteen. It doesn't take much to lose your competition edge. I could never get to county standard again, but I can still manage a good running tumble." I felt the ghost of a pull behind my belly button, the ache of newly healed fingers on my hand.

Jason traced his fingers from my knee up to my thigh, moving my borrowed sport top up with them. "In one of those little leotards that leave your butt cheeks peeking out?"

My nipples hardened at Jason's touch. "In a very little, skimpy leotard, if you like."

Jason bent forward. I put my hand on the back of his neck and tasted the slight orange tang in his kiss.

He breathed into my ear. "Bed, baby? I've got some of my body oil for you to try."

I looked into Jason's eyes and saw his bed-eyes full of want for me and gave him my bed-eyes back. "Please."

Jason stood, offered me his hand, put his remote in his pocket with the other and picked up his glass that now contained only ice. I put my hand in his, walked with him to his bedroom and he pressed on his remote. The spotlight to light the mirror over the bed came on.

Jason put his glass on the bedside table and lay on the bed. I lay beside him. He kissed my lips, picked up my hands and held them above my head. "This will be nicer if you can't wriggle away."

I looked into Jason's eyes. "How nice?"

Jason gazed back. "Very not nice."

"Yes, then."

Jason kissed my lips, walked over to his wardrobe and came back with a soft belt. I pulled Jason's top off

over my head and held my hands out in front of me.
Jason wrapped his belt around my wrists and I watched
in the mirror as Jason pulled the belt through the
headboard. My reflection stretched its arms up and my
breasts strained and raised. Jason knotted the belt and
traced his finger around their fullness.

"Perfect, baby. Just made for me."

I breathed deeper. Jason took his T-shirt and trackies
off and shook ice from his glass into his mouth. I looked
up and watched Jason's reflection move the ice around
his mouth and the back of his head move over my
nipple.

I gasped as Jason's frozen lips fastened onto my
nipple and sucked. I tried to move and couldn't. He
sucked on my other nipple and sensations raced
between my thighs from the combination of ice and my
hands being bound. Jason kissed me with cold lips. "Oil
now, baby."

Jason picked up a bottle from the bedside table,
tipped oil into his hands and massaged it, soft and
slippery, into the roundness of my breasts and over
each of my nipples. He gazed into my eyes in the mirror
and blew over my nipple.

It heated where Jason's breath touched. My eyes
widened as I pulled on my bound hands and my
shoulders came up off the mattress. Jason blew over the
fullness of my breast and my voice caught in the back
of my throat at the warmth and I arched my back as the
heat built. Jason took more ice into his mouth, licked
my hot skin and I pulled on the belt as his tongue froze
the heat.

"Shit! Jason."

He kissed my neck. "Where next, baby?"

I pressed my body against his. "Anywhere and everywhere…"

Jason kissed across my shoulder. "Sweet."

Jason dribbled oil down my body and followed with his mouth—small breaths followed by small nips from his teeth. I moaned as I pulled my hands, wanting more. Jason held my legs, sucked fresh ice into his mouth, dripped oil onto my pubic mound and breathed on it. I bucked against the mattress as his icy lips followed the heat.

"Jason… Oh…"

He stroked his fingers, cold from holding the glass, down my center and into the wet warmth inside. I wanted to part my legs, to move against his fingers and couldn't against the hold of his hand. Jason pushed his fingers inside me. "You need me in here, Ness?"

My chest heaved, my breath coming fast. "Please, now."

"Yes, now, baby."

Jason straddled my thighs, dropped a little oil on my clitoris and bent his head to blow. I shouted as it heated. Jason pushed his cock inside me. I wrapped my legs around his thighs and moaned as he pinched my nipples and bit my neck. I moved with him, hip to hip, pulling on the belt and shouting loud enough to wake the flat above as my orgasm raced through my groin and into my thighs. "Jason, fuck!"

"Yes, tell me. I love hearing you come."

"Oh, Fuck! *Yes*." I mewled and whimpered as my muscles tightened and aftershocks throbbed between my legs.

Jason breathed deeper, pumped harder and groaned out his release. "Ness…so, sweet." Jason stilled and released my hands, his breath fast in my ear. I wrapped my arms around him and panted as I ran my hands down his back. Jason eased his cock out of me and rolled to his side with me in his arms.

"Jesus! What is that stuff?"

Jason smiled and passed me the bottle. "I came across it originally in the States. I can order it online. Look at the name."

I read *Emotion Lotion, Cinnamon* and handed it back.

"That's so cheesy. They do a whole range of flavors, do they?"

"At least half a dozen, although I can't say I much fancy either the bubble gum or candy floss. It just gets warm if you rub it in, but hot if you blow on it." Jason put the bottle down beside the bed and tightened his arm around me. "Stay, Ness? I'll be okay to drive by about six. I'll get you home in time to get ready for work."

I cuddled closer to him and faced what I had to explain to the only man I'd felt strongly enough about to do so since Tim. "I can't. I don't sleep-sleep with anyone but myself."

Jason cupped my butt and lifted me up higher on the bed so my face rested on the pillow alongside his.

"What? Never? Why?"

"Bad dreams. I fight in my sleep. Lash out. You don't want to be anywhere near me when I do. It's much better all round if I've only got my duvet to beat up."

"Who are you fighting, Ness? The person that knocked you off your feet and hurt you?"

A tremor ran down my spine. I dug my fingernails into my palms and let the words out. "Yeah, that's the one. And it wasn't just me. It was Jules, too. We were walking home after a night out at the end of our first year at uni and took a short cut through the park. Two guys came up behind us. We didn't see or hear them coming. They never threatened us or gave us the chance to hand anything over. They just went for us, put us down and took our bags and jewelry. It was sudden, violent and we were both badly hurt." My skin goosebumped as I fought to keep the images out of my head. Jason squeezed his arm around me. "Now I re-live it all in my sleep sometimes. I don't know why. Jules doesn't and she was as badly hurt as me. I fight back like I did at the time, only then I didn't know how to and now I do."

Jason tucked me in tighter to his body and held his heat against my shivered skin. "How bad were you hurt, baby?"

"Battered and bruised from the punches to my head, broken ribs from the weight of him when he sat on me. He broke my fingers to get my ring…" I moved Jason's hand to my stomach and put his finger on my belly button. "That's not the one I was born with. They didn't undo the jewelry when they took it. They just ripped it off…"

"Ness…"

"The surgeon was good, though, as was the dentist that did Jules' implants to replace her missing teeth. Neither of us has much visible scarring. Because our skin was so young, they said."

Jason tightened his arms around me. "Were they ever caught?"

The shivers left my flesh as the telling of the attack itself was over. "No. Their DNA is on file from skin cells they found under our fingernails but there wasn't a match then and there hasn't been one since. The police think they followed me and Jules when we left a nightclub that night — that they must have seen our jewelry in a better light first and known it was the real deal and not fake fashion stuff."

Jason held me closer and kissed my lips. "No wonder you didn't take the tour of floor two."

I breathed easier at Jason's kiss. "I don't have a problem with jewelry itself as such. Just, for me, I couldn't bring myself to wear anything again so valuable that someone would hurt me to get their hands on it."

"And when you fight in your sleep? I couldn't stop you?"

I ran my hand over his muscled shoulder, so powerful compared to mine. "If you were awake and realized I was starting to dream, maybe. But if you were asleep and not expecting it…"

"What would you do? Show me?"

I looked into Jason's eyes.

"Make a move then. Do something. I'm awake now. I can't retaliate unless you do."

"What? Do something to you that might hurt you? I can't." I kissed Jason lips. "I know. A toughie, isn't it? When you think you might do something that you didn't mean to and hurt someone you didn't want to. I'll sleep with you, but I won't sleep-sleep with you, and if you find it's not enough, then just let me know. You won't get anything back from me other than total amnesia that we ever did so."

"Ness…"

I kissed Jason's lips to stop his words. "Don't. I've just laid a bundle of crap on you, let alone the other stuff I trail about with me that you already knew about. Take some time to think it over. I'll use your bathroom then I'm going home."

I scooped up Jason's sport top on my way to his en suite, leaned against the door as I closed it and saw the clothes I'd stripped out of wet, hung on Jason's heated towel rail. I felt them and found them nearly dry. I hung Jason's top in their place and re-dressed.

Jason called through the door. "Ness. You okay in there? Can I get you anything?"

The heat hit my face as Jason asked. I gritted my teeth and dug my nails into the palms of my hands against the unidentified 'him' that had landed all this shit in my life. Then I breathed in deep through my nose and kept my emotion out of my voice as I answered. "I'm fine. Could you call me a cab?"

I opened the door, picked my hairbrush up from beside the bed and walked through to the kitchen. Jason, re-dressed in his trackies and T-shirt, sat at the breakfast bar drinking from a bottle of water, another unopened bottle standing in front of him. I put my hands on Jason's shoulders and kissed his neck. "Thanks. I could do with that."

Jason turned and lifted me to sit on his lap. I put my arm around his neck as he asked for my lips. I tasted his tongue — cold from the water — and his sweet breath and I gave him everything I could back. Jason's phone hopped about on the breakfast bar and we pulled apart. I stood down from his lap while he read the message. "The cab's outside."

I smiled and picked up the bottle of water. "I'll drink it on the way home."

I walked to the front door and Jason put his arms around me. "I don't need time, Ness. I would have taken the chance on the sleep-sleep option, given the choice. But I'll take just sleep-with if that's better for you."

I kissed Jason and smiled a small smile. "It's for the best. I also puke when I wake from my dream and I'm afraid I don't always make the bathroom."

I stepped over the doorstep, walked to the lift and texted Jules from the cab to tell her I was on my way home. The flat was silent when I let myself in and I took myself to bed.

Chapter Seven

I woke in the morning ahead of my alarm and was ready for work so early that I had time for a second coffee before I left the flat. Jules walked into the kitchen as I poured it and she rubbed her eyes.

"You're up early. How did it go at Jason's? Did he cook something good?"

"Yeah. He can certainly cook. He made us a chicken stir-fry from scratch." I poured Jules a mug and handed it over. "Jason asked me to stay over, though. I had to tell him why I couldn't and gave him his 'get out of jail free' card."

Jules winced. "Ouch! How'd he take it?"

"Okay, I think. He's not heading straight for the hills, anyway. He said he would have taken his chances on sleep-sleep."

Jules smiled and sipped. "There you go then. He must really like you."

"Maybe, but then again, Jason doesn't know what I could actually do to him, does he? It's one thing to think

183

I might kick out and flail around a bit, but I don't how long liking me would last if he knew that with one sharp slap from me he'd be KO'd then puke his guts up alongside me."

Jules looked at me over the top of her mug. "Hey, what's wrong with a bit of dual puking? I call that true togetherness, myself."

I dipped my fingers into my mug and flicked coffee at her. "Oh, yeah. And perhaps we could have his and hers buckets and mops. Then I could clean up his puke and he could clean up mine."

Jules laughed. "So show him a couple of non-puking moves. Just give him a dead arm or something."

"I don't think he can see past the 'I'm a really big guy and you're a girl and really, really, small' bit, not that it matters whether Jason knows what I could do to him or not. I'm no keener on hurting him than he is me, so I still won't be sleep-sleeping anywhere near him. Did you get a message from Mark?"

"Yeah. So, are we going to The Vine tonight, my angel?"

"Oh, absolutely, my angel. I'm meeting Jason there. Well, I think I am, although we arranged it before I dropped my bundle of crap on him, so I'll see whether he's still coming with or not when I get to work."

"Let me know. It doesn't sound much like he's about to head off into the sunset, though."

"I hope not, but I tell you one place he is about to head off to."

"Go on, then."

"China. Next Sunday."

Jules grinned. "Oh, they are just going to *love* him out there!"

I laughed. "Oh, aren't they just! It's work but it's also the Gabriella thing. I'll catch you up with it all at wine o'clock, but I'd better get out of here and into work now."

"Sure. And my lips will remain firmly sealed at the gallery about anything to do with Belmond's, if it involves that."

I kissed Jules' cheek and she kissed mine.

"Probably safest, given how efficient and accurate your rumor mill is. Later, babe."

I let myself out of the flat into fresher morning air cleared by the heavy rain and was early enough to knock on the window of the boutique shop and persuade the owner to sell me the horseshoe charm for Jilly, even though the shop wasn't officially open. I requested a coffee from the machine on my way past, took it to my desk and smiled good morning at Annie and Maisie as I sat down.

Maisie stared at my face. "Vanessa, is that lipstick on your cheek?"

"It shouldn't be. There wasn't any when I put my makeup on this morning. Whereabouts?"

Maisie passed me the compact mirror from out of her bag. I saw a small smidge of pink on my cheek, dabbed it off with my fingertip, closed the compact and handed it back.

"Thanks, Maisie. Jules must have got me this morning when she kissed me before I left for work. There must have been a bit in the corner of her lips left over from last night."

I pulled my keyboard forward and logged on to the payroll system. Masie carried on looking at me.

"Something else?" I asked.

185

"You were chatting with Jason. Did you ask him? You know… How long he would be away in China?"

"Oh, yes. Sorry. I forgot to say, didn't I?"

Maisie nodded.

"They go on Sunday and fly back next Friday, so all week."

"And in the lift?"

"Chinese table manners. What they do instead of using a knife and fork — that type of thing."

Maisie smiled. "Well, yes. I suppose that's all right, although I can't say he can carry on chatting to other girls like that once we're going out together, even if it is *only* you."

I kept my face blank, not knowing whether to laugh or be offended over the words 'only you'.

"Okay, fine. Well, you just let me know if that ever happens." I turned to my screen and carried on with my work.

My phone vibrated at nine-fifty with a message from Dad.

Going through the tunnel in about 20 mins.

Okay. Logging on now.

I called up the DeRay brokerage website on my phone, logged on to Dad's trading account and laid my phone beside my keyboard so I could glance at the share price, even though I knew Dad had a price alert in place and my phone would sing if the price hit the mark.

Jason walked past fifteen minutes later. Maisie called his name. "Jason. Sorry, but these figures look wrong again. Would you take a look? I could print off a hard copy and bring it into your office with a coffee for you, if you like?"

Jason walked closer. "Have you checked them properly this time, Maisie?"

Maisie looked at Jason, her eyes wide and blue. "I'm sure I have."

Jason stopped walking as he reached my workstation and looked at Annie. "Check Maisie's spreadsheet against her input data, please, Annie. If you don't find any transposed figures or input errors, you can leave the hard copy on my desk and I'll check it myself later."

My phone danced on my desk as Annie nodded. I picked it up and Jason looked over my shoulder. I tapped on the icon for the dealing screen, highlighted the line for five thousand American Small Companies shares and tapped the icon to sell. The screen gave the message *Transaction Processing, Transaction Successful* then a reference number. I tapped on the icon — *Done* — backtracked out of the dealing system, logged off and looked over my shoulder at Jason. "And that's the easy bit over with."

"Good one for the bottom line. I was just going to the machine. Do you want to get a coffee?"

"Sure. Maisie, Annie, do you want me to bring you a drink back?"

Maisie looked at me and smiled past me at Jason. "That's so kind of you, Vanessa. Yes, thank you. I'll have a coffee, please."

Annie shook her head.

I walked out of the office with Jason. He glanced at me as the office door swung shut behind us.

"Is it just me or was that a little odd?"

"Ah, apparently I'm allowed to talk to you with big smiles all round because it's only me."

"Only you? What? As in, no competition?"

I smiled. "Well, I thought that at first, but then I added up some of the things she's said and what I've said back and I think she believes that I'm no competition because Jules and I are an item."

We arrived at the coffee machine and Jason put the code in. "How did she come to that conclusion?"

"I think because she never hears me talk about any male other than my dad. I've never mentioned any of my previous boyfriends and I leave out anything that concerns you, so all Maisie hears is 'Jules this' and 'Jules that'."

Jason handed me my coffee and ordered his own.

"Then yesterday, Maisie only heard one side of the conversation when I was teasing Jules about using her nipples to get the info you wanted at work and today Jules left a bit of lippy on my cheek when we pecked goodbye this morning."

Jason choked on his coffee. "Her nipples! This I've got to hear about. How?"

I laughed. "John Southall's a bit in love with Jules' chest, so she perched herself on his desk under the air con vent and got her nips up and perky against her top then pumped him for info while his mind was elsewhere and he drooled."

I put the code for Maisie's coffee into the machine as Jason laughed, took the cup from the dispenser and turned to walk back to the office.

"And believe me… Jules has got one hell of a chest. She could take your eye out with one of her nips when they're up and ready to go."

I swung my butt at the office door to open it. Jason took its weight from me and followed me in, still laughing. Maisie smiled over my shoulder at Jason as I put her coffee down on her desk.

"Annie found my little mistake for me. My input is all okay now, Jason."

He straightened his face and turned toward his office. "Really? I thought she might." Jason walked on.

Maisie watched him go. "I've never seen him laugh like that in the office. He's got the most perfect teeth, hasn't he? What did you say that he found so funny?"

Muscles tightened in my stomach as I thought, *Oh yeah, absolutely perfect* and my mouth answered, "Jules' nipples. I was telling Jason how perky they get sometimes."

Maisie's mouth opened, closed then her lips moved. "Well, really! I'm not sure that's an appropriate subject for discussion in the office."

I shrugged and pulled my keyboard forward. "Well, Jason doesn't mind so I don't see why you should or even what it's got to do with you, really."

I put my earbuds in and music on, worked through until lunch, bought a take-out salad in the canteen and texted Jules while I ate it.

All okay with J today. Been having a laugh. Tell you later.

Good. Can't wait for wine o'clock. Work so slow today. See you at home.

I worked on until just before five. My phone vibrated with a message from Jason as I put my stationery away in my drawer.

You out of here now? What time at The Vine tonight?

Sure am and 8ish?

See you there.

I smiled goodbye at Maisie and Annie, caught the bus home and opened the front door to my flat just after six to silence. I was the first one home. I headed to my bedroom, showered and Jules' key rattled in the front door as I dried my hair. I pulled a wrap on over my underwear and filled two glasses in the kitchen as Jules walked in through the living room door.

"Hey, babe. How was your day?" she said.

"Quite funny this morning, boring this afternoon."

Jules picked up her glass, drank a mouthful, kicked off her shoes and took another sip. "God, I needed that. I think we only had two people in through the door all day. I'm sure this afternoon was at least ten hours long."

"My afternoon was a bit like that, too, although at least I can have my music on."

Jules tucked her legs up beside her. "But a ha-ha morning? What happened?"

I did the same and picked up my glass. "Well, Maisie's decided she's quite happy for me to chat to Jason now because she thinks we're a couple."

Jules snorted into her wine. "How did she work that one out?"

"Because I've never mentioned any of my previous male friends and I talk about you and leave out the hours I spend with Jason. So, all she hears is 'Jules this' and 'Jules that' and 'Jules and I are going to…'"

Jules grinned. "We were talking about my nipples yesterday, weren't we?"

"And Maisie only heard my half of the conversation. And you left a bit of your lippy on my cheek this morning. You couldn't have taken your makeup off properly last night."

"Oops. I was that knackered last night. I only gave my face a quick once over with a couple of makeup wipes."

I laughed. "I'll put her right tomorrow. From what Annie's said, Maisie's not the type of girl to laugh at her own mistakes, so as tempting as it is to run with it and use it as cover for what's really going on, I won't. But how you used your nips to tease the info out of John yesterday was what made Jason laugh in work today."

"I hope he was suitably impressed with my diversionary tactics."

"You'll have to ask him tonight. Had we better eat before we go out? Have we got anything?"

"Yeah. I picked us up a prawn salad yesterday then you ate at Jason's and I had a burger with Ben. It's in the fridge. I'll get it."

Jules came back from the kitchen with the pre-dressed salad in its supermarket container and two forks then put the plastic bowl on the sofa cushion between us.

"So, Gabriella?" she asked.

I dug my fork into the salad and speared some prawns. "Well, firstly, it is Jason that owns the new artwork…"

Jules looked at me, her fork suspended halfway to her mouth. "It is? Why didn't anyone know there was any?"

"Because Jason didn't know himself until a couple of years ago. Everything his mother left to him was held in trust and Jason didn't see the portfolio of her work that he'd inherited until he turned twenty-five."

"He's got a whole portfolio? Bloody hell!"

I nodded. "But Jason's not selling anything. The piece is to be made because they've found a jeweler skilled enough to do so."

"Shit! Really? The piece I heard about is going to cost a small fortune just to produce."

I chewed a mouthful of salad and swallowed. "That makes sense. When Jason went to Spain — before I knew about Gabriella or her artwork — he said that the prospective asset being offered at the trade fair would be a large financial undertaking for Belmond's. What is it, by the way?"

"Jason hasn't said?"

"No. But it's more that I haven't asked."

Jules washed a mouthful of prawns down with another swallow of wine. "Well, the rumor says very sparkly and very, very expensive. A diamond and platinum bridal tiara, very heavy on high-end, first-class diamonds."

"That makes sense on the Chinese marketing front, given that they are all absolutely mad out there for anything to do with big, white weddings. But that aside, Jason thinks that someone might be thinking of nicking the artwork for the value of the thing itself when it's out of the care of the bank. The artwork has got to go to China with the sales team, so Jason's decided he'd better go with."

I looked at the time on my phone as I put my fork down. "It's too late for me to knock on Paula's door now. Mark said they'd be there around eight. Is that good for you or do you need extra time?"

"No, an hour should be fine. I'm not going overboard with the makeup. The rain might have cleared the air a bit but it's still hot and there's no air con in The Vine."

"I'm thinking the same on the clothes. I can't really see past shorts. I'll wear my black lacy ones with the bobble fringe."

"With you on that. Shorts…and I'll go Timberlands with mine. My hair's going up off my face again, as well."

I frowned as I thought through my inevitable shoe problem of high shoes with shorts looking just too over-the-top for a wine bar on a weekday night.

"I'll wear my short boots with the chunky heel, I think."

Jules put her glass on the coffee table. I stood mine alongside it, walked to my bedroom, dressed in my shorts and a T-shirt, put my hair up, made up my face then stepped into my boots. Jules, ready to go in shorts and a top tied under her breasts, arrived at my bedroom door and we left the flat and headed to The Vine. John walked over to serve us as we stood at the bar.

"A bottle of Raimat and two glasses?" he asked.

"Please," Jules said.

I took my card from my purse, handed it over, sat on the stool beside Jules and poured once our bottle and glasses arrived. Jules swung around on her stool.

"Simon and Mark at two o'clock. Mark's waving."

"Okay, girlie. Let's go."

I picked up my glass and our bottle and put them on Mark and Simon's table, hugged and kissed them then sat as Jules did the same. Mark looked me up and down, then Jules.

"Ness, Jules, my angels. You're both looking gorgeous, as usual. It feels like forever since we've seen you, doesn't it, Simon?"

Simon smiled. "No, my love. It was the flight back that seemed like it went on forever."

"First class was full so we had to take business seats and we couldn't even sit together. An overnighter back from the States with just a flimsy screen between you and some stranger's bad breath when the seats are down bed-style. Never again, I'm telling you," Mark said.

I laughed. "Bad organization. That's unusual for you two. I take it the fashion house was picking up the tab?"

"Of course, my angel. You know we don't fly long-haul unless someone else is paying for it. Tack your vacation on to the end of the assignment that includes paid travel. That's the way."

"We saw your pics on Facebook. How was Vegas? Did you play? Win?" Jules said.

"The runway show at Caesars was out of this world," Simon smiled.

"And we played some fab craps after the show," Mark added. "The Americans are just so much fun when they play. The noise! The whooping! All the cocktails…" Mark reached over the table, took my hand and held it. "But enough of that, Ness, my angel. I heard a whisper of a new man."

"Oh, did you? Jules wouldn't have told you, so Paula, I presume?"

Simon nodded at me behind Mark's back.

"She said he's a bit of a looker. Where did you find him? Is he coming in here tonight? Why aren't you dressed up like the dog's dinner?"

I laughed. "The dog's dinner! When do I ever dress like the dog's dinner?"

Jules grinned. "Woof, woof! Can't you see your own tail wagging, Ness? She found him at work." Jules glanced over my shoulder. "And he's just walked in."

Mark turned in Jason's direction, raised my hand to his lips and nibbled across my knuckles. "Oh, yes. Very pretty. I approve. A little jealousy is always a good thing to get a guy going, my angel. Would you like a little snog?"

I laughed and took my hand away. "No, not unless I was looking to make him piss off, which I'm not."

"Are you going to introduce us?" Simon asked.

"Not until I've said hello myself. Jules, I'm going to the bar. Keep this pair under control, will you?"

Jules smiled and picked up her glass. "If either one of them moves in the next fifteen minutes, I'll trip them up."

I picked up my handbag, walked to the bar, slipped my arms around Jason's waist and breathed in freshly showered skin and Hugo as I kissed his cheek. Jason rested his hand in the small of my back and kissed mine.

"You good, baby?"

I pressed my body against his. "Yeah."

I sat on a stool and hung my bag by its strap on the back rest. Jason sat beside me. John put our previously half-finished bottle and two glasses on the bar and Jason poured. The street door opened. Ben walked in and headed over.

"Hey, you both good?"

I offered Ben my cheek for his kiss and kissed his back. Jason and Ben nodded at each other and Ben glanced at Jules.

"Ness, while I've got the chance... Jules said she's away with you next weekend?"

"Yeah, we're going to help the peeps keep order at the baby bratlet's birthday sleepover. Why?"

"My folks are having a family lunch thing on Sunday. I'm going to ask Jules if she'll come with me. Do you think she will?"

"You can but ask. She hasn't said anything to me to make me think she'd say no, if that's what you're asking. We can leave the peeps early enough to be back for mid-morning Sunday if she says yes."

Ben smiled. "Okay. Good. I heard from James today. I need to run a demo defense session for a couple of new female constables. Are you free tomorrow evening? Can you do the session?"

"Sure. Jules didn't say anything about it. Where are you running it?"

"I only got the call from James before I came out. I'll use the gym at the block."

"Is it an open or closed session?" Jason asked.

Ben shrugged. "Open. They always are. No trade secrets about what we do."

"What time?" Jason asked.

I looked at Ben, glanced at Jules and kept my guesswork to myself until I could get hold of Jules on her own.

"About eight. Pop by if you want a look. You might like what you see enough that you'll pass on the word to girls you see at your gym or wherever."

My phone vibrated in my bag. I took it out and read a message from Jules.

He's in the loo and will be with you shortly. Brace yourself!

I blew Jules a kiss as Mark exited the gents. He walked over, hugged Ben and smacked his lips on his cheek. Ben laughed and wiped the spot with his fingers. "Get off, you silly sod. You've only been gone for two weeks. No kissing unless you've been out the country for at least a year."

Ben punched Mark lightly on the top of his arm and walked over to Jules. Mark put his arm around my shoulders and smiled. "So, Ness, my angel. You've had quite long enough to do the necessary, so here I am."

"So, I see. Perhaps I should have told Jules to sit on you instead of tripping you up."

"No, my angel. That wouldn't have worked. Now, if you'd told Ben to do so, you might have stood a chance." Mark looked at Jason. "And this is?"

"Jason," I said.

Mark held his hand out and smiled. "Hello, Jason. I'm Mark, and if Ness didn't warn you I'd be over then she should have, because I always do."

Jason took Mark's offered hand.

I looked at Mark. "Don't even think about it."

Mark shook Jason's hand and let it go. "Spoilsport." Mark nodded in Jules' direction. "We live in the flat below theirs. Met them in the lift the day they moved in. Hopeless, the pair of them. There was nothing for it but to step in and chivvy them up a bit. Take them out and about with us…"

Simon arrived at Mark's side and Mark slid his arm around Simon's waist. "And talking of the devil. This is Simon. The other half of my 'we' and 'us'. Simon, this is Ness' friend, Jason."

Simon held his hand out and Jason shook it. I looked sideways at Jason. He smiled back at me.

Mark looked at Simon. "I've just been telling Jason about when we first bumped into our angels."

Simon raised his eyes to the ceiling. "Bloody hopeless, the pair of them."

Jules walked up behind Mark and Simon, put her arms around their waists and wriggled her hips until she stood between them.

Mark knocked his hip against Jules'. "Pushy little thing she is now, though."

Jules shimmied as a phone peeped beside her. "Excuse me. I don't push any bit of me anywhere it's not wanted."

Simon took his phone out of his pocket. An alarm flashed on the screen.

"Mark, home, my love. Early shoot tomorrow and you're still jet lagged. You're going to look like hell if you're not knocking out the z's in the next hour."

Simon looked at me, Jason and Jules. "A Christmas catalog. Photos in the park. They're starting as soon as it gets light around five so we won't look too hot and sweaty in our Christmas sweaters. You see any fake snow around tomorrow and you'll know where we've been."

I smiled. "You two are always one season away from the rest of us. I'll wish for real fake snow for you. You are so going to boil."

"Ah, but it will be with real brandy egg nog, so life won't look so bad by lunchtime, my angel," Mark said. "Kiss, please, before I go?"

I put my face up for Mark's lips and he kissed me, moved over to Jules and I kissed Simon's cheek and watched them walk out of the street door, leaving a waft of Armani behind them. Ben came out of the gents as I picked up my glass. He put his arm around Jules' waist and looked at the door closing behind Mark and Simon.

"They've gone already?"

"Early photo shoot in the morning," Jules said.

Ben looked at Jules. "Talking of an early start…"

Jules put her arm around Ben. "Come on, then. We'll walk back to yours."

Jules leaned toward me with lips puckered to kiss my cheek. I caught the look in her eye as she bent but tilted my cheek toward her anyway. Jules pushed her lipsticked lips hard against my cheek and left a slick of sticky pink on it.

"There you go, my darling, sweet, honey-pie. No washing it off now. I won't be up as early as you in the morning to give you another."

I gave Jules the full dramatics back, one hand over my mouth, the other over my heart. "But you're just about to betray me again" — I hiccupped and sniffed — "with a man!"

Ben looked at Jason. "I did mention mad as a box of frogs last Friday, didn't I?"

"Only frogs? You sure?" Jason laughed.

I wiped Jules' lipstick from my face with my fingers as they walked away, picked up my glass and glanced sideways. Jason smiled.

"So, yes, my angel. They are a lovely couple."

"Yeah. They are. Jules and I moved into the flat at the start of our second year at uni. We were both just about healed up after our little surgical repair jobs but we found it difficult to go out at night, especially after dark. Mark and Simon noticed that we never went anywhere, so they used to turn up and make us. They took us everywhere with them for a while, then Jules and I signed up for self-defense classes and it all got better from there."

"Doubly lovely, then. Are you okay with me coming to watch you do your moves tomorrow?"

"Sure. As Ben said, it's not a secret. Want me to flick-flack over the mats for you while we're there?"

Jason picked up my hand and traced over my knuckles with his thumb. "Will you be wearing your little skimpy leotard?"

"Street clothes...but I could be wearing it underneath and not wearing the street clothes after the session."

Jason kissed into the palm of my hand. I ran my fingers along his jawline. "Do you want to walk back to mine?"

He smiled his assent. I gestured to John for the tab, did the necessary on the chip and pin and slipped my hand into Jason's back pocket as we walked out to the street. He put his arm around my back and I let us in through the front door of my flat ten minutes later. I took my feet out of my boots and picked up the empty salad bowl and dirty glasses as Jason sat on the sofa. I took them to the kitchen and came back with two clean glasses and a bottle of wine.

I poured and passed Jason his glass, my hips level with his face. He took the glass and put his other hand on my hip, tilted his face forward and pressed it into my groin, his breath warm through the material of my shorts. I stood still.

Jason looked into my eyes. "Yes?"

My heart pumped faster as I gazed back. "Yes."

Jason put his glass on the table, leaned forward and nibbled my pubic mound. I put my hands on his shoulders to steady myself as he eased my shorts down and off then grazed his teeth over the satin of my thong. My breath came faster as he eased my thong out the way and tasted my skin.

Cassie O'Brien

I tightened my fingers on his shoulders as he delved deeper, past the lips covering my sensitive center and licked and sucked on the softness inside. Then he teased my clitoris with the tip of his tongue.

"Jason...yes!"

"You taste good, baby. I want to feel you come with my mouth."

I whimpered as he eased my thong down and positioned his lips over my mound. "You're certainly getting there."

Jason slipped a finger inside me, then another, stroked and sucked my pussy. I ground against his fingers and pushed my pelvis forward as the muscles inside me throbbed. "Oh, that's good."

He teased his tongue over my clitoris and sucked.

I closed my eyes as my back arched. "More... Yes, more."

He fixed his lips over my pulsating center and sucked while he worked his fingers inside me, up and down, and I shouted out.

"Fuck, yes!"

Jason lifted me to lie on the sofa, unzipped his jeans, pushed them and his boxers over his hips and freed his cock. "Again now, baby." He pushed my T-shirt up, the cups of my bra down, fastened his mouth on my nipple and sucked. I moaned as he tugged with his teeth, gripping the fullness of my breast with his hand. "I'm going to fuck you now, baby."

"Please, Jason."

I wrapped my legs around his thighs as he put the head of his cock inside me and thrust. I pushed my hips against his and Jason began to move fast and urgently. I writhed as my muscles contracted and I shouted out my second climax, not sure whether it was two or one that had rolled on. "Fuck! Fuck!"

Jason groaned. His muscles tensed and strained beneath my hands. "Ness, my beautiful girl."

I eased my legs down and stroked his back as we panted. He took his cock out of me and moved onto his side, his arm underneath me. I curled my body into his and he stroked my skin under my T-shirt until my eyelids fluttered and my muscles twitched when my brain caught up.

He tightened his arm around me. "It's okay, baby. Don't worry. I wouldn't have fallen asleep, too."

I lifted my face for Jason's kiss and traced the outline of his mouth with my fingertip as our mouths parted. "You have the most beautiful mouth."

"It's yours, baby. Whenever and wherever you want it."

I smiled, sat up straighter and rearranged my clothes as he replaced his underwear and jeans. I moved under the curve of his arm as he picked up his glass and my phone vibrated in my bag. I reached over the side of the sofa, took it out and opened a message from 'DD'.

Home now. Mum will phone you tomorrow to tell what she bought for Jilly.

Okay. I got her pressie yesterday. I'll tell Mum tomorrow.

Jason handed me my glass as I pressed Send.

"Why a double D for your dad? You don't call him Dad DeRay, surely?"

I smiled. "No. And it doesn't stand for his Christian name, either. My dad's Alan. My mum's Sally. DD is a

Jilly-and-me joke. Our nickname for him is Darling Daddy."

"Oh, yeah. How did that come about then?"

I sipped my wine and thought about it. "So, an all-boys school and no little sisters. Were there no little girls around when you were growing up at all?"

"Nope. Alien species, as far as I was concerned."

"Hmmm. How to explain it if you don't know what little girls are like, anyway?" I smiled as I pictured how Jilly and I competed for Dad's attention when we were young, how we would ask him to buy something we wanted rather than ask Mum. "Do you want me to show you instead of telling?"

He smiled. "Go on, then."

I put my glass on the coffee table, sat sideways across Jason's lap and slipped my arm around his neck. "Okay, so you've got to remember I'm only six years old, and whatever I say, you've got to reply, 'Yes, darling'." I gazed into his eyes, fluttered my eyelashes and made my voice little-girlie. "Daddy?"

Jason hesitated. I nudged him. "Yes, darling," he finally said.

I laid my head on Jason's shoulder and peeked up at him. "There was a new Barbie doll on the telly tonight."

"Yes, darling."

I snuggled closer and rubbed my cheek against his neck. "She was really pretty. An' she's got dark hair like you and me an' not yellow like Mummy an' Jilly."

"Yes, darling."

I cuddled in to Jason's chest. "An' if I could have one, I'd never ask for a real horse again." I sat straighter, opened my eyes wide and gazed into his. "Please, Daddy? Pleeease."

"Yes, darling."

I picked up my wine and dropped the girlie voice. "Done deal, then."

Jason laughed. "And that's what you and Jilly used to do to your dad, is it?"

I slipped off Jason's lap and smiled. "The first person a little girl flutters her eyelashes at is her daddy. If we're not born doing it then we've normally got if down pat by the age of two. And as for 'used to'? You don't suppose we're not still both at it?"

"Oh, God. Your poor dad!"

"Nah, he likes it. And he knows exactly what we're up to. All daddies do."

"You must be looking forward to seeing your…ah, peeps on Friday?"

"Yeah. I am. I picked up the baby bratlet's present this morning. Do you want to see it?"

Jason nodded. I put my handbag on my lap and felt around inside it for the small paper carrier bag. He peeked in.

"Jesus, Ness. How much stuff have you got in there?"

I opened my handbag wider so he could look in, spotted the paper bag and pulled it out.

Jason laughed. "Yep, as suspected. The gutters of Bombay are cleaner."

"Hey, what can I say? I've had this bag a long time. Even I don't know what's lurking in the bottom of it."

I handed Jason the carrier bag. He opened the small box inside it.

"Very pretty. Your sister doesn't feel the same way about jewelry as you do, then? Given what happened."

"No, Jilly's fine. She likes her sparkly stuff. Jules bought her a white gold pendant to match the charm. It has to be gold, according to my mum. Fashion jewelry turns your skin green, then you'll be in real trouble as gangrene will set in and you'll be dead by morning from blood poisoning, for sure."

Jason smiled. "The type of person jewelers send up prayers of thanks for. Does Jules come home with you a lot?"

"Quite a bit. Her peeps are divorced so she's only got her mum and grandma living close. Her dad met someone else and emigrated to Oz. That's why we went that way on our gap year – to go to his wedding. So now, when Jules comes home with me, she borrows my peeps."

"Is that why Ben was a bit hesitant about asking her to go with him on Sunday? Because she hasn't got loads of family?"

"Ah, a bit but not really. It's more that Jules and I have never done the 'meet the peeps' thing."

"What? Never?"

"Nope. Never got close. My mum's convinced we'll both still be living in our flat in our eighties, gumming gruel together and borrowing each other's incontinence pants."

"Well, you'll meet mine tomorrow. He's coming into the office."

"Nope. I don't think that I can count that as one. I'll only see him walking through the main office to your goldfish bowl."

My phone vibrated on the coffee table. Jason looked at me. "Jules?"

I picked up my phone and nodded. Jason lifted me to sit on his lap, I put my arms around his neck and offered him my mouth until Jules' key rattled in the front door. I stood as her footsteps sounded in the hall and took in the smile on her face when she walked into the room. "You're going then?"

Jules held her hand up. I high-fived her.

"Double whammy. Two in one week. Way to go or what?" she said. "Hi, Jason," she added.

I laughed at the Cheshire cat smile on her face. "Well, there's a medal headed in your direction, for sure."

Jules shimmied her hips. "I wanna a silver one at least. You'd better get your butt down to Paula's, girlie. At this rate you won't even have a bronze sticky star to shout about, let alone a nice, shiny badge. I'm going to take my smug, triumphant butt off to bed. See you in the morning, babe. Night, Jason."

She walked out. Jason put his shoes on and followed me down the hallway to the sound of Jules trilling and gurgling in her bathroom. He put his arms around me at the front door.

"So, she's going on Sunday. What's the other one that's tipped her into happy land?"

I tilted my face up to kiss Jason goodnight. "She was a very, very brave, good girl. She knocked on Ben's front door."

"Got a real scary front door, has he?"

"Oh yeah. That's the one. I knew you'd be impressed."

Jason bent down, let my tongue into his mouth and kissed my lips as we parted. "Tell me tomorrow?"

I nodded and opened the front door. "Sure. See you then."

"Night, Ness. See you in the morning."

I watched Jason walk toward the lift and clamped my lips against the urge to call after him and ask him not to go. I shut the front door, walked to the living room, picked up my phone, switched off the lamps then got ready for bed and a night of only having my pillow to cuddle, as usual.

* * * *

Jules was standing in the kitchen with the cafetière ready to go when I arrived there before leaving for work in the morning. She poured me a mug.

"Thanks, babe. I thought you weren't getting up as early as me this morning."

Jules smiled. "I'm a bit pumped. I couldn't sleep any longer."

"Good for you, girlie. And now I've got the chance to ask. Ah...you and Ben didn't set tonight up on purpose to make a point to Jason, did you?"

Jules peeked at me over the rim of her mug. "Ah, well, sort of...just a little bit...but not actually on purpose."

I narrowed my eyes at her. "Spill it, you."

"Well, you said Jason didn't know what our defense stuff is all about and it didn't matter because you're still not going to sleep-sleep with him anyway, but you weren't sure how long it would be until he got pissed off about it. I told Ben that and Ben said, 'Yeah, but if he knows what Ness might do to him, he might be able to live with the sleep-sleep bit and not get pissed off about it. So, if I get the chance, I'll mention a training session in front of Jason and if he likes Ness enough, he'll want to know what it's all about and he'll ask to come and watch.'"

Jules ran out of breath and sipped her coffee. "You're not cross, are you, babe? The James bit was true. He did phone Ben last night out of the blue and ask him to set a demo up for that new police constable that he's started seeing and her friend. You know what James is like over girlie self-defense since he worked in Victim Support, even if he does have to keep it off the record."

I blew Jules a kiss. "No, I'm not cross, babe. As long as it's the real thing and not a stage-managed event just for Jason's benefit. It'd be obvious if it was." I drank the last mouthful of coffee in my mug. "But, Jules, please tell Ben not to invite Jason to join in a role play or anything — no 'Do you want to see how it feels?' type of stuff. Jason wouldn't want to do it but it would put him on the spot, if you see what I mean. Just keep him out of it, please."

Jules stood to attention and saluted. "Message received and understood. I will pass it on to command central."

I flicked coffee at Jules from the residue in my mug then put it on the work top. "I'm out of here before you get the chance to lipstick me again. I'll see you later."

Jules smiled. I closed the front door behind me and put my handbag on the floor beside my desk an hour later, smiled good morning at Annie and Maisie, poked through the limited contents of my drawer and found a pen.

"How was your night, Vanessa?" Annie said. "Maisie and I just chatted online. Did you go out?"

I nodded and left Jason out of my reply, as usual. "Yeah. Jules and I went to our local bar and saw a couple of friends back from the States."

"The States? Were they on holiday out there? Did they have a good time?"

"Not on holiday. Working. But they had a good time. They always do."

Annie sighed. "I'd love to get paid to have good time. What do they do?"

"Fashion models. They were in Vegas for a runway show."

"Would I recognize them? Have you got a pic?"

I took my phone out of my bag, scrolled to my pic of Mark and Simon and turned my phone toward Annie. Her eyes widened. Maisie stood, walked around the workstations and looked over my shoulder.

"I see those two in magazines all the time. And they're gay, aren't they? Like..." Maisie patted my shoulder and walked back to her desk.

"Like?" I prompted.

Maisie smiled with a hint of a wink and nodded in my direction. "Like... I have realized, you know."

I tightened my stomach muscles against a threatened laugh at Maisie's pointed nod and resisted the urge to play it further. "Yeah, Jules and I like them very much. So does Jules' boyfriend, Ben. And although I don't have a boyfriend as such, my male bed friends like Mark and Simon, too."

Annie grinned. "Bed friends?"

I counted James and Ryan, even though I hadn't had sex with either of them since I'd met Jason, and I smiled. "Just a couple of really good mates of mine. None of us has met that special person yet, so we...just sort of settle for each other when we feel like it."

Maisie pursed her lips, wrinkled her nose and made a noise that could have been either 'ew' or 'yuk'. "I couldn't do that. If I commit to someone enough to allow them to sleep with me, I expect the same back. What I've got to offer is precious. I don't give it out to just anyone."

I looked at Maisie and tightened my stomach muscles again. "Okay. Well, good for you if that's the way you feel, but do try not to look down your nose at the rest of us for having a little fun with someone we like very much but know isn't the person we want to have a full-on relationship with."

Maisie smiled and picked up the drink carrier. "Yes. Sorry. I forget sometimes that other people aren't as perfect as I am. I expect Jason would like a coffee by now, don't you? I'll just stop by and ask."

I bit down on my lip and pulled my work tray forward. The flesh and blood version of the photo in the Belmond's brochure walked into office a little bit later—a man, tall for a generation earlier that had never seen the inside of a gym, with eyes—the green of which identified Jason and Peter as father and son—not obvious behind a pair of thick-framed glasses.

Peter Belmond walked toward Jason's office and I glanced around and saw every face but mine fixed on either their desk or their computer screen.

I looked at Annie and she whispered to me. "Mr. Belmond doesn't talk to the staff, not unless he's got a query. You know, like on some figures or something."

I mouthed *okay*, turned my face to my screen and carried on inputting figures until my work tray emptied of timesheets and I looked up again. "I'm going downstairs to get a sandwich. Do either of you want me to bring anything back?"

"Ham and cheese on brown, please," Annie said.

"Thanks. I'll have the same," Maisie added.

I dropped my phone into my handbag and took out my coin purse. Annie leaned down to pick up her own bag.

"Don't worry. I'll get these."

"We'll get yours another day, then," Annie said.

I rode the lift down to the canteen, added a Caesar wrap to the order and took the sandwiches back to the office. I handed Maisie hers and walked around to my workstation. A pair of male legs and a small, neat butt stuck out of it, the body they belonged to hidden in the leg space under my desk.

I handed Annie her sandwich. She took it as the legs backed themselves out and stood, attached to a smallish man, although not as small as my dad, with thick, well-cut chestnut hair, hazel eyes and the longest, sootiest lashes I'd ever seen on a man or a girl if they weren't glued on.

"Sorry. We're doing our periodic check of the computer cabling to all the monitors. Annie said you were at lunch so I did yours first."

"Okay. Have you finished or do you need some more time?"

"Done now. Thanks."

I nodded and Annie smiled. "Vanessa, this is Craig. I told you he works in IT, didn't I?"

I smiled at Craig. He smiled back at me and moved to Annie's workstation. Annie wheeled herself backward on her chair and watched Craig's butt as she ate. I unwrapped my own sandwich and he stood upright again ten minutes later.

"Thanks, girls. I could reach Maisie's cable from Annie's workstation, so I'm done with your section now."

Craig fluttered his sooty eyelashes in Annie's direction. She gazed back and her cheeks pinked up. "Is it still okay for me to come round to yours tonight?" Craig said.

Annie nodded and he winked at her and walked off to the accounts payable workstations. Annie scooted her chair nearer her desk and sighed. "He's only got to look at me like that and, well…"

I smiled. "I know. It's a bugger when you get one with the eyes, isn't it? One look and your knees turn to jelly.

One look back and your innards start doing the samba and yelling, 'Yes, please'."

Annie laughed.

Maisie broke off a piece of her sandwich and popped it into her mouth, bypassing her lipstick. "Guys are always saying that to me. Well, not exactly those words. It's more like once I look at them, they can't pull their stares away from me."

"Your eyes are one of your best features, especially because you make them up so well." Annie smiled.

"I've posted a video online for those that want to get the look."

I tuned out, put my purse into my bag and searched for my phone. I found it zipped into the inside pocket, unlocked it and saw a message from Dad in my inbox.

You and Jules bring your laptops and iPads home with You. Gary is coming to run a security scan Saturday.

I tapped back.

Okay. Will do.

I glanced up, thought of Annie's occasional glances in my direction then in Jason's and decided that in the future I would make sure that where I was, my phone would be, too. The office door opened and Peter walked in. Annie coughed. Maisie stopped talking. Annie looked at her screen. The buzz in the room silenced and I pulled my keyboard forward, put my music on in my ears and began working. My phone vibrated just before five. *Jason.*

Shall I come to yours about 7:30?

Sure. I'll see you at mine.

I tidied my desk, said goodnight to Annie and Maisie and legged it out of the door against the silence of a library and the polite, careful voices of those still answering their phones.

Chapter Eight

The bus arrived at the same time as I did at the bus stop and, for a welcome change, caught various traffic lights on green, so I let myself into my flat well before six. I walked to my bedroom, opened a drawer in my chest of drawers and pulled out a Lycra bodysuit cut high on the leg and thin-strapped, without the sleeves of a competition leotard.

After I showered, I put street clothes on over the body suit and made up my face lightly with my hair in a high tail. Jules opened the front door as I picked up a pair of five-inch wedge-heeled shoes and walked into the hallway.

Jules smiled. "Hey, girlie. You're ready early."

"I know. Amazing but true. Every light was green all the way home. I'm going to have a glass of wine. Do you want one?"

"Please. I didn't stop at the shop. Did you?"

"No. But there's the emergency pots of dried noodles in the cupboard. I'll do them while you change, if you like?"

Jules nodded and walked into her bedroom. I boiled the kettle in the kitchen and left the noodles to soften while I took two glasses of wine from the shelf and opened the bottle. I took the noodles into the living room and passed a pot to Jules when she sat beside me, having changed into a skirt and sleeveless shirt.

"Did you get a text today from Dad? About taking our laptops and iPads with us this weekend."

Jules twirled her fork through the noodles. "And our phones for Gary to check?"

I nodded and wiped a noodle off my chin. "There was a bit of funny business at work with my phone today. I found it somewhere I'm sure I didn't leave it. It's happened a couple of times now. I go somewhere, and when I come back, my phone's not where I thought I'd left it."

"I don't suppose I have to ask who might be trying to take a peek at it?"

"I can't think of anyone else that would want to. Maisie and Annie see Jason and me chatting, so it's not too far-fetched for them to suspect I might have his mobile number on my phone. I wouldn't put it past Maisie to borrow it for a while and try to unlock it. She's pretty keen to get hold of Jason's phone number."

"And if they manage to do that, they're going to find out you and Jason are doing more than chatting."

"And I let Maisie know today that you and I aren't an item, so she'll be on the look-out again."

"You could just tell them you're seeing Jason. Get it out in the open. Mop up the hissy fit Maisie will throw and get it over with."

I shook my head. "No. No way am I becoming the office's prime source of entertainment because that little fact has come out. I might be seeing quite a bit of Jason at the moment, but nothing's been said by either of us about doing the actual, going-out-together-exclusively thing. I saw his father today. He was in the office."

"What was he like?"

I put my pot down and picked up my glass. "I can see why people don't realize they're related. Gray hair, older, thick-framed glasses… And when he came in, it was a bit like being back at school, like when you get one of those teachers that walk into the classroom and it falls silent."

Jules put her pot alongside mine and looked at the time display on the iPad.

"As you said, he is older. He might be a bit old-fashioned that way, I suppose. What time is Jason getting here?"

"Around seven-thirty."

Jules swallowed the end of her wine and reached for her shoes. "It's twenty past. I'll go down. I said I'd meet Ben in the gym a bit early. Shall I leave the front door on the latch for him?"

I nodded and put my shoes on. Jason called my name fifteen minutes later. I walked to the kitchen for a fresh glass and poured wine into it as he walked into the living room. I lifted my face for his kiss.

He smiled at the wine as we separated. "Serious stuff, then, this self-defense?"

I handed Jason his glass and sat on the sofa with my own. "Yep. But we try to keep it a bit like it might be if we ever had to use it, hence the street clothes. And we would probably have been out and maybe had a drink and we might have just eaten dinner."

Jason sat beside me and looked at my noodle pot. "That's not dinner. Is that really all you're going to eat tonight?"

"Hey…there's nothing wrong with a good old noodle."

"There's nothing wrong with my noodles. I don't think I can say the same about yours. Come to mine tomorrow and I'll cook you something that doesn't have 'dehydrated' or 'monosodium' in the list of ingredients?"

I threaded my fingers through Jason's. "Yes, please. You can keep up my intake of healthy food anytime."

"Is there anything I should avoid? Anything you don't like to eat?"

I gritted my teeth and shuddered. "Goat. I've tried various bit and pieces of it from the cheese to a goat curry because it's about on every menu nowadays, and I just can't do it. It tastes really sweaty and rather weirdly hairy to me. I tell waiters when I eat out now that I'm allergic to goat to save the embarrassment of coming across a bit of it hidden in a dish and gagging before I have to spit the mouthful back out."

Jason laughed. "How are you with fluffy baa-lambs?"

"Absolutely fine. They're woolly, not hairy."

I finished my wine and put my glass on the coffee table. Jason swallowed and stood his empty glass alongside mine.

"Bo-Peep's friend it is, then."

I looked at the time display on the iPad and we walked out to the lift. Jason asked while we waited for it to arrive, "So, James. Your local community police officer…?"

I smiled. "Mine and Jules' victim support officer before he couldn't take any more of it and moved to blues and twos."

The lift doors opened and we stepped in.

"I did wonder."

"Why he's interested in self-defense or whether I've slept with him?"

Jason put his arms around my waist. "Both."

I put my arms around him. "Then both. James is committed to anything that might help someone not become a victim because of the job he used to do, and because of it, we became friends that have sex when it suits, although not for a while now. He's first and foremost a good mate. Is that a problem for you?"

Jason bent down and kissed my lips. "Hey, you've met Mrs. N. History is history."

I stepped out of the lift, entered the code on the number pad beside the gym door and pushed it open. James stood at the matted exercise area at the far end of the gym beside two girls, one of whom I'd seen a photo of and one I didn't know, who were chatting with Jules and Ben. I put my hand in Jason's and we walked over.

James detached himself from the group. "Hi, Ness. This is Jason, is it? Come and meet Cheryl and her friend, Emma."

I tilted my face for James to kiss my cheek and pecked his back without letting go of Jason's hand. "Good to see you, babe. Yes, this is Jason."

Jason and James looked at each other. James smiled. Jason nodded. I held on to Jason's hand as we said hi to Cheryl and Emma then let go of it to lean forward and kiss Ben's cheek. Ben kissed mine and punched Jason lightly on the top of his arm.

"Hey, my man. You came. Thanks. Plonk your butt against the wall there and I'll get on with it."

I smiled at Ben as Jules leaned forward and pecked Jason. "I'll sit with Jason for now. Demo with Jules and call me in when you need me."

Ben nodded and I walked with Jason to the side of the gym. We sat on the floor with me in between his legs. James, Cheryl and Emma sat beside us. Ben stood facing us with Jules to his side and directed his speech at Cheryl and Emma.

"So, James has told you a bit about this? It's defense, not attack. Do what you can. Give yourself enough time to run away."

They both nodded. Ben continued, "There are over forty pressure points all over a human body that you can use to defend yourself with and it doesn't take strength — just speed and accuracy. Less than seven seconds is best. I'll demo with Jules but she'll only tap when she hits any of my pressure points or this demo will be a short one."

I leaned back against Jason and watched Jules and Ben move through the mechanics of the technique, with Ben making a move and Jules countering, until Ben looked at James. "So, that's basically how it works. James, do you want to play attacker?"

James nodded and stood. Jules gave James her back and walked forward. James slipped his trainers off, padded up behind her on silent, sock-clad feet and wrapped his arms around her at chest height. Jules spun within in his arms to face him and kicked the pressure point to the side of James' knee. His leg crumpled and Jules chopped her straightened hand down on the median nerve on the inside of his arm as he fell. James hit the floor with a dead leg and an arm dangling at his side.

"Hell, Jules. Just the leg would have done it." James grimaced.

Jules looked at James trying to flex some life back into his arm and she laughed. "Yeah, like you've never come back at me because I didn't take enough of you out the first time. I'm not falling for that one again."

Jules kneeled and flexed James' leg for him.

Emma looked at Cheryl. "I think I could slip that knee one in on some of the weekend drunks resisting arrest without them even realizing I had," Emma said.

Cheryl nodded. "Especially when they're struggling against our arrest hold and their mates decide to join in." Cheryl looked at me and held her arm out. "Would you show me? I'd like to know how effective it is."

I nodded. "Sure. But not like that. It's defense, not attack. You'll have to take a swing at me or something."

Cheryl pushed herself to her feet and walked nearer the center of the gym. I squeezed Jason's hand, stood and joined her.

"If I show you the arrest hold, you can put it on me and I'll fight against it, if that's okay?" Cheryl said.

"Sure. That sounds fine."

Cheryl walked behind me and put her hand on my upper arm. "So, I would start by trying to escort you to the waiting van, and if you struggle, I will twist your arm up behind your back and put my other hand on your shoulder to try to keep you still."

Cheryl completed the maneuver, twisting my arm up behind my back, her other hand on my free shoulder. "But a lot of drunks are big guys, well tanked up, and I can't always hold them as I can't use any more force than this. Twist the arm up any higher in anything less than an open-bladed knife attack and it'd be me that'd be up on a charge of using undue force."

Cheryl let go of my arm. I put the same hold on her and she twisted her shoulders against my restraint then kicked her leg backward. I moved my knee alongside hers at the same instant and knocked the bone of my kneecap hard on the same pressure point that Jules had used to disable James and released her arm as her leg collapsed.

Cheryl's eyes widened as her butt hit the floor. "Ow and shit! That was bloody good! Just one good tap that nobody could call undue force, even if they saw me do it."

Emma stood and walked closer. "Can I take a shot?"

I nodded. "Sure. Don't tell me what. Just go for it."

Emma shot her arm out, her hand curled into a fist. I stepped back and smacked the fingers of my straightened hand down on the inside of her wrist. Emma's arm dropped as she squeaked but she didn't give up and took a swing at me with her other arm. I caught it, held it straight and smacked the flattened fingers of my other hand beneath the bulge of her upper-arm muscle. Her arm fell to her side, deadened like her other.

"Fuckin' ow!"

I stepped away and Jason's eyes widened as a belt wrapped itself around my neck from behind. I spun on the balls of my feet within the belt's restriction, jabbed two stiffened fingers into the soft spot under Ben's Adam's apple and slapped the straightened fingers of my other hand firm and hard against the nerve endings underneath his ear. His eyes rolled up and he hit the floor.

I kneeled beside him and heard three different expletives behind me as I waited.

James walked past me toward Cheryl and Emma. "So, that's what I was telling you about last night for if someone went for you high on drugs or something, rather than it being just a troublesome arrest. If Jules had tried to break my hold, she'd have lost. If Ness had tried to grab the belt, she'd have lost because we're stronger. But if you know the technique and you're quick enough, you can stop an assailant bigger than you in less time than it takes to get either your baton or your mace off your belt."

Ben sat and pulled his knees up. "Damn. I thought I had you that time."

Jules walked over and sat on the floor beside Ben. I rubbed Ben's arm, left him with Jules and sat beside Jason. Jason put his arm around my shoulder as Emma said, "Well, I can see it's effective, but it's hardly regulation."

James shrugged. "I told you that this is all off the record and bugger the regulations. You come across some mile-high crackhead that launches himself at you because he knows you're just about to take his pipe and what are you going to do about it? Fumble with your belt? You know what the guys would do."

Cheryl glanced sideways. "Um…perhaps the shop talk should be left for later, James?"

James winked at me over the top of Cheryl and Emma's heads. "Sure. Do you want to go and have a pint or two at the local bar?"

Emma and Cheryl nodded and stood. James, Emma and Cheryl said goodnight or goodbye with thanks all around and walked out of the gym. Jason tightened his arm around my shoulders. "So, what would 'the guys' have done?"

"Not much more than you'd expect, guy on guy — make sure heads bounce a few times against the pavement as they take them down, make sure they leave quite a bit of nose and chin behind on it when they stand them up and all with the normal solicitous enquiries as to the state of sir's health. They're supposed to call for back-up if a situation gets sticky, but a lot of the time they're stretched pretty thin and there's not any around."

Jules and Ben walked over. "I'm going home to get showered, babe," Jules said.

"See you there later, then," I said.

I looked at Jason as the door shut behind Jules and Ben. "Were you okay watching us do that?"

Jason lifted me up to sit on his lap. "Yep. Why? Who hasn't been?"

"I've known the subject to make the odd guy or two a little insecure."

"Their male ego couldn't take it?"

"That…or a slight nervousness that I might just forget myself and deck them just because they've sneezed unexpectedly or something."

Jason cupped my butt cheek. "I can't say that occurred to me, as you didn't deck me when my hand first ended up here."

I tensed my butt muscles and twitched my cheek in Jason's hand. "And if I'd done that instead of leaving the pub?"

Jason slipped his hand up inside my skirt. "I'd have followed you straight out of the pub and anywhere else your cute little butt wanted to take me."

I tilted my head for his kiss. He traced his fingers around the outline of the moon of my butt check left naked by the high cut of my Lycra bodysuit. I looked into his eyes as we parted.

"You want more of it?"

Jason's irises darkened as I asked. "Yes, baby. You want, too?"

I gazed back. "Yes. To feel you everywhere. On all of me. Every inch."

Jason breathed a little deeper. "When?"

I traced my finger over the outline of Jason's lips. "Tomorrow night, before we eat."

Jason sucked on my fingertip and nipped his teeth on the pad of it. "Take me to bed now?" he asked.

I took my finger back and kissed Jason's lips. "Yes...but first." I slipped off Jason's lap, took my shoes, skirt and top off, handed them to Jason and rotated my ankles, shoulders and neck. "Ready?"

Jason smiled. "Go, Buff..."

I took a short, four-step run-up into a front walkover, tensed my legs muscles, swung my arms and jumped high into twisted, spiral salto then landed, jumped two back connected handsprings and finished near the gym door with a back tuck roundoff.

I looked at Jason. "Buffy enough for you?"

Jason walked over and put his arms around me. "Beautiful, baby."

I buzzed my lips over Jason's, took my skirt and shirt back and stood in his arms as we took the lift up. Music sounded through the closed sitting room door as I let us in and Jason followed me into my bedroom. I put my key down on my dressing table and smiled as I saw some of my clutter had been pushed to one side and an open bottle of wine and two clean glasses stood in the space.

Jason shut the door behind us and I turned toward him, pushed my skirt down and pulled my T-shirt off, my nipples hard against the Lycra of my bodysuit. Jason peeled off his top. I sat on the side of the bed and breathed deeper as Jason unzipped his jeans, eased them and his boxers off and freed his erection.

I lay on the bed with him beside me and slipped the straps of by bodysuit down over my arms and pushed the fabric beneath the rise and fall of my breasts.

"So pretty, baby."

I murmured as he found one nipple with his fingertips and the other with his mouth. I ran my hands over the contours of his shoulders as he sucked and nipped on one while he teased and tugged the other. I arched my back, pushed my breast forward and mewled as Jason responded with a harder pinch. He cupped the fullness of my breast, sucked, lifted his head and asked, "I can?"

I looked into his eyes. "Yes."

I closed my eyes as Jason fastened his mouth on the full moon of flesh and sucked to bring the blood to the surface and leave his mark there. He pushed my bodysuit down and sucked on the flesh of my belly then on the plumpness of my pubic mound while he slid his fingers inside me to stroke — and I moaned.

Jason kissed up my body. I reached for his erection, circled my thumb over the head of his cock as he lay over me and parted my legs for him to ease his cock inside me.

I wrapped my legs around his thighs and murmured as he moved his cock in, "Oh, babe, that feels good."

"Yes, baby, so good," he responded.

Jason took his weight on his knees and held my hands. I ground against him hip to hip with my breasts pressed against his chest and gripped his hands tighter when he bit down on my shoulder to leave his last mark on me.

"Oh, fuck!" I moaned out the waves of my orgasm as Jason's thrusts shortened, put my mouth on his shoulder, bit and sucked.

Jason groaned. "Ness, let me feel you. Fuck!" he said as he came.

I relaxed my grip on his hands, my chest heaving. Jason eased his cock out and rolled to his side. I lay across his chest, waited for my breathing to slow and kissed the blood bruise I'd left on his skin. "Below the collar line. No giveaways at work tomorrow."

Jason tightened his arm around me. "And you?"

I looked at my breast and belly and smiled. "Good for work but I don't think I'll be wearing my bikini at home this weekend."

"Would you normally?"

"If it's still this hot, yep. The pool cover will be off at least until the rampaging sixth form arrives. But I've still got my all-covering school swimsuit in a drawer at home. I'll wear that if I want to swim, so my mum doesn't have to withdraw my application to the St. Mary of the Blessed Virgin Convent for Hopeless Cases."

Jason laughed. "No, not a virgin surely? You're nearly twenty-four. They can't think that."

I smiled. "More a case of willful ignorance from both sides. Hang on. I'll pour us a glass of wine for which we can thank the blessed — also a virgin — St. Jules, who left it in here."

I picked up my bodysuit and stepped into it, poured two glasses of wine and took them over to the bed. Jason put his boxers on and held his arm out. I moved underneath it and passed him his glass.

"So, what did you think when you saw Peter today?"

"I can see why people don't connect the dots. You look more like your mum, apart from your eyes, and that's not obvious because of your father's glasses. He certainly had quite an effect on the office, though."

"Didn't he? It went so quiet. I didn't notice before when my office had the solid stud partition."

I smiled and sipped. "It was a bit like the headmaster had just walked in. What's he like out of work?"

"He's okay. We tend to steer clear of each other's personal lives, but we get on fine if it's something we've got in common, like the company."

"So, you've never done 'meet the peeps', either?"

Jason shook his head. "No, not that way round, but I went out with Caz for a couple of years, so I met her family quite a few times."

I looked at Jason. "Why did it finish?"

"It was me. Caz wanted to do the whole marriage and babies thing and I couldn't go there. You think I'm neat and tidy, but as Mrs. N hinted with the tissue thing, Caz was pretty obsessive on that front and I just couldn't imagine any child having a very good time of it."

"Was it rough? Breaking up?"

"Yeah. It was. It was really bloody awful actually getting the words out to finish it, and for a while afterward, even though I knew I'd done the right thing. Have you ever had a bad break up?"

"Nothing that serious, just a guy I was seeing at the time my life went pear shaped that couldn't take it and headed for the hills. It hurt quite a bit at the time, but as we were both barely twenty, it would have ended anyway."

"And nothing more serious ever since?"

"No, nothing that didn't just run its course and fade away. All the guys I've known since Tim I'd be happy to bump into again and catch up on what we've both been doing since we last met, for which I'm truly thankful. I didn't much like being dumped, and the thought of having to do it the other way around is enough to make my blood run cold."

Jason looked at our nearly empty glasses and I nodded. He swung his legs off the bed, brought the bottle over and topped them up.

"You might always manage to avoid it."

I moved back under Jason's arm when he sat. "Yep. If it ever came down to it I could suddenly win a once-in-a-lifetime, can't-possibly-turn-it-down prize in a competition that might even include a one person, one-way ticket to Timbuktu," I said.

Jason laughed. "No. I meant not all relationships end. Your mum and dad are still going strong, aren't they? They must have been together for quite a few years?"

"Yeah. Married for twenty-six and together for a year or so longer than that. Most of my peeps have done okay on that front. Well, except for Grandpa Ted who now lives in Spain with his second wife, Jenny, but being as he was married to Granny Alice, no one blames him for that."

"What's up with your granny? Is she hard work or something?"

"Not exactly hard work... More like difficult to keep up with, but..." I peeked sideways at Jason, reached over and tickled my fingers under his chin. "I think it was the whiskers that finally finished him off."

Jason grabbed my hand and kissed it. "Whiskers? Really? A real scary lady then is she, your granny?"

I giggled. "Oh yeah, for sure. No big, bad wolf would stand a chance if he knocked on my granny's door. She'd whip him inside and have him for dinner before he'd even managed to get the words 'What beautiful, big' out of his mouth."

Jason laughed. "Is that why front doors are scary?"

"Not Granny's to me. I've got a key for that one."

"So, front doors are scary if you can't let yourself in?"

"It's more the standing outside and waiting for a door to be answered. When Jules and I were attacked, they took our phones and we couldn't call for help. We had to bang or ring on a load of doors before someone finally came and opened it. We were both in quite a state and it seemed to go on forever."

Jason tightened his arm around me and I snuggled closer. "Standing there just brings what happened that night back, and we've both avoided doing so ever since. It's also the other reason why we have trackers on our phones. If our phones went missing like that again, Gary from the security firm Dad uses would go find whoever had them, hopefully before they managed to unlock them and disable the app."

"Big guy, is he, Gary?"

I smiled. "No. Not really. Just fit. They all are at the firm and Gary's hot on the techie stuff. He's checking our laptops and phones on Saturday, and I think I might ask him to up the security on my phone. It's gone walkies a couple of times at work lately, and although I'm ninety-nine percent sure it's only Maisie trying to take a look, my dad still won't like it. He'd pretty cautious over any hand-held anything that gets used to access his trading accounts."

Jason frowned. "You think Maisie's been taking your phone?"

"More like borrowing it for a while, and I couldn't say so absolutely. But I've found my phone where I haven't left it a couple of times now and I can't think of anyone else that might like to take a gander at what's on it. She sees us chatting. She might just wonder whether I've got your number. I had to 'fess today that me and Jules aren't really a gay couple when Maisie presumed a step too far, then I found my phone where I hadn't put it when I left it in my bag under my desk while I was out of the office later."

"I'll give it until I get back from China, but I think I'm going to have to give in and hand this over to Jenny."

I smoothed the frown lines between Jason's eyes with my fingertips. "Don't worry about it while you're away. I'll make sure I keep my phone with me from now on. There is one more thing, though…" I hesitated as I thought about it some more.

"About Maisie?" Jason prompted.

"Yeah. It's just something she said that I didn't think much of at the time, but now…"

"And…?"

"It was when she was trying to find out how you get into work, and it wasn't so much what she said but how she said it. She said she'd checked and you didn't carry car keys. I asked her how she'd done that and she turned quite pink while Annie turned her head away real quick so I couldn't see into her eyes anymore. But then Maisie recovered and managed to laugh it off. I thought she was just sheepish and bit embarrassed at the time."

"Do you think she's searched my office?"

"While Annie kept an eye out? Yeah, I'm wondering. It was before your windows went in, so if she'd managed to slip inside your office, she could have had a good old poke around."

"I really don't like the thought of that. Not so much my desk but I don't always put my suit jacket on if I'm away at a meeting in another office. Oh, bloody hell, my wallet would have been in it, too!"

I looked at Jason's expression and giggled. "Oh, dear. You carry condoms in your wallet, do you?"

Jason pinched the side of my butt. "So...?"

I squeaked and laughed. "Well, if it's Maisie that's been moving my phone, she's been through my handbag, too, and there's certainly a couple of little foil packets lurking in the bottom of that."

Jason squeezed my butt. "Oh, you have, have you?"

I laughed and kissed Jason's nipple. "They're probably a little crumpled around the edges now, but to quote my mum, 'Don't you ever come home and tell me you're pregnant because you got carried away and he didn't have anything for him. If you don't want the result of the input, take responsibility for the output.'"

"Yes. Well, that's one way of putting it. And that was your mum, was it?"

"Yep. That's my mum, and even though I'm obviously a virgin, she still gives me a nudge occasionally to check that I haven't forgotten, just in case."

"You've never told her that you're on the pill?"

I held Jason's hand in mine and rubbed his finger along the surface of my upper arm over the tiny lump under my skin. "Not the pill. The idiot jab, although why it's called that I've got no idea. You can't go travelling for a year carrying a load of little white pills in your backpack, let alone trying to keep up with it all as you cross different time zones. Jules and I had it done before we went away. Two years of not worrying and no mucky monthlies to deal with. Win-win as far as I'm concerned."

Jason touched the tiny bump and looked closer at my arm, although there was nothing to see above the skin.

"That sounds pretty good. I've never known any girl who's had one of these. Why don't more women have it done?"

"I think because it lasts two years, and although you can have it taken out if you change your mind, it can take up to a year to get back to a monthly routine. But if you're sure you don't want baby bratlets in the foreseeable future or you've done that bit, I don't know why you wouldn't. No regular bellyache, no mid-month mood swings, let alone not having the messiness of it all."

Jason gazed at my body. "None?"

"No, none," I breathed back.

Jason placed his glass on the table beside the bed and put his head between my legs, his breath warm through my bodysuit.

"And no time that I couldn't do this?"

Jason nibbled on my mound through the Lycra. I put my glass down and leaned back on my pillows. "Not at all."

"Or this?"

Jason pushed the Lycra aside and my breath caught in the back of my throat as he nibbled and nipped. He pulled my bodysuit off and pushed his boxers down. I used my momentum to push him onto his back and straddled him, my hands on his shoulders. I kissed and nibbled his bottom lip.

"I think it's my turn to fuck you this time, Mr. Peterson."

Jason breathed deeper and let me pin him down. "Baby... You are a very bad girl."

I teased my nipple across Jason's lips without it being close enough for him to be able to suck on it or draw it into his mouth. "With you, my bad man."

I raised my hips so Jason's erection moved down the crease of my butt cheeks and teased my wetness over the head of his cock.

His chest rose and fell faster. "Ness..."

I took my weight on my knees, put the tip of Jason's cock inside me and slipped down the length of his shaft slowly, inch by inch, until I had all of him inside me.

He closed his eyes. "Yes. Take me, please."

I rocked my hips fast to feel his cock on every soft part inside of me. My eyes were closed and I was breathing hard. I panted as I ground my hips down and moaned as the throb built and I took everything I wanted from Jason's cock. His muscles tensed under my hands as mine tightened between my legs.

"God, baby. Oh, fuck," he called out as he came.

"Jason, yes," I whimpered as I followed.

I moved in short bursts against his shaft to prolong my climax, whimpering as each orgasmic aftershock ran through me. Jason reached for me as I stilled. I lay on his chest with his arms around me and panted, still impaled on his cock.

Jason stroked his hands down my back until my breathing slowed. I eased myself off his cock, lay beside him in his arms with my arm draped over his chest, my leg over his thigh and breathed the scent and feel of his skin against mine into the long-term place of happy moments in my head.

Jason traced his fingers over my skin. My muscles relaxed under his touch, my eyelids getting heavy. Jason tightened his arm around me.

"I'm going to have to go, baby. I'm going to end up falling asleep here if I don't."

I kissed Jason's chest, uncurled myself and reached for my wrap.

"Don't get up. Stay there and I'll let myself out," he said. He swung his legs off the bed and got dressed. Jason tucked the quilt around me, leaned down and kissed my lips. I put my hand on the back of his neck and asked for more. He stroked down my face when our lips parted.

"Sleep well, baby. I'll see you at work tomorrow."

I smiled up at him. "See you in there. You sleep well, too."

Jason walked out of the door and a stupid tear slid down my face as he closed it. I turned to my pillow and gave it a few more as I fell asleep.

* * * *

My alarm trilled at seven. I jumped into the shower, looked at Jason's blood mark on my shoulder nestled under the strap of my bra as I dressed and judged that the wider straps of my old-school swimsuit would keep it hidden over the weekend. I banged on Jules' door on my way down the hallway. "Thanks for leaving the wine and glasses, babe. See you back here after work."

Jules mumbled bye and I let myself out of the flat, caught the bus and walked into the office at just after nine. I dropped my phone into the breast pocket of my shirt as I sat and pulled a pile of internal post envelopes toward me. My phone vibrated as I pulled the first batch of timesheets out. *Jason.*

Hey, you. Good morning. Grrr. No coffee machine for me today. Peter coming in again.

Hey, you, back. Good morning. No worries. I'll see you later.

Jason's father, briefcase in hand, walked through the office half an hour later. Annie looked at Maisie. "That's unusual these days, isn't it? Two days running."

Maisie watched over my shoulder. Ten minutes later, one of the guys I saw working in the Facilities Management office when I dropped their hard copy off each day walked through the main office and into Jason's.

"Mr. Belmond's taken a brochure or something out of his briefcase and they're all looking at it," Maisie said. "Now Lee's looking at something on the inside of the window," she added.

I remembered what Jason had said about his father when the windows were added to the stud wall. "I'm guessing window blinds, then."

"What makes you say that?" Annie said.

"Just something Jason said when the windows first went in about the chairman still using the office and not liking open plan."

"Well, he can close the blinds all he likes when he's using the office. We were all more than happy to have him behind a solid wall and not watching us when he was here full-time before Jason joined the company. Weren't we, Annie?" Maisie said.

Annie nodded. "Yeah. He *is* the chairman who owns the company, after all, not just a normal department head who just works here like the rest of us."

"And here he comes now," Maisie added.

Annie and Maisie turned their gazes back to their computer screens as Peter walked past. I reached into my bag, took out my ear buds, turned my music on and worked on until Annie tapped me on the arm just after twelve.

"I'm doing the coffee run. Do you want one?"

"Sure. Thanks, Annie."

Annie put my coffee on my desk when she arrived back from the machine and I looked at Maisie while I sipped. "Maisie, I'll work through lunch and finish early tomorrow if that's okay?"

Maisie nodded. "It's fine. Any special reason?"

"I'm going home for the weekend for my sister's birthday. I'd like to get changed here before I go. I won't have time to go back to my flat to do it and the family will already have arrived for dinner by the time Jules and I get there."

"Do you want something bringing back? You could eat at your desk and still be working," Annie said.

"No. I'm good, thanks. I'm eating out tonight so I'll pass on anything else until then."

"With one of your, ah…friends?" she asked.

Maisie tutted. I smiled and answered Annie but directed my reply at Maisie. "Yes, and the only one of my friends I'm seeing at the moment, if that makes things any better for anyone."

I finished my coffee and carried on with my work. Maisie and Annie pushed their chairs away from their desks and picked up their handbags at one. Annie looked at me. "You sure?"

I nodded and Annie patted her stomach. "Flat for tonight?"

I smiled. "Something like that."

I put my ear buds in, worked on through with two more coffee breaks and the same number of glimpses of Jason's butt as he walked through the office, until it was time to pack up my desk. I caught the bus home and called to Jules as I let myself in. She answered me from the living room. I walked through and Jules poured wine into a glass for me.

"Hey, babe. Did you have a good day?"

I sat beside her and sipped. "So-so. Jason's cooking for me tonight. I'll have this and get ready. You?"

"Yeah, really good. I'm just so pumped now that it's more official between me and Ben."

Jules reached into her handbag and pulled a new toothbrush in its wrapper out of it.

I laughed. "Way to go, girlie! Tonight?"

Jules smiled. "If you don't mind?"

I put my arm around Jules' waist and hugged her. "Of, course not. Are you sure you want to come home with me this weekend? I can hold the fort there if you want to stay with Ben?"

Jules squeezed her arm around me. "No. I'm coming with this weekend, but after that, I'll consult with Ben on any invites. Arrange stuff—not always together but more like a couple would."

I held my hand up and Jules smacked a high five on it.

"So, what time are you going to Jason's?" she asked.

"I'm just heading over when I'm ready."

"Whoa, girlie. A bronze star for you, for sure."

I chinked my glass on Jules'. "Yep. For sure."

I took my glass with me to my bedroom, left it on the dressing table and sipped while I made up my face after I'd showered and dressed in a hug-to-the-hips skater skirt and a crop top. I looked in the mirror after I dressed and smiled at the way my skirt floated out around my thighs, then threw jeans, tops and underwear into a holdall for the weekend and called a cab while I finished my wine. My phone vibrated with a message from Jason as I cut the call.

I'm home. What time are you coming over?

I messaged back.

?? Bronze star for me.

Waiting for you, baby.

My phone vibrated with my *cab waiting* message as I took my glass through to the kitchen. My knees gave their first tremble as I walked into the living room as I read it. I looked at Jules sat on the sofa.

"My cab's outside. Here goes."

"Good luck with the door, babe. Let me know." Jules smiled.

I breathed in deep. "You did it and so will I."

Chapter Nine

I climbed into the back of the cab and, half an hour later, my heart beating out of my chest, I buzzed Jason's flat number at the street door. The street door hummed open within one second of me saying 'hi'.

"Hey, you're here."

I pushed the door open, rode the lift up and stepped out of it to see Jason standing in his open front door. My heart didn't stop racing but the reason for it changed as I walked toward him and into his arms. I lifted my face to the sound of the distinctive electric whine of Mrs. Noakes' scooter.

He lifted me, swung me inside and pushed the door shut. "I don't think so. Not tonight."

I opened my mouth for his tongue and pressed my body against his. He held me close to his chest and moved his lips to my neck.

"Well done, baby. I expect you could do with a glass of wine after that?"

I breathed in deeply. "Yeah…please."

I walked ahead of Jason, my skirt moving in time to the sway of my hips reacting to the music playing in Jason's kitchen. I looked over my shoulder as I put my bag on the breakfast bar then perched on my stool.

"Kylie?"

Jason kissed my shoulder as he walked past to his side of the breakfast bar. "Yep. I saw her at Glastonbury the year I left uni and she's been on my playlist ever since."

"And the vid with the little gold shorts?"

"Absolutely…although the leotard with the long boots was pretty good live. Have you been?"

I shook my head. Jason filled a glass and put it in front of me.

"No. I went to the Isle of Wight mud fest for my eighteenth the year I left sixth form. Is it all it's cracked up to be?"

Jason sipped and started to behead green beans with a small, sharp knife. "Yeah. Really good. I went again with the guys last year and saw Dolly. She was amazing. Played just about every instrument going, including the sax."

"I love just about any music that's got a sax in it. Do you play anything?"

"I learned to strum a bit on the guitar when I was at school but not now. You?"

I smiled. "You wouldn't want a performance of the only thing I've ever got a note out of. We had recorder lessons in year six. The peeps spent the next six months with ear muffs on as I trilled away, most of the time out of tune."

Jason put the beans in a pan, the discarded tops and tails in the bin and took the chopping board and knife to the sink. "I think the music master at school wished he'd had some every time I opened my mouth to sing. He used to ask me to just mime in assembly in the end rather than growl over the rest."

I laughed. "I so want to see your yearbook."

"When you show me yours."

"I am bringing it back with me this weekend. You can have a gander at Spotty Luke if you like. He's in it."

Jason sat on the stool beside mine and picked up my hand to kiss it. "Oh, is he? And did you really have zits and braces?"

I ran my fingertips along Jason's jawline. "No, not by then. The pill had cleared up the zits and my braces came off at seventeen."

Jason took my hand to his mouth. "I knew it. You're going to look like a little cutie in yours…"

I leaned in closer. "Except for the cross-eyes and knock-knees."

Jason closed the gap between us, looked into my eyes and moved his fingers to circle my knees. "Oh, yeah. The worst case of both I've ever seen."

I put my hand on the back of Jason's neck, my heart rate accelerating as I tasted his mouth and he traced over the lace of my pants with his finger.

"You want me, baby?"

I parted my thighs and breathed into Jason's neck. "Yes. Everywhere. Very much."

"Bed or sofa, sweetheart?"

"Sofa. I'll keep my shoes on so I'm not too short for you."

Jason kissed my neck. "I'll get the gel from the bedroom."

I reached into my bag and Jason smiled as I took my own gel out of it and gave it to him. We walked to the softly lit living room and I turned to him, pulled my top over my head, unfastened my bra and let it drop. Jason stepped closer. I stepped back. "Your turn."

Jason's gaze didn't leave mine as he put the gel down on the sofa back and took his T-shirt off over his head. I ran my eyes down Jason's torso and looked at his jeans. He unfastened the zip and let his erection free as he shrugged them off. I stepped closer, ran my hands over it then kneeled in front of him, took the head of his cock into my mouth and sucked.

Jason murmured as I covered him. I stroked my fingers over and under his balls and up through the parting between his cheeks. He entwined his fingers in the back of my hair and his breath hitched as I circled my finger at the center of his butt.

"Ness…yes."

I reached for a squirt of gel, circled my fingertip over the spot between his cheeks and Jason breathed faster above me. I moved my fingertip in, angled toward Jason's tummy button, and felt my way until I touched more roughly textured skin.

I stroked over the bump it covered and he groaned at my touch. I massaged over and around it, sucked his cock and ran the fingers of my other hand over the fullness of his balls. Jason's breathing rasped to small moans in his throat. I eased my mouth and finger away and he stood upright then reached his hand down for me. "You, now, please, baby."

I wriggled my pants and skirt down and off, stood and passed Jason the tube of gel, turned and held onto the sofa back, my heart beating fast as I waited for his touch. It was soft and cool with the gel, and I moaned as he found the blossom between my butt cheeks, circled it with his finger, eased me apart and put the rounded head of his cock, wet and slippery, inside me.

I closed my eyes, gripped the sofa back and a thousand nerve endings fired up and began to sing as he moved his shaft in, slowly, inch by inch.

"Jason…"

It was secret, deep and intense. Jason filled me and moaned out his own pleasure as he did. "That's good… So sweet."

Jason rocked against me. I moaned and pushed back against him. He moved faster and I groaned. Jason reached around to the front of me, slid two fingers inside my pussy and stroked in time to the movement of his pelvis. The shock waves of my climax spread as I fisted my hands into the sofa cushion and called Jason's name from the pit of my stomach. He groaned out a last thrust as I panted and whimpered.

Jason stilled, slid his fingers out and eased his cock away. I slackened my grip on the sofa and toed off my high shoes as my knees wobbled. He put his hands on my waist to steady me, scooped me into his arms and sat us on the sofa. I cuddled into his chest, his heartbeat as rapid as mine against my cheek.

"God, Ness. That was sweet. I've never been touched like that before."

I kissed Jason's neck and snuggled closer. "Beautiful for me, too. You liked my touch?"

"Yes, baby. Very much."

"You want more another time when you're off your feet?"

Jason tightened his arm around me. "I'd love more. Why off my feet?"

"Orgasm can last several minutes. It can be a bit of a knee trembler."

Jason kissed my lips. "Double yes then."

I kissed Jason and rested my cheek against his chest.

"How did you find out where the spot was? Not from Mark and Simon again?" he asked.

"No. A guy I met just before I left uni. Quite a bit older than me and rather more experienced on the subject of advanced bed bouncing activities."

Jason smiled. "How much older?"

"Early forties to my twenty. A lecturer in a different subject to mine. I learned quite a bit about what I liked and didn't on the bed front with Doctor Who...ever. I can't quite recall his name just now."

"So, you found out you liked sex this way. What did you find that you didn't?"

I sat a little straighter. "That I can't bear anything that tickles, like those furry mitts or the stick thing with the feathers on the end. All they do for me is to give me an overwhelming urge to scratch my skin. And I don't like being spanked—far too repetitive on the same spot. Ouch, ouch and not sexy for me."

Jason laughed. "I can't say I've ever had the least urge to indulge in either of those. Anything else?"

"Yep. Clamps—whether for nipples or anywhere else—blindfolds, sticky tape and anything to do with gags. Tried them, didn't like them, don't get them. What about you?"

"I can't say any of that has come my way but the thought of the anywhere else clamps is making my eyes water."

I giggled and prompted. "So...?"

"So...on the ouch front, I slept with someone who took strips of skin off my back with her fingernails, which for me was the equivalent of the doing the ice bucket challenge while having sex. Then there was another girl at uni who, when she pulled her Christmas sweater up and over her head, I realized was a firm believer in *au naturel* on the body hair front and, unfortunately, on the deodorant front, too."

"Ew, babe. Not the pits! No!"

"Needless to say, I legged it before the jeans came off and I caught sight of whatever else was coming my way."

I laughed and snorted. "Straight through the door, cartoon style?"

"Yep. I just hoofed it on that one. Didn't even hang around long enough to do the polite, 'Oh, I'm sorry. My dog just died. I've got to go,' bit."

I giggled. "Your dog?"

"Yep. I've never had one but I've had to bury Fido a few times."

"Jason. That's outrageous. Poor Fido!" My tummy chose that moment to make a 'you've only fed me a pot of noodles since yesterday' grumble.

Jason kissed my shoulder. "You need feeding, baby. I'll wash up and put the dinner on."

I kissed Jason's lips and stood. "Thanks. I'll use your other bathroom."

Jason smiled and we went our separate ways. I heard the shower running in the bathroom next door as I flushed and checked my makeup in the mirror.

I walked back to the kitchen and topped up our glasses as Jason walked in, changed into thigh-length shorts and a T-shirt. He kissed my neck as his way past then turned the oven on to heat. "It won't take too long. I got everything good to go earlier."

I picked up my glass as Jason opened the fridge and took out an oven dish with a rack of lamb crusted with a herb mix on it.

"That looks good. When did you learn how to cook? Did they do lessons at your school?"

Jason set a dish of sliced potatoes in a creamy sauce beside the lamb, sat on a stool opposite me and picked up his glass. "No such luck. Cooking was for sissies at my school. Real men played rugby and would have stuffed any such wimp's head down the toilet and flushed."

I looked at Jason and asked the question with my eyes.

Jason laughed. "No, I did not get my head put down the loo."

The oven beeped an electronic alarm. He stood and put the lamb and potatoes into it. "But as for the cooking, I sort of got into it because I had to when my mum was ill. I found I liked it. So, I cooked on the holidays at home and never admitted to it at school."

"She was ill for a long time? Your mum?"

Jason sat and took a mouthful of wine. "From when I was twelve until just before I turned seventeen, and much as I hate to admit it, Mum was ill for so long that it just became sort of normal, just the way things were at home. I wish I'd realized it but I didn't. The courier's bringing her artwork over from the bank tomorrow afternoon. I know it's not your thing, but do you want to have a look at it when it arrives?"

I reached for Jason's hand and smiled. "Yeah. I'd love to see it...or anything your mum worked on." I squeezed Jason's hand and let it go. "I just wouldn't want to wear it."

"You know what it is, then?"

"To quote my lovely friend Jules... A platinum tiara, very sparkly, very expensive and very heavy on high-end diamonds."

Jason laughed and swung around on his stool as the oven gave another electronic peep.

"That'll be the one. Jules' rumor mill is spot on. The courier will deliver the artwork of it to Nick Davies rather than the post room and he will bring it to my office and hand it over to me like I've never seen it before. I've had a word with him and we're going to make its arrival a bit obvious." Jason took the lamb out of the oven and put his green beans in a steamer. "We want to see if we can't stir the pot a little for anyone that might have their eye on it. If I've got to go all the way to China, I'd rather it was for something to happen rather than not."

Jason put the lid on the steamer then went on, "Peter will turn up. That's the reason for the blinds, by the way. Our chairman has decided that with the time difference between us and Beijing, he ought to come into the office full-time while I'm away."

I picked up my glass and smiled. "That'll thrill everyone. The headmaster on site for the week."

"I know. I've told him about that, too. If this turns out to be an inside job, it might be something to do with the fact that none of the staff has any other incentive in the company other than that we pay their wages."

"What would you do?"

"Put a percentage of the profits aside to be shared. The harder everyone worked then, the more there would be for everyone all round."

"But Peter doesn't see it?"

"Not yet, but don't worry. Peter might be stubborn and arsy but he's got a successful business brain, and by the time I've finished with him, he will."

Jason brought the lamb over to carve it into cutlets and I looked at the plate.

"Ah, small-sized girl here."

Jason looked into my eyes and smiled. "Yes, baby. I know."

Jason turned to the cooker top and de-glazed the pan with a splash of red wine then dished the food onto plates with my dinner a third of the size of his and brought our dinner and cutlery to the breakfast bar.

"Are you all ready to go for tomorrow?" he asked as he sat beside me.

"I threw some stuff into an overnighter before I came over. I've just got to add shoes and my laptop in the morning. I won't have time to go home, so I'll change at work and go straight to Victoria from there. I'm meeting Jules at six. You all good to go for Sunday?"

I breathed in the aroma of roasted meat and cheesy, garlicky potato.

"I've put some gear in the spare room ready to pack. It'll be pretty hot and sticky out there, from what I've checked on the net."

I cut a piece of lamb and put it into my mouth. "This is good, babe. Thank you. And don't forget to take something for those sudden heaven-opening moments, even if it's only one of those disposable festival waterproofs that sit flat in your pocket until you shake them out and use them. What hotel are you booked in to?"

"The Grand. Only five minutes from the convention center."

"I think I saw that one when we visited the Olympic stadium. It overlooks the Bird's Nest, doesn't it?"

Jason nodded and cut into his layered potato. "Apparently, when the smog clears enough for you to actually be able to see it. I've read the reviews of the hotel online and it looks business-type okay, with big rooms, modern, western-style breakfast, but I've read lots of differing reports on the Wi-Fi. Some say good but more say it's slow and quite unstable."

"That might make it difficult for you to stay in touch with Peter and the office."

Jason cut his beans, speared some on the end of his fork and offered them to me. "The office with Peter in it will run on as well as it always did for years. I was hoping that even with the time difference, I'd be able to Skype you at home next week, though."

I took the beans from Jason's fork, looked into his warm, green gaze and swallowed hard. "I'll be there if the connection's good enough. Shall I Skype you tomorrow from the peeps?"

Jason smiled. "Yeah, if you get the chance. I'll be here getting the flat ready to be left."

"I should. It won't be too mad tomorrow night. It's only family dinner. The noise and bedlam isn't until Saturday."

I carried on eating until I felt full but not overly so, rinsed the plates for Jason to stack in the dishwasher then sat at the breakfast bar to finish my wine while Jason set his coffee machine to grind.

"Have you got any Glastonbury recordings saved?" I asked.

"I've got the recording from last year still on the system. Do you want to have a look at it with the coffee?"

"Yeah. I wouldn't mind a sofa bop to Dolly to shake down my dinner a bit. Who else did you see?"

"Ed Sheeran, straight after Dolly, but I had to miss Sam Smith. He was on the other stage at the same time, but I saw the Kaiser Chiefs on the Friday and I caught Fat Boy Slim's set on Saturday. It's so big there, though—so many stages—that you never get to see as much as you think you will. Do you want anything else to go with the coffee?"

"Some of that orange liqueur would be good."

Jason took the coffee cups from the machine, passed me mine and filled a beaker with ice. "It's in the other room."

I followed Jason into his sitting room and sat cross-legged on the sofa. Jason passed me a glass of iced Cointreau that he poured from his everything-else unit and sat beside me with his remote in his hand. The telly lit up with scenes of a huge crowd and a diminutive figure in rhinestone-covered white spandex.

"Lord, where were you in all that lot? Could you even see her?"

Jason pointed at the mid-point of the television. "We got in place quite early. Not that you'll see us, but we nabbed places center stage and only about fifty lines back."

Dolly opened her mouth and sang the opening line of *Nine to Five*. I bounced my butt, sipped ice-cold orange and hot coffee and laughed when I saw the mud. "Jeez! And I though the island was bad. Was it like that all weekend? You must have been stinking."

Jason smiled. "Just a bit, but everyone does. We went in Tim's car but apparently the trains back are a nightmare for anybody that hasn't been at Glastonbury. We didn't bring anything back with us, just left the lot behind for the charity collection."

I watched Dolly rev it up and I trilled, not loud enough to be heard over the top of Dolly, while Jason sipped and mimed alongside me until Dolly got to the opening bars of *I Will Always Love You*. I looked at Jason and picked up my glass. "I'm not even attempting a mime on this one."

Jason put his arm around me, tucked his hand under my butt and lifted me to sit on his lap. "Or me. Kiss instead then, my angel?"

I put my glass down, put my arms around Jason's neck and offered him my lips. Jason reached out his hand, picked up his phone, selfied our faces close together and murmured as he put it down, "That's better than Jessica Rabbit lips."

Dolly sang out the last bars of her song as we broke apart. Jason skimmed his fingertips over my nipple pressed against my top.

"Bed, baby?"

"Please."

I followed Jason out of the sitting room. He picked up his remote from the arm of the sofa. I picked up my gel from the back of it. Jason sat on the side of the bed and reached for me as I put the gel down within arm's reach and stood between his legs. I took my top off, unfastened my bra and let it drop to the floor.

Jason peeled off his tee, pulled me closer and fastened his mouth on my nipple. I steadied myself on his shoulders as he sucked one then the other and urged my skirt and pants downward. I stepped out of them and Jason lifted me to lie on the bed. I closed my eyes as he sucked between my legs and mewled as he moved his fingers inside me. I ground my pelvis against them.

Jason lifted his head. "Now, baby?"

"Please, yes."

Jason took his shorts off. I picked up the gel and asked, "You want more?"

Jason lay beside me on the bed. "Yes."

I put the gel on the bed behind me and kissed Jason's lips. "Lie on your side, babe. I'll move on you."

Jason lay on his side and I on mine facing him, stroked his erection as I parted my legs, draped one over his thigh and eased his cock inside me. I tightened the grip of my leg around his thigh and rocked my pelvis into a rhythm back and forth. The rise and fall of his chest in my eye-line increased. I reached back for the gel, squashed the tube in my hand, reached over to Jason's butt and stroked my gel-coated finger down the center of his cheeks. Jason's breath hitched at my touch. I circled my finger and eased the tip of it inside.

"Yes, Ness."

I added the tip of my middle finger and moved my caress deeper. Jason moaned. I angled my fingers, touched the bump and massaged the surface of it as I rocked. His muscles tightened and tensed.

"Ness. Fuck, yes."

I circled my fingertips over and around Jason's hot-spot, moved my hips against his, felt the sensation build in between my legs at the sound of his orgasmic groans. I ground my pelvis harder against his and rolled his climax on through the spasms and aftershocks of my own. His voice shortened into small, incoherent moans. I kissed Jason's chest and withdrew my fingers then lay still for the minutes it took for his heart rate to slow and his breathing to soften. Jason opened his eyes.

"Jesus. Ness…"

I kissed his lips. "Stay there, babe. I'll move."

Jason closed his eyes and took a deep breath in. "God, baby. You weren't joking about the knees…"

"You ready?" I smiled.

"Just about."

I eased away from Jason's cock, wriggled higher up his body and nestled under his arm.

"Stay with me a little longer?" he asked.

"For a while. Do you want to dim your lights?"

Jason reached for his remote, pressed and the floor lights softened. "That was so beautiful, baby," he sighed.

I snuggled against him until his breath evened out then lifted my head and looked at his face, relaxed in sleep and so beautiful that my heart contracted in a spasm that was almost painful. I allowed myself another minute tucked tight against his warmth, then slipped out of his embrace and padded to the bathroom.

After I turned off the light, I opened the bathroom door and crept out of the bedroom to find my shoes and bag, rummaged in my handbag until I found a good, old-fashioned pen and a piece of paper and wrote Jason a note to tell him I didn't want to wake him just to say I was going home. I added kisses and a smiley face, crept back into the bedroom and left it under his remote.

I shut the front door gently and called a cab from the lift. It arrived in good time. I checked the time on my phone alarm as I closed my bedroom door, got into bed and fell right asleep.

* * * *

My phone vibrated before my alarm with a message from Jason.

Sorry, I fell asleep on you, baby. Just woke up and read your note.

I smiled and messaged him back.

Good mornin', babe. And don't be sorry, please. Happy that you did. x

See you at work soon. x

I logged onto Facebook and posted my 'happy birthday' to Jilly, put my feet to the floor to test my 'walk of the tender' and smiled when I could feel where Jason had been last night without it being noticeable when I walked.

After I showered, I dressed for work, added my laptop, shoes and makeup bag to my weekender and dropped the iPad into it as I walked through to the kitchen for a coffee. I pushed it under my desk an hour later as I sat, smiled good morning at Annie and looked at Maisie's empty chair.

"No Maisie?"

Annie pointed her finger downward and mouthed, *loitering*. I pulled my keyboard forward. Maisie walked into the office ten minutes later and beckoned to Annie as she sat. Annie leaned forward. I tuned in, too, without taking my eyes from my screen.

"He does drive in. I've just seen him in his car waiting for the barrier to raise at the entrance to the car park. Beautiful car. Just what I'd expect—a BMW convertible, the bigger one, not the small, low one. Navy blue paint, cream interior. He had the roof down."

"He must keep his key fob on him then," Annie muttered.

Maisie nodded, smiled and shook out her hair. "I am just going to look sooo good sitting alongside him in that. Can't you just see it, Annie? The breeze running through my hair. My big Dior sunglasses on. Put your thinking cap on. Surely, between the two us, we can come up with some reason that would let Jason offer me a lift in it to somewhere or the other today."

Annie nodded. "I'll give it my best shot."

I carried on with my work and Jason walked past my workstation a few minutes later. Maisie lifted her head and gazed after him while she tapped her fingernail on her tooth before her focus went back to her work. Half an hour later, she lifted her head again. "Annie. Time for a loo break."

Maisie stood and Annie followed her out of the office. They walked back in twenty minutes later and exchanged smiles as they sat. My phone vibrated with a message from Jason shortly after eleven.

Time for a coffee?

I replied and stood.

Sure. See you there.

"I'm just going to the loo, Annie."

I walked out of the office, ignored the ladies and walked to the drink machine. I ordered a black coffee as the office door opened and Jason walked out. I handed him the cup when he reached me, put the same code in again and said, "You good?"

Jason smiled, "Yeah. Very. You?"

I took a deeper breath in. "Yeah. Very. How was the traffic this morning?"

"Bad enough to make me remember why I bike in and don't bring the car. It took me at least twice as long as normal to get here. The courier is coming in at two. Wander into the office after? I'll make up an excuse for you to come in."

"Sure, and by the way, Maisie saw you pull up at the barrier to the car park this morning. She rather likes your car, or more particularly, the thought of herself in your front passenger seat."

Jason smiled. "No way is that going to happen, but I was going to say I'm leaving early once the artwork's arrived. I could run you to Victoria on my way home if you want to take a chance on the traffic?"

"That'd be good. Thanks."

I took a sip of my coffee as Jason turned to walk back to the office. I turned, one step behind him, and the office door opened. Maisie stepped out, fixed her smile on Jason and walked toward him. I watched, just shielded from Maisie's sight by Jason. Maisie put her foot to the floor and wobbled her ankle. I stepped alongside Jason as I took a guess and held out my coffee cup as Maisie drew level with him. "Would you mind…?"

Jason reached out his hand. I put my cup into it, stepped across him as he took it and put my hand under Maisie's arm to support her weight as she lurched sideways and stumbled. I held on to her arm and put my other hand around her back to support her.

"Oops, Maisie. Are you okay? You nearly fell and twisted your ankle there."

"Ah, yes. Thank you, Vanessa. I'm fine. I'll just get my coffee."

I smiled at Maisie and took my cup from Jason. "No harm done then. I'm glad you're okay."

Maisie walked on to the coffee machine. Jason opened the office door and stopped at the empty-of-other-ears space occupied by the photocopying machine to the side of it. "I take it that it was me that was meant to catch her?"

"I'd have thought. I don't think she noticed me standing behind you or she'd have saved that one."

Jason shook his head. "I'd have walked straight into it if you hadn't noticed what she was about to do."

"She had a little practice wobble on her shoe and gave the game away."

We walked to my workstation.

Jason asked, "Will you print off an extra copy of your input today? Bring it into the office this afternoon?"

"Sure."

Maisie walked into the office as Jason walked away and huffed at Annie as she sat. "Vanessa's just gone and spoiled it all. She bloody well stepped in and caught me when I stumbled instead of letting Jason do it."

"Spoiled? Spoiled what?" I asked.

"We had it all planned and you spoiled it. I was going to twist my ankle so Jason could have an excuse to hold me, and I would be hurt just enough to have a tear or two in my eye. Then I'd say I thought my ankle should be examined at the walk-in clinic and Jason would have offered to take me."

"Are you sure he wouldn't have just had you sit on the floor and called for a first-aider?"

"No, he wouldn't. He'd have done what I've just said he would, and what were you doing there anyway? I've told you he's just waiting for his chance to ask me out. How's he supposed to do that with you hanging around? Just steer clear for a while, will you? Give the man his chance."

Maisie thumped her mouse onto its pad on the desk. I shrugged and carried on with my input until Annie and Maisie stood up at lunchtime. "We're going to get a sandwich from the canteen," Annie said. "Are you going out or can we bring you something back?"

I looked at Annie then Maisie and decided I'd had enough of Maisie's ongoing fairy tale to last me for the rest of the day.

"No, thanks. If I want anything I'll get it myself." I turned back to my screen.

Maisie gave a little cough. "Ah, I'm sorry if I sounded a bit off earlier."

I looked at her.

She continued, "But believe me. I know men and I know how they react to me. Jason would have done just what I said he would, so I was a bit miffed at you for getting in the way, even if you were only trying to help. Let us get you a sandwich or something? You got ours the other day."

Maisie smiled at me. I didn't smile back.

"Well, now that you've raised the subject, I'll just straighten something out for you. My catching you was not accidental. If what I did saved you from spraining your ankle then that's good, but I did what I did because I guessed what you were up to and I did it on purpose so Jason didn't have to."

The smile left Maisie's face. "*Have* to? How do you know he didn't want to? What? Are you an expert now just because you chat with him?"

"No, Maisie. I'm not. But neither am I the type of person who's just going to stand by and watch someone get ambushed like that. It's sneaky."

"Sneaky?"

"Yeah, nearly as sneaky as the things some people will do to try to get hold of a phone number."

Maisie flushed. "I have no idea what you're going on about."

I pasted an insincere smile onto my face. "Of course not. Do enjoy your lunch. See you when you get back."

Maisie walked off with Annie. They came back at two, followed into the office by a uniformed security guard carrying a slim black case walking through the office accompanied by an older man with thin and delicate hands. I carried on with my work and printed my hard copy off at three.

"Annie, I'll just drop these off."

I used the stairs to fill a little time then walked past my station and on to Jason's office with the spare copy he'd asked for when I returned, sat the other side of his desk and handed him the printout. "Going straight in the recycle bin, are they?"

Jason smiled. "The lot of it's going in the recycle bin shortly. It's next on my list to look at. That's why your job was only a temporary contract—just until we can get a bio-entry time management system in place, and as I don't suppose data entry duty was ever on your long-term career plan, I presume you won't mind about that at all."

"Funnily enough, it's not and never was. I nearly strangled Liz at the agency when I realized what she'd stitched me up with."

Jason laughed. "I don't blame you. I'm falling behind getting it sorted, though. If you get a chance while I'm away, flowchart the processes for me, will you?"

"Sure. Have you got a graphic on the system or do I have to play with graph paper and stencils?"

Jason looked at me. "Being as we are still churning out manual settlement checks, what do you think?"

I smiled. "I reckon I'll use the graphic on my laptop and email it to you."

Jason picked up the art case, unzipped it and opened it flat on his desk to display a tall three-tiered tiara. The way it had been drawn gave the illusion that the tiara was floating above the canvas, a three-dimensional object that would be both solid and ice cold if I touched.

"Wow. That's beautiful. How did she get it to float like that?"

Jason smiled. "When it's made, the diamonds in the tiara will look like they're suspended in mid-air, too. That's her trademark. She designed a setting that attaches to the back of the jewel and is invisible from the front, so you get the illusion that the jewels are just floating of their own free will within the piece."

I looked back at the drawing and thought 'magic' and Harry Potter or Disney Princess. "No wonder you need an exceptional jeweler to be able to craft it."

"Especially because a tiara has to look as good from behind as from the front. The back will look like a fine web of platinum filigree," he explained.

"Brides all over China will be swooning at the very thought of it. The sparkle and the diamonds will really stand out against the contrast of black, black hair," I said.

"You must be able to read her mind. One of her other notes to me was that if I made this, to do it for someone with dark hair, not blond like mine."

"They'll love it."

Jason looked over my shoulder. "Peter's here."

I stood and stepped away from the chair. "I'll leave you to it if he hasn't seen it before."

Peter walked into Jason's office before I had time to leave and he nodded at me as he walked toward Jason's desk. He took in a sharp breath then puffed out as he looked. "Yes. Beautiful, don't you think? One of her best."

Jason looked over Peter's shoulder at me as his father took his glasses off, pulled a linen hankie from his pocket and polished the lenses as he blinked.

"What time?" Jason asked me.

"I'll get changed in a few minutes."

"I'll come and get you when I see you're ready."

Peter stopped polishing and looked at me. "Beautiful, isn't it?"

I smiled. "Stunning."

Peter turned his eyes back to the tiara and I walked to my desk. Maisie looked up. I answered the question in her eyes before she got her first word out. "Talking about his plan to make my job redundant, for which I can hardly wait. I'm going to get changed."

I picked up my weekend bag and headed for the ladies, changed my fitted office skirt for my jeans, adjusted my makeup to a more evening look, exchanged my shoes for a pair with higher heels and walked back to the office.

Maisie and Annie sat with their desk drawers open, putting pens and note pads away to leave their workstations weekend tidy. Annie looked up as I sat and neatened my own desk. "You look different out of work clothes. Good different, I mean."

"Thanks. I expect you do, too."

Maisie looked over Annie's shoulder. "He's closed his laptop. Get ready, Annie. You ask me what time tonight, I'll say Barrio around ten then I'll say to him—"

I stood, shouldered my travel weekend bag, walked out of the office and heard Maisie and Annie launch into their pre-prepared speech as the office door swung shut behind me.

"Barrio for cocktails at ten. Oh, hi, Jason. Have you heard of Barrio's?"

"Can't say I have. Have a good weekend."

I looked over my shoulder as the office door squeaked and paused until Jason caught up with me.

"Barrio. I don't think so," he said.

"That's why I came on out. I thought you might get buttonholed if you stopped by my desk."

Jason lengthened his stride. "Double-quick time on the walking?"

I sped up. "And maybe the stairs rather than wait for the lift?"

"The stairs it is. Pass me your bag. It's slowing you down."

I let it slip from my shoulder. Jason took it, added its handle to that of the art case and we moved faster. The door at the head of the stairs swung shut behind us and we slowed our pace.

The parking bays were weekend-empty of cars as we pushed through the door at the bottom. I spotted Jason's car from Maisie's description, parked on its own in the middle of the back row. Jason unlocked it, popped the boot and stowed the hand luggage. "I won't put the roof down so we can get your bag out of the boot when we get to the station."

"That's fine with me. I don't know how you managed to breathe through the traffic fumes this morning."

"Don't worry. I regretted it just about every yard here, especially every time I got caught at the rear of a bus at a traffic light and couldn't move away from the exhaust like I can on my bike."

I smiled. "Good practice for smog central next week, though."

Jason drove to the exit ramp and out into the London crawl. We made the train station ten minutes before I was due to meet Jules, pulled up in the set-down bay and I reached for him as he leaned over the central console and put his arms around me. I closed my eyes for his goodbye kiss and tried to take in enough essence of Jason to last me a week until a car tooted behind us.

"We're getting hooted at again," he said.

I stroked my fingertips along his jawline. "Pop the boot then and you can let Mr. Impatient have your spot."

It clicked and I opened the door after one last hug and got out. "Thanks for the lift. Speak to you tonight."

"Speak later. Have a safe trip home."

Chapter Ten

Jules was waiting under the departures board, her back pressed up against a pillar, two tickets in her hand. We hurried to the platform and managed to get the last two adjoining seats in a packed carriage. I scanned our fellow travelers and saw no chunky, brown-eyed male who to my mind would also have rotten teeth from the breath I had smelled — just Friday-weary commuters — and I relaxed a little.

I picked up my holdall as the train pulled into Chi and Jules followed me out of the carriage. We exited the station into the summer evening air, fresh with the tang of salt, although the station was a couple of miles from the coast. Mum was parked in a short-stay parking slot. I opened the rear door, jumped in, leaned forward and kissed her. "Hi, Mum. How's the birthday girl? Hopping?"

Jules climbed in beside me, shut the door and did the same.

"Hi, darling. Jules, how are you, sweetheart? Jilly's bouncing on cloud nine. She had her first driving lesson this afternoon. Everyone's arrived. Dad will be serving dinner around nine."

Mum started the engine and had us home in twenty minutes. I dumped my travel bag with Jules' in the hall then kissed and hugged Dad, who stood at the oven, on my way through to the sunroom behind the kitchen. Jilly, perched on a high stool at the breakfast bar, screeched when she saw me and Jules hugging Dad behind me.

"Ness! Jules! You're here. I had my first driving lesson. The instructor was really pleased. He said it was excellent for a first drive. Have you brought my presents?"

I kissed Jilly's cheek and unzipped my handbag. "Yes. I have. Happy birthday, bratlet. Here you are."

I handed over my present and card. Jules handed Jilly a gift out of her handbag. "There you go, Jilly. Happy birthday."

A small pair of chubby legs rushed toward Jules and two small arms wrapped around her knees. "Aundy Jules. Aundy Jules. Aundy Sally says I can sleep in your bed with you tonight if'n I'm a good girl. An' I am. An' I can, can't I?"

Jules picked up Natalie, my cousin Lucy's daughter. "Of course, you can, Nat."

Natalie wrapped her arms around Jules' neck. Jules kissed the curls on the top of Natalie's head.

"An' we can watch *Peppa Pig* inna morning. An' *Paw Patrol*, if'n you like," she said.

Mum stood two glasses of wine on the breakfast bar in front of us. "Sorry, Jules. I hope you don't mind. Bobby's been keeping Lucy and Adam up for hours at night. We're trying to give them the night off so they can get a few hours' sleep."

Jules cuddled Natalie. "It's fine. Really."

Mum looked at me. "Will you stay up and feed Bobby around one? Then you can move him and his travel cot in with me and Dad and we'll do the next one."

I nodded and Jilly squealed as she took the wrappings off her presents. "I love it. It's just what I wanted. And a matching pendant. Thank you." Jilly jumped off her stool, threw her arms around me then Jules, picked up her boxes and danced off to show them to Dad.

I picked up my glass and drank. Jules stood Natalie on her feet and did the same, then we moved off around the room to kiss and say hi to two aunts, an uncle and Granny Alice. We stayed to chat with two of my cousins who were full of plans for their start at university in October until the noise of crockery being placed on the breakfast bar gave us notice that food was about to be served.

"Just don't leave it too late to book your first-year accommodation," I said, as our group broke up.

"Yeah," Jules agreed. "For the first year, at least. Then you'll be more familiar with your uni city and where it's safe or not to be."

I looked at the time as Dad put a plate of carved roast beef on the heated tray, saw it was nearly ten and sat on a stool at the breakfast bar alongside Jules as plates filled and everyone looked for somewhere to sit and eat. Mum beat Dad to the last empty stool beside us by less than a second and she laughed. "There's the quick and there's those that have now got to go sit with my mother." Dad smiled and took his plate with him to perch on the arm of Granny Alice's chair. Mum picked up her fork. "Slide my glass over, will you, Jules? If I'd stopped to pick it up, Al would've had his butt on this stool before me."

Jules slid Mum's glass to her. Mum speared a pea and looked at me then Jules over the top of her fork. "So, girls, all good in town with you two, is it?"

I looked at the pea then at Jules. I sipped from my glass. Jules sipped from hers. We both nodded at my mum.

"Yes, fine," I said.

"All good, thanks," Jules echoed.

"Lovely party in Camden, was it?" Mum said.

Jules and I both nodded and watched the pea wobbling on the tines of Mum's fork.

Mum looked at me. "And you seem to have been back to Camden a couple of times since" — she turned to Jules — "without you. Although you do seem to quite a fascination with a flat a few hundred yards from your own."

Jules gave in, laughed and let the existence of Ben out of her mouth. "Yes, Sally. That's where Ben lives and I'll admit it now that me and Ben are a little way down the road to being an item. I like Ben very much and I'm going to meet his family on Sunday."

Mum dropped her fork and wrapped her arms around Jules. "Jules, darling. I know it's been tough. I'm so happy for you. I always knew you'd get through it. Have you got a photo of him?"

Jules took her phone out of her pocket, scrolled down the photos then passed it to Mum. I looked over Mum's shoulder at a full-body shot of Ben in tight sport wear, looking his gorgeous best.

Mum swallowed as she looked. "Well…goodness." Mum passed Jules her phone back and fanned herself with her hand. "Lovely man as well, is he?"

I laughed. "Jules won't puff it off but Ben is in every way as gorgeous as he looks."

Mum picked up her wine and smiled at Jules. "Worth waiting for then, I'd say."

Jules smiled and put her phone away. "Yeah. I think so, too."

Mum picked up her fork and waved the pea at me. "So, Camden?"

I thought of Jason and the heat hit my cheeks. "Well, I've sort of met someone I like but I've haven't known him for as long as Jules has known Ben."

Jules laughed, flicked a pea at me and swallowed a mouthful of wine. "His name is Jason, Sally, and Ness met him at work."

I flicked two peas with double gravy at Jules.

Jules flicked double peas back at me and grinned.

"Is he as nice as Ben, darling? Would either of you bring them home to say hi?"

I shrugged. "Too early to say."

Jules smiled. "Yeah, sure I would."

I picked up my knife and fork and ate my beef while Jules told Mum a little more about Ben, then I rinsed plates and cutlery at the sink for Jules to stack in the dishwasher. I followed her through to the sunroom after we shut the door on the last plate and picked up our glasses.

"Sorry, babe, for letting that out in front of your mum. I wouldn't have carried on and said any more."

I blew Jules a kiss. "I know that. Don't worry about it. You're just a bit of an over-excited fruit bat at the moment and I'm happy for you."

A crease line appeared between Jules' eyes. "What if they don't like me on Sunday, Ness?"

"They'll love you and I don't think Ben would have invited you if there was the smallest chance of that."

Jules' worry line disappeared. "No, he wouldn't have, would he? Not Ben. I'll just pop upstairs and phone him, check that he's okay."

Jules took her glass with her and I sat beside Granny Alice.

"Ness, darling. How's work? Is it all going okay?" she asked.

I nodded as Jilly perched herself on the other side of Granny. "Granny's going to Spain on Monday to stay with Grandpa and Jenny for a few days."

I smiled at Granny. "They'll be glad to see you. It's the first time this year, isn't it? Who are you taking with you, Richard or Barry?"

Granny shrugged and sipped. "I haven't decided yet. Whichever one of them offers to take me out for the best dinner tomorrow night, I expect."

"I'd pick Richard. He's still got all of his hair," Jilly said.

Granny raised her eyebrows at Jilly. "Ah, but it is real or stuck on with glue? That's what you've got to ask yourself."

I joined in. "And what about the teeth? Do they come out at night and into a glass of water beside the bed?"

Dad snorted as he walked past.

Jilly screwed up her face. "Ew. You two are grossing me out."

Granny laughed. "But I haven't even started on the subject of his incontinence undies yet."

Jilly squealed, "Ew! No!" and fled.

My phone vibrated in my pocket as I laughed. I unlocked it and saw a message from Jason.

How's dinner? Is your sister enjoying her birthday?

I blew a kiss at Granny and she turned to talk to Lucy as I tapped in my reply.

LOL. She was until about a minute ago, but Granny's just grossed her out talking about incontinence pads!

Eek. Still sounds like hell.

LOL again. Don't even get me started on the false teeth and wig! Will you still be up later to Skype?

Waiting for you whenever you are ready.

Mmmm. I wish. x

Wish too. x

I looked up from my phone. Two aunts, one uncle and assorted cousins stood up to say goodnight. I kissed them on their way past. Jules walked in and Natalie detached herself from her mother. "Aundy Jules, can we go to bed now? I'm tired."

Jules picked Natalie up. "Of course we can. You'll turn into a pumpkin if you stay up much longer."

I looked at the time on my phone as Mum looked over my shoulder and did the same. "Jilly, get moving. I know it's still your birthday for another fifteen minutes but your late night up is tomorrow," Mum said.

Jilly didn't object and followed along behind Jules, who was carrying Natalie out of the room. I looked and saw Bobby's pram was empty.

"He's already in his travel cot in your bedroom, Ness," Mum said.

"Okay. I'm off."

I blew a kiss at Granny, walked upstairs, used my bathroom, put on PJs with a short-sleeved, all-covering top then sat on my bed with my laptop and pressed Call on Jason's Skype icon. He appeared, sitting at his breakfast bar in his kitchen as the webcams connected.

"Hey, you. You had a good night?" I asked.

"Hey, you, back. Yeah. The flat's good to be left," he smiled.

"You got dishpan hands there? I can't imagine what you've been up to that it's taken you all night."

Jason smiled. "No, I don't suppose you can. That's your bedroom at your parents' place, is it?"

"Yep. It's never been changed since I left home. You might have had *Buffy*, but I had *Twilight*. I've still got Edward on the wall."

I tilted my laptop so Jason could see my *Twilight* posters with at least three of my teenage crush, Robert Pattinson. I righted my screen.

Jason's gaze moved to the side of my bed. "What's that on the table beside your bed?"

I flicked my eyes toward the conical shape plugged in on my bedside table, the warming light flashing on the front of it and I smiled.

"Ah, that belongs to Bobby, the man I'm sharing my room with at the moment."

"Really? Where is he then? I don't quite see him on the cam."

I blew a kiss at the screen. "Oh, ye of little faith. Hang on. I'll wriggle down the bed and show you."

I shuffled down to the foot of my bed and tilted the webcam toward Bobby, asleep, his small fists curled and his arms thrown up either side of his head in his travel cot.

"Jesus, Ness! Is that a baby in there?"

I tilted the screen back toward my face, looked at Jason's expression and laughed as I wriggled back up the bed. "Yep. This week's special offer—buy one, get one free. Jules has got the other one—Bobby's sister, Natalie. She's four."

"Who do they belong to?"

"My cousin Lucy and her husband Adam. They were here for dinner and the kids are sleeping over tonight. I'm feeding Bobby when he wakes then lobbing him into my mum and dad's room for them to do the next one."

I looked up at a soft tap on the door and Jules walked in. "Have you got a nappy pant for Natalie in Bobby's changing bag, babe? She's just nodded off without one and I don't want her to pee all over me in the night like she did last time."

I nodded toward the bag on the floor beside my bed. "Down there. Have a rummage. If there's not one, fold up a bath towel and stick it under her butt."

I looked at Jason as Jules unzipped the magic bag.

"Buy one, get one free with extra free pee this week, is it?" he asked.

Jules pulled her hand out of the bag with a nappy pant in it, lay across my bed and waved it at the screen. "Hi, Jason. Not with one of these. You good? Looking forward to China?"

Jason shook his head at Jules as Mum called out. "Ness, Jules. Are the kids okay?"

"Both asleep. I was just getting a nappy pant for Natalie," Jules called back.

"Okay. Goodnight, everyone," Mum said.

Jilly answered. "Goodnight, Mama. Goodnight, Jim-Bob."

Jules looked at me and asked the question with her finger — *me or you?* I pointed to her to go first.

"Goodnight, Elizabeth," she said.

Jilly called out, "Goodnight, Mary-Ellen. Goodnight, Erin."

I joined in, "Goodnight, Elizabeth. Goodnight, Mama. Goodnight Jim-Bob."

"Yeah, yeah and goodnight, John-Boy. Now shut up, will you? Damn house full of women and the only other two males in the house are already knocking out the Zs."

"I heard that, Alan DeRay," Granny Alice said.

"Oh, God! Are you still awake, too? Get your teeth in that glass and a curler in under your chin, will you?"

Jules grinned at my screen and mouthed to Jason, *Granny*.

"You will pay for that in the morning when I dribble in your porridge."

"Sally, tell her. I hate it when the drool runs down her chin."

Mum laughed. "Go to sleep, the lot of you. Some of us really do have to be up for porridge patrol in the morning."

Jules waved her nappy pant at Jason as she rolled off the bed. I mimed at Jules to close the door, looked at Jason sitting in his cool, clean, kitchen and wondered if he would like to be in our warm chaos with its background smell of roast beef or whether he'd run a mile from it instead. I smiled at the screen and Jason smiled back.

"Ah, am I missing something here? Erin, Mary-Ellen?" he asked.

"So, no cheesy telly for you when you were young either, then?

"Apart from Buffy, sadly not."

I puckered Jason a kiss. "Go on YouTube sometime and type in *The Waltons*. Have you got much to do tomorrow before you go?"

"Not a lot, but it'll be one of those odd, out of sync days. My flight's so early that the taxi's coming at three Sunday morning."

"Go wear yourself out down at the gym and get half a bottle of wine inside you by seven, then."

"It's on the list. You and Jules will just be gearing up, ready to go by then."

"Yeah. We'll—"

Bobby opened his mouth and wailed. I wrinkled my nose at Jason and mouthed *damn*. The pitch of Bobby's wail went up a notch.

"Sorry. I'd better see to him. He'll only get louder."

Jason smiled. "Sounds like you'd better. Call me tomorrow when you can?"

"Sure. Speak tomorrow."

"Night, Ness. Sleep well."

I closed my laptop, picked up Bobby and snuggled him as I fed him his milk. Bobby fell back asleep as I burped him. I laid him on my bed, carried his travel cot into the peeps' bedroom on soft feet so as not to wake them and took Bobby to join them. Duty done, I got under my duvet and didn't hear another thing until I opened my eyes in the morning just after ten.

I swung my legs out of bed to the sound of the front door closing, dropped my phone into the pocket of my bathrobe and Mum smiled at me as I walked down the stairs.

"That's Lucy and Adam just gone. I sent Jules back to bed to catch a couple more hours. She's been up being *Peppa*'d by Natalie since five-thirty," Mum said.

I followed Mum through to the kitchen. She set the coffee machine off while I sat at the breakfast bar. When it was ready, she put two coffees in front of me and sat on the stool beside mine. I picked up my cup, breathed in the aroma and sipped. Mum did the same and glanced sideways at me.

"So, Jason? You work with him, then?"

I nodded.

"And he lives in Camden, does he?"

"Yep."

"And that's who you were chatting with last night before Bobby woke up, was it?"

"Might have been."

"And you haven't got a photo of him on your phone?"

My cheeks heated as I thought of the only pic I had of Jason on my phone. "Nope."

"Ugly then, is he?"

"Very."

Mum looked at my heated face and laughed. "Well, soul of discretion as he is, you'd better delete any photos if Jason's so ugly that you wouldn't want Gary to come across him later."

Jilly walked in through the kitchen door. "Who's ugly?"

Mum smiled and fibbed with the fluidness of years of practice in avoiding an issue. "Not who, what. The design for a new apartment block they want to build near where Ness lives."

I took my coffee cup to the sink. "I'm off to get changed. I'll swim for a while before I shower."

Jilly looked out of the window at the pool. "I'm not swimming today. It's going to take me hours just to get ready."

I swam for an hour in my all-covering school swimsuit, showered, dressed in shorts and a T-shirt, tucked my phone into my shorts pocket and bumped into a yawning Jules on the landing as I walked downstairs.

"Why is it that I can stay up until five and feel fine the next day but get woken up at five and I'm just knackered?" she said.

"That's *Peppa Pig* for you. You'll feel better after a coffee."

Jules sniffed. "And I think I can smell your dad cooking bacon for brunch."

Granny Alice's head appeared around the edge of her bedroom door. "Just what I could do with before I go home and early enough that it won't spoil my appetite for dinner with Richard tonight."

"Oh, you've decided then?" I said as Granny followed us down the stairs.

"Yep. Barry just offered a bar meal at the local. Richard offered fine dining at the Manor Hotel."

Jules grinned. "No contest, then, Alice."

We sat in a line along the breakfast bar, drank coffee and watched Dad flip bacon and eggs in two large frying pans. My phone vibrated in my pocket. Jules looked over my shoulder as I opened a message from Jason.

Hey, you. Are you having a good day? Just back from the gym. Did the small, noisy thing enjoy his late-night supper?

Hey, you, back. Yes and yes. Bobby's deserted me and gone home now, though. Had a healthy swim and in the kitchen at the moment with Jules and Granny watching Dad cook an unhealthy brunch.

She's taken her curler out and put her teeth in then, I hope?

I smiled at Granny and she smiled her perfect, beautifully whitened teeth at me and mouthed, *who's that?*

"Just a friend I was talking to on Skype last night who overheard you and Dad giving each other a bit of stick."

I carried on typing as Jules grinned.

For sure, although the smell of the bacon is making her mouth water and that's not always a happy thing. But not to worry as Bobby's left a bib behind, so she's sorted.

Aaargh. I really needed that. I was just going out to eat.

Enjoy, babe. At least you're not here mopping it up! Shall I Skype you later? Before Jilly's party if you are going to sleep early because of your taxi time?

That would be good. What time does the party start?

I'm not needed until about nine but I'll Skype you 7ish when I go upstairs to get changed?

Mmmm. Getting changed. Yes, please.

Bad man!

I put my phone in my pocket and looked at Jules. "I didn't ask. Was Ben okay last night?"

"As gorgeous as ever."

"Ben? Who's Ben?" Granny said.

"Go on. Show Granny the photo."

"I will if you do," Jules said.

"In your dreams, girlie. I've already had to tell Mum…far too ugly."

Jules laughed, pulled her phone from her pocket and showed Ben's pic to Granny.

"Yes. Well. Has he got a free and available grandfather, by any chance?"

"Grandfather, yes. Available, unfortunately not." Jules smiled.

Dad put plates of brunch down in front of us and Gary arrived as we finished eating. Jules and I fetched our laptops and iPads and handed them to him, sitting at the desk in Dad's study. He held his hand out. "And the rest."

I looked at Jules and she wrinkled her nose at me. We took our phones out of our pockets and handed them over.

Gary smiled. "Thank you. I will, of course, not comment or laugh too loudly when I check them."

I sidled out of the room with Jules and shut the door behind us. "What have you got on yours?"

"A couple of vids of me and Ben, not for sharing but too special for me to want to delete them. You?"

"Just the one of us arsing about when we got the…ah, birthday pressie we gave to Mark and my pic of Jason."

Jules laughed. "No, not the birthday pressie? Please tell me you deleted that vid."

I shook my head as laughter and a shout sounded through the study door. "No! Surely not! Really!"

"Nope. But hey, you have to leave something on there to relieve his boredom."

Jules grinned. "That should keep his mind off the vid of me and Ben."

I held my hand up for a high five. "You'd think."

I followed Jules into the kitchen and we started to set up Jilly's party venue by removing anything breakable or remotely alcoholic from the sunroom. Jilly sat at the breakfast bar and concentrated on the rather more important matter of organizing her playlist. I stopped on my last pass through the room to remove two bottles of liquid potpourri that wouldn't taste good, even if diluted with lemonade, to have a look over her shoulder. Jilly tilted her iPad in my direction.

"What do you think? Too much Little Mix or not?"

I ran my eyes down the list. "No, it's well broken up. You can't have too much Little Mix. They're fun, but I'm not sure I'd have that slower Stan Smith track in the middle of them."

Jilly's cheeks colored a little. "That one's for Josh, but you're right. I'll move it to later."

Dad walked into the kitchen with a large-chain pizza menu in his hand and gave it to Jilly. "I think six of the largest should do it. Make me a list of the toppings you want and I'll do an online order in advance. Although why you wouldn't let me make them —"

"Dad! You can't serve homemade pizza at a party. Everyone will think I'm a geek!"

I smiled at Dad and walked off with the pot pourri, saw his study door ajar and slipped in. Gary looked over his shoulder at me. "Don't worry, Ness. I've nearly finished if you need anything back."

"Thanks, Gary. But I really came about something else."

"Fire away."

"I don't think it's anything to do with Dad, but I think someone at work is trying to unlock and take a peek at my phone."

Gary turned in his chair. "Think? Or know?"

"Think. And I think they're after personal data, not business data. But I couldn't say absolutely for sure, so just in case…"

Gary nodded. "Okay. I'll add another layer of security to your phone then come and tell what I've done when I've finished."

I thanked Gary and closed the study door. A little while later, Gary brought our laptops, iPads and phones into the kitchen as Jules and I placed extra Wi-Fi speakers around the sunroom. Gary picked my phone up off the top of the pile and offered it to me.

"Okay, so unlock your phone with the numerical code as normal then press star then hash. If you don't within thirty seconds, the phone will switch off. If you switch the phone back on and put the code in incorrectly a second time, the tracker will send a message and the firm will send someone out to see what's going on."

"Thanks, Gary. I won't forget the extra code."

Gary leaned forward. "Good…and, by the way, just what was the blow-up cow doing to the blow-up pig?"

"You don't want to know, but just think of the sounds of squeal and moooo and the fact that the recipients live in the flat below ours."

Gary laughed and walked out of the kitchen. I looked at the time on my phone and mimed a drinking motion at Jules. She nodded. I filled two glasses with the end of a bottle from the previous night. Jules sat on a stool at the breakfast bar and glanced around the empty room. "I'm going to phone Ben before things get started. When are you speaking to Jason?"

"I said I'd Skype him before the party. His flight is early, so he might be asleep later."

Jilly popped up from behind the sofa at the end of the sunroom. "Gotcha. Jason, is it?"

I looked at her. "If you're down there because you've just hidden your bottle, I'm going to have it."

"Ness! No! I was, ah…just checking the speaker."

Jilly stood with a bottle-shaped bump on the front of her bathrobe and side-stepped out of the garden door. Jules laughed and picked up her laptop and glass. "I think I might go and see what Ben is up to."

I did the same. "With you, girlie."

I followed Jules up the stairs, pulled blue jeans, a sleeveless button-through shirt and underwear out of my holdall and took a shower. Hair dried and makeup on, I put a bathrobe over my underwear, lay on my stomach across my bed, opened my laptop and tapped on Jason's icon. He answered on the third ring, lounging back on his sofa, a glass of wine in his hand. I blew a kiss at the webcam and showed him my glass. "Snap."

Jason smiled at me and muscles all over me tightened as I smiled back and made a wish.

"Have you had a good day? I'm on my second glass," he said.

"Yeah. We've got everything good to go for Jilly. Did you wear yourself out at the gym?" I asked.

"I did a couple of hours but I'm not sure it's helped. It's left me feeling more buzzy than tired, so I'm having a couple of glasses to try to wind down."

My bedroom swung open. Jilly, dressed in tight white jeans and a gold crop top, sauntered in. "Ness, have you got any eyelash glue? The one that came with my new set is rubbish."

"On my dressing table."

Jilly began to pick through the make-up on my dressing table. "Your mascara's better than mine. Oooh, I've looked for a glitter eyeshadow like this one for ages."

I smiled at Jason. "Nothing is safe from her nimble fingers."

Jilly sat down on the side of my bed with a collection of my makeup in her hand. "Who's that? He Who Must Not Be Named or my vodka's going down the toilet?" Jilly poked her head around the lid of my laptop. "Hello, Jason."

Jason smiled. "Hello, Jilly. I thought I didn't have a name?"

Jilly took my wine glass out of my hand, swallowed a mouthful and gave me the glass back. "Ah but I was hiding behind the sofa listening in when she said your name to Jules earlier, hence the toilet threat."

I looked at Jilly. "Where'd you get the vodka from, anyway? Dad said he'd got cases of WKD in and that was your lot."

Jilly took my glass and swallowed another mouthful. "So, I offered to go shopping with Granny last week and hid it under her stuff in the trolley then offered to pack her bag for her at the end of the checkout."

I laughed and flicked Jilly's shoulder with my thumb and finger. "Brat. Checked the lavender bush in the last half hour, have you?"

Jilly handed me my glass, jumped up off the bed and scooted toward the door. "Ness, no! You can't have found it already."

Jason laughed. "Know that bush well, do you?"

I smiled. "Absolutely. Great place to stow a bottle, especially if you've already been caught trying to hide it behind the sofa. Where did you hide yours?"

"Ah, geek central here until uni. I didn't."

"Aw, babe. What? Nothing?"

"Nearest I got to illicit drinking was a packet of seriously non-alcoholic wine gums."

I toasted Jason with my glass. "I think you probably made up for it at uni and I expect most of the beer-swilling first fifteen are probably great big lard-asses now."

Jason smiled. "I did and I hope so. I sometimes wonder how I got out of uni with a first-class degree, not a third. I'm sure when I took my finals I was still pissed from year two."

I giggled. "Right. Add your graduation ceremony and ball pics to my list. I wanna see them."

"If I get to see yours."

I put my glass down, stood and dropped my bathrobe to the floor. "See my what?" I turned my butt toward my laptop, picked up my jeans, wriggled them on, added my shirt and lay across my bed.

"Jesus, Ness. I wish I could just reach through this screen."

"Mmmm. Fully interactive cybersex. Now there's a thought."

Jules opened my bedroom door and let in the full throb of the beat from downstairs.

"Sixth form in full attendance down there, babe. I think most of them got some down their throats before they even got here."

"Vodka patrol coming right up, girlie."

Jules called out. "Sorry, Jason. Safe flight and enjoy China. See you soon."

"Thanks, Jules." Jason looked at me as Jules walked out of the room. "I'm wishing China and everyone in it to hell at the moment."

I reached my fingers toward the screen. "Let me know how it's going tomorrow?"

"Yes, baby. And you?"

"Yes, my lovely man. Now get some sleep. You've got to be up at silly o'clock."

I blew Jason a kiss, swallowed hard as his face disappeared and walked downstairs into the noise. Three girls sat on the bottom stair chatting and another two loitered in the cloakroom. I shooed them back into the party room. Dad brought the boxes of pizza in at nine-thirty. I looked at Jilly's boyfriend.

"Josh. If any of that hits the ceiling and I will personally come and stomp on all your heads when you've got your sleeping bags out later."

Josh laughed and nodded. I nudged Jules and took two bottles of water out of the fridge. We took our wine glasses with us, exited to the garden, toured the bushes, tipped out half the contents of the bottles we found and topped them up with water. I sat at the garden table. Jules sat beside me and we listened for any sign of discord in the buzz as we sipped.

Mum wandered out with her glass and sat opposite us. "So, Jules, love, what time is your do with Ben tomorrow?"

"It's lunch. Ben's calling for me around twelve."

"Don't wait around in the morning then. Dad and I can sort this lot out and wait for their parents to arrive," Mum said.

"Work out how much time you need to get ready and find what train time would be best," I said.

Jules nodded and tapped on her phone. "I could do with getting the ten past eight if that's not too early?"

"I'll drive us to the station. Dad will drive Mum to the station later and pick my car up."

"Just creep on out then. Don't wake the sleeping babies," Mum said then picked up her glass. "So, Jason?"

I clamped my lips together.

"Don't give me that look, Vanessa DeRay. I don't want to know the ins and outs of whatever, but this is the first guy's name you've let escape in nearly three years. We've all lived through this. At least spit out the basics."

"Like?"

"Like what does he do? How did you meet him at Belmond's? How old is he? Reassure your old mum. She worries."

Jules laughed and I gave in. "Okay. Chartered accountant. Twenty-seven. Has a flat in Camden."

"So?" Mum prompted. "Tall? Short? Fat? Thin? Hair?"

"Tall. Over six feet and blond. I like him very much and I think he likes me as well, but that's where it stops. I only *think*. It could go somewhere or nowhere. I'm hoping for somewhere" —I shrugged and sipped—"but I don't know."

Mum patted my hand. "You've told him about the attack? What it has left behind?"

"Yes, she has and Jason's been okay with it all, hasn't he, Ness?"

"So, far, babe. But this early…who knows?"

Laughter sounded inside the sunroom and the first piece of pepperoni hit the window. Jules and I walked inside, rounded up all the pizza boxes with any uneaten contents and took them away. An hour later I held the first head over the pan while Jules handed out tissues to the girl crying on the bottom stair, supported by two of her outraged friends.

At one, Dad blowtorched marshmallows and Jules and I chivvied the party guests into their sleeping bags, turned on the movie and left them to it as Mum and Dad walked up the stairs to bed. I sat at the breakfast bar beside Jules and picked up my glass.

"Do you need to go to bed, babe? I can get some sleep when we get home tomorrow but you've got to go straight back out."

Jules sipped. "Yeah, I'll finish this and go up. How's it going to be next week? When you can't see Jason?"

"Double, double doggie dollops. It already is" — I swallowed my last mouthful of wine and put my glass down — "although no one will know it apart from you."

Jules put her glass beside mine and held her little finger out. "Pinky swear."

I linked my smallest finger around hers and shook. "Pinky swear. They're all fairly quiet now. Let's go up to bed."

Jules followed me up the stairs and I hugged her outside her bedroom door.

"See you good and early in the morning, girlie. They are so going to love you tomorrow."

Jules kissed my cheek. "I hope so, babe. See you in the morning."

I closed my bedroom door, dug around in my cupboard and came away with my yearbook and a couple of photos, added them to my packed holdall, climbed into bed, woke with my alarm at six-thirty and texted Jason before I put my feet to the floor.

All on time for you? Everyone get to the airport okay? Have a safe flight.

All here. Just boarding. Phone or text you tonight when we've landed. Have a good trip home.

I decided to save my shower for when I got back to the flat, dressed and went to see if Jules was up. She was zipping her toilet bag into her overnighter as I opened her door.

"All good to go?" I asked her.

Jules nodded.

"I'll get my bag." I walked back to my bedroom, picked up my holdall and padded quietly down the stairs after Jules. I took one of the keys to my car out of the kitchen drawer, clicked the front door shut softly behind us, rolled up the garage door and reversed Daisy out. Jules put our bags on the back seat and climbed in. We arrived at the station in plenty of time to park and get the eight-ten back to Victoria Station.

Only a handful of day tourists occupied the train when it pulled in and Jules and I had an empty carriage to ourselves all the way back. The concourse at Victoria was nearly empty of milling travelers as we walked through and climbed into a cab outside.

I looked at my phone while Jules gave the driver our address. "Not bad. It's not quite ten yet. You'll have plenty of time to get ready."

Jules nodded and gripped her knees with her hands. "I'm getting pretty nervous now. Do you think it's out of order to sneak a glass in around eleven before I go?"

"Lord, no. I'd definitely need to. You can always clean your teeth again before you go so you don't already smell of alcohol when you have to do all the *hello, pleased to meet you* kissy stuff."

I paid the driver when he pulled up outside our block. Jules let us in at the street door and called for the lift. I opened our front door and Jules walked straight to her bedroom. "I was thinking of my stretch, tight-fit green dress with a linen short-sleeved shirt tied at the waist over it. What do you think?"

"I think good. It hints sexy and gorgeous but without being too much so for a lunch with the shirt over it. You'll knock them dead, girlie."

I dumped my bag in my bedroom, walked to the kitchen and thought of Jason while I put the kettle on. He'd be three hours into his thirteen-hour flight and I wondered whether he'd been served breakfast or the more normal fare. I sat on the sofa to the sound of Jules' hairdryer. Jules called as it switched off, "Okay, wine open and good to go in about half an hour."

I walked to the kitchen, picked up a bottle and two glasses, opened it and left it on the coffee table to breathe. Jules walked into the living room forty minutes later.

I picked up the bottle and poured. "You look beautiful, girlie."

Jules picked up her glass and swallowed as Ben called from the front door. Jules kissed him and they shared the end of Jules' wine between them before they left. I stood my empty glass alongside theirs, walked to my bedroom, plugged my laptop and phone in to charge then caught up on some missing sleep.

* * * *

I woke at three, took myself down to the gym for a two-hour sweat, showered, wandered out to the hot chicken shop for a spicy wrap and ate it as I caught up with Mae, Beth, Mark and Simon on Facebook. My phone vibrated just after ten. *Jason.*

Hey, you. Here and in taxi on the way to hotel.

Hey, you, back. How was the flight? And the time warp?

Flight boring but at least business not economy seat. Bit weird to find it 5 a.m. here and the day about to start, not finish.

Are you straight into it? Or a day off to adjust to the time zone?

Straight to it. Check in. Breakfast then over to the conference center. Speak to you tomorrow for you and tonite for me.

Have a good day. Speak soon.

I closed my laptop and took a book to bed, woke well in advance of my alarm and figured the time difference to one o'clock lunchtime in Beijing. My phone vibrated with a message from Jason just after seven-thirty as I dried my hair.

Hey, you. You awake yet? Just at the end of a lunch meeting here.

Hey, you, back. Just getting ready for work. Polite lunch or messy?

Very polite. What time are you back from work tonite?

Around 6.

I should be finished dinner by then. I'll try and Skype you?

I'll load my laptop when I get home. Hope to speak to you then.

The office was quiet when I arrived. Peter sat behind Jason's desk in the goldfish bowl. I put my phone in my pocket and picked up the drink carrier. "Coffee anyone?"

Maisie and Annie both looked up.

"Yeah, why not?" Annie said.

"Yeah. We'll come with," Maisie said.

They followed me out of the office. I put the first code into the machine, handed Maisie her white without and tapped Annie's code in. Maisie sipped and sighed. "He's only been in there twenty minutes. We're all going to be climbing the walls by Friday."

I handed Annie her coffee. "That bad?"

"You can just feel it, can't you?" Annie said. "Nobody talking. Nobody saying what they did over the weekend. No buzz. It's like a morgue in there already."

I took my cup out of the machine. "The window blinds are going in this afternoon. Will that make it better?"

"I hope so. How was your weekend? Did your sister enjoy her birthday?" Annie said.

"Yeah. It was good. Jilly's party was okay. Just a couple of pukers and a few tears to sort out. How was yours?"

"We had a good time on Friday, didn't we, Maisie? Honestly, there were at least three guys that couldn't take their eyes off her and trailed along behind her all night."

Maisie's eyes lightened and she smiled. "Yeah, they did. It's just a shame that we didn't bump into Jason. I thought I'd said the name of the bar clearly enough, but I guess I didn't."

"Did you chat with any of the guys trailing after you?" I asked.

Maisie shook her head.

"You could be missing out on a guy that's perfect for you," I offered.

Maisie dropped her empty cup into the bin and smiled at me. "No, sorry. I'm not interested. I already know who that is. He'll miss seeing me this week. I'm sure that'll be enough for him get over his nerves and ask me for a date when he gets back."

I shrugged and walked behind Maisie and Annie toward the office. Derek walked out of the office door. His cheeks turned a pale-rose color as he walked past Maisie.

Annie giggled and looked at me. "I still can't imagine *him* with a six-pack, dressed in tight black leather."

I looked over my shoulder at Derek's disappearing back. "What? When?"

"Craig told me Derek's a gamer out of work. He plays those fantasy role-play games online and that's what his avatar looks like."

I shook my head. "Nope. I can't get my head around that one. I wonder if his avatar blushes. Does Craig play as well, then?"

"No. But some of those games have a secret hidden key in them that you type in to get extra power and things. Derek sometimes picks Craig's brain to help him get it."

Maisie pushed the office door open and muttered under her breath, "Sad sap."

I followed Maisie into the office, put my ear buds in as I worked on through to lunch without any further chat. The window-blind fitters turned up as I ate a sandwich at lunchtime, and by four, a low hum returned to office as the blinds swung shut.

Maisie looked up from her keyboard. "Thank God for that."

Peter didn't appear for the rest of the afternoon and I logged off at five, opened the front door just before six, opened my laptop on the coffee table and poured a glass of wine. My Skype icon didn't ring as I sat on the sofa but my phone did. *Jason*.

I smiled as I answered it. "Hey, you. Was the Skype connection not good?"

"Hey, you, back. I haven't tried. There's a problem with my laptop. I'll have it looked it at when I come home. I won't use it again until then."

"What's going on?"

"Perhaps a bit of a coincidence or maybe a lucky break, but the trade fair's a mixed bag of different businesses and the company at the stand next to ours is an IT outfit. I got to talking to the guy there today and he offered to run a little demo of their latest security scan on my laptop. It picked up an issue. From what he could tell, an ad hoc piece of coding has been installed on my laptop to copy some of my personal data."

I heard the bead of worry in Jason's voice. "What? From emails?"

"Yeah. Emails, Word documents and goodness knows what else. He offered to get rid of the coding but

I've left it on there. I want to know more about it and what it does. Do you think your dad's security guy would take a look at it?"

"Sure. I'll get Gary's number from Dad for you."

"Thanks, Ness. I've turned the Wi-Fi connection off on my mobile to cut the link between it and my laptop as well, just in case. I'll use my phone this week as a standalone."

"Are you thinking someone in the IT office has coded the spyware?"

"Might be, but that's the problem. It doesn't have to be. Plenty of people can code that have never been anywhere near an IT department for their job. I'm hoping that whoever it is might have left a little footprint behind."

I sipped and heard Jason do the same.

"Gary's good. If they have, he'll find it and avoid any little self-destruct trip hazards that might be embedded in it," I told him.

"It might give me something to take to the police if he does."

"What about the artwork itself? Has anyone made a move in that direction?"

"Not that I've spotted, but I'm only really just finding my feet. My body clock's still out of sync with the time difference."

I smiled at my phone. "It'll be better tomorrow, when you've had a night's sleep Beijing time. How is the hotel?"

"The hotel's as expected, but you were right about my height standing out over here. The convention center itself isn't too bad. There's lots of Western business interest there but walking to and from it today was a bit more than uncomfortable."

"Petted all the way?"

"Not so much. I think I'm so much bigger than the locals that it makes them hold off on the touching front, but the staring? I don't like it, Ness. It makes me feel a bit like I did back at school — a bit of a freak."

"Aw, babe, no. Never that."

Jason's voice deepened. "I miss you, baby. I'm in bed now and wishing you were, too. It's only been four days since you were and already it seems like more than a week."

I rested my head against the sofa back, closed my eyes and summoned Jason, naked, into my mind. I saw him looking at me, the green of his irises dark with his want of my body, and I breathed a little deeper down the phone. "Yeah. Me, too. Nice bed, is it?"

"Far too nice. It's got a you-sized empty space in it."

My heart jumped a beat. My lips and arms joined in and ached. "I so wish, but it's nearly just another night gone. What time will you be up in the morning?"

"Around seven for breakfast at eight, then we've got a lunch meeting arranged with Ju-long Linn, who owns the company that Mike is hoping to do the main business with."

"I'll just be going to bed then and asleep through your lunch," I said.

"What are you up to tonight?" he asked.

"I'll eat with Jules when she gets home then we've said we'll meet Mark and Simon in The Vine for a glass."

"Text me before you go to bed, baby?"

"I will. Sleep well. Speak soon."

"Speak soon. Night, Ness."

I cut the connection and Jules called to me as she opened the front door. "Hey, babe. I picked us up a pasta salad."

"Never mind that. Get in here and tell me more about the party."

Jules' eyes sparkled as she walked in through the living room door. "Oh, it was so, so good, Ness. Ben's family were just gorgeous. So welcoming. I never felt like a newbie with everyone chatting, laughing, talking and kids running everywhere."

I held my hand up. "Way to go, girlie."

Jules smacked her hand on mine. "I'll put the salad in the fridge and get changed."

I showered, dressed in blue skinny jeans and an off-the-shoulder top then walked through to the living room. Jules, dressed in jeans and a tight vest, brought in the pasta salad.

"Sweet chili chicken. Okay?"

I mixed the chicken around in the pasta. "Good for me. Thanks, babe."

Jules dug her fork in. "So, how was it in work today with Jason's father being in the office instead of Jason?"

"Pretty dire at first. You could have heard a pin drop. But better once the windows were covered. Jason phoned me just before you got back from work. He's found an interesting little piece of spyware on his laptop. Ad hoc, not something that's come in from the net. He wants Gary to take a look at it when he gets back."

"What's it spying on, as if I couldn't guess?"

I smiled. "Jason thinks so, too. He said it records his personal data."

"Someone's determined then. Has he got any idea who, yet?"

"Not yet. That's what he'd like Gary to look for. Plenty of people can code. Pre-prepared on a memory stick, the spyware could have been installed onto Jason's laptop in a just a couple of minutes while he was out of his office."

My phone vibrated on the coffee table. Jules' vibrated on the arm of the sofa. I picked mine up and saw a message in my inbox from Ryan. Jules showed me the same name in hers. We opened the messages together.

Hey, all. I'm home and sitting in The Vine. Anyone coming in for a glass tonight?

Jules smiled. "You ready to head down?"

"Yeah. Let's go and find out what he's been up to. I bet he's got a few stories to tell us."

Chapter Eleven

Jules pushed open the door to The Vine twenty minutes later and I followed her in. Ryan, tan and lean, his hair as black as mine, stood with his back against the bar, talking to his audience of Steve, Paula and Ben.

"And the rocket festival at Yasothon? Well, just totally amazing." Ryan smiled at me and Jules as we walked over. "Long time, no see, you two."

I kissed Ryan's cheek. Jules did the same and Ben poured us each a glass from the bottle. Ten minutes later, Mark and Simon walked through the door with Nick and Josh — Ben's tenants — one step behind them and our circle of stools expanded, with Ryan holding center stage as he took us with him back to Thailand. I pulled my phone out of my pocket as he reached the elephants at the Mork Fa waterfall, saw that it was one a.m. and texted Jason.

Hey, you. Good morning. You up and about and brekkie time for you?

Hey, you, yes. You under your quilt now?

Not yet. Still at The Vine. Everyone's called in.

Tinkerbell, Captain Hook and the angelic pair?

For sure. With Jules and Ben. And Josh and Nick and Ryan just back from Thailand. And I refuse to believe the elephant stuck its trunk where he just said it did!

Eyes watering over my bacon here.

I saw the male faces in our circle in various stages of wincing while Jules and Paula laughed. I took a quick pic and sent it to Jason with a text.

Yep.

Ouch! Nellie looks like she's been very naughty. Phone you after work again?

Yeah, please. Going home shortly.

Speak tonite. xx

Enjoy your lunch. Until later.

I put my glass on the bar. "I'm out of here, guys."
Jules and Ben stood their glasses alongside mine.
"With you, girlie," Jules said.
Ben offered Jules one arm and me the other. I blew kisses over my shoulder at the others still finishing their drinks and walked with Ben and Jules over to the street door and home. I kissed Jules' cheek then Ben's

as Jules shut the front door behind us and messaged Jason as I pulled my quilt over my legs.

Under my quilt now. Wish you were too. x

I so wish too. x

I put my phone beside my bed and turned my face to my pillow.

The moon hid behind the trees to leave the path a dark trip-hazard of exposed, misshapen tree roots for us to find. I grabbed Jules' hand to steady myself and giggled into the warm night air as I stumbled. Jules giggled beside me.

"Shouldn't 'ave had the last one, Ness."

"The B-52 or the pinta pina colada?"

Jules lurched against me as her shoe snagged and caught. I laughed and pushed her upright again.

"Both. Should'a got a taxi, though."

"Only gotta get through the par –"

Jules' chin hit her chest and her knees crumpled as the back of my head exploded with pain from a curled fist that I glimpsed out of the corner of my eye as my legs gave way. My butt hit the path and my scream joined Jules'. I screamed again, kicked out with my foot and caught the thigh of the chunky male, closing the gap between us with the high heel of my shoe.

"Fuck! You bitch!"

The man made a grab for my ankle. I bought my other leg up, caught his thigh again with the heel of my other shoe and screamed louder. Jules' shrill cry cut off with a crack of bone on bone.

"What the fuck are you doin', man?"

"She's kicking me."

"Just shut 'er the fuck up!"

The man lurched forward, dropped his weight onto my legs, used it to stifle my struggles and cut off my voice with a hand clamped over my mouth and nose as I writhed beneath him.

I fought for breath, aimed desperate fingernails at the brown eyes showing beneath a knitted hat pulled down low and flashes of light swam before my eyes as a swinging arm connected with the side of my head.

"Get the fuck on with it! I've got the other one's jewelry and bag."

My lungs cried out for air, the hand left my face and I screamed into darkness as the tiara left my head.

"No! You can't have it — "

My eyes fluttered open and I sat up. My bedroom light turned on and I blinked in the brighter light at Jules standing in the doorway.

"Ness, you okay? You didn't make the bathroom?"

Jules looked at the floor on the side of my bed. I blinked the last whispers of the dream away. "It changed. It was different. It didn't go through to the end..."

Jules pushed my bedroom door shut and sat on my bed. "It changed? What? You haven't been sick?"

"It stopped before the worst bit, after he says, 'get the jewelry'. I wasn't wearing my jewelry. I was wearing the tiara I saw on the artwork. Then the dream finished and I woke up."

"Oh, my God! Way to go! What are you thinking? That because the tiara doesn't really exist, the dream had nowhere to go?"

"Maybe that and maybe that nothing's happened to the artwork yet."

"Jason must really be under your skin if what might happen to him has overridden what happened to us in your head. Will you tell him?"

I shook my head. "No. I'm not laying that on him. If Jason and I carry on seeing each other, it's got to be for reasons other than this."

Jules squeezed my hand. "Sorry babe, but I take your point. If nothing does happen to the artwork and it goes back to the bank safe and sound, then that particular worry goes with it and you might still get the full nightmare back."

I returned the squeeze. "Yeah, I know, happy as I am to have escaped halfway through tonight. Go back to bed. I'm fine and you've got to be up for work in a couple of hours."

Jules turned my light out and I lay back on my pillow, tossed and turned then gave up just after six and got up for an early shower. My phone vibrated as I sat at my dressing table to put my makeup on.

Hey, you. Good morning. You up and getting ready for work? Just finishing lunch here again.

Hey, you. Yep and yep. How's lunch? Polite or messy?

Very polite. Very long. Mr. Linn and his eldest daughter who runs Linn's sales team. I know now why I don't work in sales and marketing!

Tell me tonight?

For sure. Speak later.

I finished my makeup and had time for two mugs of coffee before leaving the flat to catch the bus to work. I smiled at Maisie and Annie when I saw the blinds closed as I sat and waited for them to leave the office to do a coffee run at ten before I dialed Dad at home.

"Hi, darling. You've called from work. Is everything okay?"

"Yeah, everything's fine, but it's work I'm calling about. Someone here has a problem with their laptop and they'd like Gary to check it out. Could you text his contact details to me so I can pass them on?"

"Serious enough to involve Gary, is it?"

"I think so. A nasty piece of spyware has been installed on the laptop, possibly by someone in-house."

"Ah, yes. Best get it checked off site then. It wouldn't happen to be Belmond's F.D.'s laptop, by any chance?"

"How do you know he's that?"

Dad laughed down the line. "Because Belmond's have a fairly comprehensive 'contact us' listing for their staff on their website and there's only one Jason on it."

I tutted. "There might be another one not listed from the cleaning service or the catering franchise."

"Oh, yeah, and they all have laptops full of the type of confidential data that would need Gary's services, do they?"

"Absolutely. The recipe for the chef's secret salad dressing and where the cache of spare furniture polish is hidden."

Dad laughed again. "Oh, absolutely vital. I'm sure Belmond's would come to a grinding halt if either of those got out."

The office door opened. Annie and Maisie walked in. "Got to go. A couple of pairs of interested ears on the horizon here."

"Okay, darling. Gary's details coming straight up."

"Thanks, Dad."

I cut the call as Annie handed me a coffee. Then I forwarded Dad's text to Jason when it came in but with some extra kisses after I sipped. I carried on working until my phone vibrated just before lunch. I answered a call from Liz at my employment agency.

"Hi, Liz. Something up?"

"Hi, Vanessa. Not as such, but I'm in a bit of a fix and I'm trying to rally some troops."

"Fire away then. What for?"

"I'm hosting a seminar here on Thursday morning. I've got HR from a couple of big potential clients coming in and I need a full room. I've had so many pull outs. Would you attend? Just for the morning, please? If I clear it with Belmond's HR?"

"Yeah, I suppose I could, as long as Belmond's is okay with it. What time?"

"Thanks, Vanessa. It'll be much appreciated next time something juicy hits the books. It's a nine o'clock start and don't worry about Belmond's. I'll get straight on to them now."

"See you Thursday, then. Bye." I ended the call and looked at Maisie. "That was my agency. I won't be in Thursday morning. I've got to attend a seminar."

Maisie looked over my shoulder at Jason's office. "I should have Jason's contact number. This should be cleared with him. I'm a section leader. I should be able to speak to him in person when things like this come up."

I shrugged. "My agency has already squared it with HR here, but you could always have a word with Mr. Belmond if you're worried. He's doing Jason's job while he's away, isn't he?"

Maisie pulled her eyes away from Jason's office. "No, no. That's fine if HR knows about it." Maisie gazed over my shoulder. "Still, I expect Jason would welcome a phone call from me. It's nice to hear a voice from home when you're away. Dawn's posted on Facebook that she loves the hotel. I could have chatted to Jason about it. See if he does, too."

I left Maisie to gaze her daydreams into thin air and pulled my keyboard forward. Annie smiled as the office door opened and Craig walked in. He perched on the side of her workstation, winked and smiled at her.

"Do you want to get out of here for an hour and get some lunch?"

Annie nodded. Craig looked at Maisie and me. "My treat, girls, if you want to come with."

Maisie stood. "I could do with an hour out of here today."

Annie picked up her handbag. "Vanessa, are you coming?"

I hid a yawn behind my hand as my restless night caught up with me. "I won't, thanks. I didn't sleep well last night. I'll take a shorter lunch and leave a bit early."

I visited the canteen after they'd gone, bought myself a snack and ate it at my desk. Annie and Maisie walked into the office just after two. Maisie looked at the closed blinds of Jason's office as she sat and put her phone on her desk. "Dawn's just posted that they have a free evening out there at the moment. They're going to hit some bars in the city. I wonder if Jason's with them. Oh, God! Door alert."

Annie and Maisie turned their faces to their screens as Peter walked past. I worked on, printed my hard copy and took the chance when I dropped them off to ask each of the offices that received them a few questions about what they used them for so I could complete my flowchart for Jason. I walked out of the office before five and opened the front door of the flat before six.

Jules called from the living room as I shut the front door. "Hey, babe. How was your day?"

I walked into the living room and Jules poured me a glass.

"Nothing good, nothing bad. Liz phoned from the agency and I get to jib out of Belmond's input duty on Thursday morning for a seminar. What about you?"

"I had a good one. Lots of people through the door and Ben had free time, so he came over and we went out for lunch. We've managed to book back-row seats for the cinema tonight. Do you want to come with?"

I sipped and sat on the sofa. "No, I'm good. Thanks, babe. I've got something work-related I said I'd do for Jason. I'll get on with that tonight."

Jules smiled. "Okay. I picked us up some supper. The deli had their garlic mushrooms in white wine and cream in the chiller so I bought us some."

I toasted Jules with my glass. "Wow. Real posh nosh."

Jules chinked her glass on mine and assumed her best totty voice. "I think I should get the table cloth and candles out."

I stuck my nose in the air. "Oh, absolutely! And I will iron the napkins and we shall dine with our pinky fingers up and drink champagne out of our crystal flutes."

Jules mirrored my move with her nose. "Baldrick, have we got any or is there a fault in your cunning plan?"

"Damn it, yes! One plate, two forks and a lump of kitchen roll coming straight up."

Jules laughed as my phone vibrated. I giggled as I answered it, blew Jules a kiss when I heard Jason's voice and took my glass with me to my bedroom.

"I can hear Jules laughing—and you. What's set you two off?"

"Our range of fine dining facilities—or, more, our lack of them. How's you? Just finished fine dining yourself, I hope."

"Yep. Well, not fine dining but better than lunch. I had dinner, Western style, in the hotel with another interested party."

"Not out bar hopping in the city with the rest of your merry band, then?"

I heard the smile in Jason's voice. "Nope. How did you know that's where they were?"

"Maisie's in touch on Facebook with someone called Dawn."

"She's one of Mike's marketing team who seems to be enjoying herself immensely, unlike some of us."

"Lunch was that dire, was it?"

"Oh, God, it was awful! I'd walk to and from the convention center all day long rather than sit through another lunch like that. I'm really not cut out for this polite sales and marketing stuff. It went for just about ever, and the more I heard, the more I'm not sure about Mr. Linn and his company. That's why Mike and I had dinner with the marketing guy from another company tonight."

"What's putting you off Linn's?"

"Mainly because what they seem to have in mind is a mass production. I know we're a bit along that way ourselves for the non-commissioned pieces in the showrooms, but at the end of the day, our pieces are still all hand-worked and Linn's wants to use laser robotics."

"And the other interested party at dinner?"

"Is about to back a film to be produced by a major American studio. One of those adult, fantasy-type epics and they'd like to feature the tiara as the magical object in it. A version of it would be made as part of the film's merchandise afterward and it would be our workshops that would produce them, although the contract won't be worth as much as the percentage deal Linn's are offering."

"So, you've been sitting there working it through?"

"Yeah. We're hosting dinner for Linn's tomorrow night and I'll speak to the film production company again sometime tomorrow. What are you up to tonight? Going out?"

"Not tonight. I should really go do an hour in the gym but I've got a few friends I need to catch up with, so I'm jibbing out and doing that with a couple of glasses instead."

"Feeling the effects of your unexpected late one last night? What have you eaten? Not more dried noodles?"

I laughed. "Excuse me. It's fine dining here tonight. We have mushrooms in white wine and cream."

"Cooked by?"

"By the local deli."

Jason laughed. "Thought so. I'll cook them properly for you when I come home."

Jules opened my door. "Sorry, babe. Supper in five before I go?"

I nodded.

"Go and eat, baby. It's nearly two here. I ought to sleep."

"You should. Speak tomorrow?"

"I'll text you in your morning after my lunch."

"Have a good one. Sleep well, my angel."

"Never that when I'm thinking of you."

"Thinking of you, too."

I blew a kiss the phone, cut the connection and walked into the living room for supper. Ben arrived just as I wiped a last piece of bread through my sauce and I loaded a flowchart graphic on my laptop as they walked out of the door. Three hours later I saved the completed file, shut my laptop and cuddled up under my quilt against Jason in my imagination.

* * * *

I woke when my alarm sounded and used the bathroom. My phone vibrated as I dried my hair.

Hey, good morning, you. Have just finished a great lunch. Feeling the buzz from it. Wish you were here with me.

I smiled at my phone.

Hey, good morning, back. Wish too. Up and out of bed and getting ready for work here.

Mmmm. Bed. Call you when I'm back from dinner with Linn's tonight? x

Mmmm. Yes. Speak later. x

I finished getting ready, smiled good morning at Maisie and Annie when I arrived at work, and with nothing more difficult than another bout of repetitive input to occupy my brain, let my thoughts roam over to Beijing and Jason while I worked. I picked up a ham sandwich at lunchtime, thought of Jason just starting dinner as I sat at my desk with it and hoped that his dinner with Linn's would be less tiresome for him than his lunch with them had been. I tossed my wrapper into the bin when I finished and worked until just before four when Maisie's phone vibrated on her desk. She moved her fingers over the screen and swore under breath. "What the fuck?"

Annie walked around to her workstation and looked over Maisie's shoulder. "Shit! Show them to Vanessa, Maisie. See what she thinks."

Maisie glared at her phone and held it out. "Dawn's posted these on Facebook. Looks cozy, don't you think?"

I took Maisie's phone, looked at the screen and came face to face with Jason dressed in a dark suit, a white shirt, a blue-and-silver striped tie, his eyes clear and green looking out at me and standing next to a Chinese girl wearing an embroidered silk dress hugged tight to her small, neat body. Her arm was through his, her brown eyes gazing up at him. I read the words underneath the picture. *Dinner at Tiger Lily restaurant. Jason and Su Linn.*

I scrolled down and saw Jason and Su Linn sitting side by side at a restaurant table, Jason's hand laid on the table top with Su Linn's fingers resting on it while she smiled up at him as he gazed at her, his eyes warm and green. The expression in them was one I knew and couldn't be mistaken for anything else. My heart raced and my hand shook. I took a deep breath and managed to keep my hand steady as I handed Maisie her phone and shrugged. "A bit, but I don't see the problem. Jason's a single guy."

Maisie flicked her finger on Su Linn's face. "Dawn said this girl, Su Linn, is the daughter of the guy that owns the company that Belmond's is hoping will place the big order. I'll forgive him this one as he's away, but once we're going out together, he's not going anywhere like this again on his own."

I thought of what I knew about Jason and looked at Maisie. "I'm guessing here that Jason and Su Linn didn't know Dawn was taking the photo? That Dawn picked up her phone as if she was looking at something else on it and just snapped the pics without saying anything?"

Maisie glared at her phone. "I suppose so. She's not likely to have asked them to pose for her, is she? Why? Do you think they could get her in trouble?"

"I'm thinking they might. It's one thing to cop a cheeky shot and share it with your friends, but Dawn's posted those pics online for everyone to see. It's a company business trip that Dawn's on, not a private holiday."

Maisie smiled. "Good. I hope they do. Dawn posted those pics on Facebook just to wind me up because she knows how I feel about Jason. Girls like her are just so jealous of me that they can't help it."

I thought of Jason. "How long ago were they posted? You could give Dawn the heads-up and she could delete them before too many people see them."

Maisie looked at her phone and didn't. "About three hours ago and no way. Definitely not. Dawn can get everything that's coming to her, as far as I'm concerned."

I sat at my desk and picked up my phone. My heart raced as my head begged, *please, don't have*, and I messaged Jason.

Maisie's just shown me her phone. Dawn has posted pics of you on Facebook that I really don't think you're going to want out there.

I put my phone in my pocket, tidied my desk, opened the door of the flat shortly after six and sat on the sofa with a glass of wine. My phone beside me on the sofa arm, I leaned back and closed my eyes as it stayed silent of Jason's promised after-dinner phone call or any message from him to say why he hadn't. The photo of him and Su Linn had wedged itself into my mind.

I opened my eyes as Jules' rattled her key in the front door lock and realized that I'd been sitting for more than an hour with thoughts of a me-sized empty bed and a me-shaped available alternative going round and round in my imagination until nothing but the obvious remained. I picked up my glass as she walked into the sitting room.

"Hey, babe. Do you fancy going out?"

"Sorry. I'm away with fairies here. I saw some pics of Jason in China at work today. I was sitting here mulling them over."

Jules walked into the kitchen. "I'll get a wine. Did Jason send some pics to your phone?"

"No. I haven't heard from him since this morning. Maisie got some pics on Facebook from one of the girls on the marketing team out there."

"Any good? What were they of?" Jules sat and took a mouthful of wine.

"Ah, no, not good really. They were of Jason out having dinner with a girl called Su Linn, both looking totally wrapped up in each other."

Jules coughed as she swallowed. "Shit, babe! I didn't see that one coming."

"No, neither did I. That's why I've been sitting here thinking it over."

"And how are you feeling about it?"

I pushed the pics out of my head, took a breath in through my nose to combat the rolling motion in the pit of my stomach and took a big chug from my glass. "Like a bit of an idiot for reading the situation with Jason wrong and thinking that what we had going on between us was special enough that Jason wouldn't want to have sex with any other girl but me at the moment the same as I don't want to have sex with any other guy but him."

Jules squeezed my hand.

"Ness, are you absolutely sure Jason was up for sex with this girl? I really thought he was more into you than that."

I chugged a big mouthful from my glass as the photo on Maisie's phone floated into my mind and I saw Jason looking down at Su Linn with the same look in his eyes that I saw when he wanted me. "Jules, I saw the pics, and believe me. Jason looked more than happy to be exactly where he was with Su Linn. The pic might as well have had speech bubbles on it. Her gazing up at him, *Come to bed?* Him, *Yum, yes please.* I sent Jason a text when I saw the pics to tell him they were on Facebook but he hasn't replied and it's two in the morning over there now."

Jules looked at me. "So, you're thinking that Jason's either ignored your message or not even looked at his phone because he's busy with Su Linn as the desert course?"

"Yeah. I am. I texted Jason nearly three hours ago. They must have had a decent phone signal at the restaurant or Dawn couldn't have posted the pics. I know the one at his hotel is okay. He should have received my message in one place or the other by now and replied if he's not, ah…otherwise occupied."

Jules topped up our glasses. "So, what are you going to do?"

"To tell you the truth, babe. I don't know. I don't think I can do friendly friends with Jason and share him with other girls. The thought of what Jason's probably doing with Su Linn as we sit here talking about it is absolutely churning my guts up."

Jules looked at my face. "You're thinking of letting him go, aren't you?"

I ignored the roll of my stomach, along with the unpleasant thump of my heart and nodded as I swallowed two mouthfuls of wine, one after the other. "I think I might have to. We both know it doesn't work when one person cares more than the other, and much as Jason has been great about it so far, I still carry my own personal world of shit around with me. If what we've got isn't as special as I thought, then Jason will meet someone else who isn't carrying the baggage I am in the end and leg it like Tim did. Letting Jason go now will hurt, but not half as much as hanging on and still being around when that happens."

"I'm sorry, Ness. I really am. But don't make your mind up until you've heard what Jason's got to say about the pics. Let's get out of here. Go down to The Vine. I expect you'll get a message one way or the other sometime tonight."

I thought about it and looked at Jules as my stomach informed me it would still like to be sick. "Would you mind if I didn't? I don't think I can pretend I'm okay in front of everyone in the bar."

"I'll stay home with you then."

313

"No, Jules. It's fine. I wouldn't mind some time alone to think what I should say to Jason, depending on what he says to me."

Jules finished her glass and stood. "If that's what you need, then sure. But let me know if you hear anything as soon as you do. I can always run home if you need me."

I gave a small smile. Jules left the room and came back ready to go an hour later. I switched the telly on for some background noise after she left then glanced at my phone every ten minutes until I gave in and took a shower at eleven.

After I changed into short pajamas, I wandered back into the living room to watch some more telly with an occasional restless circuit of the sofa as my heart raced and my knees wobbled as more time passed and it became more obvious that whatever else Jason was doing, it hadn't involved looking at his phone all night. Jules opened the front door just after midnight. "Nothing yet?" she asked.

I shook my head. "Not a bean. How was The Vine? Do you want a coffee?"

"If you're having one."

I nodded. "One cup then I'm giving up and going to bed."

I boiled the kettle, poured it onto the coffee in the cafetière and took it with two mugs to the coffee table. My phone vibrated on the arm of the sofa and my hand shook as I picked it up and opened a message from Jason.

Sorry. I've only just looked at my phone. Thanks for the heads up. I'd best get downstairs to breakfast, find Dawn and sort it.

I handed my phone to Jules. Jules frowned as she read. "That's it, is it? What do you think?"

I poured the coffee. "Only just looked at my phone from eleven in the evening until seven in the morning? I wonder why that was, is what I'm thinking. And if there's any other reason for not looking at your phone other than the one I'm thinking of, why not say? My text warning him the pics are dodgy has sat there unanswered on his phone for hours."

Jules squeezed my arm. "Sorry, babe. But hang in there at least until Jason's seen the actual pics. You really like Jason, so see what he says before you make up your mind whether to cut and run."

"Maybe, but not tonight. I've done enough sitting around waiting to hear from Jason today. My phone's going in my drawer on silent and the way I'm feeling right now, I might or might not get around to looking at it tomorrow." I put my mug of untasted coffee on the table. "I'm going to hit the sheets, Jules, and I mean it. I'm not looking at my phone again tonight. Whatever Jason wants to say to me can wait now on my wanting to hear it. I'll see you in the morning."

"Night, Ness. Try and get some sleep."

I buried my phone in the middle of my underwear, set my manual alarm clock in place of my phone alarm, tossed and turned for most of the night, slept through the unfamiliar ring tones of my alarm and woke late for Liz's seminar. I rushed down the street to jump on the bus after the quickest of showers, realized I'd left my phone at home with my knickers and thought, *Sod it*.

Liz was waiting in reception with a clipboard when I arrived at the agency's office. She ticked my name off her list, smiled and gestured to a table that stood at the side of the room.

"Thanks for coming, Vanessa. There's tea and coffee if you'd like some."

"Thanks, Liz. Could I use your landline to make a quick call? I've left my mobile at home and I should let my flat mate know that I have."

Liz nodded. "Sure. On the desk. Dial nine for an outside line."

I dialed Jules' number, got her voicemail, told it I'd left my mobile at home and I would pick it up as I left the seminar at lunchtime before I returned to work. Liz called everyone in to the meeting room as I put the handset down and I sat on a seat at the back and didn't hear more than one word in ten of the presentation as I wondered whether Jason had called or messaged me yet.

The bus took forever to get home through the midday traffic and it was nearly two as I let myself into the flat. I retrieved my phone from my drawer and saw two missed calls and two messages from Jason, a message from Jules and no voicemail. I opened Jason's message sent to my knickers at one-thirty in the morning.

I've just seen the pics. They've been deleted now. I'm sorry you had to see them, baby. I'll call you.

I viewed my call log and saw a missed call from Jason at one thirty-five as I'd tossed and turned in bed and another at nine as I'd arrived at the seminar and opened Jason's second message sent two minutes after his missed call.

Wanted to talk to you about Su Linn, not just text. Call me?

I opened Jules' message.

Have had Jason on the landline at work. Call me.

I called Jules and she answered on the third ring.

"Hey, babe. Where are you?"

"I've just got home and looked at my mobile. Why did Jason ring you?"

"Because he couldn't get hold of you on your phone and he tried the office and they told him you weren't in work. He knew where I worked so he tried here to ask where were you and were you okay?"

"And you said?"

"That you had other things to do at your agency this morning and had left your phone at home, so wouldn't be answering it. Then he said he'd had problems with his phone last night."

"Did he? Go on then, spit it out."

"He got a cab back to his hotel and there was a pile up and he got stuck in a traffic jam for over three hours with no phone signal, and while he was in it, his phone battery died, and when he got back to his hotel, he put his phone on to charge then fell asleep, which he didn't mean to do."

"Jason didn't say where he was when he got in the cab? Like the restaurant?"

"No, sorry. You thinking he could have still have been doing bedtime with Su Linn but maybe not all night?"

"Yeah. I've had a couple of texts from him but nothing in them that tells me anything different than the pic of him gazing 'come to bed' at Su Linn. What did you say to him when he asked you if I was okay?"

Jules apologized. "Sorry, Ness. I laughed. Jason has seen his face in that pic now. If it's anything different to what it seems, he should have let you know, and he surely knows it's not okay to do bed bouncing with another girl without at least dropping a hint in the direction of anyone else he also happens to be sleeping with."

"You'd have thought. What did you say after you laughed?"

"I wasn't too bad. I put on a false, happy voice and said. 'Oh, Ness is fine. Why wouldn't she be? It just might have been a little politer to give her a heads up before the event rather than let her walk into it cold.' Then he said okay and he'd call you later then hung up."

I breathed in deeply as my heart beat in time to my stomach rolling over.

"Then I'm not going to take his call. Jason's a free agent and he can sleep with whoever he likes but I don't want to hear him say it. You were right when you said Jason's under my skin. I can't do friendly friends this time. I'd rather let him go than share him with other girls."

"Ness, shouldn't you at least take his call?"

"I can't, Jules. I can't get what that pic is telling me out of my head, and if sleeping with Su Linn is what Jason comes out with, I'll blub. If I don't take his call, he'll text instead and I can answer it without sounding like a sniveling idiot."

I looked at the time and saw two-thirty.

"I'm not going to bother going into work now. It's so late that it's not worth it. I'll phone Liz."

"Okay. I'll see you at home. I won't be late."

I phoned Liz and invented a sudden severe migraine, changed out of my work clothes, poured an early glass of wine, sat on the sofa and sipped while I looked at the blank screen on my phone. It vibrated with an incoming call half a glass later. *Jason.* My heart thumped harder, my stomach joined in and I wanted to be sick as I ignored my phone's soft buzz. It jumped again a couple of minutes later with a message.

Still not got your phone? I want to talk to you rather than just text to tell you about Su Linn. I'll try to call again in a little while.

I didn't reply as my head told me, *eek, no thanks* but finished the end of my glass and walked to the kitchen to top it up as Jules opened the front door home from work early. I poured a second glass, handed it to her and took another mouthful of mine as we sat on the sofa and I passed her my phone. Jules read Jason's message thread.

"Sorry, babe. I see what you mean. There's nothing here on Jason's texts to tell you any different to the pics and this last one? Just the wording of it. He wants to tell you about Su Linn. That doesn't sound good to me. Jason would think you'd be cool with hearing about someone else he's sleeping with, wouldn't he?"

I picked up my glass and chugged. "Yeah. Why, wouldn't he? I've found his previous history on the subject nothing but a hoot and Jason knows that James has been a friend with benefits. When we found out about Cheryl that night in The Vine, it was only with smiles all around."

"You haven't replied. Are you going to?"

"I am, but it's difficult. Finding the words to say, 'It's fine, I'm cool, no sniveling idiots here,' when I'm not and I am. Think I've got it now, though."

I took my phone from Jules and typed in my reply.

I'll pass on the courtesy call, thanks. A text before the pics would have been appreciated but Jules let me know you had traffic and phone problems, so no worries. Have fun if you're out tonight.

Jules read over my shoulder. "Well, he won't be able to mistake that for anything other than 'I'm cool. I don't give a shit.'"

"Okay. Good. I need to be able to face him fake it in work next week."

I pressed send. My inbox pinged five minutes later.

Ouch. Sorry, and point taken. I kept anything about the pics out of my texts because it would have taken an essay. Should have said something rather than nothing, though. Just wanted to talk to you.

Jules looked over my shoulder as I read. "Perhaps he hasn't slept with her then."

My heart squeezed in my chest and I picked up my glass. "Perhaps... What would you do if it was Ben?"

"Now that we're going out-out, I'd just ask. Before? Well, it just wouldn't have come up, would it? There's unwritten rules for sleeping with friends and both sides know what they are or you steer clear in the first place."

I swallowed a mouthful and put my glass down. "You're right. Jason and I have never said we're going out-out together, so I can't ask. I can only go friends with benefits, casual rules."

I tapped.

As I said. No worries. Essays etc. not needed for something that's no concern of mine.

My phone vibrated five minutes later.

Ow, and double ouch. But got it. I won't phone if you don't want me to. Out of here now. See you when I get home.

Jules slipped her arm around my waist. "Sorry, babe. You okay?"

"Not really. My innards are doing a shake, rattle and roll of the non-dancing kind. But it's my choice. It's me that can't share. I need to go and work this off for a while."

"You okay for Ben to come over? We were going to order some food in but I can cancel or we can do it at his."

I blinked to stop the threatened tears from forming. "Whichever suits you, babe. I need a bit of solitary tonight. I'll use the gym and swing straight into bed after."

With my trainers on, I let myself out of the flat and into the gym then lifted, pushed and pulled weighted pads until my sweat poured and my knees trembled with a threat to refuse to hold my weight any longer.

I let myself in to the flat, showered the sweat away, lay on my bed, loaded the selfie Jason had sent me from Spain on my phone screen and allowed the tears to pour down my face in a silent torrent until my eyes promised to look like two bruised gooseberries in the morning if I didn't stop. I blew my nose, turned my pillow to the dry side and the hours crept past.

Chapter Twelve

I opened my eyes to daylight and realized my gym work had rewarded me with some unexpected sleep. Movement outside my bedroom told me Ben and Jules were up and I walked into my bathroom and looked in the mirror at the bit-too-large panda eyes and puffy skin but nothing that some extra concealer and foundation couldn't cope with.

Once I'd showered, I dried my hair and peered into my dressing table mirror to see the hot, steamy water had reduced the puffiness of my skin, although not the dark shadows under my eyes, picked up my concealer and worked my makeup over my face.

Jules called through my bedroom door. "Out of here, girlie. Coffee's still hot in the jug in the kitchen."

I tested my voice and found it didn't squeak. "Thanks, babe. I'll grab a cup then I'm out of here, too."

The front door clicked shut as I zipped up my skirt and slipped my feet into my shoes. The intercom in the hall buzzed as I poured a coffee and I ignored it in favor of my phone's vibration and a message from Jules.

Doggie doo-doo? Brace yourself, girlie! Have just seen J in the lobby. He's on his way up.

My hand shook as my heart leapt. *He's flown home early!* My head interrupted. *So, what's changed?*

The intercom sounded again. I took a deep breath in and walked to the front door telling myself, *Okay. Play it cool. Do not act like an idiot.* I reached for the door latch, pasted every ounce of 'not-bothered-friendly-friend-surprise' I could manage onto my face and employed my best interview technique as I swung the door open, focused my gaze on Jason's nose and smiled.

"Jason? I thought you didn't fly home until tomorrow? Sorry. You've caught me just as I'm out of here."

Jason reached out his hand. I ignored it and he winced.

"Ouch and double ouch, Ness. The pics really upset you, then? I thought they had, although it took me a while to get it."

I shrugged against the harder thump of my heart. "Nothing about me that's looking upset here, I think."

"Apart from that you're not looking at me."

Jason put his finger under my chin and tilted my face. I gazed at his forehead.

"The pics weren't true, Ness. Dawn snapped them out of context."

I lifted my chin off Jason's finger and bit it, hard. "How lovely of you to say so…eventually."

Jason re-offered his finger to my lips. "Again? If it means you won't shut the door in my face."

I looked at Jason, saw the same dark shadow beneath his eyes that I had disguised by my makeup and stepped back a pace.

"The coffee's still warm if you want one?"

The start of a smile lifted Jason's lips as he stepped over the doorstep and followed me to the kitchen. I filled a mug, handed it over and took mine to the sofa. Jason sat beside me. I toed of my shoes, tucked my legs up beside me, shuffled farther up the sofa as I did and widened the gap between us. "So?"

Jason put his mug on the coffee table and held his arm out.

"No. I need you closer. It's why I wouldn't text it."

I looked at Jason, saw the crease of a worry line in between his eyebrows and shuffled closer. Jason took my mug, put it beside his and scooped me onto his lap. I breathed him in and wrapped my arms around his neck. Jason spoke into my ear.

"Su Linn might have been looking at me like that but I wasn't looking at her, sweetheart. I was looking at you…at the pic of us on my phone. She tried to pick my phone up. I covered it with my hand and Dawn snapped the pic. The first pic was just another lucky shot, taken just before I removed Su Linn's arm from mine for about the twentieth time."

I pressed closer and nuzzled Jason's neck. "I thought you wanted to tell me you'd done bedtime with her. I didn't want to hear it."

"I should have told you before I went away, shouldn't I? I don't want anyone but you, baby. It's been that way for me since the start. I'm only yours. You mine?"

I held on tighter. "Yes. Only yours and only mine. I can't share you with anyone else."

"No sharing, sweetheart. You're mine. I'm yours."

I tilted my face for Jason's kiss and sighed as our lips parted.

"Take me to bed, please. I've missed you so much."

"Yes, my beautiful girl. I've wanted you so much this week."

Jason walked us to my bedroom and over to the bed. I tugged on Jason's tee, searching for skin as he lay beside me, unbuttoning my shirt. I shrugged it off and then my skirt and underwear as Jason shrugged out of his jeans and underwear, his cock erect. I was damp with my need for him.

I reached for Jason and parted my legs to his fingers. Jason lay over me, withdrew his fingers, replaced them with the tip of his cock and moved the length of his shaft inside me. I moaned as he filled me.

"Jason, I need you."

"Sweetheart, yes. I need you, too."

Jason kissed my lips. I wrapped my legs around his thighs and lifted my pelvis to feel his cock on every inch of softness inside me, ground my hips against him as he thrust—hard, fast and urgent. Jason groaned. His movements shortened and I moaned it out as muscles in my groin tightened. "Jason... Oh, God!"

"Ness, yes."

I stilled, panting. Jason kissed me "I bumped my flight when you didn't pick up my calls but I didn't really get it until your last two texts. You told me one-on-one relationships hadn't come your way and I should have known that if I didn't say anything about the pictures first, you wouldn't ask, even if they had wound you up."

I stroked my fingers along Jason's jawline. "I didn't need an essay just for you to say."

Jason cupped my face. "You okay now?"

I smiled. "I am now. What about you? Are you tired? Did you sleep on the flight?"

"I didn't sleep much. I just wanted to get home and come to find you."

"Do you need to sleep now?"

Jason moved my hand to his mouth and kissed it. "No. I think I'd better stay up and get my head back in UK time."

"Tough one. East to west travel is the worst."

"I'll try and work through it. I could get my laptop over to Gary and drop the artwork in to work. It's going to stay on floor two for a few days with Nick and Harry before it goes back to the bank. Perhaps I'll have a word with Peter while I'm there."

I leaned up on my elbow. "Did you decide which company to work with?"

Jason smiled. "Xiao Pictures, the film company. I like the quality control we'd still have over the product and the extra jobs it will mean here. I told Mike I was coming home early and left him to work on the detail of the contract."

"Do Linn's know yet?"

Jason nodded and pushed his body higher up the bed. "Yeah. They were fine. Business is business. Win some, lose some, and although I could have worked with Linn's, I'm glad I don't have to."

I sat straighter and curled my legs beside me. "Nothing happened to the artwork while you were there, though? You brought it back with you?"

Jason took my hand and circled his thumb over my knuckles. "Yeah. I called in at mine and dropped it off in the flat with my suitcase before I came here. It'll be safe enough while it's in Nick's care on floor two, but

I'll be happier still when I can take it back to the bank. Why were you at your agency? An interview?"

"No. An employment seminar. A favor for Liz. She said she'd return it next time a graduate interview came up."

"Stay at Belmond's, Ness. Don't leave. A lot of the office working practices have fallen behind. It's going to be a full-time job bringing them up to date. Stay and do it with me. You could take your certified exams while you do."

I smiled. "Does this count as my first naked interview?"

Jason kissed the end of my nose. "Yep. And mine. First and only one, though, I hope."

"Then yes and yes."

"Good. I'll ask Jenny to work on the details and tell Peter this afternoon. I'll see you in there?"

I looked at the time on my phone.

"I should get there by one if I jump back in the shower now. I'll ring HR and excuse my lateness before I leave."

"I think I'll be there around three by the time I've picked up my laptop and been to see Gary. I'll be finished by five at the latest. Come to mine tonight? I'll have the car with me to bring the artwork in. We could come back here after work if you want to change then drive over to mine?"

I nodded. "Sure." Jason kissed my shoulder and swung his legs off the bed. "I'll head off and see you in the office. I'll bring you a coffee when I get in."

I put my feet to the floor and reached for my wrap. "Because?"

Jason picked up his clothes. "Because without putting an announcement in the staff magazine, the office might as well start getting used to the fact that we're on intimate coffee drinking terms."

I smiled. "Okay, but I think I'll forgo the brandy with this one."

"Then I shall bring you something more publicly acceptable."

I stood on tip-toes and nibbled Jason's chin. "Oh, will you? Then I'll see you in the office soon."

I wrapped a towel around my hair to keep it dry, showered the musk of our sex away and re-dressed for work. I bought a hot sausage roll and ate it at the bus stop, texted Jules what had happened with Jason for the length of my bus ride and walked past Gabriella's necklace in reception a few minutes after one. I lit up the lift call button and Jess walked out of the canteen door alongside the girl that sat opposite her in the accounts payable section.

"Hold the lift for us, Vanessa."

I put my foot in the way of the door. Jess smiled her thanks as they walked in. I pulled my foot away and the lift door closed.

"Thanks, Vanessa. I don't think you know Kallie, do you?"

I smiled hi at Kallie. She smiled at me. Jess looked at Kallie. "So, how do you think she did it? Screenshot and Photoshop?"

Kallie glanced at me.

Jess smiled. "Vanessa's okay. Don't worry. She won't pass the gossip back to where it's come from on this." She raised her eyebrows in my direction. "In fact, I think Vanessa really might like to hear this one."

Kallie smiled. "Okay, then."

Our floor arrived and we stepped outside.

"Come on. Coffee machine," Jess said.

We walked down the corridor and gathered in a circle around the coffee machine.

"I take it your Facebook news is up to date?" Jess said.

I took my cup from the dispenser and nodded. Jess tapped her own code into the machine and nudged Kallie. "Go on, then."

"Well…" Kallie said.

Jess and I leaned forward to listen.

"I was in the loo before I went to the canteen, in the end cubicle where the door outside doesn't show red when you lock it, and Maisie and Annie came in. I heard Annie giggle as I opened the cubicle door, and if looks could kill, when I came out" — Kallie ran a finger across her neck and pointed to the floor — "but I saw what was on Maisie's phone in the mirror and the Chinese connection isn't in that pic anymore, but Maisie certainly is."

I looked at Jess. She looked at me. I shrugged. "Pics aren't always true or even what they seem in the first place."

"You know that for sure?" Jess said.

"Yep. Absolutely."

"Why do I get the impression that you two are having a different conversation than I am?" Kallie said.

Jess laughed. "Because we are. Go on in. I'll walk back with Vanessa."

Kallie walked away with her coffee. I waited with Jess until Kallie pushed through the office door and we set off walking.

"Have you talked to him on the phone or something then?" Jess asked.

"Or something. Jason will be in the office this afternoon." I pushed the office door open.

Jess took the weight of it from me and nodded in Maisie's direction. "Hissy fit time?"

"I hope not, but I'm not holding my breath."

"Get your crash hat and body armor on, then."

I smiled. "I doubt it will come to that. After all, she might break a nail."

Jess laughed and we walked toward to my workstation. Maisie looked up as I pulled my chair out and sat. "I thought you said you weren't in work only yesterday morning."

"I did phone the agency yesterday. They'll have told HR here. Sorry if they didn't let you know as well."

Maisie tutted. "The weekly paid staff's overtime hours have to be input today or they'll be missing from the overnight payroll run."

I pulled my work tray forward. "It only takes half an hour. Surely you or Annie could have fitted it in if I wasn't here?"

"Certainly not. You're here to do the data input, not us."

I began to enter the figures of extra hours worked by cleaning staff into the payroll system with one eye on the time on my phone. The office door opened a few minutes after three and Jason walked into the office, his laptop bag on his shoulder, a cup of coffee in each hand, dressed in suit trousers but tieless and wearing an 'I'm not officially in work today' short-sleeved shirt.

Jason stopped at my workstation and put the coffee cups down. Maisie looked up. Annie looked over. Jason took his laptop bag off his shoulder and unzipped it. "Did you get some lunch?"

I nodded. "Sure. A hot sausage roll from Greggs."

Jason shook his head. "As suspected. Something quick with double grease so you could get here by one."

Jason reached into his bag, took a fruit pot of grapes and strawberries out of it and put it beside my coffee, picked up his own cup and walked to his office.

Maisie watched Jason walk away then looked at me. "What the hell? You knew he was back. What's going on? You had better bloody well not be…"

I peeled the lid off of the fruit pot. "Not be what?"

Maisie hissed across the desk. "He's mine. You know it. I've told you often enough. You had just bloody well better not have."

I looked into Maisie's eyes. "And as I've told *you* more than once, saying 'he's mine' isn't enough to make it true. Jason's not yours and never was. He's a single guy. I'm a single girl. The rest of it is no concern of yours."

Maisie stared a full glare of icy blue. "You won't win this. He'll realize in the end that I'm the one and when he does, you'll find out you're just another girl he's wasted his time on, like the one in China."

Maisie stood and looked at Annie. Jess appeared at my workstation and perched her butt on it. "Annie…loo. Now," Maisie said.

"All good here with you, Vanessa?" Jess said.

Annie walked out of the office behind Maisie. I offered the fruit pot to Jess. She picked out a grape and put it in her mouth.

"I saw her give you the evil eye and thought I'd wander over. Are you okay?"

I picked out a strawberry. "Yeah. I'm good. Thanks, though, Jess."

"It won't do any harm for her to know that someone else in the office is watching your back."

I smiled and held the fruit pot out again as my phone vibrated in my shirt pocket. Jess took another grape and walked toward a round-eyed Derek gazing in our direction and her own desk. I looked at my phone and read a message from Jason.

How'd that go down?

Not too bad. Only minor hissing, although I think I'm off the invite list for the pub and Zero One from here on in.

And me? He says hopefully!

Unfortunately not, my angel. You will realize your error shortly and I will be in the dustbin.

Make it a big wheelie bin then so I can jump in alongside you.

I smiled at my phone, pulled my work tray forward, moved my fingers over my keyboard and ignored Maisie and Annie when they returned to their desks. My phone vibrated at four-thirty. *Jason.*

Good to go in ten?

Sure. Caught up on what I needed to do.

I logged out of the payroll system and knew Jason had left his office when Maisie's gaze darted over my shoulder. I stood and smelled Hugo as I pushed my chair under my desk.

"Ness. You ready to go home?"

I turned and smiled. "Sure am. Everything for the payroll run is good to go. I'll catch the rest up on Monday."

"Back to yours first then home to mine?"

I nodded.

"We'll catch Jules if the traffic's not too bad." I stepped alongside Jason.

He looked at Annie and Maisie as we began to walk. "Night. Have a good weekend."

I glanced over my shoulder in the general direction of our workstations but looked at Annie.

"Night. Have a good one. See you Monday."

Jason pushed the office door open. I stepped through and Jason followed me out.

"What do you think? Enough that she'll get the message and will have wrapped her head around it by Monday?"

"She's got the message, but as for wrapping her head around it? I don't know. Not after what I heard from Kallie today and what she said to me after you came into work this afternoon."

Jason pressed the call button for the lift and waited for the doors to shut before he asked. "What did Kallie say?"

"That she saw Maisie's phone in the loo. She's screenshotted the pics of you from Dawn's Facebook and Su Linn's not in them anymore."

"She's Photoshopped her out?"

"And herself in."

Jason frowned. "Damn. And I can't do a thing about it. Dawn deleted hers because Mike made her understand how much trouble she'd be in if we lost the deal with Linn's because of the potential embarrassment factor she'd created for Su Linn, but I've got no such hold over Maisie's private phone."

I smoothed the crease between Jason's eyebrows with my fingertips. "She'll keep them to herself. Kallie said

Maisie was furious when she realized she'd caught sight of her phone."

"Because she's embarrassed?"

"I'd have thought. It's a pretty cringy thing to be caught doing, but at least it's diverted the office buzz away from Dawn's Facebook pics. All it's about now is Maisie and what she's done, rather than what the picture she altered was of in the first place."

The lift stopped and Jason held out his hand. I slipped mine into it and we walked through the car park toward his car.

"That's good, but I'll see Jenny again on Monday. I mentioned to her that I may have a problem with one of my staff when I saw her earlier about your new contract. I can ignore the eyes that follow me everywhere and turn down any amount of coffee, but Maisie's antics are really starting to give me the yips now. Jenny will know how to go about putting her straight."

Jason unlocked the car and I clicked my seatbelt on as Jason did the same, started the engine and drove to the ramp. A motorbike revved up behind us and I looked at it over my shoulder.

"That's what you should have if you want to beat the traffic."

Jason looked in his rearview mirror. "I've never ridden one or even been on the back of one. Have you?"

"I've been on the back of Gary's. The security firm uses them all the time to get where they need to be and cut through the traffic."

Jason engaged the gear and drove past the uplifted arm of the barrier. "He seemed to know what he was up to when I saw him earlier. He said to give him a day or two and he'll get back to me."

"If anyone's left a little marker behind them, Gary will find it."

Jason turned in to my cul-de-sac, nosed his car into a parking space outside my apartment block and I opened the front door of the flat to the sound of Little Mix and Jules' shout from her bedroom.

"Woohoo, girlie. It's Friday."

I smiled at Jason as I called to Jules. "Woohoo back, girlie. Jason's with me. You got your knickers on in there?"

"Yep. Just finishing my face. I'm quite decent."

I walked to Jules' bedroom. She sat at her dressing table, gluing on one half of a set of false eyelashes.

"Did you have a good day, babe?"

Jules smiled into her mirror. "Yep, the gallery was fun today. I'm going to Ben's as soon as I'm ready. Hi, Jason. You good?"

Jason smiled and nodded. "Happy to be back from smog central, thanks."

"I've just come back to get changed, then we're going to Jason's."

I blew Jules a kiss and walked into my bedroom. Jason put his arm around my waist as he followed me in.

"Bring your change of clothes with you? Get changed at mine? We could go out after and have something to eat?"

I kissed Jason. "Okay but I'll lose the work skirt and change my shoes."

Jason sat on the side of the bed. I up-ended my holdall and tipped out the contents of my visit to the peeps, picked up my makeup bag, yearbook and photos, put them back in and added my hair dryer and straighteners. Jason took my straighteners out, straightened the electric flex, wound it around the hand grip, put them back in and reached for my hairdryer. I laughed.

Jason smiled. "Get used to it, you. I'm neat."

"But does mess drive you mad?"

"No. I like it. I was never allowed to touch Caz's stuff. Move anything of hers by as much as an inch and she'd make a point of moving it back to within a millimeter of where it had been before."

I opened my wardrobe door. "Well, fill your boots with mine, although I do have a good tidy-up occasionally, you know."

Jason looked around my bedroom. "Like when?"

I followed Jason's eyes and smiled. "Like when it needs it. Once every couple of months or so."

I pushed hangers along the rail, took my scarlet, thigh-length, stretch Lycra dress from its hanger and threw it to Jason, followed it with a seam-free sport thong from my drawer and changed my work skirt for jeans.

Jason zipped up my holdall. I strapped on black platform sandals, called goodbye to Jules and Jason had us back at his flat in just over half an hour. We rode up the lift. Mrs. N. was sitting on her scooter, waiting outside it when the doors opened.

I smiled. "Are you waiting to get in? I'll hold the door."

"No, dear. I'm not waiting for the lift." Mrs. Noakes looked at Jason. "I'm waiting for you, dear. I came out when I saw your car." She moved her gaze back to me. "Although it's very nice to see you again, dear. I saw you last Thursday, of course, when you arrived in your taxi then again when you went home. But that was over a week ago now and I must say..." Mrs. Noakes looked at Jason and snorted.

I bit down on my lip.

"I was beginning to wonder. I mean, not that it hasn't been an entertaining parade to watch, of course, but really, it would be nice to meet a familiar face in the lift that a person can chat with."

Jason squeezed my waist as my shoulders shook. "And you were waiting for me because...?" he prompted.

"Because you had one of those motorcycle couriers try to deliver your pizza about half an hour ago, dear. I directed him to the porter's room after he asked me if I had a spare key to your flat so he could leave your delivery. I suppose it might not be too cold by now."

Jason smiled. "Okay. Thanks. But the pizza company must have made a mistake and delivered to the wrong address. I'll ring them and let them know."

Mrs. Noakes reversed her scooter and I asked, "Which pizza company was it, Mrs. Noakes? Did you notice?"

"I did look, dear, but the box was plain brown with just the picture of a pizza on it, and the delivery man didn't have a logo on his jacket, either. Just those black leathers that motorbike riders wear and the crash helmet. Big pizza, though, dear. One of the giant size. Shame if it goes to waste. Still, the porter might like it if the pizza company doesn't want it back."

Mrs. Noakes waved and motored off. Jason let us in to his flat and dropped my bag inside his bedroom. I followed him to the kitchen, perched on my stool and Jason poured wine into two glasses.

"Well done, Mrs. N, but I don't think I'm going to find a box of cold pizza in the porter's room, do you?"

I sipped from the glass Jason slid over to me. "If there was ever any pizza in it in the first place. Nice size box for the artwork, though, even if trying to con your way in through somebody's front door is hardly the most cunning plan in the world."

Jason sat on the stool beside mine and pressed his remote. Adele's voice floated out of the speakers. "It might have worked. Neighbors have keys. Some would have opened the door and waited outside while he took it in. In and out with some excuse for still having the box with him. Taking it away for recycling or something."

I threaded my fingers through Jason's. "Somebody doesn't realize you've taken the artwork into work and it's safe on floor two."

"Good job somebody didn't know it was here on its own and in plain view this morning, then. They might have tried a bit harder to get in."

"Give Gary a ring if you think somebody might try again. Get him to put in one of his CCTV tricks on your front door. You could get some footage to take to the police."

"I will, and I'll try to find out who at work rides a motorbike, including who might have been on the one that followed us out of the car park tonight."

I stroked my fingers down the side of Jason's face. "Are you sure you still want to go out tonight? We don't have to if this is worrying you."

Jason held my hand to his mouth and kissed into my palm. "No, it's fine. I still think this looks like a wishful amateur, and the artwork isn't here."

I unfastened the buttons on Jason's shirt and traced my fingertip down the center of his chest. "We should get changed then."

Jason's eyes darkened as my fingers neared his waistband. He stood and offered me his hand.

"Yes, baby, we should."

I put my hand in Jason's and unbuttoned my shirt with the other as we walked to the bedroom. I dropped it to the floor as I sat on the side of the bed and added my bra and my jeans. Jason added his shirt to the pile and I put my arms around his waist, urged him closer, put my tongue into his belly button and traced it down the line of golden hair to the waistband of his trousers. "I want to taste you."

Jason stroked his hand down the back of my hair. "Please."

I unfastened Jason's trouser clip, eased his zip down, pushed his boxers and trousers over his butt and fastened my mouth over the end of his cock.

Jason threaded his fingers through the back of my hair.

"Ness, yes. Don't make it nice."

I bypassed the soft oral foreplay and sucked harder, putting my hands at the top and the base of his shaft and giving his cock a squeeze of pressure as I moved them back and forth.

Jason rocked his hips, his hands stroking the back of my hair. I sucked harder with a small twist of my hand, the throb in between my legs building as I moved his cock in and out of my mouth.

His abs tightened along with his fingers in the back of my hair. I moved my hand from the base of his shaft to my center to give myself the last jolt I needed to climax with him. He groaned and his cum filled my mouth.

"Ness... Oh, baby..."

I sucked softer, rubbed myself and my climax pulsed through my pelvis as I swallowed. I kissed Jason's cockhead and released it from my mouth. Jason sat beside me on the bed, put his arm around me and took me with him to lie sideways across it.

"So sweet, baby."

I kissed Jason's chest. "You taste beautiful."

Jason tightened his arm around me.

"How's the jet lag? It's still early. You could sleep for a while."

Jason kissed the top of my head. "Not yet. I don't want to fall asleep with you in my arms and wake up and find you're gone."

I cuddled in closer, thought of possible intruders — wishful amateurs or not — of how the time lag worked on long-haul travel, east to west, and knew there was no way I would leave Jason on his own in deep, zoned out, jet-lagged sleep tonight.

"Sleep if you need to. I won't go. I'll be snuggled up against you when you wake."

"Yes, sweetheart, please."

Jason pushed his trousers and underwear over his feet, moved the right way around on the bed and pulled the quilt down. I cuddled into his arm and he pulled the quilt over us both.

"Baby, if you fall asleep, too, and if you dream, I'll deal with it the same way Ben does when he gets crated. I'd rather that than have a you-size empty space in the bed."

I kissed Jason's chest. "And the puke?"

"Hey, I've got a washing machine behind one of those doors and I know how to use it."

I relaxed into Jason's arms and found a floaty, dreamy half-sleep as Jason's breathing became regular and even. I came to every so often to brush my cheek against his chest or move my thigh on his before I drifted back off to happy land in my head and the bedroom filled with the light of a late evening and darkened into full night.

The hours slipped away and I opened my eyes as Jason stirred, to see early July daybreak lighting the room. Jason tightened his arm around me. I stroked my fingers down his waking erection pressed against my thigh.

Jason murmured, still half-asleep. I tilted my hip and teased the head of his cock with the wet early-morning want between my legs. Jason's smile tilted the corners of his lips and he moved me to lie on top of him.

"Yes, please."

I parted my legs to each side of his hips and eased his cock inside me, slid down the length of him and rocked on his erection. Jason asked for more with his hands on my hips and I rocked faster, pushed down on his cock harder, angled my hips for more friction and moaned when his shaft hit the place. "Oh, God, that's good."

Jason moved his fingers to my nipple and pinched. I moaned louder. "Please, more…"

He squeezed my breast, pinched my nipple harder then tugged. I gave my climax voice as the throb pulsed in between my legs and he worked magic with his fingers on my breasts. "Jason. Oh, fuck!"

Jason held my butt. His muscles tensed beneath me. "Ness… My baby."

I laid my face on his shoulder, panting, and he breathed hard into my neck. I lay still until my heart stopped thumping and kissed his lips. Jason opened his eyes and smiled at me.

"Beautiful way to wake up, baby. I haven't slept for too long, have I? If it's just getting dark."

I brushed my lips over the night stubble on Jason's jawline. "Hey you, good morning. It's not getting dark. It's getting light."

Jason felt his chin. "It's morning? I've slept all evening and all night?"

I smiled. "That's east to west long-haul for you. How are you feeling now?"

"Hungry, but what about you? Did you sleep? You must be starving, too. We didn't go out and eat."

"A bit and a bit but I liked it. You're rather more gorgeous to cuddle into at night than my normal two options."

"Of?"

"Of my pillow or Mr. Brown, my bear at home at the peeps."

Jason looked into my eyes. "Enough that you'd risk it again?"

I gazed back. "If you're sure you would."

Jason kissed my lips. "Yes, baby. I'd risk a lot more than that to fall asleep with you cuddled in tight to me all night and wake up like we did this morning. You're mine, I'm yours and the rest of it doesn't matter compared to that."

I swallowed hard as my heart tapped a double beat. Jason stroked his hands down my back. "I've got to move, sweetheart. I need the bathroom."

I rolled to my side. Jason swung his legs out of bed and opened the bathroom door after the flush of the loo. "Do you want to swing back to yours while it's still early and pick up a change of clothes? This time on a Saturday morning it would only take about fifteen minutes each way. We could have breakfast after."

I looked at the puddle of clothes lying beside the bed.

"That'd be good. My shirt's well past its sell-by date and I didn't bring a toothbrush."

"There's a toothbrush in the pack the airline handed out in the drawer under the sink."

I picked up my jeans and shirt, took my clean thong out of my holdall and smiled over my shoulder at Jason as I walked into the bathroom.

"But at least not yesterday's underwear."

I used the bathroom, dressed and walked into a tidied bedroom, the quilt turned back, my yearbook, phone, makeup bag, straighteners and hairdryer on the top of Jason's chest of drawers, my dress and bra on a hanger on the wardrobe door with my shoes standing underneath it. I smiled at the sight of my bra, picked up my shoes and phone then walked through to the kitchen to the sound of grinding coffee beans.

Jason put two coffee cups under the spout as I perched on my stool, then brought them over and sat on the stool beside mine.

"Are you still going to give Gary a call later?"

"I think I will. What's the firm's call-out turnaround time like?"

"Fast. If you call him this morning, he'll be out this morning. Apart from being good at the techie stuff, it's one of the reasons Dad uses the firm."

"To keep an eye on you and Jules?"

I put down my empty cup. "Not so much an eye on and not just me and Jules. It's more that Dad's put a couple of things in place that any of the family could call on if we ever needed the cavalry to arrive pronto."

Jason took my cup with his to the dishwasher. "Yeah, I can see why he'd do that. You good to go?"

I put my hand in Jason's and tapped a message to Jules as Jason drove to tell her I was coming home but heading straight out again. We arrived at my flat in under twenty minutes. I opened the front door to sleeping silence and closed my bedroom door behind us.

Jason sat on the side of my bed and opened my bag. I passed him a couple of clean T-shirts, leggings and clean underwear. Jason picked up my wrap, folded it into the overnighter and spoke in my ear.

"What about tomorrow? Do you want to get out of the city for a while? Brighton's only a couple of hours. We might catch some breeze there."

I breathed Jason in and my heart thumped as I murmured back. "Um, the peeps are on the coast not far from Brighton. You want to go by with me and say hi?"

Jason kissed my neck. "Yes, baby. I'd like that."

"I Skype home on Saturdays. I'll bring my laptop and let them know."

I passed Jason my laptop and charger, opened another drawer and handed over a pair of shorts, found my Vans under the bed and added them to the bag, closed the front door softly behind us and Jason had us parked at his flat fifteen minutes later.

"Where do you want to eat? I need to do some shopping but I've got eggs or there's a café about ten minutes away that will be open by now."

I looked at my creased shirt. "I'll take an egg, I think, rather than go out before I've showered and changed."

Jason swung his legs out of the car and I followed him in, dropped my overnighter off in the bedroom and perched on my stool. Jason beat up eggs and we shared a breakfast omelet between us with more coffee. Jason took his phone from his pocket and looked at the time. "I'll give Gary a ring."

"I'll hop in the shower, then."

I walked through to the bedroom, rummaged in my holdall for leggings and a T-shirt, looked at my bra dangling from the hanger and smiled as I wondered whether my clean knickers would have joined it the next time I looked.

Clean, with hair washed and plaited, I took my laptop with me to the kitchen. Jason looked up from stacking the dishwasher as I walked in smelling rather better than I had when I'd left it.

"Gary said he'll be here before ten. He's copied my hard drive onto a spare of his own to work on and cleaned up my laptop so I can have it back."

I sat on my stool. "Has he found anything yet?"

"Yeah. A nasty piece of self-destruct code that would have been triggered if I'd let that guy use his pro forma anti-virus to try and delete the spyware in China. It would have ripped through my data files and turned the lot of them to meaningless junk."

"Ouch. Do you think this is starting to sound more like IT pro code?"

"I thought so, but Gary's not quite so sure. He said although that piece of code was well written, other sections of it are quite naïvely put together. The code could have been made to do a lot more than just search my data files for certain key words if the coder had thought it through."

"What words was it looking for, as if I can't guess?"

Jason smiled. "All the obvious ones. Gary said he'll bring the list over with him when he comes to install a set of his own particular brand of spyware this morning."

Jason moved my plait to one side with his finger and kissed my neck.

"You smell good, baby. I'd better get my stinky self in the shower and get this grizzle off my face."

I turned and put my arms around him.

"I'll load my laptop and see what posts I've got on Facebook. You'll be glad to have yours back?"

"Just a bit. I loaded my old laptop and changed things like my banking passwords before I went to see Gary yesterday, but I bet I'll have work emails coming out of my ears even though Peter sent a memo around last week to say that I had a problem connecting to the hotel's Wi-Fi and not to bother emailing me until I came back."

I kissed Jason's stomach and lifted the lid on my laptop as he walked out of the kitchen. I sent Jules a text to say I'd call her later then looked at the latest posts from Mark and Simon and laughed at their July Christmas pictures in the park.

Jason walked into the kitchen, clean shaven with a handful of laundry that included my thong and he kissed my shoulder as he walked past. "I moved some of my stuff around and put yours in the top drawer of the chest."

Jason added his handful of laundry to his washing machine and set it off.

I smiled. "So, my knickers aren't hung on hangers all around the bedroom?"

Jason nipped his fingers on my butt and sat on the stool beside mine.

"No, my messy one, they are not. And your dress is now hung in the wardrobe alongside my shirts and your shoes are on the shoe rack behind the end wardrobe door with mine."

I raised my butt from my stool and kissed his cheek.

"Then, thank you for tidying me up."

The door buzzer sounded in the hallway. Jason went to answer it and came back with Gary, who put a black case on the breakfast bar, opened it and handed Jason his laptop.

"Hi, Ness. You good?"

I nodded as Gary took a glass-ended, short, slim, metal tube out of his case.

"If I replace the spy hole in your front door with this, you can get a live feed from it on your phone. It's motion sensitive. Anyone approaches your front door and it'll start to record until it senses a lack of movement for longer than five minutes. Two-way, it will record up your hallway as well, so you'll have proof if you need it that the premises were actually entered."

Jason looked at the replacement spyhole.

"Looks good. What's its power source?"

"Two small titanium batteries. I'll show you how to get the lens off on the hall side of the door and fit them. The app that I'll install on your phone will tell you when they need replacing. The recorder plugs into the mains then into your router."

"It's in the sitting room. I'll show you."

Gary picked up the spyhole and followed Jason out. Jason walked into the kitchen a few minutes later. "I'm making Gary a coffee. Do you want one?"

I looked up from posting to Mark. "Thanks, babe. That'd be good."

Jason stopped to look over my shoulder at Mark and Simon. "Nice sweaters."

I smiled and scrolled upward. "What about this one in the Santa pants?"

Jason laughed. "Okay, but I don't think many guys wear a snowflake bobble hat and scarf with just their underwear." He tugged on the end of my plait and put his hands on my shoulders. "Are you going to update your status on there?"

I smiled over my shoulder. "Yep. Are you ever going to post anything on yours again?"

"Yep. I'm going to post you."

"Why did you stop? Caz?"

Jason kissed on the top of my head. "Yeah. It wasn't helping either of us to move on when we broke up and it felt too mean to block her when it was me that called it off, so I changed my profile pic to a generic sunset and haven't logged on since — more now because I got out of the habit rather than anything else. Do you want to go out tonight for the dinner neither of got to eat last night?"

"Yeah. That would be good."

Jason took a tall glass cup from the cupboard above the coffee machine and made Gary a latte. Gary walked into the kitchen as Jason put it on the breakfast bar and pressed the machine for two, straight black.

"Have you got your phone? I'll download the app."

Jason handed his phone over. Gary tapped on the screen, laid it on the breakfast bar and picked up his coffee. "So, as to your unexpected pizza delivery. It was no trouble to get to your front door without you having to buzz me in. I just loitered on the street for a while as if I was looking at my phone and took a video of the keypad when a resident entered the code to open the door."

Jason set my cup in front of me and sat with his own. "Yeah. That would be easy enough to do. Nobody covers the keypad with their hand like they would at a cashpoint or a chip and pin."

"The IP address for the coder is anonymous. It could be anyone's Hotmail account under the name 'Dark Rider at'."

I sipped a mouthful. "What else for a black leather-clad pizza-delivering biker?"

Gary took a printed list out of his pocket. "Nothing too unexpected on the keywords the code is looking for other than...who's Tim?"

"Tim?" Jason frowned. "He's a good friend of mine from university."

"A close enough friend that maybe if you got a shout for help or a request to meet him urgently somewhere, you'd just drop everything and head on out?"

Jason nodded. "Yeah. I would. No question."

"Let Tim know not to contact you by email then. The spyware's interested in the emails you two exchange with each other. I'm suspecting it alters the content of them but what it wants to do with them I can't say yet. I'll let you know if and when I do."

"Okay. Thanks. I'll give Tim a ring and let him know."

"Your laptop's clean and okay to use now, but I'm keeping up a little fake noise from the corrupted copy of your hard drive to keep our coder from realizing his spyware is now obsolete. I'm presuming you'd like to know who tried to do this, even if they don't succeed?"

"Yeah, I would. I don't want to spend all my time at work wondering who it was and whether they'd try again."

Gary looked at me. "Ness, just in case. Don't forget to show Jason your phone."

"Sure. Just as soon as you're out of here."

Gary picked up Jason's phone. "Okay. All good to go. I'll walk you through it."

My Skype icon rang as Jason and Gary walked out of the kitchen. Mum's face appeared on the screen. She was sitting at the breakfast bar at home when I accepted the call.

"Hi, Mum. Where's Dad and Jilly?"

Mum wrinkled her nose. "Your father's braver than me. He's out giving Jilly a driving lesson in Daisy."

I winced back. "Braver than me, too. Poor Daisy."

Mum looked over my shoulder and tapped on her phone. "You're at Jason's?"

I nodded and breathed in a bit deeper. "Yeah, I am and ah...I thought I might come home tomorrow because um...Jason said he'll drive us down."

Mum's eyes widened and her whole face smiled. "You're bringing him home to say hi?"

The heat crept up my cheeks. "Um...yes."

Mum laughed. "Okay. good. Granny will be here. She's back from Spain and looking after Natalie for the day."

I smiled and let my lungs relax now that the words were out. "I'll text you in the morning and let you know what time."

Jason and Gary walked into the kitchen. I blew Mum a kiss. "Got to go. I'll see you tomorrow."

Mum blew me a kiss and I cut the Skype connection as Gary closed the lid on his case. "Okay, I'm out of here. Call me if anything else turns up or I'll call you when I've played with the code a little more."

I waved at Gary's departing back and waited for Jason to let him out. He sat on the stool beside mine after he had and looked at the live feed from the front door on his phone.

"That's a real neat piece of kit he's put in. What did Gary want you to show me on your phone?"

"Not so much show as tell, because by the firm's rules, Gary can't share details of one client's arrangements with another, but what he would have liked to have said is that if anything turns unexpectedly nasty, like say half a dozen six-packed goons turn up, if you unlock my phone twice with an incorrect code, the tracker alerts the firm and the cavalry will arrive pronto."

Jason smiled. "Not that I'm expecting any six-packed goons, but that's good to know."

"The correct code's five, seven, two, nine, star, hash."

Jason leaned closer and kissed my lips. "Two, one, one, nine."

"Your door number and…?"

"And the age I was when I first got to pop my cherry."

I giggled. "Aw, babe…"

Jason pinched my butt. "Pack it in, you. I was a September baby and already nineteen when I started uni."

"Don't worry. You didn't miss much. Early teenage sex isn't much to write home about."

"Not with…?"

I squeezed Jason's butt. "No way. And my yearbook's in the bedroom, so I hope you know where yours is."

"Yes, I do, but for now I think we should head on out. I need to do some shopping."

I hopped off my stool. "Come on then. Show me what real shopping's all about."

Chapter Thirteen

Two hours later I sat on my stool, sipped from a bottle of water and watched Jason unpack three bags of shopping that didn't feature a single pre-prepared pasta salad. Jason seared tuna steaks for our lunch and my night of light dozing caught up with me as I put my knife and fork down and yawned. Jason took my plate and stacked it on his.

"Sofa, baby? I'll put something on the telly that we can nap to or we're not going to make it out of the door again tonight."

I nodded and followed Jason to the sitting room. Jason toed his shoes off and lay on the sofa, his head on a cushion. I unlaced my Vans, joined him and snuggled into his arm as he pressed his remote and turned the telly on. I snaked my hand inside his T-shirt to touch his skin as my eyes refused to focus any longer, then stirred later to hear the sound of a hard ball hitting a bat and Jason breathing softly beside me. I closed my eyes and cuddled in again.

I opened my eyes later to see Jason awake and watching the television over the top of my head. He kissed on my hair.

"Hey, you. You feel better for that?"

I nuzzled my lips on his neck. "Hey you, back. Much. What time is it?"

"Just before five."

I untangled my legs from Jason's, stretched and wriggled higher up the sofa. "I'd better give Jules a ring and let her know what I'm up to."

Jason sat up straighter. "And I'd better have a look at my emails. It'll only bug me up this evening if I don't."

I swung my legs to the floor and stood so Jason could do the same, walked through to kitchen, sat on my stool and picked up my phone while Jason sat opposite me and lifted the lid on his laptop. Jules answered me on the third ring.

"Woohoo, girlie. Have I got to order you a nice, shiny medal?"

I smiled at my phone. "Nearly but definitely tomorrow."

"Are you staying over at Jason's for a sleep-sleep over tonight, then?"

"Yep. We're going to see the peeps tomorrow." I held my phone away from my ear against the volume of Jules' shout.

"What! Really! Yay! Who's going to be there?"

Jason's eyes flicked up from his screen as I pulled my phone away. I put it back to my ear as Jules' volume went down on her last sentence.

"Mum says Granny Alice is home, so she will."

"Not too many to scare Jason off, then?"

"It should be okay. I'm sure Mum will bib and pad her up."

I heard the smile in Jules' voice.

"Jason's there and in earshot, is he?"

I kept my face straight and nodded at my phone. "Yeah. For sure. But she's not too bad if you keep topping up her gin."

Jules laughed. "Playing along but doesn't believe a word of it?"

"Absolutely. Can't do it with someone who does."

"Let me know, babe. I'd love to have bought Ben along too but we've arranged to go to my mum's for tea," she said.

"Eek! Let me know how that one goes, girlie."

"Will do. Speak tomorrow."

Jason looked over the top of his laptop as I cut the connection. "Gin now, is it?"

I sighed and nodded. "Yeah. Sorry. I forgot to mention that one, didn't I?"

Jason looked into my eyes. "Knits, does she? Granny. Possibly sitting in her little rocking chair?"

I gazed back, tensed my stomach muscles against the tickle of a giggle and gasped. "Good lord, no! We wouldn't let Granny loose with a pair of knitting needles. They've got sharp, pointy ends! And as for a rocking chair" — I sighed — "well, motion sickness is a terrible thing."

Jason shook his head and laughed. "And you said Fido was outrageous. Poor Granny!"

I relaxed my tummy and let my smile into my eyes. "Yep. How are the emails? Were there as many as you thought?"

"Just over a hundred, but only about twenty I've got to answer by the time I've deleted the nonsense and some figures I've got to send to Peter."

"How did he feel about the China deal? Was he disappointed not to be doing the business with Linn's?"

"No, he was fine about it. Actually, more than fine. The thought of my mother's work being out there, high profile and on show again? Well, let's just say Peter wasn't disappointed and also more than happy that you were staying on when he read your resume and saw a degree from UCL."

I stood and smiled at Jason.

"I thought your father looked...well, a bit more than fine when he first saw the artwork of the tiara. I'll just use the loo."

I used the en suite and slid the top drawer of the chest open to find my shorts, jeans, T-shirts and underwear stacked neatly to one side of it, my makeup, dryer and straighteners lined up on the other. I looked at my makeup bag as I closed the drawer and walked through to the kitchen. Jason looked up from his laptop.

"Is there a chemist nearby? I've just remembered Jilly's still got my eyelash glue from last weekend."

"About a ten-minute walk if you turn left when you leave the flat. They don't shut until seven."

Jason opened a drawer and offered me the door key he took out of it. "Take the spare."

I walked around the breakfast bar, took it and kissed his cheek. "I won't be long."

He put his arms around me. "Keep the key, baby. You don't have to stand outside waiting to be let in."

I leaned against Jason in the V of his legs and nuzzled my mouth on his neck. "You sure?"

"Yep. You?"

I looked into his eyes. They were beautiful and looking at me. "Yep."

I smiled over my shoulder as I left the kitchen and he turned his attention back to his laptop. I dropped the glue off in the drawer when I returned half an hour later, added a bottle of conditioner to the rack in his shower and walked to the kitchen to find Jason still tapping away on his keyboard. I picked up my handbag, dropped my purse into it and added his key to those already on my keyring. Jason raised his eyes from his work.

"Did you get what you wanted? I won't be much longer doing this."

"Yeah, they had what I wanted, and don't rush. I'll go and start getting ready. It'll take me longer than you."

Jason smiled, pressed on his remote and John Legend sang out of the speakers. "I'll bring you a glass of wine in when I've finished."

It didn't take me long to dress after I'd showered, with only a smooth sport thong and my red dress to pull on. I found a socket within reach of the mirror, dried my hair and began to straighten it. Jason walked in, put a glass of wine on the chest of drawers and brushed his lips on my shoulder on his way to the wardrobe.

"You've been quick," he said.

I smiled into the mirror. "It's the face that does it. You'll be gorgeous and good to go before I will."

Jason took clothes out of the wardrobe, laid them on the bed and was showered, dressed and smelling lovely before I'd finished straightening my hair. He kissed my shoulder as he left the bedroom. "I'll go give Tim a ring while you finish."

Forty minutes later I strapped on my shoes, looked into the mirror and saw hair lying flat down my back, my dress tight and clinging in all the right places, big eyes and red, red lips to match my dress. I tucked my extra photos inside my yearbook, then took it and my wine glass through to the kitchen.

Jason looked up, patted the seat of the stool between his legs and picked up his phone. "You look beautiful, sweetheart. Let's do a pic."

I put my glass and book on the breakfast bar, took my phone out of my bag and perched between his legs. Jason held his phone out and took several pics, then took more with my phone. We put our phones side by side and I picked one of me laughing at Jason when he'd nipped his fingers on my butt, loaded Facebook and changed my profile pic and status.

Jason looked at me then his phone. "Here goes then. God knows what I'm going to find on here after more than a year."

Jason logged on and his profile page loaded with a picture of a generic sunset, a list of older posts from Caz with nothing posted back and a last post from her, dated three months previously. I looked at a blue-eyed brunette, toned but taller and bigger all over than I'd imagined she would be, sitting on a sofa displaying a small but unmistakable baby bump. Jason smiled as we read the words that accompanied the pic. *In case you ever log in again, just to let you know. Happily married now.*

"I'm glad to see that one," he said.

I picked up my glass as Jason changed his profile page and my phone vibrated on the breakfast bar. I looked at a rolling list of posts and logged out of Facebook. "I'll look at those later. Where's this yearbook of yours?"

Jason stood from his stool. "Have you got your graduation pics?"

"Yep. One from the ball."

"Okay. I'll get mine from the sitting room."

I took the loose photos from my yearbook and turned them face down.

Jason sat beside me and handed me his book. "Page twenty. And no laughing, you."

I found the page, looked at a younger Jason—all bones and angles as he'd told me he would be—and bit down on my lip when I saw the shoulder-length mop of soft waves and curls on his head.

"Aw, babe. You've got hair like your mum," I smiled.

"Unfortunately, yes. If it grows any longer than it is now, I look like a girl."

I giggled. "No, my angel. It's really nearly cute."

Jason laughed and flicked his finger on my butt. "Get out of here, you. No, it's absolutely not. Show me you looking like a cutie in yours, then."

I picked up the first of my loose photos. "Okay. But you can have a look at me first at my fifteen-year-old geeky best, if you like."

I handed Jason a group shot from a school trip with me, small and undersized, standing at the end of the line of other pupils and smiling through a mouthful of braces, a fair smattering of spots and much shorter hair, cut with a thick, full fringe that did nothing to flatter my face.

Jason grinned. "Oh, yeah. Yep. I can see why this one probably doesn't make it out of the drawer too often."

I pointed at the figure standing in the middle of the line—glasses, greasy hair and, like me, small with an even better smattering of spots. "There he is. Luke."

"Jesus, Ness. Ew!"

I laughed. "He looks better in the yearbook. We all do."

I handed it to Jason and he flicked through the pages of pupils dancing, playing sports and laughing. He stopped on the page headed *County Colors* and the pic of me frozen in time in my competition leotard, twisting high in the air in the midst of a full multi salto tumbling pass.

"Hey, Buffy. That looks good."

I smiled and flicked a few pages over to a group shot taken in the common room. Half a dozen of us in three groups of two, leaning against each other back to back — Luke, still small, but clean and shiny and without his glasses, me, fringe gone and hair long down my back, teeth straight and not a spot in sight.

Jason looked at Luke. "Were you dating him by then?"

"No, I never dated Luke as such. We just did the kissy bit when we were younger."

I turned over two more pages to the team shot of the first fifteen rugby team and pointed to the figure in the back row. "I was dating that one."

"Oh, were you? And?"

"And, yep. That's my equivalent of your Emma."

Jason smiled, closed the book and handed me his graduation ball photo. I saw a girl, tall and elegant in a strapless evening gown that fit tightly to her knees before it swirled out from knees to floor, her hair straightened into black, soft waves, her face pretty with a dusting of gold makeup to highlight her skin's natural tone, her arm threaded through Jason's.

"She's very pretty. Did you date for a while?"

Jason pointed at the girl's hand. "One time only."

I looked and winced. "Ouch, babe. And she dug those into your back, did she?"

Jason nodded. "Oh, yeah. Did she ever."

I looked again. "Ow and ouch! They should be classed as dangerous weapons, not fingernails."

I handed Jason my last photo and Jason opened the cardboard cover to see me dressed in a floor-length version of the dress I was currently wearing, Jules in a similar full-length in green with Mark and Simon stood one each side of us. Jason laughed.

"You took the angelic pair to your graduation ball?"

I smiled and put my empty glass down. "Yes and no. We did go to the ball and stayed for the dinner but then jibbed out, hoofed it back to The Vine and had our own party there."

Jason put his glass beside mine, stood and offered me his hand. I dropped my phone into my handbag and put my hand in his.

"Aw, baby. You didn't get to stay for your own graduation ball."

I laughed. "No aw about that one. We had an absolute riot and most of our friends ended up in The Vine with us on an all-nighter."

Jason smiled as we walked down the hall to the front door. "Glad about that one, too."

I followed Jason out of the street door and he turned away from Camden center and walked towards Kentish Town.

"Local's preference?" I asked.

Jason squeezed my hand. "Yeah. Most locals stay away from the center of Camden itself. Too full of city-cruising tourists. I thought we could see if Joe's Kitchen have a table. It's an American bar-diner type of place."

"Sounds good."

Jason stopped outside a restaurant and opened the door onto a bar of red brick with red banquette seating, rustic slatted wooden tables and a wonderful savory smell. With only two to seat, the server managed to find us a small table and Jason ordered short ribs with mashed potatoes and onion gravy from the big plate menu and I ordered a braised beef chili cup from the small plate section.

Jason eyed my dinner when it arrived. "That's not very much."

I offered Jason a taste of my beef from my fork. "It's plenty. I can't remember the last time I ate three times in any one day."

Jason offered me his fork, laughed when it dripped gravy on my chin and dabbed it off with his napkin. We shared the two plates between us and with Jason's bigger appetite, finished eating at the same time.

"Coffee here, baby? Or…?"

"Or, please."

Jason smiled, motioned for the bill and followed me out when he received his card back.

I slipped my hand in his and we walked through late-evening, still-warm summer air back to his flat. Jason let us in and I followed him through to the kitchen. He put the coffee machine on to grind.

"Hot or cold to go with?" he asked.

"Yesterday's inappropriate hot, please."

Jason kissed my shoulder on his way past to the sitting room. I took my phone out of my bag, logged on to Facebook and smiled at the likes and the thirty-seven new posts in various forms of 'oh', 'my' and 'God', then frowned at a friend request from Annie and muttered under my breath. "I think not."

Jason walked into the kitchen with two glasses of brandy. "Something up?"

"Nothing drastic. Just a friend request from Annie that I'll pretend I never received because it's probably come via Maisie."

Jason put the brandy down and carried the coffee over. "I emailed Jenny today. I'm seeing her first thing Monday morning. It'll be sorted soon."

I sipped my coffee, took a smaller sip of brandy after it and relaxed as I felt the warmth in my throat. "She's good, then? Jenny?"

Jason sat beside me and picked up his glass. "Yeah. I think so. Better than if I try to do it myself. Jenny will make the point but in an impersonal way that Maisie won't be able to ignore but won't be able to take offense to."

"From what I've heard from Jess, you're the only guy that's turned Maisie down for just about ever. I think that because she doesn't definitely know you're not going anywhere near her, it's sort of keeping her going."

Jason picked up my hand and kissed the back of it. "She'll know by Monday. Bed, baby?"

I smiled and followed him to the bedroom, peeled off my dress and lay on the bed as Jason unbuttoned his shirt and took it off. My breathing increased as he stepped out of his boxers, lay beside me and teased his fingertips over my nipples.

"You need my mouth hot here?" he asked.

I breathed harder. "Yes."

Jason filled his mouth with hot coffee and covered my nipple. I murmured as he sucked on one and pinched the other. Jason picked up his brandy glass. "Baby, I need to be between your legs."

I moaned as his mouth, warm with alcohol, covered my mound and he sucked. "Jason…"

His tongue probed deeper. I writhed against it. He pushed his finger inside me and added another. I pushed down and panted, "Fuck me, please."

Jason kissed up my body.

"Yes, baby. I'm going to fuck you now."

I whimpered as he put his cock inside me, pushed against him as he thrust and writhed as his pinch on my nipple released my climax.

"Baby, yes…"

"Jason…"

I rested my cheek on Jason's chest as he eased away and onto his side. He kissed the top of my head when our heart rates slowed. "I've got to move now and clean my teeth and I don't want to."

"Neither do I and I've got to take my makeup off, too."

Jason swung his legs off the bed. "Best do it before we fall asleep."

I put my feet to the floor. "Okay. You use the bathroom and I'll clean my face."

I pulled my eyelashes off, used makeup wipes on my face while Jason used the bathroom then brushed my teeth after he finished. I snuggled in under his arm as he pulled the quilt over us, curled in close to his body and draped my arm over his chest. Jason put his other arm over me and held me tight.

"Sleep well, baby."

I sighed, closed my eyes and breathed Jason in as I drifted away.

My foot caught under a branch that wormed its way underground then snaked its way up again in a knobbly hoop. I grabbed Jules' hand to steady myself and giggled into the warm night air as I stumbled. Jules giggled beside me.

"Shouldn't 'ave had the last one, Ness."

"The B-52 or the pinta piña colada?"

Jules lurched against me as the heel of her shoe snagged and caught. I laughed and pushed her upright again.

"Both. Should've got a taxi, though."

"Only gotta get through the par —"

Jules' chin hit her chest and her knees crumpled. She fell as the back of my head exploded with pain from a curled fist that I glimpsed out of the corner of my eye as my legs gave way. My butt hit the path and my scream joined Jules'. I screamed again, kicked out with my foot and caught the thigh of the chunky, male closing the gap between us with the high heel of my shoe.

"Ness, sweetheart. Wake up, baby. It's not him. It's me. I'm here."

My eyes fluttered open. Jason was holding me close. He stroked his hand down my back and through my hair. "You stopped it. You knew," I said as my eyes filled.

"You lay so still cuddled up to me. It woke me when you started to move. I knew when you started to struggle," Jason replied.

My first tear splashed onto Jason's chest.

"Don't cry, baby. It's okay. I'm here."

"Not crying. Nope. Not doing that."

Jason held me tightly while I did anyway, then mopped up my face. I snuggled close against his body once more with his arms around me and we slept through until after eight. Jason looked out of the window as we stirred.

"It's a beautiful day out there."

I opened my eyes, wriggled up his body, buzzed my lips over his morning stubble and ran my fingers down the length of his erection. "Yes, it is. Is this for me?"

Jason stroked down my body and between my legs and found wetness waiting for him. "Oh, yes. I think it is."

I turned onto my back, put my arms around him and parted my legs. He searched farther inside me with his fingers and found my breast with his mouth. I murmured as he sucked on my nipple and his bristles scratched on the soft skin of my breast.

"Oh...that feels good."

He moved the roughness of his chin over my breast, teased my nipple with it and I breathed harder.

"You like?"

"Mmmm...morning stubble. Yes, please."

Jason buried his face in the valley of my breasts, moved the fullness of them against his face then over one nipple then the other.

I mewled in the back of my throat as the roughness of his face on my flesh caused a tremble between my legs. "Oh, good..."

Jason bit my nipple, tugged with his teeth and teased his chin over the extended nub. Then he eased his cock inside me. I moved my pelvis up to meet his, breathing hard as he bit down and pushed his shaft farther in. Jason thrust and I ground against him and moaned, my breasts alive with the burn from his face. He moved faster, breathed harder and I gave my climax voice as the shock waves spread from the center of me and out. "Jason... Oh, fuck!"

Jason's thrusts shortened and he moaned, "My baby...yes."

I panted against Jason's neck as he stilled, breathing hard above me. I stroked my fingers down his back until he rolled onto his side and I cuddled into his arm.

He ran his fingers through the length of my hair. "Nice?"

"Mmmm. Face hair that doesn't tickle? Definitely not."

Jason buzzed his chin against my shoulder. "Have I left you with stubble rash?"

"It doesn't matter. I like to see and feel where you've been on my body. I'll cover it up from other eyes if I have any."

Jason tightened his arm around me. "Bad girl."

I nuzzled my lips into Jason's neck. "With you. As much and as often as you like."

"Coffee?" Jason smiled.

"Please."

Jason slid out of bed and walked over to the bedroom door. I giggled. Jason looked over his shoulder. "Camera out there now."

Jason opened a drawer and took out a pair of boxers. I picked up my wrap and walked into the bathroom as Jason pulled his underwear on and I walked through to the kitchen after I'd used the loo.

Jason put a coffee in front of me as I sat and buttered toast for us to share. Once we were showered and dressed in shorts and T-shirts, we were good to go an hour later. Jason took his car keys out of a drawer and we headed down to his car.

We flew through London, which was light on traffic because of the weekend, and my stomach started to flutter as I saw the signs for Worthing. My heart joined it as we arrived at the peeps and Jason parked at the end of the drive. I opened the car door to the sound of squeals coming from the back of the house. *Jilly.*

I smiled at Jason, took his hand, walked with him around to the back and looked at a normal hot Sunday for the peeps. The pool cover was back, Dad was throwing Jilly backward into the water, Mum was sitting in a chair to one side of the pool deck to avoid the splash and Granny Alice sat beside her. Granny looked over, noticed us and nudged Mum. Mum jumped up and walked over — willowy in her bikini, her arms outstretched.

"Hello, darling. You made it here in good time."

Mum wrapped her arms around me and kissed the top of my head and offered Jason her hand. "You must be, Jason. I'm Ness' mum, Sally."

"Pleased to meet you," Jason said as he shook it.

Granny was one willowy step behind Mum and said, "Hello, Jason. I'm Alice."

Jason looked at me. I gave him my best wide open, innocent eyes but couldn't keep the laugh out of them. Granny looked at Jason then me and side-swiped my arm as I let a giggle escape.

"She's been telling you I've got dribbly whiskers, hasn't she? The wicked moo."

Jason smiled. "Ah, yeah. Sort of."

Granny threaded her arm through Jason's and led him over to the pool chairs with Mum following along behind. "I only promised that when I'm old, I'm going to grow some, come and live here and dribble all over them. Now every time I see them, they're inspecting my upper lip."

Dad climbed out of the pool, shucked the wet off his head and I hugged him as Jilly climbed out behind him, stood close to me and shook water all over. I tickled Jilly's belly with my fingers. Dad tipped her into the water while she was off balance and she squealed, "Ness! Dad!"

I walked with Dad toward Jason, who was sitting a pool chair beside Granny.

"Dad, this is Jason," I said.

Dad sat in a chair opposite Jason, held his hand out and they did the man-shake thing. I sat beside Jason. Mum stood behind Dad's chair, put her hands on his shoulders and kissed the top of his head. "Drink? Al? Jason?"

Dad pulled Mum's hand forward and kissed it. "Thanks, Sal. A coffee would be good."

I looked at Jason. He nodded. "Yes, please, Mum. Both black, no sugar."

Dad leaned back in his chair. "Did you have a good trip down?"

Natalie ran out of the sunroom door, calling before Jason could answer, "Aundy Ness, Aundy Ness. Where is Aundy Jules?"

I held my arms out and kissed Natalie as she reached me. "She's not here this time, Nat. I've brought Jason to see you instead."

Natalie gazed at Jason, then me and nibbled the top of her finger. Jilly dripped over from the pool and flopped into the chair beside mine.

"Hi, Jason. You got back okay from where ever it was you were flying to last weekend, then?"

"China. Yes, thanks. I got home yesterday."

Natalie turned her eyes to Jilly, then back to Jason.

"China? How did you find it? It was still a closed country when Sally and I travelled that way, although Ness and Jules have been," Dad said.

Natalie moved a step closer to Jason.

"Different," Jason said. "But it was a business trip, so I didn't see much of it."

Natalie took two last steps and patted Jason's knee. He looked down. Natalie held her arms out. "Up, please."

Jason looked at me over the top of Natalie's head and I smiled. "Yep. You have to pick her up, now."

Jason lifted Natalie from her feet and perched her on the edge of his knees. Natalie wriggled her butt onto Jason's lap, small and still a little chubby with the remainder of her baby fat. She gazed up into Jason's face and gave him a full blast of big, wide-open brown eyes.

"I made crispy cakes with Aundy Sally an' you can have one if'n you like."

Jason's mouth twitched. "Yes. Well, thanks. I'm sure they'll be lovely."

"But only if'n you're good an' eat up all your lunch."

"Okay. Right. I'll make sure I do, then."

Granny caught my eye over the top of her sunglasses. "Who else can have one, Nat? Can Aunty Ness? What about the special one?"

"Yes, Granny. You can, an' Aundy Ness can have the special one I only licked a little bit if'n she's good, too."

I mouthed *thanks for that* to Granny and smiled at Natalie. "Thanks, Nat but perhaps I should take that one home with me for Aunty Jules."

Natalie nodded and settled against Jason's arm, her head on his chest, put her thumb in her mouth and rubbed her cheek against his T-shirt.

"She'll nod off now. She's due her nap," Granny said.

Natalie's eyelids fluttered closed and Jason glanced down at her un-nappy-panted butt. Mum walked out of the sunroom door with coffees to one side of a tray and a plate of sandwiches on the other. Dad stood and took the sandwiches from the tray to lighten the load.

I grabbed the towel from the back of Jilly's chair, draped it over Natalie, lifted her from Jason's lap and laid her on a sun lounger under the shade of its parasol. Mum passed out paper napkins and we all helped ourselves as the plate went around.

Dad looked at Jason as he picked up his sandwich. "Ness said you came across a piece of spyware on your laptop. Did you get hold of Gary okay?"

Jason nodded as he bit down.

"Ace is a good outfit and Gary's one of their best," Dad said.

"He's unpicking the spyware for me and upping some personal security. It looks like my personal data's been accessed to run a scam on one of Belmond's assets that I own."

"An in-house purchase, was it?" Dad said.

I swallowed hard on my mouthful of sandwich but Jason didn't hesitate and said it straight out. "I inherited a half-share of Belmond's and certain assets associated with it from my mother. Peter Belmond's my father."

Dad picked up another sandwich, glanced at my face and didn't probe that any further. "And your father's laptop? It's clean?"

Jason nodded. "Peter — my father — doesn't come into the office that often now. His laptop's not really been around for anyone to get to, and the prospective scam will be over with by Wednesday at the latest when my mother's artwork goes back to the bank. It's being held in a secure area at work until then, although I'd still like to know who at work tried to do this."

Dad nodded. "If your prospective scammer has left any tracks in the sand Gary will find them."

Mum looked at Jason. "Your mother was an artist?"

Granny smiled. "I'm guessing Gabriella Delaney?"

"You've heard of her?" Jason asked.

Granny smiled. "I remember all the brouhaha in the press when she designed and made the jewelry the Duchess wore for her wedding."

Jason smiled. "And refused to wear the family heirlooms."

Granny laughed. "Who wouldn't? They were so old-fashioned and looked like they weighed a ton."

I put my plate and cup on the table and looked at Jason. "Do you want to walk through to the beach?"

Jason nodded yes and mouthed at me, *loo?*

I smiled and stood. "This way."

I walked ahead of Jason into the house, took his hand as we walked through the sunroom and into the kitchen, gleaming and as hi-tech as his own, cream granite not black and three times the size. Jason looked at the appliances as we walked.

"No wonder you're not allowed to touch this lot."

I smiled. "I couldn't even tell you what most of it does."

I led Jason up the stairs and opened the door to the perfectly preserved time capsule of my teenage years. Jason walked into my en suite and I looked out of the window at the sea, calm and nearly empty of sails on a day with only a whisper of breeze. I heard the flush. He stood behind me, put his arms around my waist and looked at the view from over my head. I leaned back into him.

"It's a lovely place, Ness. There aren't many people using the beach."

"It's always quiet. Mainly residents and dog walkers. There's no cafés or shops to bring the tourists in. You've got to go farther down the coast for that. How are you finding the peeps?"

Jason nuzzled my neck. "It's fine. They're lovely, Ness."

Jilly's voice floated through the open window. "How come she's allowed and you won't let me and Josh use my bedroom?"

Mum's voice answered, "Because…"

"Because why?"

"Because I said so."

I smiled at Jason and we walked downstairs. I took Jason's hand, led him through the garden to the conifer screen at the back of it and opened the gate onto the pebble beach. A slight breeze cooled my face as I pulled it shut behind us, the sea in front of me a rare true blue reflection of the cloudless sky above.

Jason gazed seaward. "Do you swim in it, Ness?"

I shook my head and walked with Jason to the tide line. "No, we don't really. It looks lovely today but the seaweed's quite ew here. We use the pool to swim in and the beach to walk on. I love it best in the winter. High tide and stormy."

I stopped at the water's edge, crunched the pebbles flat with my foot and sat. Jason sat beside me and winced as an un-flattened pebble edge caught his butt. I slipped my arm around his waist and leaned my head on his arm. He put his arm around me.

"Do you want to go away for a few days somewhere hot later in the year?"

"Somewhere hot enough that I might have to rub your sunscreen on for you?"

Jason squeezed. "And perhaps some of that after-sun oil?"

I tilted my face toward him. "Yeah. And perhaps some of your oil, too."

Jason put his lips on mine and I threaded my fingers through the back of his hair as we kissed.

"You want to head back to town soon?" I asked when we broke our kiss.

"Yes, sweetheart. Whenever you're ready."

We got up and I slipped my hand into Jason's while we walked back to the peeps. I opened the gate and Jason followed me in.

"Mum, we're going to make a move now and get back to town to be ready for work tomorrow."

"Okay, darling."

I hugged and kissed the peeps, picked up Natalie and held her out so she could kiss Jason. Jason pecked Mum and Granny goodbye, smiled at Jilly and shook Dad's hand.

"Bye. Thanks for lunch."

"See you again, Jason. Ness, I'll call you in the week," Mum said.

I put my hand in Jason's and we walked around the side of the house to the car. He put the roof down after he started the engine. I turned the music up against the noise of the wind rush, put my sunglasses on then regretted my choice of untied hair when the wind direction changed as Jason drove over the chalky hills of the South Downs and I ate mouthfuls of my hair for most of the way home. Jason turned the engine off in his parking space when we arrived and replaced the car top. I took my not-Dior sunglasses off and pulled strands of hair off my face.

"Thank you. That was lovely, especially across the top of the Downs."

Jason laughed. "Hair up next time, I think."

I puffed more wayward strands out of my mouth as I opened the car door.

Jason let us into his flat. "Wine?"

"Please. It's after wine o'clock, for sure."

I followed Jason to the kitchen and sat on my stool. Jason poured, slid my glass over then sat opposite me.

"Have you always lived in that house, Ness?"

"Yeah. The peeps bought it when they first got married, although it didn't look like it does now when I was small. They've done a lot of work on it over the years. What about your father? Does he still live in the house down the road from your mum's?"

Jason shook his head. "No. Both houses were sold when I went to uni. Peter has a small barn conversion in Surrey. It's got to be near a first-rate golf course for him."

"What's it like? A good conversion?"

Jason shrugged and sipped. "I wouldn't know. I've never been there."

"What? *Never?* Where did you go for holidays and Christmas and things when your mum's house was sold?"

"I stayed at my digs in Exeter while I was at uni and sometimes at Tim's parents' place. The money from mum's house sorted out my first flat for me when I first started work in London. It wasn't a problem. I didn't want to stay with Peter. It was a bit late for the dad-son bit by then and I did see him three or four times a year when he'd book into a nearby hotel for a night or two."

I shook my head and sipped. "I can't wrap my head around it. My family's a noisy bunch, always crowding into one house or the other, and the ruder we are to each other, the more it means we care. I can't imagine that if anything ever happened to the peeps that someone in the family wouldn't take over and suck me and Jilly in."

Jason smiled. "But at the end of the day, you get what you get and not having much of a family is what I'm used to."

I put my hand over Jason's and squeezed. "I could offer you a lend of Granny on every other weekend, a share in a sister whenever you'd like to take her off my hands and assorted cousins freely available on any given nights of the week at a very reasonable rate of dinner, if it includes a bottle or two."

Jason smiled. "And this week's special offer?"

I chinked my glass on Jason's. "Buy one, get two free. Granny's just been out to Spain to stay with Grandpa Ted and Jenny, and they've got another spare bedroom if you want to go with them on their next bargain-bucket weekend."

Jason laughed and stood. "Bucket class? Eating my knees? No, I think I'll pass on that one. Thanks. I'll put the oven on for the chicken."

I smiled and picked up my glass. "How are you doing it?"

"I'm going to stuff chicken breasts with garlic butter, wrap them in pancetta and roast them."

"That sounds lovely. I'll give Jules a quick text and see how they got on at her mum's."

I moved my fingers over my screen, gave Jules a quick update of my day, asked about hers and said I'd be home in the morning. Her reply said Ben hadn't headed for the hills after the visit, although she'd been lacing his running shoes up for him at one point. I laughed. Jason looked up from bashing chicken laid between two sheets of plastic film with a rolling pin.

"Ben didn't leg it from Jules' mum's, but it was close at one point, she said."

Jason smiled. "Because…?"

"Because, unlike Granny, really, really, Jules' mum is more comfortable with her horse, dogs and cats than she is with meeting new people. She can come across as quite stiff and sort of snottily polite with people she doesn't know."

"Definitely not like your granny, then. Does she really go and stay with her ex-husband and his second wife?"

I put my phone on the breakfast bar and smiled as I thought of Granny and Grandpa.

"Yeah, she does. Granny and Grandpa separated because they felt like they'd become more friends than a married couple, but as they both felt the same, there were never any hurt feelings floating around to mess things up, so the friends bit has never changed."

Jason placed a sausage of garlic butter onto the flattened chicken and made a parcel of the chicken and pancetta with the butter at its heart.

"It's the best way to be if it's over, I suppose. Are you okay with broccoli?"

I nodded and Jason slid the chicken into the oven, put tiny potatoes and greenery into a steamer and dished everything onto two plates half an hour later while I topped up our glasses.

I slipped off my stool when we finished eating. "I'll rinse, you stack. I'm even allowed to do that much at home."

Jason found a horror movie on Netflix for us to watch after dinner. I lounged on the sofa, sideways across Jason's lap, and found plenty of chances to hide my face in his chest at the gory bits while Jason laughed at me for being a wimp. Jason turned the telly off at the end credits.

"Bed, baby?"

I put my arms around his neck. "Yes, please."

He traced his fingers up my bare thigh and stood with me in his arms. "I want to bite your butt."

I kissed his neck. "Just my butt?"

"No, lots of places on all of you."

"Mmmm, please."

Jason lay me on the bed and peeled off his T. My heart rate increased as he undid his shorts and I saw no boxers. I took my T-shirt off over my head, wiggled out of my shorts and turned onto my belly. Jason parted my legs and kneeled in between them.

"Sweet, baby." Jason squeezed and moved over one cheek then the other to nibble and suck.

I murmured as he moved his mouth to the soft flesh on the inside of my thighs then moaned when he flicked his tongue between my legs, followed with his teeth and nipped.

"You like, baby?"

"You have the most beautiful mouth."

"Turn over, baby. Let me taste more of you."

I turned onto my back and Jason fastened his mouth on my nipple and sucked, moved down to my belly with brief nips and kisses and on to my pubic mound. I tightened my fingers on his shoulders as he fastened on my center and I whimpered as he pushed his tongue deeper inside.

My back arched as Jason joined his tongue with a fingertip to circle and rub my clitoris.

"Oh, God! Jason…now, please."

He moved up my body, eased his cock inside me, held my hands and pinned them with his above my head. "Baby, let me feel you. Hear you."

I writhed as Jason thrust inside me and I ground my pelvis against his, shouting it out as he bit my neck and my orgasm raced through me in rhythm to the blood pounding through my heart. "Jason. Fuck! Yes."

Jason's thrusts shortened and he tightened his hands on mine. "Ness, that's beautiful."

I wrapped my arms around him when he released my hands, stroking them down his back as we breathed hard. I snuggled under his arm and draped my leg over his thighs as he moved to his side.

"Good, baby?" he asked.

I kissed his chest. "Yeah. Very. You?"

"Yeah. Very. I think I've left a hickey above the collar line on your neck."

I touched the spot where Jason's teeth had been. "I'll dab some makeup over it if it is."

I lay still in Jason's arms and he ran his fingers through my hair until my eyelids started to close. "I don't want to, but I'd best get up to do my teeth."

Jason kissed the top of my head and I used the bathroom then cuddled back under his arm as he got back into bed after doing the same.

"I'll run you home in the car early enough to get changed for work in the morning if you like?"

I snuggled closer and yawned as I wrapped my leg over Jason's thighs.

"It's okay. I'll run back in the morning. I haven't been to the gym this weekend. I could do with the stretch."

"Alarm's set. Sleep well, sweetheart."

I smiled against Jason's chest. "And you. Until the morning."

My muscles relaxed under the touch of Jason's fingers down my back and I slept until his phone alarm trilled at six, pressed close against his warmth for a minute and slid my legs out of bed. Jason sat up and yawned as I walked out of the bathroom, swung his legs to the floor as I pulled on my leggings and a tee and stopped for a kiss on his way to the bathroom.

"I'll see you in there."

"See you soon."

I loaded Google's *Walk It* map on my phone and headed out with a bottle of water from the fridge to sip from as I ran, opened the front door to my flat before seven and heard Jules' hairdryer. She put it down when she saw me reflected in her mirror and grinned.

"Woohoo you, girlie. Your gold medal is on order for sleep-sleep for sure. What changed?"

I smiled at Jules' reflection. "I'll put some coffee on and tell you. Where's Ben?"

"He had a couple of private clients to see before they start work and he zipped off early. It's why I'm up at stupid o'clock. I'll be with you in two."

I put my hand on the half-full cafetière in the kitchen, found it still hot and poured coffee into two mugs. Jules, dressed in her work-day uniform of blue jeans and a shirt, sat on the sofa. I handed her a mug, sat beside her and tucked my legs up.

"Go on then. Spill it. How?" Jules said.

"Well, on Friday Jason had a bloke turn up at his flat and try to con his way in with a fake pizza delivery. It didn't work but he was so zoned out from the travel then staying up all day that I knew he wouldn't wake if anyone tried anything overnight, so I stayed and dozed on and off while he slept." I sipped and pictured Jason sleeping. "And I liked it, Jules. I really liked it—

being cuddled up against him all night and being there in the morning when he woke — and so did he. So, when Jason said he'd rather get crated and puked on than keep waking up alone, I risked it and stayed."

"And it was fine and you didn't dream."

"But I did, Jules. I don't know if the dream was lurking because we'd been talking about it but I started to dream on Saturday and it woke him, and he woke me before it even really started."

Jules grabbed my hand and squeezed. "Ness. That's good, isn't it? What was it that woke Jason up? Did he say?"

"I was cuddled against him with his arms around me, so when I started to dream, I started to struggle and that woke him up."

"So, it should all be okay as long neither of you moves away from the other in your sleep."

I tightened my hand around Jules'. "Yeah. Fingers crossed that neither of us gets too hot or something, but I love the feel of Jason's skin on mine, and I snug up to him like a little limpet. I think I might wake up myself if Jason turned over in his sleep and moved away from me."

Jules' eyes softened into pools of liquid brown. "Yeah, I sleep spooned into Ben's back with my arm around him. He likes to feel my breasts squashed up against him, although sometimes he likes to pillow his head on them for a while before we turn over and get comfy."

I giggled. "I bet he does."

Jules smiled. "I can't believe it sometimes. Who knew we'd each have a proper boyfriend in our lives like this even a few months ago?"

"Not me, for sure. How was it at your Mum's?"

"Like she always is when she meets someone new — stiff, polite and the best china out for tea."

"Pinky fingers up and ironed napkins all around?"

"Absolutely, but I'd warned Ben, so he just let it all float over his head, and it'll be better next time when a second visit means it's sherry time."

I looked at the time on my phone. "Damn, I'd better jump in the shower and I wanted to know if your mum's cat Lucky did her usual. Catch the rest up at wine o'clock later?"

Jules laughed. "Definitely wine o'clock later. I want to know more about fake pizza, let alone how the fan club is now that Jason's back."

"And I've got a bit to tell you on that one, girlie."

I walked to my bedroom, showered, put on my work shirt and checked my collar line in the mirror. Jason's blood mark showed just above it, so I covered it back to nearly skin tone when I made up my face from the overflow on my dressing table.

Jules put her head around my bedroom door. "Out of here, babe. Have a good day."

"And you. See you back here tonight."

Jules shut the front door behind her and I slipped my feet into black leather shoes with an office-respectable heel and followed her out ten minutes later.

Chapter Fourteen

Jason sat behind his desk as I walked into the office a little before nine. I dropped my phone into my shirt pocket as I sat and waited for a reaction to my arrival from either Annie or Maisie.

Annie glanced over and smiled a quick smile. Maisie muttered under her breath without looking up. "F'in' bitch."

The state of play established, I pulled a pile of internal post envelopes toward me to open. Jason walked past my workstation half an hour later and back again an hour after that. Maisie answered the office landline on her desk fifteen minutes later and looked at Annie as she replaced the handset.

"I've got to pop to HR for a minute. They didn't say what for. I'll tell you when I get back."

Maisie walked away from her desk. Annie watched her go and looked at me. "I don't suppose I've got to take too much of a wild guess what for?"

I shrugged and didn't answer.

"It's been going on between you and Jason for a while, hasn't it? Couldn't you have said something earlier before it came to this?"

"Sorry, but I've done nothing but try and let Maisie know she didn't stand a chance where Jason's concerned, if you'd like to think back. And if you thought I might have given you an on-going progress report about my relationship with him for the rest of the office to enjoy before this point, you're about as far down the road marked stupid as Maisie is."

Annie sighed and nodded. "Yeah, I know you did, but Maisie's so pretty that I always thought she'd get there in the end. I still can't quite wrap my head around why he doesn't like her back."

"It happens. Accept it and move on. There'll be a guy out there somewhere for Maisie that'll do more for her than just look good standing beside her. Help her find him."

"Yeah. I suppose…"

Annie looked up and her eyes widened as the office door opened. I followed her gaze.

Maisie stalked in, every molecule of her body stiff and rigid. She sat, gave me two eyefuls of glittering ice across the desk and hissed, "This is down to you, you stupid cow. You're going to get this back in spades one day and I'm going to enjoy every damn minute when it does."

"Maisie? Are you okay? What happened?" Annie whispered.

Maisie looked at Annie and kept her voice low. "Miss Jealous Bitch here has stitched me up. She can't cope with the competition so she's had a little whine at Jenny. God, the girls in this office just can't take it!"

"But, Maisie, Vanessa hasn't left her desk this morning. It must have been Jason that went to HR," Annie said.

Maisie hissed back. "Then she must have wound him up to do it. Apparently, I can't help the way I feel but I should try and keep it to myself because I'm embarrassing people. Well, I don't have to look far to know who the only person is that could be."

I put in my earbuds and pulled my keyboard forward as Maisie slammed her mouse onto its mat. My phone vibrated in my pocket ten minutes later. *Jason*.

You okay? Meeting Gary off site for lunch. Come with at one?

I'm fine. Not happy when she came back but expected that. See you at one.

I carried on with my work. Maisie left her desk at eleven and returned five minutes later with two coffees. I gave it another half an hour, left the office and fetched my own.

Derek stood beside Maisie's workstation as I arrived back at my desk, his cheeks a pretty shade of rose. "About what I said on Friday… Um…perhaps a coffee? Ah…perhaps at lunchtime?"

Maisie flicked her eyes in my direction as I sat. "I'll think about it," she told him.

Derek walked away. I dropped my empty cup into the waste bin, put my ear buds in and didn't look up from my work again until one. I stepped alongside Jason as he arrived at my desk and walked out of the office with him.

"How has it been this morning? You could move to a different workstation if you like?" Jason said as the door swung shut behind us.

"No, it's fine. I got a bit of a mouthful when she got back, but I haven't heard another word since and I'd stay sitting just where I am, no matter what, because I'm bit of a stubborn cow like that."

Jason smiled. "Yeah. I would be, too." Jason pressed the call button for the lift. "Gary will be in Costa just after one."

Gary nodded as we walked in through the door and Jason put the tray down with our toasted ham and cheese sandwiches and coffees ten minutes later. Gary swallowed his mouthful of panini as we sat. "Ness. Jason. You both good?"

I smiled and Jason nodded. "What have you got for us?"

"Well, I've been following the code to find out why the interest in Tim and found that it extracts words and phrases from the emails you exchange with him. I'm thinking you might receive one from Tim at some point setting up the scam and it will appear genuine because it will have been put together using Tim's own words and phrases that will hit the right chord with you."

"I'll look out for it."

"Do you still want to find out who's behind this, rather than just stop the theft?" Gary asked.

Jason nodded. "Yeah. If I can. There's no allocated parking at work, so I'm not getting anywhere fast trying to find out who our biker could be. What are you thinking of?"

"I'm thinking of turning the email lure back on the perp to see if we can draw him out. A fictional one from you to Tim that drops rather guessable hints that the artwork will be alone and unattended in your empty flat tomorrow evening—which it won't be because your place will have me sitting in it."

Jason frowned. "Yeah. I could go for that, but I don't want to risk the actual piece. I'm sure you'd stop him from taking it, but the artwork could be easily damaged in the event of struggle and I can't go for anything that allows that to be a possibility."

Gary smiled. "I thought you might say that, but you don't have to risk the artwork itself as long as the perp thinks that you have. You could put something else in the art case and it would still be an attempted burglary if he opens it and finds not the artwork but maybe something intriguing enough to make him want to lift it out."

Jason nodded. "Okay. Yeah. I can do that. We've got a display frame in the workshop that shows all the different cuts we do on various stones. It looks impressive but the majority of the stones are semi-precious and their total value is only about two or three thousand, although an untrained eye would probably add another zero to that from the look of the thing. How do you want to work this?"

Gary thought for a minute then said, "With just enough fuss for it be noticed, get the artwork case into your office tomorrow. Take it home. Return to the office without it. Go where you've said you'll be when you finish work."

"Ness and I could call into the local bar and stop off for a drink on our way home from work."

Gary shook his head. "Too close. Your perp might have a mate on the lookout to make sure you're really out the way. You want to let your perp relax a little. I wouldn't be surprised if he didn't have a tire iron or something similar in his excuse of a delivery bag if he turns up. He must know from his last visit that the internal locks on the front doors at your place are an easily popped single Yale, but let's let him think he's got a bit of time to enter and search for what he's looking for."

"Okay. Then we'll head for Ness' flat and watch the live feed on the phone. But I'm heading straight back the minute I catch sight of him. It takes around twenty-five minutes at a fast jog."

Gary smiled. "Don't worry. He won't be going anywhere once I've got my hands on him. He'll still be there if you want to give him a whack."

Jason laughed. "No. That's fine. I don't mind thumping anyone in the heat of the moment because I've got to, but I won't do it cold just because someone's pissed me off. I'll settle for seeing who it is and handing them and the camera footage over to the police. Thanks."

"Good. I'll go back to the office now and get the dummy email from you to Tim ready to go from your corrupted hard drive. I'll be at your front door bright and early before many people are up to see me do so. Around six?"

I looked at Gary. "Watch out for Jason's neighbor, Mrs. N. She's a bit lonely and entertains herself by watching the comings and goings at Jason's flat. She'll be up by then and she'll also jump straight in if she spots anything going on in the communal hallway later."

Jason added. "She's disabled and rides an electric scooter. She can be a bit of pain, but as Ness said, she's lonely and I'd hate to see her get caught up in any of this."

"Okay. I'll get the office on to it. See what they can come up with to keep her entertained and out of the way."

Gary stood up and fastened his jacket. "So, I'll see you in the morning. Phone me if anything changes."

I smiled and finished my coffee. Jason tipped the lunch debris from our tray into the bin and I followed him out of the door. "Are you okay with Gary's plans?"

"It goes against the grain a bit to have to stay out of the way when it's my flat that might get broken into, but I get the point."

I squeezed Jason's hand. "We can head straight out the minute you see the first sign of someone on the live feed. Jog on ahead of me. I'm built for a hundred-meter dash, not the marathon. I'll catch up with you as soon as I can."

"If there's any point to it I will, but as Gary says, it'll all be over then but the shouting."

Jason opened Belmond's street door and we rode up the lift. Jason pushed the office door open. "Stay at mine tonight? I'll cook."

"Yes, please. I'll go home first, pick up some clothes for the morning, have a quick catch-up with Jules then come over to yours."

Jason walked with me to my workstation and looked at my handbag. "Got your key in there in case you're back at the flat before me?"

I reached in and pulled out my fluff-ball key ring. "Yep. Yours, mine, the peeps and Granny's."

I dropped my keys into my bag as Jason walked away, put my phone in my shirt pocket and sat. Maisie watched Jason's rear view all the way to his office then muttered. "You might think you've covered that mark up on your neck but he'll see it in the end and know what you've been up to behind his back."

The words were out of my mouth one second before my brain caught up and kicked me for replying, "Yeah, yeah. Like he really knows nothing about it."

"You're a disgusting little tart that sleeps around. Don't try and tell me Jason would do something like that. He wouldn't."

I pasted a small false smile on my face. "Well, none of it is your business either way. Now, I'm going to keep it civil during working hours. I suggest you do the same."

Maisie looked at me with a smile that was as false as my own. "Oh, I will, when there's anyone else around to hear me, but as there's not at the moment, piss off."

"Lovely," I said.

I carried on with my work and Maisie did the same. We worked in silence until Annie walked into the office. She smiled at Maisie as she sat.

"God, it was packed in Costa. Did you make Derek's day and have that coffee with him?"

Maisie nodded. "Not someone I normally like to be seen with, but he told me some stuff that I needed to hear so it was worth it."

"Really? What stuff?"

Maisie looked at me, stared for just long enough to make her point and turned her face toward Annie. "Not for here. I'll tell you tonight."

Annie took her phone out of her handbag. "Great. I'll text Craig and let him know. I'll come over to yours and we can meet Craig there."

I put my ear buds in, worked on until I printed the hard copy of my input figures off at three and managed to spend over an hour dropping them off. Annie stepped out of the lift as I walked past it, returning to the office.

"That's the post dropped off. Have you only just finished taking the printouts around?"

I looked at Annie and lied. "Yeah. Sorry. I dropped them twice and had to take the time to put all the pages back in order."

Annie lied back with a grin. "Yeah, I know what you mean. All of my envelopes slipped right out of my hands just outside of the IT office. It took me at least half an hour to pick them all up."

I pushed the office door open. Derek looked up and moved out of Annie's chair. I sat and filled the remaining minutes of my working day putting timesheets in order for filing, left the office at five and opened the front door of my flat just before six. Katy Perry gave it her best roar as I walked down the hallway. Jules sat on the sofa varnishing her fingernails.

"Did you have a good day, girlie? How was the gallery?" I asked her.

Jules smiled, blew on her nails then said, "Really good. We had a sixth form art class in this afternoon and one of the girls' work was so good I've put her name on my watch list for a few years' time. How about you?"

I walked to the kitchen for a glass, filled it from the open bottle on the coffee table and kicked my shoes off as I sat. "Fairly action-packed, what with Maisie and everything, but I'd better catch you up with what I haven't told you about Friday first."

Jules put her feet up on the coffee table and picked up her glass. "Go then, girlie. So, Friday…"

"So, on Friday, Jason wanted to stay awake to catch up to UK time, so we went into work for the afternoon and Jason thought that without making a song and dance about it, it was time that the office found out we were seeing each other." I sipped a mouthful of wine as Jules grinned. "So, I got into work first and Jason stopped at my desk when he arrived and we sort of made it obvious without actually saying so that we'd already seen each other that morning."

"And Maisie?"

"Has altered the pics of Jason and Su Linn so Su Linn's not in them anymore but she is."

Jules spat her mouthful of wine back into her glass. "Shit! You're joking! And she let someone see them?"

"Yep. One of the girls in the office caught sight of them on her phone."

"And when she realized you're actually going out with Jason?"

"She hissed at me a bit but still along the lines of *I'm going to end up going out with Jason not you,* so I gave her a bit back and she stopped talking to me, which was fine, but…"

"But?" Jules prompted.

"But Maisie *is* out of order on this, isn't she? It's not just me? Because of how I feel about Jason?"

"Yes, babe. She is. Jason's made it quite clear he's not interested, and even if Jason wasn't going out with anyone at all, it's gone on for too long and worse, the longer it's gone on, the more Maisie's stepped up the ante."

"Okay, good. So, I told Jason about Maisie altering the pictures and he asked Jenny in HR to have a word with Maisie this morning. When she came back to the office afterward, she declared that I was a jealous bitch who'd stitched her up, then after lunch, I was a tart who must be sleeping with someone else as well as Jason because of…" I touched my neck and Jules laughed.

"Because fictional Jason wouldn't do such a thing," Jules guessed.

I raised my glass to her. "And fictional Jason is alive and well in Maisie's head, although I'm the only one that's copping for that at the moment. But I'll take any amount of it if the message has hit home enough that she tones it down in front of everyone else and stops giving Jason the yips."

"So, will you tell Jason what Maisie's being saying to you? That she hasn't given up?"

"Yes and no. Yes, I'll tell Jason that I don't think Jenny's having a word with her has worked but without making too much of it. Jason's got more to sort out than Maisie at the moment."

"Is that why you met Gary at lunch? What did he say?"

"Well, the artwork's going back to bank on Wednesday, so Gary asked Jason if he wanted to set up a little something to try to draw out our prospective thief."

Jules smiled. "And Jason said…?"

"Yes, of course."

"How is he hoping to do it?"

"Gary will send an email from the copy of Jason's hard drive that still has the spyware on it saying that the artwork will be at Jason's flat tomorrow, only it won't. Then Jason will go out and leave it in his flat, only the flat won't be empty. Gary will be in it. And we'll see who, if anyone, turns up."

"And where will you and Jason be?"

"Gary says he thinks Jason's got to be where he's said he'll be, so we'll be here watching the live feed on

Jason's phone then jog over to his if we see our phony pizza-delivering biker arrive."

"You'll get the chance to see Gary in action if he does. I'll try to get back from work in time to have a peek in on Jason's phone for that one."

"Yeah, see if you can. Now, what about your mum's cats, Lucky and Bilbo? What did they do?"

Jules laughed. "Nothing compared to what's going on with you, but you would have laughed so much."

I smiled. "Go on then, spill it, girlie."

"So, we're all sat at the dining table for formal tea and the eggshell china's out and Ben's doing his best to get his finger through the handle of the cup without breaking it and Lucky jumped up onto his lap and did what Lucky always does."

I laughed. "Made love to Ben's crotch with her claws out and gave his bollocks a good old kneading while she purred?"

"Yep. And Ben didn't want to bat her away in case it offended my mother, then Bilbo jumped up and joined in. I had to bite down on my napkin to stop myself from laughing but, bless him, Ben carried straight on through, only slightly goggle-eyed while I shoved the damn cats off his lap."

"Oh, God! I'd have to have excused myself and legged it to the loo like I did when the vicar came to tea. Ben deserves more than a sticky star for that one."

Jules laughed. "For sure. What time are you going to Jason's?"

I looked at the time on my phone. "I'll get some clothes for the morning and head on out. I'll see you here tomorrow evening."

"I'll grab Ben on my way home. See you tomorrow, babe."

I changed back into my morning running clothes, re-packed my work skirt and shoes and another clean shirt into a carrier bag and hit the streets. Half an hour later, and rather less fragrant than I'd been in the morning, I let myself into Jason's flat and pulled my earbuds out.

Jason, changed and smelling rather better than me, poked his head around the kitchen door. "Hey you. You're back."

I fanned myself. "Hey, you, yes. And I ran back, so I'd best jump straight in the shower."

"Wine in here when you're ready."

I made up my face with a light touch, after I'd showered, took underwear, jeans and a clean T-shirt out of the drawer and walked through to the kitchen when I'd dressed. Jason smiled and I put my arms around his neck and my face up for his kiss.

Jason put his hands around my waist, lifted me up to perch on the breakfast bar to kiss me without having to bend down then passed me a glass of wine.

"How was it with Maisie in work this afternoon?"

Jason stepped to his oven, took the lid off a pan on its top and stirred a herby tomato something.

"Still hissy with me and still not giving up on you, but as she only found out this morning that you won't be asking her out this side of the next ice age, I don't think that's much of a surprise."

"No, I suppose not, but I hoped for a fairly instant response. Jenny said that as this is informal for now. She felt she could speak to Maisie without any HR jargon and Maisie should have got my message loud and clear."

I sipped and thought about what Jules had said. "I think that's some of Maisie's problem. It's your message, but the guy in Maisie's head isn't you. He only looks like you."

Jason put the lid back on the pan. "I'll give it until next week, and if nothing's changed, I'll speak to Maisie to try to dispel that particular illusion in person. Nothing formal, although I'll ask Jenny to sit in so there's a neutral third person in the room."

"You might not have to. The guy in Maisie's head hasn't asked her out because she's so beautiful and lovely that he won't risk asking in case she says no. If that particular bubble's been popped for her fictional you, you can't exist either, although he's been hanging around for a while, so it could take a bit of time for him to pack his bags and leave."

Jason smiled. "Well, his eviction notice has been served, so I hope he gets the message and moves out soon. What time do you want to eat? This will be ready in twenty but I can slow it down if you're not hungry yet."

I sniffed the air. "Whenever it's ready, please. It smells lovely. Can I do anything?"

Jason opened a drawer, took a cheese grater out of it and offered it to me. "If you're sure this won't turn into a lethal weapon in your hands, the parmesan's in the fridge."

"I shall do my best not to give you a side order of grated fingertip with it" — I took the grater from Jason's hand and jumped down off the breakfast bar — "although I've never used a little, sharp one like this. Ours is a box grater."

Jason held his hand out. "I knew it. Give it back, you."

I held the grater behind my back, danced a quick side-step past Jason and laughed. "Nope. You said I could have a go. You're not getting it."

Jason opened a drawer, took out a first-aid box, flicked the lid up and poked the contents with his finger. "Plasters, bandages, nine-nine-nine on speed dial. Go on, then. I'm ready."

Jason looked at me. I straightened my face, saluted with the cheese grater and side stepped over to the fridge. "Roger, that. It's a dangerous job but someone's got to do it. I'm going in."

I opened the fridge door, looked for the Parmesan and saw the wedge of hard cheese that Jason had bought in the deli on Saturday through the clear lid of a plastic food box. I put my hand into the fridge and picked it up.

"Careful there, soldier. That's a mature *Parmigiano stravecchio* you have there. Fully ripe."

I lifted the box out of the fridge, popped open the lid and held the box at arm's length away from my nose as I spluttered, "Bloody hell, Jason! You're not kidding on that one."

Jason laughed and dropped strands of pasta into a pan of boiling water. "Leave the lid off for a couple of minutes. The smell will disappear."

I flicked the lid off, put the box down on the worktop, stepped away from it holding my grater and sat on my stool at the breakfast bar. Jason looked at me as I picked up my glass, put the grater down and nudged it over in his direction with my elbow. "Sorry. I'm not that brave. No way am I going anywhere near that monster again until it's been reduced to small grains and on my dinner."

Jason smiled, picked up the grater, rubbed the cheese against it over his pot of sauce, drained the pasta, stirred the two together and tipped the contents into two pasta bowls.

I twirled my fork through the mixture and tasted.

"Oh, this is good. I was sure that cheese was going to bite me back."

Jason dipped his fork into his bowl. "No, sweetheart. That'll be me."

I glanced sideways at him as my nipples hardened at the thought.

He looked at my chest. "Bad girl."

I smiled, twisted another mouthful of pasta around my fork and managed to eat my way through half my bowl. Jason swapped bowls with me and ate the rest of mine, then I rinsed and Jason stacked the dishwasher.

"Coffee and…?" Jason asked.

"Coffee and your choice with ice."

Jason set the coffee machine off, filled a beaker with ice, left the kitchen and came back with two chinking brandy glasses of creamy stuff.

"Bailey's. It's slightly less alcoholic than the rest, if I've got to set the alarm early."

I sipped, swallowed and the warmth hit the back of my throat. "Doesn't taste it. The *rest*? How many different ones have you got in there?"

Jason put the coffees on the breakfast bar and sat beside me. "Plenty, including the inevitable one that tasted wonderful in the Caribbean but at home tastes so sickly that I wonder why I haven't poured it down the loo yet."

I guessed. "Pineapple?"

"If only. Thick, yellow, banana."

"Ew, babe. It sounds sticky."

"You could hang wallpaper with it. They mix it with rum and lime out there."

"Okay. I'm game for a laugh. Mix me one on Saturday and I'll give it a go."

"Okay, but you've got to mix me one."

I laughed. "Coquito. Tasted fantastic in Puerto Rico at Christmas, totally the most disgusting thing ever if you try and mix it yourself when you get home."

"What's in it?"

"Apart from white rum? Coconut cream, condensed milk, egg yolks and some other delicious, yummy things."

"Condensed milk and egg yolks? Ew! Barf juice or what!"

I laughed, finished the last mouthful in my glass, let an ice cube into my mouth and offered Jason my lips when it melted. Jason put his lips on mine and I ran the tip of my cold tongue over his bottom lip.

"Yes?"

Jason breathed in a little deeper. "Yes."

I picked up my glass of ice. "A glass of hot water to go with?"

Jason filled a tumbler and passed it to me. I put both glasses on the bedside table, stripped off my leggings and T-shirt and sat on the side of the bed. Jason moved his gaze over my body as he took off his T. My heart thumped as he popped the button on his jeans, sped faster as he shrugged out of them and his cock, hard and ready, appeared.

I patted the bed alongside me. "On sideways, babe, so, I can reach the glasses."

Jason lay across the bed. I kissed his lips, moved my tongue down his chest, over his belly, down to his cock then licked and sucked. His breathing deepened.

I stroked his balls with one hand, put a sliver of ice in my mouth with the other and played my icy tongue on the nerve endings there where my warm hand had been. Jason took in a sharper breath.

I heated my hand around the glass, ran my cold tongue over his cockhead and eased his foreskin forward with my warm hand. Jason's abs tightened. "Ness…"

"More or stop, babe?"

"More…"

I nipped my teeth into the crease of Jason's thigh, nibbled through the golden hair of his pubic mound, heated my mouth, fastened my lips over his cock and sucked. Jason breathed faster.

I sucked harder, heated my hand around the glass again and cupped his balls, then melted ice on my tongue and flicked small, quick licks where my hand had been. Jason's muscles tensed. "God, Ness."

I moved my lips up his erection, wrapped my still-cold mouth over his cock, sucked and worked my hands on the length of his shaft, hummed in the back of my throat as he murmured and breathed faster. "Ness, please…"

I kept up the rhythm of my hand, moved my tongue up his body and kissed his lips. "Fuck me?"

Jason groaned, turned and pinned my shoulders. I parted my legs. He ran his fingers between them, opened me and thrust the length of his shaft in.

I arched my back to meet him. "Hard, please, babe. Don't hold back."

Jason moved fast, pounding his cock inside me, holding my shoulders down. I writhed underneath him, moaning as his cock hit deep, his pelvis slamming again and again against mine. His muscles tensed. I tilted my head for his teeth on my neck and shouted as he bit down. "Oh, Fuck! Shit! Yes!"

Jason groaned low in his chest and released my neck. "Ness… My lovely, girl." He breathed hard against my neck. "Jesus, baby. What you do to me…"

I panted into his. "And you me. The way you read my body…" I held on tight and lay in Jason's arms until we breathed normally.

Jason stirred and kissed my shoulder. "I'll set the alarm for five-thirty if Gary's getting here around six."

"You feeling okay about tomorrow?" I asked him.

"Yeah, fine. Apart from setting the scene and pretending to bring the artwork back here, it won't really involve us, will it? Whoever it is will show — or not — and Gary will deal with him if he does."

"You'll have the police around if he turns up and breaks in," I said.

"If he does, the CCTV footage will be there. That should make it pretty open and shut. You want the bathroom first or me?"

I yawned. "I'll go first. I might nod off otherwise."

"Someone been wearing you out?"

I kissed Jason's lips, nibbled his chin and swung my legs off the bed. "Bad man. And I've got another hickey." I had my shower then he went in.

I curled against Jason when he got into bed. Jason put his arm around me and stroked his hand down my back. I closed my eyes, relaxed under his touch and didn't stir again until his phone alarm trilled in the morning. Jason kissed the top of my head.

"Much as I don't want to, I'd better move. Stay there, baby. I'll shower and make the coffee."

I dozed for a while to the sound of water running, opened one eye to watch Jason get dressed then sat up and stretched as he zipped his suit trousers and sat on the side of the bed to put socks on his feet.

"Okay. I'm up." I put my feet to the floor to Jason's smile.

"Coffee and toast ready when you want them."

Jason straightened the pillow and turned the quilt back as I closed the bathroom door. I dried my hair to the smell of brewed coffee and walked through to the kitchen to see Gary sitting at the breakfast bar drinking a coffee with his laptop open. Jason slid my cup over as I sat, buttered a slice from a mountain of toast and pushed the plate forward.

Gary picked up a slice and bit down, chewed, swallowed then said, "Morning, Ness. You good?"

"Fine, thanks. Did you see any sign of Jason's neighbor when you got here?"

Gary shook his head. "She might have caught sight of me at the street door but there was no sign of her in the hallway, so she won't know which flat I'm visiting. She'll be out later, visiting a couple of places to give her opinion on their suitability for disability access. Dinner afterward to say thanks, that type of thing."

I smiled. "Did she take much persuading?"

"Not a lot. Liam and Lisa are running back-up for me today. They'll make sure she has a good time."

"You think *you* might need back-up?" Jason said.

"No, probably not," Gary smiled, "but I'm a cautious guy. You don't last long in this industry if you're not. I'll set another camera up in your living room when you go to work. We'll put the case on the unit you've got in there. It won't quite be in plain sight but visible enough to someone that will be looking for it."

Jason nodded. "Okay. I'll send you a text when I leave work with it. I'm going to have forgotten something I need from here and use the lunch break to come get it and take the chance to bring the case home with me because I'm going to Ness' after work."

Gary picked up another slice of toast. "Good."

Jason put his coffee cup down and I did the same. "Ready, Ness?"

"Sure. See you later, Gary."

I followed Jason out to the lift and Jason nosed the car into the morning crawl and cut the engine as he pulled into a parking bay well over an hour later.

"It shouldn't take quite as long to get home at lunch. I'll Tube it back."

I shut the car door and walked with Jason to the lift. "I forgot to put my running shoes in my bag. Could you bring them back with you?"

"Sure. I'll put mine and some trackies in the bag to get changed at yours."

Our floor arrived and I walked with Jason into the office. Maisie's gaze flicked up to Jason's face as we arrived and followed his rear to his office from under half-lowered lids. I picked up the drink carrier and dipped my toe in to test the temperature of this morning's water. "Coffee, anyone?"

"Thanks. I could do with one," Annie said.

"Not until I know where your hands have been," Maisie replied without looking up.

Annie looked at Maisie with a small shake of her head. "Maisie. Remember what Craig said about…you know."

"No, then."

"Charming. Annie, do you still want one?"

Annie glanced over at Maisie's face. "Um…"

"It's fine if you don't."

"Ah, well. Perhaps not then, although thank you for asking."

I walked out of the office and used the ladies. Jess waved at me from the coffee machine as I exited it and she laughed when I reached her. "I know I shouldn't but I can't help myself. Who on earth is does she think she's kidding over Derek? Poor bugger! It's all smiles and whispers when she talks to him but you've only got to see the look on her face change when he walks away to know that she doesn't like him any more than she did before and is just using him to prop up her ego and cover her embarrassment at being caught doing what she did to the pictures."

I asked the machine for a coffee. "Why him, though? Derek seems nice enough but Maisie's all about appearances, and he's hardly up to her standards on that front."

Jess grinned. "Because he was available and on tap, I should think. Her focus has been elsewhere for so long that she hasn't got her normal guy or two dangling, just waiting for her to click her fingers. I just hope he doesn't take it too hard when she gets someone better-looking on her hook and drops him."

I took my coffee out of the dispenser. "I suppose."

I walked back to the office with Jess, drank my coffee and carried on with my work. Nick Davies walked through the office with the art case in his hand at eleven. Jason walked out of his office with it at twelve-thirty and stopped at my workstation. "I've left some paperwork at home that I need. I'll run the car back and get it, drop this indoors and we can go straight to yours tonight. Anything you need from mine, apart from your shoes?"

I smiled. "Just them, thanks. I'll use Jules' things if I need to."

"Okay. See you later."

Jason walked away and Maisie muttered at her screen, "Enjoy it while you can, but he's mine and I know it."

I ignored the comment and moved my fingers over my keyboard. Maisie and Annie picked their handbags up at one and walked to the office door. Derek stood and hurried after them.

"Ah…Maisie. Have you done your quarter end accrual journals? Um, I could do them for you if you like."

Derek's voice cut off as the door swung shut behind the three of them and the office quieted as people came and went for lunch. Annie walked into the office at two, sat and looked at me. "She's still cheering herself up in Miss Selfridge" — her cheeks flushed a little as she added — "and I just wanted to say sorry about the coffee and all that, but Maisie's my best friend. I have to be on her side and do what she needs me to do."

"I wouldn't expect any different. You do what you need to. It's fine."

Maisie sat at her desk half an hour later. Annie looked at the carrier bag standing beside her handbag.

"You found something you liked? What did you get?"

Maisie fanned her face with her hand. "The most amazing pair of jeans. You wait until you see them. Tight all the way up and they make my legs look like they go on for just about ever."

"I'll look forward to seeing them on."

Maisie giggled. "I'm looking forward to wearing them, nearly as much as I'm looking forward to seeing someone's face when they get dumped."

"Maisie…" Annie said.

Maisie gazed over Annie's shoulder at Jason's office. "It's me he wants really. I know it. He just needs to be sure I'll say yes."

I tuned out Maisie and her daydreams, put my ear buds in and printed my hard copy off at three. Jason arrived at my desk with his laptop bag and a small holdall travel bag as I shut my desk drawer at five.

"Ready, Ness?"

"Sure."

I waited for the office door to swing shut behind us before I asked.

"How was Gary?"

"Working on his laptop in the kitchen. He's set the other camera up and he's got a couple of windows open on his laptop to keep an eye on them while he works. How are we getting back to yours?"

"There's a bus at twelve past."

"Lovely."

I grinned at the fixed smile on Jason's face. "Better than the tube from here. The bus is nearly door to door."

We managed to get two seats together at the back of the bus and it chugged us home through the bus lanes.

I opened the door to my flat a little after six. "No music. Jules isn't back yet. I'll jump in the shower quick."

"Yeah, why not? We could be sitting here for a while or even all night if Pizza Man doesn't take the bait. You go first. I'll watch the phone, then we can swap."

Jason sat on the side of the bed with his phone in his hand. I turned on the shower, soaped up and washed my hair, brushed it into a high tail then slipped my leggings and top on. Jason handed me his phone and changed places with me in the bathroom. I looked at my own phone, saw thirty percent and called through the bathroom door.

"I'll give my phone a quick boost. My charger's at yours but Jules' is in the living room. I've got your phone with me."

"Okay, I won't be long."

I opened the bedroom door, heard movement in the living room and called out as I walked down the hall.

"Jules, can I borrow your charger, ba—?" My words dried in my mouth as I walked through the living room door and saw Maisie inside the room. "Maisie? What are you doing here? How did you get in?"

Maisie moved her hand and I saw a pistol-shaped object in it—not a gun but something of a similar shape with a feathered dart on top of it. I lodged the phones in the back of the sofa cushion and stepped to the side of the sofa to close the gap between us. Maisie waved the gun-shape at me.

"No closer."

"Maisie, where did you get that? Put it down before you hurt yourself."

"No. He said you'd say that when he gave it to me with your key."

"Who's *he*?"

Maisie shook her head. "No way. He said you'd ask that one, too."

I looked at Maisie's flushed face, her eyes over-bright, and tried to keep my voice calm as my heart rate sped up and the hair on the back of my neck prickled. "Why have you come here?"

Maisie laughed, sharp and shrill. "Priceless! I told you it would be me in the end and I told you I would enjoy every damn second of it when it was!"

Jason's voice called from the hallway. "Ness. Who's that? You okay?"

Jason walked into the living room, a towel wrapped around his waist. Maisie turned toward Jason and she gazed at his upper torso.

Jason stilled as he looked at Maisie's face then at her hand pointed in my direction. "What the hell?"

Maisie turned her over-bright gaze toward Jason and smiled, her hand still pointed at me. "It's okay. I got your email. I'm here. Don't worry."

"Maisie, whatever that is, put it down."

"No. It's fine, really. He said it won't hurt her, only put her to sleep so she can't stop you leaving with me."

Jason looked at his phone propped up on the sofa cushion then at me. "A diversion to make sure I didn't come home unexpectedly."

I nodded and my heart beat harder as my thoughts raced. I looked at Maisie and judged the distance. "I'd have thought. With something in hand to keep us busy for a while. We might have just chucked her straight back out of the front door else," I said.

"What are you two going on about? Stop it. This isn't right. Jason, I'm here like you wanted."

I looked into Jason's eyes, dropped mine to his towel then looked at the floor. Jason's gaze followed mine.

"Ah...I could get there myself instead," he winced.

I rotated my ankles and loosened my shoulders. "Sorry, Angel. Buffy has the best chance. She's closer."

Maisie's voice rose. "Buffy? Angel? What? This isn't the way this is supposed to go. Jason, look at me, not her."

I tensed my leg muscles, ready to move, looked at Jason and waited.

He moved his hand and untucked his towel.

I sprang high as Maisie's mouth dropped open and her gaze fixed on Jason naked. I twisted as I jumped, curved my torso out of the way and angled my landing toward Maisie. She released the dart as her head spun back to where I should have been standing. I landed at the same time as the dart buried itself in the wall behind me and Maisie shouted, "No!"

Maisie's voice cut off as I smacked her hard on the nerve endings under her ear. I stepped back as she fell and the dart gun dropped from her hand. Jason picked his towel up from the floor as I toed the gun away.

"Fuck! She actually fired the bloody thing!"

I kneeled beside Maisie and checked her pulse under her ear. "She's out cold for now. Do you want to do the thing on my phone? Ace will get here faster than anything else."

Jason wrapped his towel around his waist and picked up my phone. "I'll do it while I throw my trackies on."

"Leave the front door on the latch so Ace can get in."

I kept my eyes on Maisie, walked backward and picked up Jason's phone from the sofa. One glance at the screen as I stepped back toward Maisie showed me Jason's front door stood ajar. I patted Maisie's jean pockets and pulled out four shiny new keys on a loop. Jason walked into the living room as Maisie began to stir.

"I didn't hear the door buzzer. How did she get in?"

I showed Jason the copied keys and handed him his phone. "My keys have been copied. She let herself in. She was already in here when I walked into the room to charge my phone, and whoever is in your flat must have another set of keys. Your front door is open but intact."

Jason tapped on his phone. "I can't see anything happening from the camera in the hall. Do you think Gary will have gotten his hands on him?"

"I'm sure so, but it could still be in progress out of the camera's range."

"I'll wait for him to contact me, then."

Maisie's eyes fluttered open. She stared at the ceiling, moved to my face then to the dart in the wall. She sat up. I looked at her hands and saw them whiten under her weight as she pulled her knees up.

"Don't try to stand or I'll put you flat on your back again," I said.

Maisie looked at Jason, her eyes unblinking, her lips tilting to the start of a smile. "Jason, tell her. Once she knows, we can still get out here. You can stop her if she goes for me when we leave."

Jason shook his head and put his arm around me. Maisie blinked. The brightness clouded in her eyes. "Jason. No. The email..."

Jason looked at Maisie with eyes as narrow and cold as I wished never to see again. "I don't care what it said. You've got eyes in your head and a brain in there somewhere that should have told you it was a bundle of bullshit, let alone that Jenny made it quite clear to you that Ness and I are together and not in the least interested in getting involved with anyone else."

The cavalry arrived in the doorway behind Jason and I nodded at Liam. Liam looked around the room. "This linked to what Gary's got going on at your place?"

Jason nodded.

"Get out of here then. I'll call the police and start the process. You'll be stuck here for hours before they get around to taking your statements if you're here when they arrive."

"They won't like it much."

Liam shrugged. "They'll get over it. Nothing more you can do here other than give a statement. I'll call Gary after I call the police. I'll let him know you've had trouble here and you're on your way over."

I followed Jason out of the room to the sound of Maisie's wail. "Jason. Don't leave. This is all her fault. Let me explain. Jason! Jason…"

I laced up my running shoes in the hall, picked up my phone and opened the front door. "Do you want to take the stairs rather than wait for the lift?"

Jason took my hand in his and walked toward the lift.

"The lift—and flag down the first available cab we see. Gary must have got his hands on whoever it is at mine or we'd have heard otherwise by now. No need for us to arrive out of breath and sweaty, let alone run a route that will still be a pedestrian collision course at this time of day."

"Maisie would probably have told you who it is if you'd have asked her."

Jason put his arms around me when we stepped into the lift. "I wouldn't trust a word that came out of her mouth after that. Are you okay, baby? I never expected anything like this to happen when we set this up with Gary."

I squeezed around Jason's waist. "No, neither did I, but I'm fine. I'd better call and warn Jules, though."

Jules answered on the second ring and I put her on speaker.

"Is everything okay, babe? We were just leaving Ben's."

"You're on speaker so Jason can hear you. Don't go home yet. Maisie turned up at ours and created mayhem. Liam's with her, waiting for the police to arrive. We're on our way back to Jason's to find out who Gary's got for us."

The lift doors opened. Jason let us out of the street door and we quick-walked toward the gates.

"That bloody girl's getting to be a real menace. What did she do? Turn up and act out one of her fairy stories?"

"Absolutely and for real with special effects. She bought a tranquillizer dart thing with her and fired it at me."

"Shit, babe! Where the hell did she get that? Please, tell me you decked her?"

Jason's released the gate and we picked up the pace a little.

"Yeah, I did. Jason distracted her so I could move and put her out. She said an unnamed 'he' gave her the dart gun and a key to our flat and that she'd received an email from Jason asking her to come to our flat and help him get away from me."

Jules snorted down the line. "But that's just ridiculous! It sounds like she totally lost the plot this time."

"It was the worst I've ever seen her. Totally acting out what was inside her own head. We're thinking whoever set this up is probably the same person Gary's holding on to at Jason's."

"Let me know when you can, babe. I'll steer clear of the flat until Liam tells me the police have finished processing it. I wonder if James is on duty. He'll hear our address for a possible assault with a weapon over the radio when the call goes out."

"Text him then. Let him know, no drama. We're out of the flat and clear but don't mention Jason's. We don't want his blue twinklers turning up there before they're needed. I'll call you again later."

"When you can. Speak soon."

I cut the connection as we turned onto the Fulham Road.

"Maisie's been like this at work before?" Jason said.

"Not like we've just seen, more like a glimpse of it. A couple of times her eyes did that too-over-bright thing while she talked as if things she wanted to be true actually were. It didn't last long, though. Two or three minutes at most, then she snapped out of it and came back down to earth."

"Somebody realized it could be more than that then, someone who knows rather more about Maisie than we do."

Jason put his hand out for empty black cab headed in the direction we wanted to go.

"I hope not. My head really doesn't want to go there."

"The IT connection is there."

I scooted across the back seat as Jason climbed in and gave the driver his address.

"My keys could only have been copied yesterday or today if your key was with them. The longest time I leave my handbag is to take the hard copy to the other offices. I hate to say it, but Annie went missing at the same time as I was away from my desk yesterday, doing something with Craig."

Jason's phone vibrated. He took it out it of his pocket and opened a message from Gary.

Got him. Cocky git. Smug like he's got an ace to play and is waiting to do it.

Jason replied.

About thirty mins away. No name?

Won't tell me. Think he's waiting for you.

Text you when we're at the door.

Jason put his phone away. "Does that sound like Craig to you? He's never come across as either smug or cocky to me."

"The few times I've seen him with Annie he's had the winky, eyelash thing going on but I'd have said confident rather than up himself. I could kick myself over my copied keys, though. I knew my handbag had been rummaged through more than once and never gave a thought about what else was in it other than my phone."

"Who would? We all leave stuff laying around in the office. Whoever it is, though, must have got Maisie to your flat on his bike then shot over to mine. She was still in work when we left. She couldn't have got to your place that quick behind us, otherwise."

"Yeah. I'm thinking that way, too. You can't straddle a motor bike in a tight skirt, and Maisie went out and bought a pair of jeans at lunchtime. Has Craig got a bike? Annie's never mentioned one."

The cab pulled up outside Jason's block. Jason passed the fare forward to the driver. "Might have. Time to find out."

Jason messaged Gary at the street door. Gary replied as we took the lift up.

Have heard from Liam. Something I want to hear. Play him if you can until I give you the nod?

Jason tapped back, turned the key and opened the front door. Gary leaned against the door frame of the bathroom door, looking toward us as Jason closed the door behind us. "He shot in here when I asked him to put the art case down and assured him he wouldn't be leaving just yet. He sussed you had CCTV on site. I offered him a seat elsewhere but he assures me he's quite comfy sitting on your loo."

"Never known anyone have a camera anywhere near their loo. It's just not the thing to do, is it? To record someone taking a crap."

I looked at Jason. He widened his eyes slightly to mirror mine as we recognized the voice. I followed Jason down the hallway and looked over Gary's shoulder. Jason did the same and said, "Yeah, you look quite comfy there, Derek. Don't forget to flush if you've used it."

Derek looked at Jason, then at me. He was leather-clad, with hair slicked, no glasses, no downcast eyes and no sign of pink rosiness.

"Oh, it's both of you, is it? I thought she might be on her way to the hospital."

I shrugged. "You misjudged your girl, then. That'll be Maisie after I decked her."

"No. Not that. The only thing I misjudged was how protective he would be over an asset owned by the company he works for. Private security. I'll admit I wasn't expecting that for what should have been a straight in-and-out insurance job."

"So, who are you? Not Derek. Your avatar?" I said.

Derek looked at his knees, half closed his eyes and blushed. "Oh, Derek exists when I want him to. It's one of more my useful props, being able to blush when I want to. My avatar gets Derek a little IT help when he needs it. IT pros are suckers for showing off if what you've asked for is a bit of code for a dumb-ass role-play game."

"You've done this before?" Jason prompted.

"Oh, well done, Einstein. This is the sixth company Derek has worked for, although he's not always called Derek."

"And you're telling us this because...?"

"Because Derek and Company have a one-hundred percent success rate and I walked into a set-up. It has pissed me off, so I want you to know I'm going to walk away from this and piss you off, too."

"Oh yeah, how'd you work that one out?" Jason asked.

My phone vibrated. I ignored it.

"You'll find nothing in Derek's life that leads back to me. The police will arrest Derek and by the time Derek's given his final performance, it'll be your word against his that you didn't give me your key and ask me to come and pick up the art case. Either way, the police aren't going to jump through hoops for what at worse will be a charge of trespass."

"And if Maisie tells them any different?" I asked.

Derek laughed. "Ah, yes. Poor Maisie. So easy to manipulate so long as what you're suggesting fits in with the story in her head. When the police interview that one, the only place she'll be heading for is the doc's. The minute she opens her mouth they'll realize her head's not in this world and anything that comes out of her mouth can't be relied on in court."

"There's still your laptop. Had time to delete my data from it, have you? The tranquilizer dart? Any more of those at home?" Jason said.

"There's nothing on Derek's cheap laptop for them to find. I don't keep my work data and props anywhere near Derek's bedsit. The emails that found their way to Maisie's spam folder from you and Tim? The tranquilizer set-up? They're nothing to do with Derek."

Gary nodded. Jason shrugged at Derek. "Oh, well, it might end up as trespass but you'll still have been arrested. I'll settle for getting your fingerprints and DNA into the system for the next time you slip up and keeping hold of my artwork."

"*Your* artwork?"

Jason ignored the question and looked at Gary. "Would you do the honors?"

Gary smiled and took his phone out of his pocket. Derek unzipped his jacket, untucked his shirt, ruffled his hair and took his glasses out. "Do excuse me if I just get ready."

Jason turned away and we walked through to the kitchen. Jason poured wine and sat beside me, his voice low to avoid the ears sitting on the loo. "Bloody git! I know I said I didn't lump people cold. I think I've just changed my mind."

"He would have liked that, I think. I bet if you'd gone for him, he'd have been straight out your bathroom in the hope that the camera would catch you attacking him."

Jason swallowed a mouthful of wine. "Probably, and he'll try and twist anything I say to the police, so I think I'll keep what we can't prove out of it."

"Give James an off-the-record heads up. That'll at least make sure the police don't just swallow the 'Derek the wimp' act. He slipped up today. He might have done so again, even if he's sure Derek's bedsit is clean."

"Okay. Yeah."

I took my phone out of my pocket and saw a missed call and a message. "Speak of the devil."

Where are you? Thought you'd know better than to skip a crime scene.

Jason read the message.
"I'll give Jules the go ahead to tell James what's been going on, shall I?" I asked.
Jason nodded so I texted James back first.

Sorry. At another one now. Go find Jules at Ben's. She'll tell you.

Then a short update to Jules.

Hey, babe. All okay. It was a guy from work — Derek. Police here shortly. James on way to you. Okay to tell him what's been going on now, but off record. More later.

The door buzzer sounded in the hallway as I read Jules' reply.

Okay, babe. Had a text from him asking where we were. I didn't tell him. Will do so now. Speak later.

A uniformed police officer walked in through the kitchen door.
"PC Stevens. Mr. Jones says he was here with your permission. That you gave him a key?"
Jason shook his head. "No. I did neither."
"You'll give a statement to that effect?"
"Of course."

PC Stevens nodded and left the room. Ten minutes later, Derek's voice sounded in the hallway. "But he did. I wouldn't have —"

A female voice answered him. "Yes, sir, but the householder has made a complaint and we have a procedure to follow. You'll have your chance to explain down at the station."

PC Stevens walked into the kitchen. Gary followed after him and put the CCTV data recorder on the breakfast bar. PC Stevens looked at a dining room chair. Jason nodded and he sat, took his official notebook out of his pocket, looked at it then at Jason. "Mr. Jones says you work at the same company, that you gave him a key to this property, asked him to come here, enter your residence and pick up an item."

"No. Mr. Jones works for *my* company. I did *not* give him a key. I did *not* ask or invite him to enter my flat."

"*Your* company?"

"I own fifty percent of Belmond's. The other half is owned by my father."

"And Mr. Jones was unaware of that?"

Jason shrugged. "I wouldn't know. Mr. Jones, as far as I'm concerned, is an employee who runs my accounts payable section. I don't know him on any more of a personal level than that."

"The CCTV?"

"Data on my laptop has been interfered with. I've had a delivery to my front door that I didn't order. I occasionally bring items of value from work here to my flat. I upped my personal security."

"And the key?"

"I did *not* give Derek Jones a key to my flat. If he has one that fits my lock, he's obtained it by other means."

The door buzzer sounded in the hallway. Gary walked out to answer it.

"Hazard a guess?" PC Stevens asked.

Jason shook his head. "No. I won't muddy the waters for you with what I think or don't."

"Two crime scenes in one day, Ness? Busy, busy," James said from the doorway.

"Just a bit, babe."

PC Stevens looked up from his notebook. "Two?"

"Miss DeRay had an intruder in her flat earlier this evening, Stevo. Armed. How about this one?"

"No. Your colleagues patted him down. He wasn't carrying," Gary said as he sat.

"I saw Jules. She gave me the history."

"Good. At least I won't have to cough it all out again tonight. It's been quite a day."

James pulled his notebook out of his pocket. "Sorry, Ness. You've still got to do this bit."

"Okay. Get ready."

James put his pen to the pad. "Go."

"Arrived home at six-o-five. Took a shower. Walked to the living room. Maisie Sealy was in it. She pointed a dart gun in my direction. Jason walked into the room and distracted her. I moved. She fired. I smacked her neck. She blacked out. Jason called my father's security company. We were alerted to an intruder in Jason's flat. We left Maisie in the care of Ace Security and took a cab here. Your colleague has the rest."

James turned to a fresh page. "Okay. Good. Jason? Just the differences will do."

"I sat in the bedroom while Ness showered then used the shower after her. Heard a female voice laugh. It sounded odd, shrill. Went to the living room to see who it was."

"Okay, thanks. I'll arrange for formal statements to be taken in a day or two. Stevo, you got what you need for now?"

"Barely, but I suppose."

"I'll fill you in when we're out of here. Ness, off the record?"

"Derek Jones is a fake. He's scammed five companies successfully before this one. No idea who he really is and he's convinced you won't be able to find out."

"Oh, is he? Well, it won't stop us trying. Out of here, babe. I'll call you tomorrow. Night, Jason. Come on, Stevo. Move your butt."

Gary handed PC Stevens the data recorder, followed them out and returned two minutes later. "Thank God it was your mate, Ness. I thought we were in for another couple of hours of that."

I smiled and sipped. "There's got to be some advantages to having a bit of previous history, even if it is only being able to take a short cut through the procedure."

Jason picked up his glass and nodded to Gary. "You driving?"

"Yeah, but I could murder a coffee."

Jason walked to the coffee machine and asked over his shoulder. "So, you heard what you wanted to hear. What was it?"

"I wanted to know that the email I sent last night is still around. Derek the Dark Rider has just let me know it's sitting on a second laptop at wherever he lives for real that he won't burn because he thinks his real identity can't be traced."

"And that's important because...?"

"When your guy let himself in with a key I thought, not good. When he found the art case and saw what was inside it, he didn't even pick it up, but you still needed to identify him, so I let him know I was there. He sussed straight away that if I'd been out of sight waiting for him, I would have been watching what he was up to on a cam. I expected him to head for the front door and I blocked it. He turned right around, found your loo and I still thought okay, job done" — Jason put Gary's coffee down in front of him. Gary loaded a pic of the tranquilizer dart on his phone — "until Liam sent me this then gave me a call and told me what had happened at Ness' place. He said that the girl that fired it is — to put it politely — off with the fairies, and I looked at Mr. Smug and thought, you think you're going to get away this — Gary flicked his finger at his phone — "then I looked at this and thought, not if I can bloody well help it, you're not."

Jason looked at the pic. "The dart's that bad?"

Gary nodded. "Don't be fooled by its appearance. It might only be a little feathered metal tube a few millimeters long, but these darts pack one hell of a punch. It's why they're on the restricted list and only available on prescription from a registered vet."

"I wonder where the hell he got it? What about the gun?"

"The firing mechanism isn't restricted. Anyone can buy one. The dart? Conned it, nicked it, smuggled in from abroad… Who knows? But it could have been filled with anything, something of his own devising. Nicked, pre-loaded from a vet, either of you would probably have been OD'd in the chiller by now."

The color drained from Jason's face.

"Shit! Ness, it only just missed you."

I squeezed Jason's hand. "Try not to go there, love. The 'could have's' and 'might have's' get stuck in your head. They didn't happen. Don't let them in."

Gary interrupted us. "And he put it in the hands of someone he knew was, quite frankly, unstable, let alone that they shouldn't be used indoors in a confined space."

Gary scrolled down his phone. "Liam sent me this while you were talking to PC Stevens."

I looked at the picture of the wall at my flat with a plate-sized area of bare brick on it.

"That's how much of your plaster it took with it when they pulled it out."

I glanced at Jason's still-white face and speared Gary with a quick, pointed look. "Very nice. I think I might have a frame put around it. So, back to the laptop and the 'not if I can bloody well help it, you're not'?"

Gary raised his coffee cup. I chinked my glass on it.

"So…?" I prompted.

"So, because I'm a cautious guy, I like things in place for just in case. So, I added a little code of my own to the email I sent to the Dark Rider. A rootkit and Trojan so I could access his data again if I needed to."

Jason picked up his glass. "So, you could get the real evidence and give it to the police."

"No, I can't. Any evidence I pull off that hard drive will have been illegally obtained. It won't stand up in court and the police won't touch it. So…" Gary picked up his coffee cup.

I narrowed my eyes at him. "So, get on with it, you, or it's going to be more than a blow-up cow that's coming your way."

Gary laughed. "Okay. So, I'll fire up the not-Derek laptop from mine once the police have had to release him for only a misdemeanor. His Dark Rider Hotmail account will visit the police national computer and make a nuisance of itself for a while, break through a couple of firewalls, try and take a peek at Derek's arrest record, that type of thing."

I smiled. "Now, that's seriously illegal."

Gary returned my smile. "Isn't it? The police hate unauthorized access to their database and they won't let that one go. They'll find out from the IP provider who Derek aka the Dark Rider really is. That alone should see him locked up for a while, and hopefully, he's so sure his real identity is safe that he'll have saved data on his, not Derek's, laptop that will help the police find out the rest of what he's been up to. When I back the Dark Rider out of the police computer, I'll destroy my Trojan code. Unlike Derek aka the Dark Rider, I'm good. There'll be no trace of me left behind."

Jason lifted his glass. "Couldn't happen to a nicer guy."

Gary zipped up his jacket and picked up his case. Jason stood to let him out.

"I'll let you know how it goes. Night, Ness."

I blew Gary a kiss and sipped my wine while I waited for Jason to come back. He lifted me onto his lap when he did. I wrapped my arms around his neck and kissed him until our air ran out.

"I know what you said about the might have and could have, baby, but it's still making my blood run cold. That dart was only ever aimed at you and it only just missed. If I'd known..."

I tightened my arms around Jason.

"I'd have still gone for her. That's the point of The Girls' Club. I avoid certain situations that make me anxious, but threaten me and I'm coming back at whoever does it. I won't *ever* be taken down again like I was before."

"You called me 'love', not 'babe'."

I looked into his warm green eyes, saw my look and knew it stood for more than just 'wow' sex. "Because I do."

"Like 'I love you'?" Jason asked.

"All of you. Everything. Every inch."

Jason offered me his lips. "And I love you, baby."

I moved Jason's hand to my breast, pressed his fingertips to my hardened nipple and tilted my mouth to his. "Practical demonstration?"

"Bad girl…"

* * * *

Four months later

I lay beside Jason on the mattress of our double-size sun lounger and watched the darting runs of Lizzie the Lizard between the arid plants of the screened garden outside our hotel room. Droplets from the solar fountain caught in the sunlight as they fell into the plunge pool at the end of the garden. I moved closer under Jason's arm.

"It's truly beautiful here. I'm glad you found this hotel."

Jason put down his book. "It is, isn't it? Although I can't quite take the credit for finding it."

I heard the smile in Jason's voice, rolled across his chest and looked up him. "Oh, yeah, you. Who found it then?"

Jason lifted me closer and kissed my lips. "I sort of stole it from Caz. From when she kept leaving wedding brochures and things around the flat."

I nibbled my lips across Jason's chin. "Bad man."

"It would be a lovely place for a honeymoon, though," Jason said.

I looked at the blue, blue sky and sparkling water. "Yeah, it would. Perfect."

Jason kissed my shoulder. "Would you like to come back for one, sweetheart? Maybe next year?"

I swallowed. My muscles tightened. My skin tingled. "Um…yes. I'd like that."

"And if I had one tiny ring made for you, would you wear it?"

My heart raced. The tingles on my skin erupted into promised goosebumps. I ignored them. "Yes. For you, I would."

Jason reached into the pocket of his swim shorts, took out a small, velvet bag and tipped a narrow band that wouldn't attract any notice from anyone at all into the palm of his hand, put the tip of his smallest finger inside it and pressed. The ring fell open in half on a near invisible hinge. "Nick Davies made it. It'll fall off if you need it to."

I swallowed as a tear threatened to sidle out of the corner of my eye. I read the words, *only yours, only mine*, inscribed in fine script on either side of the inside of the ring and blinked another one away. "It's beautiful. Did you have one made for you, too?"

Jason reached into his pocket, pulled out similar bag and tipped an identical but man-sized ring into his hand. "Yes, baby. Of course."

I took Jason's ring and slipped it onto his finger. Jason closed my ring. I breathed in deep and held my finger out. Jason brushed his lips over mine and slid it on. "I love you so much, baby."

"I love you, too…so, so much." I lifted my face for Jason's kiss and trailed my fingers over his back when we parted. "You're awful hot there. You need me to rub something on it for you?"

Jason smiled and got up from the sun lounger. I stood, slipped my hand in his and we pushed the door of our hotel room shut behind us, leaving Lizzie to stare out at the rest of the world on her own.

Want to see more from this author?
Here's a taster for you to enjoy!

From a Lady to a Maid
Cassie O'Brien

Excerpt

"Amelia. Amelia Brown. Where are you?"

I pulled my hands from the chill depths of the stone sink and wiped their numbness on the front of my pinny as I walked around the corner of the scullery into the kitchen and halted in front of the tall, bony figure of Ashton Manor's housekeeper.

"I'm here, Mrs. Price."

Mrs. Price peered at me over the top of half-glasses perched on her beak of a nose and sniffed. "Are the saucepans from lunch clean? The china from afternoon tea?"

The material of my dress cut into my armpit as I breathed in to speak. I pulled on the side seam of my bodice and eased the fabric away from my chafed skin. "Yes, Mrs. Price. I've just finished."

My movement provided some relief under my arm but tightened the material around my waist and I wriggled. Mrs. Price frowned.

"Amelia, kindly stand still when I'm talking to you. Why are you so pink in the face?"

I pulled on the front of my dress and shift to try to find a little room inside, so my chest could expand. "My clothes are too tight."

Mrs. Price looked at the stretched stitches on the side seam of my dress. "Are your laces tied at the end of their length?"

I nodded. "Yes, Mrs. Price. I can loosen them no farther."

"Yes, well...I believe it's your name-day?"

"Yes, Mrs. Price. I turned nineteen today."

"Are you sure? I wouldn't have put you at more than fourteen when I took you on as a tweenie maid last year." Mrs. Price's gaze moved down to my toes then back to my head. "Still, even I can see you've grown quite considerably since then."

"Yes, I'm sure, Mrs. Price. The day of my birth is written in the bible at home. I've grown this last year, I'm afraid."

Mrs. Price sniffed. "You can read?"

"Yes, Mrs. Price. I've had some schooling."

"Yes, well...you may have a larger dress and shifts today, as it's your name-day. Come and see me before supper. Now tidy that hair back under your cap and go and find Ellen to attend to the fires Above Stairs."

I wound a strand of my hair around my finger and tucked it under my cap. Mrs. Price walked away, her black dress rustling, and I let myself out of the kitchen door into the back yard. Cold February air wrapped itself around my body and I shivered as I trotted through damp mizzle to the sound of clunks on metal toward the glow of the oil lamp sitting on the ground by the coal shed. Ellen shoveled a last scoop into the second of two coal scuttles as I arrived.

"Ellen, you've filled mine for me. I thank you."

Ellen smiled as she put the shovel inside the coal shed and latched its door. "Well, as it's your birthday…"

I tugged on my dress and sucked in what air I could. "Mrs. Price says I may have another dress and shifts tonight. I can't wait. I can hardly breathe."

"I know. One set a year isn't enough, is it? You do know you've got to give the ones you're wearing back to Mrs. Price for the next maid who would fit them?"

"She'll be welcome to them." I winced. I gripped my scuttle handle with both hands. "Ready?"

Ellen nodded, turned down the wick of the lamp and grasped hers. I tensed my arm muscles, heaved my scuttle upward and followed her through the back yard toward the yellow glow of the oil lamp sitting on the kitchen window sill. Mrs. Price, sitting at the long, wooden table I scrubbed daily, looked up from counting a pile of linen napkins in front of her as we staggered in.

"Plenty of time before the dressing gong," she said. "Make sure you're finished and back Below Stairs when you hear it."

I followed Ellen to the green, baize-covered door that led to the flights of wooden servants' stairs that allowed us access to the upper floors of the Family's living quarters of Ashton Manor. Six flights later, I stood beside her, puffed and rested my scuttle. Ellen pushed open the green swing-hinge door that separated the realm of servant from that of Family and peeked around it.

"No sign of any of them," she said over her shoulder.

I hefted my scuttle and stepped around her onto the softness of red carpet, walked with her into a hallway of closed, polished wooden doors illuminated by whiter light from the cleaner burn of paraffin lamps suspended by chains overhead and my dress pinched me again.

"Thank the Lord. It's quicker when they're not in their bedrooms, and I could do with quick tonight," I puffed out.

Ellen stopped walking and looked me. "Your face is awfully pink. You stop here on the Bachelors' wing and just do His Lordship's. I'll run down and do the three Ladies'."

"Ellen, that's kind of you. I'll do your potty duty tomorrow morning. I'll be well by then, once I can catch my breath again."

Ellen grinned. "Fires in exchange for chamber pots? I'll take that trade anytime, I thank you. I'll meet you behind the green door on the half-landing when we've finished."

Ellen walked up the hallway toward the Ladies' bedrooms. I tapped on His Lordship's door, received no answer and opened it to find the side lamps lit, as well as the ceiling fitting. I left the door open behind me as I walked in, a signal to the room's occupant that a servant—other than his valet, Mr. Hubert—was in his room, should he return to it.

The pain shot through my ribcage as I put my scuttle down, knelt before the fire and stretched forward to rake the hot coals with the poker. My ears filled with a soft buzz and the flicker of the flames hazed before my eyes. I sat back on my heels and breathed in as deep my dress would allow when it dawned on me how close I had come to passing out face-down into the fire.

I looked over my shoulder and heard only silence from the hallway, so reached into the scooped neckline of my dress and unfastened the first few buttons of my modesty shift. My breasts billowed upward into a décolleté normally only seen on the Ladies of the house when dressed for a ball, but the cramp in my ribs eased and my vision settled. I bent forward and re-applied the poker, listening for the sound of a footstep or the dressing gong, glanced backward to pull the scuttle closer and saw a pair of male legs encased in buckskin riding breeches and soft-soled leather boots walk into the room.

I pinched my shift together as best I could with one hand, kept my back turned and carried on working the poker with the other, as if I hadn't seen a Lord enter the room, while I tried to think of a way to get my breasts decently covered again without my doing so being noticed.

"Will you be much longer?" he asked.

"My apologies, My Lord. I didn't hear the dressing gong."

"It hasn't been rung yet. I'm early."

The whisper of leather footwear on the move warned me I had no time to consider any discreet option. I weighed the idea of making a dash for the door, looked down at my chest and realized even more breast would be exposed if I jumped up to run, so decided that if I was to be discovered with more than an appropriate amount of flesh on display, it was not going to be while I was on the floor kneeling at anyone's feet.

I hung the poker alongside the other fire irons, stood and tipped the scuttle toward the flames then reached for my buttons and looked sideways at the boy, grown into a man, that I hadn't been this close to since I was seven years old. I saw no hint of recognition in his eyes, although they widened slightly as his gaze dropped to my open frontage. I recalled his attention to my face.

"If you wouldn't mind averting your eyes, My Lord."

A gleam of amusement lightened the blue of Damion's irises as he raised his gaze from my chest.

"I'd rather not. I believe I'm enjoying the view."

My heart thumped. I squared my shoulders as the servant in me sensed the offer of a quick tumble coming my way, and the woman I had been a year ago stiffened her spine and turned the offer aside in the manner I would have done then.

"Hardly befitting conduct, Sir. But as the fault is mine, enjoy away."

I put my hand on my breasts, pushed them inside my shift, refastened my buttons and picked up my scuttle.

Damion smiled. "It might have been more enjoyable if you'd permitted me to do that for you."

I didn't lower my gaze as I dipped my curtsey. "I thank you for your kind offer, Sir, but I believe I must decline. I do have a prior evening engagement that will amuse me more."

"With…?"

I stepped around him. "With the pans in the scullery that have just been used to provide your dinner."

I walked out of the room and Damion's soft laughter followed me, along with the hope that the sound of it meant the boy I had known had retained his sense of humor and Mrs. Price wouldn't be calling me to her room shortly to tell me to pack my box because of my cheek. She looked at me as I entered the kitchen.

"Ah, Amelia. Relieve yourself of your scuttle and come with me."

Home of Erotic Romance

Sign up for our newsletter and find out about all our romance book releases, eBook sales and promotions, sneak peeks and FREE romance books!

About the Author

I love:
Being with family and friends.
Writing and having the freedom to do so now child four of four has passed her driving test and is off to uni later this year.
I Like:
Any excuse to throw a party.
Any excuse to open a bottle of fizz.
Shoes in vast quantities – the higher the heel the better.
Ambitions:
To write many more books.
To own a pair of Louboutin's.
To never go near an iron or a hoover again.

Cassie loves to hear from readers. You can find her contact information, website details and author profile page at https://www.totallybound.com

www.ingramcontent.com/pod-product-compliance
Lightning Source LLC
Chambersburg PA
CBHW020633020726
47494CB00001B/174